1920

SHORT STORY

SHORT STORY 1

RICHARD YATES	*The Best of Everything*
GINA BERRIAULT	*The Houses of the City*
B. L. BARRETT	*The Family Tree*
SEYMOUR EPSTEIN	*Come to the Fair*

SHORT STORY 2

ARNO KARLEN	*The Clown*
SALLY WEBER	*The River Summer*
MICHAEL RUMAKER	*Exit 3*
GERTRUDE FRIEDBERG	*The Wayward Cravat*

SHORT STORY 3

BURTON RAFFEL	*Sicilian Vespers*
MATTHEW CARNEY	*The Drifter*
JOSEPH SLOTKIN	*The Perfectionist*
ROBERT CREELEY	*The Musicians*

SHORT STORY

3

SHORT STORY 3

SICILIAN VESPERS

STORIES BY *Burton Raffel*

THE DRIFTER

STORIES BY *Matthew Carney*

THE PERFECTIONIST

STORIES BY *Joseph Slotkin*

THE MUSICIANS

STORIES BY *Robert Creeley*

CHARLES SCRIBNER'S SONS, NEW YORK

A–8.60 [V]

PRINTED IN THE UNITED STATES OF AMERICA

Library of Congress Catalog Card Number 58-12310

PUBLISHER'S NOTE

This third volume in our annual series of short story collections presents, as did its two predecessors, the work of four highly talented writers who have not previously published their fiction in book form. These were chosen from among nearly two hundred candidates. Their variety and quality give fresh evidence, we believe, that the short story in America is as vital and significant an art form today as it has ever been, even though the market for short fiction today can rarely return a livelihood for the serious writer.

Short Story was conceived as a means of introducing each year to the book public three or four new writers, chosen in open competition. In deciding on an omnibus format it was felt that *Short Story* would have two unusual advantages: it would permit the publication of more writers than would be possible in individual volumes; and it could present a larger and more representative body of work by each writer than the usual story anthology. *Short Story 1* and *Short Story 2* were warmly received by critics and reviewers. We believe this response will grow as the series continues to reflect the vigor of the short story today and to fulfill its unique introductory role.

THE AUTHORS

Burton Raffel is a young writer with a remarkably varied background. He is a lawyer, a translator of Anglo-Saxon, French and Indonesian poetry, and has taught English at Brooklyn College, Ohio State University, and in Indonesia under the Ford Foundation program. His verse translations have appeared in *Atlantic Monthly*, *New Mexico Quarterly*, *London Magazine*, *Prairie Schooner*, and

The Antioch Review. He has published non-fiction in *The Yale Review* and in various law journals, and his own poetry in *New Mexico Quarterly* and *The Antioch Review.* He plans to devote his efforts increasingly to the writing of fiction. "What I try to accomplish for myself is a series of portraits with impact," he says, "glimpses of certain people's insides and the small, special worlds of which our society is constructed. My highest goal, I think, is understanding, and I come closest to achieving it, right now, in stories rather than in poems."

"Sicilian Vespers," one of the three stories in Mr. Raffel's section, appeared in *New World Writing #17.*

Matthew Carney has been living and writing in Paris for the past eleven years. He was born in New York, attended school and college in California, and completed his graduate studies at the Sorbonne. He has published several articles, but his fiction appears here for the first time in this country. Mr. Carney writes, "To be a vagabond, to be a writer, to be a learned man: these drives crystallized in me by the time I was nineteen and still define my life. Writing to me is art. My aim is to become an artist with this to do: to raise my level of consciousness in existence. In writing I wish to reconstruct my consciousness in forms which catch readers' attention and then affect readers' values on life, either by breaking down values or building new ones."

Of Mr. Carney's six stories in *Short Story 3*, four comprise a separate "cycle" based upon a single character.

Joseph Slotkin, a resident of California, has worked in radio as writer and actor, and in a great many other fields including newspaper reporting and teaching. He has also written for television and films, and has taught writing for both media in Hollywood. His fiction has been published in numerous periodicals, including several science-fiction magazines, *Arizona Quarterly, Discovery, Perspective,* and *Quixote.* Mr. Slotkin says of the short story, "Short stories are like solar plexus blows—the effect is single and at once. Longer works are more like little love affairs, with byplay. But I believe it is possible to fall in love from the effects of a short or long work. A single statement can often reach a receiver with as much force as a novel, if the reader is ready." . . . and of writing generally, "Writing is trying to touch another with a tool, and at times I think it is symbols reaching out to other symbols, for I believe that is what we are—symbols of what we might be and, God willing, will some day be."

All of the stories in Mr. Slotkin's section have appeared in magazines. "Your Best Interests at Heart" is from a novel in progress and was cited by Martha Foley as one of the "Distinctive Short Stories Published in American Magazines" in 1959.

Robert Creeley has gained a considerable reputation as a poet and as a teacher of writing. He has had seven collections of poems published, and his work, criticism as well as poetry and fiction, has appeared in such periodicals as *Kenyon Review, Accent, The Nation, New Directions Annual, Poetry, New Mexico Quarterly,* and *Evergreen Review.* He served as an instructor at Black Mountain College and was Editor of *Black Mountain Review.*

In writing of his short stories, Mr. Creeley says, "The story has no time finally. Or it hasn't here. Its shape, if form can be so thought of, is a sphere, an egg of obdurate kind. The only possible reason for its existence is that it has, in itself, the fact of reality and the pressure. There, in short, is its form—no matter how random or broken that will seem. The old assumptions of beginning and end—those very neat assertions—have fallen way completely in a place where the only actuality is life, the only end (never realized) death, and the only value, what love one can manage."

CONTENTS

SHORT STORY

3

Sicilian Vespers

SHORT STORIES

by

BURTON RAFFEL

Sicilian Vespers

The Russian Voice

Fatherhood

SICILIAN VESPERS

DISEASE is wholly relative: anyone can catch anything, and sickness sits more obviously on some people than on others. This was medical school, lesson one the first day out. Even Carrel Lee remembered, though med school was almost ten years behind him, and most of that time had been wrapped in a specialist garb of surgeon's white. He had cut into living flesh too often not to know how soft and pliable it was, nor could he ever again be surprised at anything the human body might contain. The world, and the flesh, were full of secret worms, and if some of them stayed silent and hidden that was their choice, not their host's. No two attackers, no two attacked, were the same.

It all started with quiet good grace, on a weekday morning just after a brief routine operation. He was stripping off his gloves, laughing to himself at his inept fumbling, when he became aware that his fingers felt loose almost to the point of being detached. He looked down, felt a strange dizziness, and got himself into a chair just before he went completely unconscious. It could only have lasted a moment, for he was still alone and robed when he came to. His hands were more responsive, now, though still quite weak, and he managed to stand up and finish the dressing process. It felt most like flu, and he did not worry. He signed himself out, told the girl he was a bit under the weather, and went home to bed.

He slept till late afternoon, drifting up out of sleep as from an opium dream, coming awake with the gentle slowness of dust falling across a pillow. The room was dim, except for a thin slash of sunlight that hung on the far wall, and there was the faint sound of music. He lay where he was, still not sure that this was not another hazy sleep vision. But the music grew more audible, though no more familiar, and he knew that he had wakened. He sat up, slowly, not surprised to find his whole body light and loose. The sickness worked that way. The music had continued to grow louder; it beat in the darkened room like something pounding inside his chest. Then he came fully, lucidly awake and realized that there was no music, that the swelling sound had been splashing out as though from him, that he was the source. The sounds faded and stopped, as he realized his responsibility for them. The room was hushed and nowhere was there anything but the half heard echoes of city traffic.

He got out of bed: it was not difficult, except that his legs moved as though the bare floor was covered with seaweed and the room was full of water. It was partly walking, partly swimming, but he got to the telephone. He did not know how ill he was going to be, but it did not pay to remain alone. Medical assistance was literally just around the corner, for his apartment was within easy walking distance of the hospital. He tried to joke about himself, on the phone, but articulation had become difficult and even simple words were too much of an effort. Everything was too much of an effort. He pushed himself back through the water-logged room to his bed, and was asleep when the bell rang. It took several minutes for him to wade to the door again.

The examination was thorough and minute; he described symptoms and reactions with faithful care and a vaguely amused sense of how odd it was to have the tables turned. He managed a slow smile, once, inwardly contrasting his elaborate abstract language with the sensations his body had been experiencing. But the diagnosis was puzzling. He knew how restlessly the mind sat in the body, and by what slender nerve filaments the whole mechanism was kept in operation. So the concepts of mental strain and mental illness were not a bit strange or peculiar. Yet to be told that he had already slipped over the edge of a nervous breakdown was queerly shocking. It was too much to have expected clear warning;

he was used to the abrupt irrelevance of disease. But his nerves, in the lay sense, had always been good, and he was aware of no strain, no shock, nothing that could have overturned the balance and sent him reeling into such inappropriate ill-health. He was not ashamed or even bewildered, but simply very surprised. Still, he accepted the findings just as, in the next week or two, he accepted the visits and the telephone calls and the mild directions showered upon him by friends and colleagues.

It was universally agreed that he had to get away. He did not protest, even as his hands grew steadier and his ears less likely to hear what no one else could hear. The danger of a relapse, with a patient on the table and a knife in his hands, was too great a risk. A cure was essential. He rejected, with some impatience, the idea of a European journey: he had no interest in being a tourist, home or abroad. The idea was pressed on him, despite his opposition. It was explained how valuable a complete break would be. He would not have to tramp through museums or visit cultural landmarks. What mattered was that he would be in utterly foreign surroundings, with few people even talking his language. He agreed, finally, when a colleague offered to arrange for a seaside room in southern Italy, in a small town where no tourists were likely to come and where nothing in particular ever happened. At least, not to foreigners. It was the ideal place for a composer with a symphony to write, for a poet with half formed poems that wanted out. Perhaps even for a painter, he was assured, for the sea was lovely, the sun was very bright, and there were low, green hills not too far inland. Sunshine and olive oil, street serenades and sea-bathing. This was the prescription to which he at last surrendered himself. He even agreed to fly, much as he hated planes, because the sooner he went the sooner he could return. And that was really all he wanted. He would pamper his body or his mind or his colleagues, as long as he was thereby enabled to return to the career his illness had so suddenly interrupted. It was that, after all, which marked out the world that counted, and was all he cared very much about. It was that to which he had long ago both abandoned and dedicated himself, with results, until now, steadily more satisfying. No one would give him a date for coming back; he realized, of course, that no one could. It was up to him, and to southern Italy. So he went almost eagerly, determined to knit up a web, this time, that no casual disorder could break. He thought himself an ideal patient, and neither worried nor doubted.

The village was everything he had been promised. The arrangements had been made exactly as planned: his quarters were in a private house, with a family where no English was spoken. The man was a civil servant, so living was not entirely devoid of graciousness. There were a number of children, precisely how many he never quite knew. The lady of the house did his washing, and his meals were served privately, on a small gate-legged table that stood in a corner of his room and, most of the day, bore a small vase regularly replenished with bright flowers. The room was small but clean, and the window looked out on street scenes that were sufficiently unfamiliar to be pleasantly attractive. He made no effort to understand what was going on, what the women were chattering about, why the small boys ran, why the occasional cars used their horns so liberally. No more did he attempt to communicate with his hosts. Sign language did very well with the woman; when something more elaborate was needed, both he and the civil servant resurrected broken phrases of schoolboy French. It was good enough: he had nothing to say, and wanted to talk to no one. He had come to rest, to let whatever raggedness had infested his nerves be smoothed over and healed. The country and the people did not concern him. He knew nothing about them and wanted to know no more than that. They had their lives and he had his. At least, he would have his if he did as instructed and returned in one reasonably unified whole.

He strolled through the town, at first, though more from a sense of duty than out of real curiosity. But he quickly learned that the seaside was a better place. For one thing, the townsfolk stared and gaped as he came by; children ran up to him, squalling out incomprehensible demands, peddlers waved their wares in his face and made vaguely inviting gestures. He could ignore it all, but it was preferable not to be bothered even to that extent. More, he found the beach genuinely restful—not just a suspension of activity, the quiet vacuum of the desert, but something so soothing that he sometimes felt he could fill a tightly stoppered vial, take it to a laboratory, and have them distill out the palpable essence of the place. It was the air, which was light with moisture and fragrance and heavy with heat. It was the clear, hot sun, the soft, cluttered sand, the steady, gentle hissing of the sea, slapping against the shore and running back to itself in unending cycles. It was the white-tipped birds, hanging over the water, flicking down in long, steep runs, occasionally pecking in the sand at respectful distances. It was even the dirty sails and the creaking of their ropes, the small, weathered fishing boats that came scraping in on the wet, sloping approaches, even the thin, dark, bustling men with their nets and lines, their baskets and their incomprehensible speech. Best of all, no one paid any attention to him; his foreignness was obvious, his unconcern at least as clear. He could sit thirty feet from an active boat crew and be as far away as China. It was like being an invisible non-human, basking in the soft climate and immune from notice.

He took to spending most of his time on the beach, sitting in the dry sand in casual clothes, his head protected by a round straw hat. He never read; he had taken some books in his valise, but never opened them. There was nothing he wanted to know, no entertainment he lacked. His instructions had forbidden the only reading he cared about; if he could not read medical journals there was no point to pretending to enjoy anything else. The books were arranged on a shelf, in his rented room, and every day they were carefully dusted and replaced. He had several times seen it done. But he did not open them, not once in all the time he was there. He simply sat in the sand and watched, or thought empty thoughts, or half dozed and neither watched nor thought. The break with the past was, as intended, complete.

There was a number of lazy, meaningless games he played with himself. He could see far out over the water without raising his head or craning, and he would count the puffs of white cloud floating slowly by, mentally assembling their future shapes and watching how well his predictions worked. When he watched: often he would abandon the game in favor of something equally devoid of significance. Or in favor of nothing. At times he would try to blend himself, motionless, into the landscape, in order to tempt a bird to peck that much closer. It worked, now and then: he developed the capacity for motionlessness to a high degree of perfection. He learned, too, how to close his eyes so that only a slit of vision remained; staring at the far horizon he could produce a rainbow almost at will. He spent long hours lifting handfuls of powdery sand and letting it slip back through his fingers, as close to one grain at a time as he could manage. He developed great skill at this art, too. He learned the value of tiny, gradual changes in posture. He would sometimes plan, a quarter of an hour in advance, how he would shift his arms, and when the moment came he would quietly relish the knowledge and control with which the maneuver was carried out. He collected nothing, however, no colored shells, no water-rubbed pebbles, no sun-stained fragments of glass, worn smooth and dull. He neither brought anything to or from the beach. He simply came, and sat, and then went as he had come, his hands and his mind about equally empty.

He was not bored. His rest-cure was not relaxation, not a vacation trip, but medicine; he took the largest doses he could. His goal was recovery, and he worked at its attainment with all the focussed concentration of which he was capable. The sun and the sea were prophylactic; stripping his mind was hygienic. The regimen was no less rigid for being spontaneous and unarticulated—for he did not encourage even thoughts about his strict thoughtlessness. He kept himself firmly blank, and there was no more room for boredom than for anything else less negative.

He had come down to the beach, one morning, just before a small fishing boat was pushed into the sea. Half a dozen scantily clad men were clustered about, and their voices were clearly audible. His eye wandered over them, like some conveniently located camera, interested as much in color and line as in what the movements meant. In the strangely clear air the panorama was very like something seen projected on a screen. He was only fifty feet away; he could have been perched in a movie seat, watching a film of this very scene. In fact, he so fancied himself: it made the distance seem much greater than a mere fifty feet, and the increased separation contributed to his medicinal isolation.

The fishermen ranged themselves alongside and began heaving the stern free of the sand. They formed an odd composition, their feet planted far back, their heads leaning almost horizontally forward. The little boat dipped slowly down, then there was a yell from the far side, where he could not see, and the boat halted, the heads resumed their position directly above the feet and bodies, and everyone clustered on the side away from him. He scarcely noticed the interruption, watching, now, the gentle swells that took the bow and softly raised and lowered it. The sails were still furled: the boat bobbed like a large stick of driftwood.

The fishermen emerged from behind the boat, gesturing and pouring out words, leading one of their number up out of the water, supporting him as he stumbled onto the beach, clutching at his shoulder, his face contorted. Lee could see it all quite clearly. He kept his poised isolation, skimming off the details and movements without interpretation or thought. He watched them trying to administer to the injured party; he knew, without knowing, that there had been an injury. It meant nothing to him. Then one of the fishermen succeeded, with the others' help, in getting a grip on the injured arm. He yanked, and the victim bellowed. Without the slightest volition Lee got to his feet and walked, with even steps, toward the struggling group. He arrived just as the treatment was about to be repeated and, without a word, pulled the men away from their injured and harassed fellow. His examination was rapid; the separation was obvious. With quick, decisive motions he manipulated the joint back into place. The victim howled and jumped, but then retreated no further. Gingerly, he moved the arm, grimacing with pain, but obviously relieved. An immense jabber went up from the others; they crowded around Lee, pointing and questioning. He endured it a moment, then calmly shook his head and began to walk off. They followed, insistent, only one of them staying behind with the injured party, now sunk into a shaken heap on the sand.

He reached his previous position, but did not seat himself. The fishermen were still with him. His manner calm, he turned to them and tried to indicate that he had no desire to pursue the contact. It was hopeless. He sighed, but could not so easily break away. His face grew warm and his temper rose. Why were they bothering him? He had very nearly succeeded in forgetting: his actions had been mechanical and quite without meaning. A word dinned at him, something like *doctorre*. He nodded, and was greeted with smiles and a new babble. There was no help for it. He raised his hand in a frigid farewell, turned, and walked off. No one followed him, this time, much to his relief. He climbed back onto the path and walked to his lodging, proceeding a little faster than had been his habit. His jaw felt tense and his hands, though steady, were clutched into tight balls. He carefully loosened them, and made them wipe the dampness from his brow. It was early and the sun was low, but he was sweating. Back in his room he felt queasy and a little faint, and stretched himself out on the hard, narrow bed. He did not close his eyes, but neither did he let himself think about the disturbance. He was still ill; there was nothing to think about, and there was only one thing to do. He had to stay in Italy, here, and keep his divorcement from life on a perfect, even keel. There could be no more digressions; he could not afford even so slight a relapse.

He lay there until his mid-day meal was brought, when he washed himself and carefully ate everything on the gaudy metal tray. Food was as important as rest. He ate slowly, deliberately, and then took his straw hat and walked down to the beach. The fishing boat was gone, and only a few birds circled quietly overhead. He seated himself and began to count the thin wisps of clouds, turning lazily in the bright sky far out over the sea. They were most like fish, today. If there were enough wind, that patch to the right would form a veritable whale. A gull cawed, the surf broke lightly on the shore, and the afternoon slipped easily by.

He was sitting on the deserted beach, a week later, trying with considerable success to ignore the children who occasionally ran by him, their bare feet plowing up a small sandstorm and their hard, high voices frightening the gulls. Where they had come from and why they came running here instead of in some schoolyard were of no concern to him; he simply wished them out of existence and automatically repopulated the beach with silence and warm sun. When the old woman waddled up to him, her face red and her lips working soundlessly, he applied the same technique to her. But she wanted his attention. After her first few words fell unnoticed, she plucked at his shoulder with irreverent urgency. He finally looked around at her.

"No," he told her in a firm, loud voice. He had found this a universal solvent. He turned his gaze back to the sky behind her, where a gull was hanging motionless on rigid wings, only the faintest twitching indicating that it and the wind were still alive.

She pulled at his sleeve again.

"No," he repeated, this time not looking around. Whatever she had to sell, whatever she wanted him to do, he could not be bothered. There was nothing he wanted to receive or to give, except silence and blank inattention.

But she would not give up and at last he did turn away from the white gull floating in the shimmering blue sky. There were tears on her cheeks and her voice was desperate. He could not understand a word she said, but he knew. It had always been the same; he had seen that look a thousand times, and the response was too deeply imbedded to be ignored. He sighed, got to his feet and followed her. When he thought to look over his shoulder, a moment later, the gull was gone, carried out of sight on its stiff wings. It was almost as though it had stayed only while he watched, kept glued against the sky by his steady, unthinking stare.

He did not have to walk very far. There were occasional dilapidated shacks all along the shore, back a few hundred yards from the water line, looking like deserted playthings set up by children, one idle summer, out of driftwood and discarded bits of metal. If he had noticed them at all, it had never occurred to him that they were inhabited, that people actually spent their lives under such sagging, gaping roofs, in a climate where, in winter, overcoats were necessary and, in bad years, snow fell. But he did not permit himself to be surprised, as she waddled straight up to just such a shack and motioned him in. Under other circumstances he might have been hesitant, or afraid, but caution was quite as irrelevant, now, as concern. He had entrapped himself; the only thing to do was to extricate himself, with as little effort as was necessary.

The interior was a single dim room, furnished with little more than several straw mats and one partly broken chair. His patient was lying on a mat, toward one corner, but sat up as he came in. He stood where he was a moment, letting his eyes adjust. It was a girl, her hair loose behind her neck, her thin face stained with tears. One arm hung very limply and there was blood on her shirt. He stepped closer. Without his bag, and the comfort of its clean, familiar tools, he felt foolishly unmedical. He looked quickly behind him, not sure what he was expecting to see. There was only the old woman, nodding anxiously and muttering something that might have been a prayer. He went down on his knees and motioned the child closer. Her lips were trembling as she edged toward him, using only the one hand; she looked ready to scramble to her feet and run.

He smiled automatically and put a hand on her shoulder. She sat very still, and then, moving with careful slowness, he took the hand at the end of the limp arm and flexed the fingers. There was no response. It might have been fright, but it might well have been a fracture. He asked her, with gestures, to raise the arm. She shook her head and he nodded. So it was not fright. Her lips had steadied; he could see that she was not as young as he had thought, but small and thin enough to pass for as little as twelve or thirteen. She was probably more than that.

She let him examine the arm, which he did with slow, gentle motions. The fracture was fairly recent, for the swelling was new. And yet not too new. These people probably could not afford to call a local doctor, and had come to him only out of mounting fear. Perhaps the blood on the girl's shirt had sent the old woman struggling through the loose sand to where he sat. How had they heard of him? It was the fisherman: he had no doubt of that. People talked.

The fracture was not a difficult one. He would be able to set it, even without the usual tools and conveniences. But the blood on her shirt was partly caked, partly fresh; whatever the wound, it was still open, and needed to be looked after. He drew the shirt away from her side and though she winced it came away easily. He hesitated, his fingers twitching as though holding a surgical scissors, then made the best of it. With a quick, strong motion—for his hands had become as steady and hard as they had ever been—he took the worn collar and ripped it through, ignoring the old woman's sudden cry of protest. He would give her another old shirt, later. Then, edging around the bloodied area, he ripped through the body of the material and carefully parted it back on both sides.

It was the first time he had ever been aware of the patient's body as something other than a vessel for illness and decay. He did not look at the wound, which from the small quantity of blood he had suspected was minor, but at the sloping line of a thin, graceful collarbone, at the round smoothness of two even shoulders, and at the astonishing fullness of her breasts. He had not expected such maturity, and he had not expected that simply opening her shirt would leave her naked to the waist. He hesitated, again, and her nipples came erect and she shivered slightly. He set his teeth in an effort to keep his hands away from her smooth, firm skin and busied himself with the two wide but comparatively shallow cuts in her side. As he worked his mind, if not his eyes, was on the fresh loveliness of her body. He was a doctor but not a doctor, she was injured but different from any patient he had ever had. Maybe he had grown too used to sick people prepared for him by experienced hands, always cleaned and strapped and exposed exactly as his efforts would require. Maybe it was his own sickness. Maybe a breast from which a tumor had to be extracted, or shoulders whose height had to be lowered or raised, were not parts of a body at all. Others of his colleagues had had trouble with female patients; he had never been disturbed. It was his sickness; it could only be his sickness.

She did not make a sound, even when he finally came back to the arm and set the fracture. Her face was very close to his, and he could see that, mostly, she closed her eyes and, panting faintly, endured as best she could. He watched for signs of shock, for pallor and unsteadiness, even as he watched her long, fine lashes when she blinked, and the gentle parting of her nostrils as her breath came and went. Her lips were full, even though clenched against the pain; her teeth were small and regular. It was difficult, when he was done, to keep from pressing his lips against hers. It was even more difficult to control his hands, which already had a limited license with her body. But he kept himself to his doctoring, and finished as rapidly and efficiently as he was able.

Nor was it a bad, or a wholly unprofessional job. The arm would heal straight: he was reasonably sure of that. And the cuts would leave scars, but not deep ones. She was still young: they would even fade a bit, in time. With a body as lovely as hers she did not need to fret about two irrelevant scars: it would be a long time before anyone with the opportunity to observe them would detect their existence. He put one hand behind her back, the other against the base of her thin collarbone, and lowered her to the mat. She opened her eyes, smiled at him briefly, then closed her eyes once more. The smile lasted only until she could not see him. He stayed a moment longer than he had to, looking down at her perspiring, half naked body. She was lying on her back and her breasts seemed less full; he felt a sudden weariness and wanted to let his head settle down against her. She was already half asleep and probably would not have minded: her nudity apparently gave her no concern. Or was she too much in pain to have really noticed? He motioned to the old woman for something to cover her with, and himself settled the ragged blanket over the small, damp body.

He got to his feet with a delayed sigh, but in fact his moment of fatigue had passed. The woman was gesturing incomprehensibly; he reassured her with a smile and a shake of the head. It was money she was worried about, more than likely, frightened at the possibility of his fee. She persisted and held to his arm, as though afraid he would break away and disappear. He let her lead him outside, then saw the little wood fire and the battered kettle. He nodded and joined her for a cup of weak, odd tasting brew that might have been tea but could easily have been chicory or bark or baked seaweed stems. They sat quietly at opposite sides of the fire, which she allowed to flicker into oblivion. There was obviously no point to talk: they had scarcely a word in common. But she seemed content, having gotten him to drink her offering, and there was no need to reassure her about his non-existent fee. She sat in peaceful, abstracted silence, drooping over the handleless teacup, her broad, hooked nose sniffing at the warm aroma, her sloping shoulders pointed toward the trampled ground, sprinkled with patches of grass and streaked with sand and yellow clay. He could see no resemblance between her sagging, wrinkled face and the girl lying inside, but that meant nothing. The connection between them could have been anything from mother or grandmother to distant relative, to no relative at all. The girl was just old enough, he thought, to have been born during the war; perhaps her parents were dead, or perhaps she had only one, her father just passing through with his battalion, loving and leaving and as quickly forgetting. None of it meant anything: the old woman could have bought the child, for all he cared, and reared her like some latter day fatted calf. Perhaps she was already turning a profit by renting the girl out. But he did care, in some strange fashion, and he forced himself to think about something else, the bright, hot day that was just as he had left it a little earlier and was inviting him back, the gulls that were swooping and calling over his head, the last red flickers in the fire and the grey ashes that the wind lifted away. Then he finished drinking and put the cup down on the grass beside him.

The old woman rose with him, and he waited while she struggled heavily to her feet. She smiled gratefully and he nodded with a casual aplomb that, in other circumstances, would have astonished him. He wanted to say something she would understand, and racked his brain for an Italian word, any Italian word.

"*Bella*," he finally said, pointing inside. It was all he could think of.

She continued to smile and did not seem shocked, which made him, perversely, a little less happy, a little more sure that her connection with the girl was not a wholly desirable one. But it was none of his affair. He offered her his hand, which she shook only after wiping her own diligently against her frayed dress, and walked off.

The beach was still deserted. He did not look back, but he was sure the woman would not have followed. He had done all he could do, and all she wanted of him. Nor did he want to fix the shack in his mind: why should he go back? He suspected himself of wanting to, and carefully refrained from turning, a hundred feet away, to distinguish this from the other dilapidated heaps that, at irregular intervals, dotted the fringes of the beach. It was better that way. Besides, how much more than fifteen or sixteen could the girl possibly be?

The sand was uncomfortably warm, perhaps because he had not followed it through the slow stages of heating. He fidgetted about, trying to focus his attention on the distant cloud banks or the wheeling gulls. It did not work. Abruptly, he decided to walk through the town before returning for his afternoon meal.

The yapping animals and the staring local peddlers and the small boys could not be more unsettling than to have his favored spot soured and inhospitable. The distractions and noises might even be help rather than hindrance, now, focussing his attention outside himself. He dusted the sand from his trousers and walked off. It did not strike him until later, when he had already sat down to his food, that there had been no reaction to the morning's episode. He had not been affected in the slightest, and had carried through, in primitive surroundings, without fumbling, without evoking any of the symptoms of his illness. He could not know what this meant, of course, but he could not doubt that whatever the meaning it was good. He was becoming himself. To prove it, he asserted his palate and ignored half the food placed before him. Why stuff the body with nutriment when it was so far along on the road to health? His landlady frowned, clearing away the dishes, but he beamed at her and nodded a benediction. He was tempted, as the euphoria bubbled up, to kiss her worn cheek in appreciation and sheer goodwill, but refrained in time. It could not last much longer, this queer, unending exile. There was light at the end of the tunnel, and he was so sure of seeing it full and clear that he felt no impatience. It was coming; it was all a matter of time.

The sun was just sliding out over the hill tops, the next morning, when he opened his eyes and knew at once that sleep was finished for the day. The light changed quickly from pallid grey to pink and then to the normal hot glare; he dutifully closed his eyes and tried to re-invoke slumber, but it was no good, he was fully awake at the first touch of dawn. He felt rested and strong, in the clear, still air, but something was quietly, steadily clanging in his head, some insistent note of barely suppressed excitement. He slipped out of bed and tip-toed across to where his clothing lay, dressing with quick, sure motions, conscious of the deft strength in his hands. He was rested, completely awake, and ready. It made very little difference what for: it could be nothing but good fortune. His streak of bad health was ending, a surface vein soon worked through; everything that came out of those mysterious depths inside him, now, was bound to be bright with gold.

He sat by the window, in the growing heat, but only vaguely aware of the sounds of the village rising, doors swinging to and fro, feet clattering across the cobblestones, cans and plates banging, cries and children and domestic animals and here and there a small truck motor, coughing and spluttering with age and fatigue. There was no question of forgetting the girl. He had known even then, from the moment he exposed her body, that this was nothing his mind would ever release, let slip back into the dim, unremembered past. A day, a year, or ten: he would never forget, whether he saw her again or not. Yet he knew he would see her again, that there had to be more.

Music drifted through his slow, fragmentary reflections; he pulled his head up with a start. He had not been aware of music since, in his New York apartment, he had sickened to the knowledge that like some insane sending station he was himself flooding the room with pulsing sound. He tensed, then realized that this was different. In a moment he saw a beggar making his way down the street below, grinding away at a small hand organ. He smiled. No monkey? No sickness? Just an old man hunting alms. There was nothing he needed, nothing he had to give. He glanced at his watch, saw that breakfast would soon be arriving, and pulled in his head before the beggar passed under the window. The music dipped past, then faded slowly into the distance.

He walked out at the usual hour, and headed for the usual spot. Everything was in place; no one had re-shaped the beach during the night, nor had he expected change. Yet he saw the quiet line of the sea with a queer new intensity, the sky seemed to curve and stretch with heightened purpose, even the tiny grains of sand were coarser, less smooth to his fingers, less willing to slip through in thin, even streams. If there were gulls he did not see or hear them, not them nor anything else that might have stirred. He sat and stared at the unmoving ocean, then did not see it, only a dazzling spark that grew and spread and finally, in a flaring fire of white heat that he knew must be roaring only in his head, pulled him hurriedly to his feet and threw him, his balance momentarily unsteady, striding down the beach to the shack where the girl was lying. He did not know which it was, nor even just where it was, but if he did not know something did, and took him on the straightest course. And as his feet pushed him eagerly through the sand, following the shore in a slow arc that seemed more a funnel than a road, the puff of white flame receded and left him with clear eyes and a determined sense of well being.

She was sitting in front of the shack, not inside it. Her back was against the door post, her tanned face held up to the sun, eyes closed, lips just barely parted. Her arms, all of her except her face and the bare, grimy soles of her feet, were covered by a tattered blanket. She did not hear him, and he stood silently watching, with doctor's eyes surprised to find her so soon about, with his own eyes incredibly soothed and gratified that she was just as he had left her, her lips as full, her hair as dark and loose, her cheeks as high and prominent. He stood for several minutes, not wanting to disturb her, until something told her that someone had come and she lowered her head and stared up at him. She looked frightened, for an instant, then returned the smile that he quickly offered. He wished, briefly, that he could speak with her, then knew that it made no difference. Without a sound he settled himself alongside her, he too leaning against the wall of the shack, his eyes closed, basking in a glow that was deeper and warmer than the sun.

He looked around at her, finally. Her glance was down. Modesty? He laughed, and she couldn't help turning to him.

"You're not afraid of me, are you?" he wondered gaily.

She blinked and ran her tongue over her lips. He leaned forward and plucked some grass, then braided it idly.

"Don't worry: I'm not going to ask for any money. My services are free." He laughed again. "Take advantage of me while you can."

She could not follow a word, but she laughed with him, the second time. He nodded approval.

"*Bene,*" he ventured, and she giggled. He shrugged, dropped the bits of grass and wiped his hands against each other. Then he pointed at where he guessed her arm must be, under the loose, bulging blanket. He raised his eyebrows and made a gesture of inquiry. She did not seem to understand. He lifted his own arm and indicated a splint, then touched his side and pretended to wince. She nodded, and he got to his feet. She sat looking up at him. He gestured into the shack and extended his hand, to help her up. Not smiling, now, she shook her head and eased herself up by backing against the doorpost. She came erect, finally, with something like a slow shudder, stood a moment beside him, small and quite shapeless in her heavy covering, then stepped through into the shack. He followed.

It was just as he had remembered it, except that they were alone. But he was not concerned about the old woman. As she hesitated, then walked to her pallet, he found himself swallowing hard, his hands warm and damp with anticipation. She sat down and he went over to her, going down on his knees and waiting. He was aware of the artery in his neck throbbing, and vaguely reminded himself that it was just an examination, a routine examination. But as she at last let the blanket slip off her shoulders, and he saw that she was wearing some kind of loose undervest, he stopped trying to fool himself. He wanted to see her as he had the day before, and his disappointment was like an ache, spinning his heart a notch faster.

He bent over the splint, which was obviously in good order, and pretended to check it and the arm, probing gently and peering with as professional an air as he could assume. It was exactly what he had expected; there was no undue inflammation, no sign of infection. He smiled at her, but again she was looking away, her lips together and her eyes down.

"*Bene,*" he repeated. She still did not move. He tapped her on the shoulder, and when she slowly turned to him indicated that her side was next to be examined. She shook her head and he opened his eyes as wide as he could, in a mock show of astonishment, smiling as reassuringly as he knew how. He let his hand fall from her shoulder and with calm purposefulness pulled the blanket away from her waist, to aid her in removing the undergarment. He brushed a bare thigh and tried not to look, but did. The undervest was all she was wearing.

Her good hand gathered the edge of the garment and, forcing himself to look only at her face, he helped her pull it carefully over her head. But even before it had quite dropped free of her long hair his head darted down and nuzzled against her belly, his arms went around her waist, and with a violent passion he could neither slow nor control he pushed her down and, neither seeking nor caring about consent, made love to her. It took only a moment. He lay across her, his breath coming in great, halting gasps, his brain whirled in an agony of fulfillment. It was a trance that receded with blessed reluctance, a pinnacle from which he descended in long, slow steps, each plateau of satisfied desire a deep well of knowledge and rounded pleasure. She lay very still; it was only after consciousness had practically returned, and he sought and found her lips, only to have her jerk her head to the side, that he realized how unwilling she had been. It did not reach him all at once. His hand groped and found her breast, which lay quiescent under his touch. That was a brief opiate, but it did not last. Her silence was too complete, the hard, shut feeling of her lips too vivid.

He released her, rolling to the side and sitting up. She did not move, gave no sign of knowing that he had freed her of the weight of his body. She was completely uncovered, the blanket under her in a tangled heap, her legs sprawled as he had left them. His hand slowly went to her thigh, and stroked along its smooth, warm length. Her skin quivered and that was all. Perhaps it was a different kind of fulfillment: he went on his hands and knees and peered into her face. Her eyes were open; tears ran across her cheeks. She blinked and cringed, seeing him. When he raised a hand to dry off the tears she rolled her head away. He squatted over her, waiting, but she would not turn back. He took a last lingering look down the length of her naked body, then got to his feet, adjusted his clothing and walked out.

He staggered, as the old woman ran head on into him and recoiled, her fat legs weaving and buckling but not spilling her down. She shook her head, dazed by the impact, tried to smile at him but gave over when she saw the distant, withdrawn expression on his face. She had a small package in one hand, which she tentatively lifted toward him, then withdrew as it became clear that he did not see her. Blinking and muttering she hurried into the shack, and he stood just outside the door, unable to either come or go, waiting. It took only a moment. He heard her coarse, brittle voice bark loudly, in fright and horror, and involuntarily he backed away. She came out at him with a rush, her face working and a knife in her hand. His mouth opened soundlessly, and his brain yammered: live by the knife, die by the knife. But before she could plunge the long blade into him he broke and ran, racing frantically over the sand while she heaved herself after him, crying and barking until he outdistanced her, ran out of her sight, ran till even her voice could not reach him. He ran far down the beach, past the village, ran until there was no breath in his lungs, until his legs would not hold him and he collapsed onto the sand. Let her kill him. He lay face down a moment, then nausea wrenched him to his feet and he took half a dozen wobbling steps toward the sea, vomiting with a shudder that threw him back down again. Let her kill him. But she did not come, and he lay there, his face twitching, his hands trembling as though from epilepsy; even when the sun went down and the trembling had eased to a steady, uncontrollable shuddering he could not move.

Fishermen found him, the next morning, surprised that he was alive. He tried to talk, but at the sight of them the trembling soared back and his jaws clattered too hysterically even for words they could not understand. They tried to help him to his feet, but at their touch his body jerked away, twitching in the sand like a mortally wounded crab. As they stood over him, jabbering to themselves, he felt tears pouring over his cheeks and was unable even to cover his face, lying helplessly on his back and sobbing with fear and understanding. But even tears were no release, did not dissolve the hooks and pulleys which tore at his twitching body. He lay there, wondering how long it would be before his mind shook itself loose, how long before he smashed some essential spring and shuddering and realization died together. It would be too long; the anguish drew a long, high cry out of his throat, a strangled protest that he wanted to bring death itself but which only drove the fishermen a step backward, fear and bewilderment in their uncomprehending faces. They crossed themselves, afraid to help and afraid to leave him, and while they hesitated he tore out cry after shuddering cry, howling in the quiet morning air like a tortured animal.

THE RUSSIAN VOICE

HARUB MILGANI did not like to write: friends who had moved on to distant places found it virtually impossible to pry even a postcard out of him, no matter how copiously and entertainingly they bombarded him with mail. They minded, but they also understood. Harub had not forgotten them, he probably thought of them often and with great affection, but to put any part of himself onto paper was so vast a chore that the United States government, his employer, had several times threatened to discharge him for failure to file required reports. The discharge never took place, perhaps because he talked so well and talking was his job, perhaps because his talk was in Russian and the government suffered from a severe shortage of people who could handle that language.

Harub Milgani also disliked thinking: his mind only seemed to him alive and functioning when it was hooked to his mouth by a direct line, pouring out an uninhibited stream of words. It may have been his middle-Eastern blood, but he valued eloquence and fertility of expression far more than precise significance. Speed, and ease of delivery, and expansiveness—these were what counted. It was not much of a professional drawback, since his words were usually authored for him by others: his primary task was to read into a Voice of America microphone, and when he was not broadcasting he was translating other people's broadcasts, Russian into English, English into Russian. There was no need for him to write, even here. He sat down alongside a stenographer, material in hand, and dictated a sight translation; later, draft version in hand, he dictated a final product. The whole thing took written form quite apart from any physical effort of his, and he was left untroubled by anything except the reports for which the government did not supply him with stenographic assistance. Or had not so supplied him: he was too valuable a man to be lost on such grounds, and his department superior argued for and finally secured a special dispensation.

He was a small, dark-skinned man, not hook nosed but with the high cheek bones and full lips of his nativc Uzbckistan. Russian was his second language, English his third: he was fond of declaring that he could not be as eloquent, in either, as in his own tongue. "But who cares about the people of Uzbekistan? You want to talk to Moscow and Leningrad. Alright, I'll talk, they'll listen." And, when the Voice was not clogged by deliberate interference, presumably they did. People always listened to Harub Milgani; it was not really possible to remain in the same room with him and avoid being washed by the slightly high-pitched organ with which he sprayed words, endlessly and abundantly, at and sometimes over everyone within hearing range. He could listen, if necessary, but only until his blood had quickened and his tongue had become active. There was no turning back after that, it was stand and fire until capitulation and flight were the only alternatives to hypnotized attention.

He had come to the United States after the war, so that both his education and his habits were European. Not Russian, not anything else, but blended, bonded European. His regiment had been one of the first to be over-run in the great German offensive against the Soviets. He was captured and sent, first to Germany, later, with a work battalion, to France. In the middle of the war the Germans had recruited minorities of all kinds into a kind of half-slave, half-free fighting force. Harub had been a sergeant until he and his company deserted, going over to the liberating Allies during a steaming rainstorm in the Italian mountains. He had been a prisoner then too, until his background was traced and proven. Then he had successfully begged not to be sent home: the military intelligence people were delighted with so useful a helper. The war had ended, the United States forces had mostly gone home, and Harub had followed them. He was a citizen, now, and an especially rabid devotee of the fascinating political game. His politics were uncertain, at least to others, but there was no doubt that he held opinions by the bushelful. It was difficult to remember enough of what he'd said, from occasion to occasion, to indict him for inconsistency. No one really tried; it was not hard to see how futile a task it would have been.

He had many casual friends and, inevitably, many committed enemies. His professional contacts were typically peculiar. His supervisors treated him with care and courtesy, suspecting that so volatile a personality was also liable to be a highly sensitized one. His work was excellent, his salary moderate, and none of them knew where they could have gotten anyone with his enthusiasm and ability, anyone who could turn out so much excellent work in so short a time. His colleagues, some of them inclined to volatility to almost the same degree, generally despised him. One sardonic Georgian, born in Stalin's birthplace, Tiflis, insisted that Harub's Russian was so poor that no one except another denizen of god-forsaken Uzbekistan could possibly have understood him; in fact, over a short-wave transmitter it was his considered opinion that no one could understand him. A few less temperamental workers respected his abilities and ignored his shortcomings. In secret, one or two even admired him. And the secretarial force, being largely female, found him enormously attractive. He had no enemies among the swollen female population of Washington, being both a bachelor and a dark, moustached, odd-flavored quantity of unknown exotica. And the cheerful friendship so readily extended him by women, almost at sight, was still more cheerfully reciprocated: if there was one thing that interested Harub more than politics, more even than Russian politics or office politics, it was women. Washington was his natural, his inevitable base of operations. He should have been deliriously happy, he should have darted from flower to flower like a perpetually drunken honey bee, but it was not so easy, there was a thorn hidden in the blossom and a canker inside the thorn.

In a word, Harub was in love with love, but not as Don Juan, not as Casanova or Romeo had loved it. For him, a cosmopolitan with some of the genes of Mahomet, women should have been an object, an instrumentality, at best a thing to be toyed with for pleasure and dropped whenever satiety was reached. Yet his highest goal, his most passionate dream, was not passion but an *amour* which would have done credit to a Provençal troubador, a love perfect and rounded, gentle and full, ripe and serene. He longed for spiritual satisfaction, for something more than the dubious joys of flirtation and lust. His search was continuous, his disappointment—but not his disillusionment—profound. The look with which he peered into a woman's soul, or as far in that direction as he was able to penetrate, had melted many hearts, deceived into thinking that what had been thus lovingly bestowed was meant for what they in fact were, rather than what Harub wanted them to be, needed them to be, longed and craved and sometimes wept for them to be. The deception was no more intentional than the efforts he unconsciously made to conceal each new unveiling from himself. It was always the same, but always going to be different. Soul would meet soul, love would be supreme, until mundane trivialities sprouted like noxious weeds, until the rough edges of unknown personalities began to grate and rub, until, finally, each new *amour* went the way of all those that had preceded it. Harub was forty and still a bachelor: the list was a long one, the trail of shattered romance wide and far-reaching, the history of broken hearts as thick as an encyclopaedic tome. He had not given up, he would never give up. What if love was never revealed to him? It was the honesty and devotion of the pursuit which mattered: only Parsifal was granted the holy grail, of all those who had travelled in its pursuit. Had they been less worthy, those dedicated knights, less holy themselves, because their search was fruitless? Harub talked his way through the constantly shifting ranks of Washington womanhood, sometimes peering, sometimes leaping, always waiting. He would never settle for less than was his, and Love's, proper due: of that one cardinal principle he was completely sure. Nothing could shake his faith, or prompt him to an act of desecration.

II

For over six years, without wanting to face what he really knew to be reality, Harub had allowed himself to be at least formally engaged to one woman, a secretary in another government office. Her name was Mary Jane Path, she was a year his senior, and he knew he would never marry her. It seemed to him, after they had engaged themselves, that he had known the impossibility of the thing even then, even before buying her a ring and letting her exhibit it on the third finger of her left hand. But she was content, she did not urge him onward, and as long as everything was thus indefinite it seemed to do no harm. And her father, a suburban doctor, was one of the kindest, warmest men Harub had ever met: he needed Dr. Path more than he needed to be rid of the doctor's daughter. There were few men with whom he had been so at home, with whom he felt such a quiet, sure rapport that, often, even speech did not seem to be necessary. Vagueness was his element, of course, he could move through it as sure-footedly as a Sherpa blazing a trail through three-dimensional rocks and peaks. It did no harm to encourage Mary Jane in return for her father's friendship, her father's deep, sustaining trust and confidence.

Dr. Path and he had met, originally, at a conference of medical men. The Voice of America had sent a team to interview several outstanding personalities, notably the inventor of a world-renowned serum; Harub had accompanied the team, and Dr. Path, a teacher as well as a practitioner, had been asked to participate by his medical colleagues. He was, in addition, the local chairman of the medical association. After they had taped what was needed the team had left, but Harub lingered, curious, impressed, and well aware that his schedule was pretty much his own to make. The vast importance of what was being discussed attracted him; so, too, did the dry calm with which speaker after speaker analyzed and re-framed the life-giving potentialities of their discoveries, describing nostrums designed to heal or check ancient and feared maladies as though dealing with the equipment of the contracting or shipbuilding industries. Unemotionalism in the face of such enormous topics could not help but intrigue him.

"You're all so calm," he had exclaimed to Dr. Path, while the recording machine was being packed away and the conferees were enjoying an intermission. "It's amazing."

"Sheer histrionics," the doctor smiled back. "We're as excited about most of this stuff as you are, but how can we say so? No one wants an enthusiastic doctor: what's needed, alongside a sick bed, is a steady hand and a moderately cheerful smile. Not too cheerful," he explained, "or else the patient will leap up and kill himself with happiness. But not too grim, lest the sick be killed by fear alone."

Harub nodded appreciatively. This was a conversation on which he had, as yet, the slimmest of holds.

"But you are speaking to each other. No one is sick, here."

Dr. Path laughed.

"We're all sick, Mr. Milgani, but it isn't as obvious as it is with the people in my waiting room. And a doctor can't change his spots any more than the leopard can: he works so hard at being medical rather than personal that he's professional even with other professionals."

"Ah," Harub replied quickly, seeing the lay of the land and moving to occupy it. "The healing hand must move independently of the heart; there can be no pulse when the pulse is being sought. It is not the priest who delivers the sacrament, not the flesh and blood of a man, but the motion of God directing Himself toward humanity in a shape which humanity can tolerate and consume. Religion cannot stop at the doorway, cannot be inside the lintels and not outside them too. The black robe is more than the actor's mask, as is the white robe of your profession." He bowed to the silent, blinking, attentive doctor. "To be a man is a wonderful thing, but to be both a man and a servant of man, a man made not-man, is more wonderful still. In order to cloak his humanness in a saving robe a doctor, like a priest, must leave part of himself out, must tailor himself to his garments, must make the outside of the church stand also for what lies beyond the flesh and blood walls."

The conference was called back to order, and Dr. Path was called back to the rostrum: Harub had been rising toward free flight, from which no mere politeness could have rescued his accidental audience. But he was not offended, and the doctor was not displeased. The gift of tongues, since the Babel-blasted tower, is no longer a mortal possession, but even its latter-day approximation is enough to bring astonishment and sometimes admiration to those less abundantly blessed. Dr. Path knew a rare bird when he caught one in his lens; Harub was obviously a phenomenon, in his way as strange and noteworthy as a gull with three wings or a robin with a green breast. At the end of the conference, which Harub sat through in perfect quiet, Dr. Path approached him without any intent to snare a prospect for his still unmarried daughter's net. He was interested, as a practical scientist, in observing Harub more closely, perhaps learning what spring, wound by what mysterious hand, kept the flow of words from drying away. He was interested, as a connoisseur of fine objects of all kinds, in the pleasure of hearing perfect talk, monologue brought to its highest pitch. And he was interested, as an ordinary human being, in what lay beyond Harub's fantastic outer sheen: could the being within glow just as brightly? Here, too, even an approximation would be worth cultivating.

Mary Jane did not inquire into her father's motives. She was a woman, as she had been a girl, of no particular attainments. Her appearance was equally unremarkable: she was inclined to be thin, yet not at all scrawny, and if her face was bland it was also regularly featured and smooth-complexioned. There had been a time, when she was eighteen or nineteen, when it would have been possible to call her pretty. The time had passed, and she was only innocuous, only acceptable, a woman one could pass without looking back yet not without being aware that it was a woman one was passing. Her job had come about in the same uneventful way: she had wanted no career except marriage, and when her school offered part-time secretarial instruction she had accepted it. She was a competent stenographer and a good though slow typist; the job was hers till she either died or retired, whichever came first. She welcomed so exotic and unexpected a bonanza as her father brought her as a younger and less desperate girl might have welcomed a gift of chocolates or a new hat: Harub was too susceptible to be wary, and then too quickly devoted to Dr. Path to be critical until almost too late. Engagement, of course, was still well this side of disaster, was a transient commitment that he knew he could somehow abandon whenever abandonment became necessary.

"You're really Russian," she had exclaimed that first evening, while Dr. Path attended to the final stages of preparing their drinks. Harub had been describing, for her very willing ears, the intricate architecture of the Eastern Orthodox cathedrals.

"Because I remember my grandfather's religion?" he answered with a smile. It was only with women, and then only with women he knew either very well or not at all, that Harub was possessed of a sense of humor. But even then it did not last long, quickly falling, a mute victim, at the feet of his oratorical fervor. "The new Czars haven't pulled down the churches, they can't afford to. It keeps people quiet, just knowing they're still there, the ancient places where spirit has once had a meaning. And where else could Stalin find a better place to store his own relics? Churches are just magnificent museums, as far as the communists are concerned. Religion!" he proclaimed, settling comfortably into the curves of the rattan chair, breathing deeply of the fragrance of Dr. Path's generously flowered garden. It was late summer, warm and, had he noticed such things, unpleasantly close; the air was overhung with the smells of blossoms and the chittering of insects. Mosquitoes and small, nameless bugs brushed their skin, in the pale darkness, as they sat and Harub talked. "There is no opiate in religion, nothing that drugs the masses. They come to it drugged and it sings them lullabies, they come to it demented and it gives their insanity a place and a point. It expresses all the humanity there is in them. They have no influence over it, except as rivers slowly cut into the rocks over which they flow. It exists, it stands and waits, and they flood toward it, not sucked down but struggling to come to where it is, struggling to arrive where it has been from the beginning and from where it will never move. Only people move, slide away from it or crawl back toward it. Religion, the great churches and the great ideas, are in fact what Peter called them, the rock on which humanity rests, restlessly, often unknowingly, but eternally."

Dr. Path came over with a small tray and they helped themselves.

"You *are* a true believer," the older man observed quietly, sitting with them. He had heard the last part of Harub's remarks as he approached.

Harub smiled.

"For myself," he answered, holding out his glass and, at intervals during his speech, sipping gently from its edge, "for Harub Milgani personally, there is neither church nor religion nor even God. I know it all, I have lived it and seen it and felt it. I feel it still, but not here." He nodded, and lightly thumped his chest. "I feel it as a man, looking out from inside my own little cage of bones and flesh, and seeing other men. I see how the people, the endless majority of every country, every country in the world, wallow in their nothingness, knowing neither themselves nor each other, knowing nothing of how they seem in the sight of God. For them, for each of us in our turn, there is the single rock, a pinnacle, a beacon, and we find our way through to it or we die."

"How true!" Mary Jane whispered in an awed voice.

"Yet whatever I see I do not see as a Russian," Harub went on, somehow remembering her original remark and turning back to wipe away its slightly unwholesome sting. "I am a Russian by fiat only, created in the Great Russian image by *ukaz* alone. In actual fact I am an Uzbekistani, and as long as there was an Uzbekistan I was of it, despite the propaganda and the beatings, despite the threats and the punishments. Here," he explained soulfully, "here is this country, of which I am legally and gratefully a citizen, I am Russian because you so label me. But I am nothing, I am an outcast from everywhere, a homeless soul without the possibility of ever finding a home."

"Oh no," Mary Jane exclaimed involuntarily.

Dr. Path brushed away a persistent insect.

"I speak as a medical sceptic, of course," he acknowledged dryly. "An American sceptic, with my soul immunized in antiseptic plastic. But you hardly seem as out of place as you say." He laughed easily. "I would even predict that, some day, you will discover that you have a great deal of affection for this brass and chrome land of ours."

Harub leaned forward, a bit of his drink trickling out and down over his hand to the ground. He did not notice, and Mary Jane pretended that she too did not see.

"Of course!" he agreed passionately. "How can you call yourself a sceptic, seeing so much, understanding so truly, how can you even think of yourself in such terms? Life is composed of two parts, spirit and affection. I have been deprived of the one; without the other I would wither, literally, physically wither. I would die. I must feel at home, here and wherever I am, or else I must leave, find somewhere else to stay and work and wait. But," he assured them eloquently, his voice rising with adept, automatic skill, "the home that you make is different, very different, from the home that makes you. In one case you are the child of the land, it holds you and feeds you and when you are grown you take strength, like the ancient giant, merely from putting your feet against it. I weep," he confided, "when people show me photographs of the Uzbekistani places I knew, once. And yet I must look, I cannot look away. But that," he announced with clarion sharpness, "that kind of home is once and forever and when it is lost it is lost forever. The other home, the one you fly down onto, come down from the air like a wandering pigeon and roost upon, that is a stepmother, earnest, helpful, but never warm. Surely I have an affection for this country and," he bowed his head briefly, courteously, "also for its people, but the pieces of my heart are held together with a different glue, a paste you do not manufacture here, not with all your wonderful machines and great cleverness at duplicating what nature alone has been making for centuries and centuries. With all your mechanical genius you cannot put together the pieces of hearts, you cannot fabricate home and love and the spirit of what I once had and have no longer." He nodded carefully. "And Russia, with its new machines, as big, maybe bigger than yours, is going to make certain that nowhere in the world is there any home but the Great Russian home. They are as foolish as you have been, they are as sure that machines can do what machines can never do, and they will lose their hearts, have already lost them, as well as make all the rest of us lose ours. My Uzbekistan does not exist; what you call Russia does not exist. There is only the communist machine and here, Dr. Path, the American machine." He produced a quick smile. "I like your machine better, you are right. It is cleverer, and it is older, and it is really almost successful at pretending not to be a machine at all. At least it tries. I have no right, in this splintered world, to ask for more." He shook his head. "I do not ask for more. I am content." He raised his glass, swished it in a slow circle while the ice clinked against itself with high pitched bell sounds, and then he smiled more deeply and drank. He was doing them the greatest of honors, though he did not put it to himself in that way. He was going to stop without having said everything, without having emptied his heart—an inexhaustible chamber, but tonight curbed, checked, restrained in tribute to the soft-spoken, courtly manners of his host. Cessation at any point, in fact, was Harub's way of attempting to duplicate that courtliness, the flattery of imitation as closely as he knew how to practice it.

"But you do understand," Mary Jane burst out. "You do!" She turned to her father, her fingers opening as she sought the words that came so readily to their guest. "It's divine, isn't it?" she appealed at last, unable to shape a declaration of her own. "It's an understanding of the divine."

Harub was not sure what she meant, but he could not be displeased and certainly he was not shocked. His eyes glowed, realizing how desperately she was striving for expression. To become aware that a woman sought contact with the same inner realities for which he himself lived was to become aware, for him, of woman as woman. Perhaps, he wondered hurriedly, neither thinking nor wanting to think, perhaps this daughter of his new and already treasured friend would become the final solution to the unsolvable equation of love.

"We sceptics can't speak of such things with authority," Dr. Path noted with a quick laugh, "but a doctor with your understanding of faith, Mr. Milgani, could be a miracle man. I don't mean a medicine man, but a worker of miracles." He nodded. "Even science admits that."

Harub's laugh was eager.

"Yes!" he echoed. It had been a long time since he'd wanted so badly to throw his arms around another man's neck, to exchange, in warm delight, the traditional kiss on both cheeks. It was difficult to restrain himself: Dr. Path so clearly knew that even an officially designated Russian was, underneath, simply a human being like other human beings. Harub had always wanted, in this adopted homeland, to reach out to his fellow citizens in affection and joy. The rebuffs had been painful, no matter how effectively he disguised them from himself. But here, in this lovely bower of humanity, this fragrant arbor of hope and comfort, he needed no fear, it was he, precisely and knowingly he, that the Paths had invited. He threw a quick side glance at Mary Jane, but did not see how, in the darkness, she trembled under his eyes.

But it was Mary Jane, when the evening was finally over, who carried him off, bundling him into her own slightly battered sedan and driving down the brief garage-way and out onto the largely deserted roads. She had been patient and silent; the talk had swirled and lapped around her without cutting away a bit of the new-sprung hope and excitement which supported and buoyed her virgin fastness. And then, at last, her reward had been easier than she could have expected. Harub had risen, suddenly aware that he was staying very much longer than was either wise or polite, and her offer to chauffeur him back had been seconded by her father and quickly accepted.

Harub sat beside her, at first, in satisfied, fulfilled silence, as rare and deeply-savored as the whole evening with this agreeable, sympathetic woman and her relaxed, encouraging father. When she spun the car easily off a side road and onto a wide parkway he laughed with pleasure.

"You drive very well," he said appreciatively. The only motor he himself could manipulate sat fixed at the base of his tongue; his mechanical skills were for all intents and purposes nil.

She succeeded in not blushing: the rapprochement for which she'd been waiting all night, and for a vast succession of nights before that, had begun. She was sure, and so excited that it was hard to keep her eyes on the road. It was only at Harub that she wanted to look.

"Thank you."

He was sitting in the middle of the front seat, not too far from her. He waved his hand deprecatingly and it just missed brushing against her shoulder.

"I have never been able to learn," he confided.

She glanced around, her smile not quite so steady as her hand on the wheel. Driving was much more a habit than such barely restrainable passion.

"I could teach you," she murmured.

Harub chuckled.

"What else do you do?" he wondered.

The revelation could not be avoided; unlike Harub there was nothing she feared quite so much as exposure. She had never had ambitions of the usual kind and this was the price she always paid.

"I write letters," she said reluctantly, putting as decorative a face on her grubby job as she could quickly invent for it. "For the government."

But Harub, in some things naively literal, was impressed all over again. A person who could write, actually write, for a living—and talk of it so matter-of-factly—was as wonderful, to him, as a horse that could speak or a shrimp that could whistle.

"How can you!" he exclaimed.

She pursed her lips, a little angry but resolved not to reveal herself. Personal injury over such trifles was a luxury she could not afford.

"It's a job," she shrugged.

He shook his head.

"I can just manage to sign my name," he confided. "You don't know what a gift you have."

She giggled, still not understanding yet seeing that he was anything but critical. It did not matter how they arrived, if they got where she wanted them to go.

"Didn't you ever go to school?" she asked, easing her foot still further off the accelerator. This was not a trip she could hurry; he would not notice.

He waved his hand and this time it did touch her, a quick passing contact that, for an instant, left her limp.

"School," he mocked. "The master would beat my hand with a stick when I wrote a letter the wrong way. I was like a small dog: I learned not to soil my paper, but only to keep from being beaten."

She found herself staring open-eyed at the road, scarcely able to see its edges or the soft winding turns it made.

"How different you are!" she exclaimed.

He laughed.

"How wrong you are," he answered lightly.

She circled the car around a deep-swung arc in the road, then, without letting herself think about what she was doing, pointed the long, smoky beams of its lights down the dark channel of an exit ramp, following silently as the ramp wound itself into a small, bumpy-surfaced country road. It did not matter where they were: she drove a hundred yards away from the highway and eased the car onto the shoulder.

Harub blinked.

"Something wrong?" he inquired.

She turned toward him, for a moment unable to speak. She shook her head and watched to see what he would do. He did nothing, the initiative was all hers.

"Would you talk to me a little?" she asked, her voice uncertainly husky. She bent forward, remembering the motor, and switched it off.

He smiled, touched and pleased.

"Gladly," he assured her, cheerful and, for his own part, still warmed by the evening she and her father had given him. "You're very good company, Miss Path." He faced around too; their knees bumped and, sitting in the darkness, the car lights all out and the motor silent, he smiled, neither embarrassed nor concerned. She was revealing herself as more and more unusual, and he did not mind such revelations in the least.

"Would you call me Mary Jane?"

He remembered her appreciative knowingness, earlier, and felt a growing interest in the unknown, almost invisible woman sitting opposite him.

"It would be a privilege," he assured her.

Somewhere in the countryside nearby a car came alive with a bang like a rifle shot. The seat rocked as she started; he put out his hand to reassure her and found himself holding her damp, slightly limp fingers in his own. She did not pull away; he could hear her breathing a little too loudly.

"It was only a car," he explained.

It took her a moment to answer.

"I know," she said.

Harub was not sure, but with a faint pressure he began to pull her toward him. Her head thumped against his chest and her free hand clung to his sleeve. He was still not sure; it was all too fast and he was the least sensual of men.

"You shouldn't be frightened," he explained, touching her hair gently. It felt surprisingly soft; she was smaller than he'd realized, smaller than he'd expected, seeing her in her father's home. "Not of the dark or of loud noises like guns or of anything. Not even of guns themselves. They're only machines, and we're human beings, we make them, we un-make them, they're only pieces of inertness for us to command."

Her head rolled hesitantly from side to side.

"Still afraid, Mary Jane?" he wondered, saying the unfamiliar name with quiet grace.

Her hand separated itself from his, then both hands went around his neck. He kissed her, willingly, and she lay against him a long time while he stroked her hair and kept brushing his lips against hers. It was oddly impersonal, he did not quite feel that it was he who was with her. Yet it was distinctly pleasurable, it was clearly of a piece with Dr. Path's easy acceptance of him. And when she straightened and took him the rest of the way home, finally, he sat a good deal closer, occasionally draping his arm across her shoulder.

Just under a month later, a month in which he had seen a good deal of both Paths, he and Mary Jane were sitting in the back row of a movie theatre she'd asked him to take her to. They generally did not go out unless she proposed it; the arrangement did not disturb either of them. Dr. Path never interfered, though Harub's attention was directed to him whenever there was a choice.

The picture they were seeing was ludicrously simple-minded. Harub held her hand, as she wanted it to be held, and smiled at the farcical ineptness being flashed on the big screen. He had seen perhaps half a dozen American movies in all the time he'd been in the country, and the professional propagandist in him took considerable pleasure in the opportunity. He found himself, quickly, planning how the Russians could most effectively satirize this arch nonsense: his pictorially oriented mind often ran to such things.

Mary Jane suddenly leaned her head onto his shoulder.

"Do you like me?" she whispered.

He did not talk to her, when they were alone—not as he talked to almost everyone else. She was, he'd learned, just as obviously sympathetic and eager as she'd seemed that very first night. It was not difficult to spend time with her, she demanded very little. An occasional word, an occasional mild caress, was more than enough. But he had also learned, though he had yet to confess it to himself, that they could never be closer than they had been in the first ten minutes, the first ten seconds, of their acquaintanceship. He did not care that she lacked opinions: that would not have been her role, in his ideal relationship. But he did care, without admitting it, that she lacked anything except a bland, continuous desire. He saw passion as a ritual of variety, counterpointed around a central core of enthusiasm and affection. Mary Jane had only one kind and one degree of enthusiasm, and he had come to suspect its depth and its sincerity.

"Of course," he whispered. "Of course I like you."

She was silent a moment. He transferred his attention back to the ridiculous antics portrayed on the screen in front of them; his mouth separated in a faint smile of superior comprehension.

"How much?" she asked again.

He kept himself from shrugging.

"A great deal," he said easily.

Her head lifted away from him.

"My father was asking," she declared untruthfully. Dr. Path was neither blind nor uncurious, but he would not have interfered in any way with his daughter and their unhurried friend. Harub could not have known; when he was with them he did not notice Mary Jane very much, and when he was alone with her he did not consider what her father might be thinking.

He blinked, wondering what she meant.

"He likes you," she went on.

He nodded firmly.

"I like him as much as any man I've ever met," he replied, back on reliable ground. "I'm sure there isn't a better man, not anywhere." Her head returned to his shoulder. But the catechism was not done with.

"He asked what you and I were planning to do," she announced.

Harub felt, uneasily, that he would have to give her what she wanted, at least for the moment. If Dr. Path really wanted it, he might even have been capable of marrying the girl; he was not ready to face that. But he would have done a great deal to keep everything just the way it had become. He would do a great deal, would do what now had to be done.

"Are we planning at all?" he hedged.

She sighed.

"Aren't we?"

He made a quick face: it would not matter, later, it was only an accommodation, an easing of tension, a way to prevent difficulties more painful than anything this decision could cause him.

"I suppose we are," he confessed. She squeezed his arm so hard that he almost cried out. But then she was quiet and he went back to watching the silly film. The next week he bought her a ring and she wore it with great but unassertive pride. There was no rush, she did not want to force matters. Now that she clearly had him she could be as patient as, before, she had been perpetually anxious. Her soul, which he had so much trouble locating at all, was at peace.

Dr. Path, seeing the ring displayed a little embarrassedly at his table, nodded and offered them a quiet smile.

"My congratulations," he said to Harub when Mary Jane was out of the room. Harub was no longer a guest; indeed, he sometimes felt as though he lived in the Path home, so frequently did he visit, staying long hours and invariably dining with his hosts. His enthusiasm was inexhaustible; Dr. Path's easy comradeship was apparently just as deep. It was a relationship to be protected and preserved at almost any cost, especially when it was his most vital link with his fellow men. And the first he had had in many years.

"Thank you," he acknowledged. It was not hypocrisy, he told himself hastily. His mind was not wholly made up; it was still conceivable that he would actually marry Mary Jane. Then he asked the doctor about a new serum, and the engagement was never again mentioned between them. It lasted over six years, six very full and contented years in which Harub and Mary Jane did not push at the transparent barrier between themselves and final fruition, each of them too pleased with the present to jeopardize the future, each of them too afraid of change to risk either a forward or a backward step. And Dr. Path, long a widower and too long bored by his home and his daughter, welcomed their indecision. Mary Jane had truthfully reported his affection for Harub: he found the younger man constantly interesting, often fascinating. He smiled at Harub's inadequacies, marvelled at his uncontrolled virtuosity with words, and took both pleasure and pride in their unspoken mutual affection. It was a queerly self-sustaining triangle, almost entirely satisfactory exactly as it was. And that was how they carefully maintained it, and themselves, while seasons and all the rest of the world fluctuated and spun; while change and variety ruled supreme they preserved their unique oasis unaltered. Their affairs seemed as regular and predictable as stars and planets, and quite as fixed in both time and space.

III

And then came Sasha Borisovna, a widow and a whirlwind, and instead of Harub and peace, Mary Jane was left with nothing, and Dr. Path was left with Mary Jane. Sasha was forty-three, inclined to be plump at every point and curve where Mary Jane was inclined to be thin, and she could speak Russian. Indeed, her attempts to speak anything else were sometimes incomprehensible. Her first husband had been a Pole, a minor diplomat in the pre-Hitler days, at the end an exile, supporting himself by lecturing on east European affairs. He had been dead over a year, and Sasha had resolved to be true to his memory: like Mary Jane's fiancé she was a true romantic. She came to Washington and did wretched but enthusiastic translating for an agricultural bureau. But after a year she met Harub at a semi-official function, heard him deliver an impassioned harangue on the Great Russians' superiority complex, and on the spot lost both her heart and her sacrificial dedication.

Unlike Mary Jane, to whom marriage was only an ideal state, Sasha had no talent for passivity. A woman of experience and some culture, she moved rapidly, making excellent use of every advantage she possessed. Harub was dazzled: it had been his conviction that all Russian-speaking women were carefully married off before they were allowed to enter the United States. He had long since resigned himself to the thought that, whoever she might be, her tongue would move in square Anglo-Saxon cadences. And along with her linguistic affinity, of course, Sasha bore the deep, miraculous imprint of that peculiarly slavic taste for the spirit, that longing for high conversation which even the warm but scientific Dr. Path could not duplicate. Sasha was Woman as Harub had not dared to dream of her, she was too good to be true, and after a hectic courtship full of endless tea-drinking sessions and almost unbroken conversation, they trundled themselves off to the Municipal Hall (both being believers only in their own unorganized, non-institutional way) and were married. The whole process had taken two weeks, during which time both Mary Jane and her father were totally, even shockingly neglected. Mary Jane had called, several times, but he had put her off, inventing excuses with that wild fluency she could not openly doubt. He told her nothing of Sasha, and though she worried she did not worry enough. And then it was too late.

The day after their marriage—Sasha agreed that there was no need for a honeymoon: life itself was their festival and celebration—Harub made his way to Dr. Path's suburban waiting room. He had no fear of meeting Mary Jane, who was surely at her Washington desk; he much preferred not meeting her, now, at all. He was there before the doctor's usual hour for seeing patients, but when he sent in his name the nurse allowed him into the softly lit, grey carpeted room where people regularly sat and awaited Dr. Path's ministrations. Harub had never seen it, his health was superb. But he took a seat on the plush couch, just like any ailing supplicant, and hoped the doctor would not be too long.

Dr. Path appeared in less than a quarter of an hour, garbed in professional white and smiling warmly.

"Harub," he greeted his friend. "I told her it couldn't be you: you haven't been sick a day since I've known you." He led Harub into his office and discreetly closed the door. "That's more than half a dozen years, isn't it?" Dr. Path waved to a chair. "Sit down. What's wrong?"

Harub settled himself with a residual sense of discomfort. But he smiled easily, crossing his legs and giving his moustache a small flick with one tobacco stained finger.

"Nothing, nothing," he murmured.

Dr. Path closed his notebook with a flourish.

"Then I won't need to take your life history," he said pleasantly. He smoothed down the starched white coat. "I didn't need this, either, I suppose. I couldn't quite believe it was you."

Harub nodded, understanding the mild reproach.

"I have neglected you," he conceded.

"Not at all," Dr. Path assured him. "We've missed you, but both Mary Jane and I quite understand that a public servant cannot always call his time his own."

Harub cleared his throat.

"I'm married," he said with lame, hopeless bluntness.

Dr. Path nodded slowly.

"Not to Mary Jane," he said after a moment.

Harub shook his head.

"No."

Dr. Path leaned back in his chair and crossed his arms on his chest.

"You haven't told her."

"No," Harub admitted, once again impressed with his friend's incisive powers, his soul-sparing ability to say what others needed to hear.

Dr. Path permitted himself a small sigh.

"You waited so long: I didn't think it was going to work. Who is she?" he suddenly wondered.

Harub almost blushed.

"A Russian lady, a widow. Her name is Sasha."

"Ah," Dr. Path smiled.

"She is what I've dreamed of," Harub said hurriedly, his tongue loosening slightly. "Always, without ever expecting to find her. It isn't love, it's more than love could ever be. Her soul is shaped just as mine, her heart hears the same invisible sounds mine lives by."

Dr. Path nodded once more.

"I won't tell Mary Jane that," he observed quietly.

Harub started.

"My god, no!" he exclaimed. "But," he added quickly, "you will tell her?"

Dr. Path shrugged.

"I suppose I'll have to, if you won't. Coward," he pronounced with a smile.

Harub shook his head.

"It would be too brutal," he explained. "Thank you for sparing the two of us." He rose. "You will see me—us," he corrected with fleeting confusion, "if you want to. I hope you do," he declared, extending his hand.

Dr. Path had risen with him.

"Of course," he answered, as they shook hands. They walked slowly to the door: the first patients would soon be arriving, and Harub too had to return to his work. "But I suppose we'd better give time a chance to smooth things over a little."

Harub nodded eagerly.

"Thank you," he exclaimed again, grasping the doctor's hand and squeezing it. "Thank you."

He hurried off, almost afraid to look back. What if Mary Jane had not gone to work that day, or for some reason had decided to come home in the middle of the morning?

He never saw Dr. Path again. A bit less than a month later he was reading idly through a local newspaper when, by chance, his eye caught a familiar name on the obituary page. "Dr. Richard Path, prominent physician, stricken suddenly; heart attack fatal to healer of many." He lowered the paper, his face so anguished that his wife rose from her chair and ran to his side.

"Harub," she cried. "What is it?"

He simply shook his head; he could not speak.

"Are you ill?" she asked, the high, smooth Russian phrases providing none of their usual solace. She shook him lightly. "Tell me," she begged, more worried by his silence than by the sudden pallor of his face, already fading back toward normalcy. "Do you want a doctor?"

He shook his head again.

"No," he said thickly. "No doctor." He dropped the paper onto the breakfast table. His head seemed to sag uncertainly forward: he put his hands against the table edge, as though to support himself. "Dr. Path is dead."

She released his shoulder, then slowly resumed her place.

"How terrible," she said fervently, the tears gathering in her eyes. Like her husband, her emotions shifted quickly and violently. "How terrible," she repeated, beginning to dab at the tears with her tiny handkerchief. She had never met Dr. Path, but that did not matter. Harub knew him and loved him, and she was instantly and totally grief-stricken.

Harub sighed miserably.

"How I will miss him," he murmured. Then he looked up, blinking. "I must call her," he announced, pushing back from the table.

Sasha tried to smile but could not manage it.

"Of course," she snuffled. "Go, Harub, go." She might have been making the sign of the cross, behind the protection of the little square of cloth; he was not sure. But he hurried to the telephone and dialed Mary Jane's number, the number that until the day before she had shared with her wonderful, departed father.

Surprisingly, she answered the phone herself.

"This is Harub," he said at once, his tongue not at all stiffened at the sound of her voice. Emotional shock spurred him into his greatest feats of verbal magic: his wife, had she been asked, could have testified abundantly to that. "I have just read, in the paper, of your terrible, terrible loss. I must come to you," he said urgently.

"No," she said flatly. "Don't."

"He could have been my father, too," he informed her quietly, his tone deep and so compelling that Sasha had to turn away her face, to hide the freshly flowing tears. "I loved him, I honored him, I cannot let you mourn alone."

"I don't want you to come," she insisted.

"Mary Jane," he went on. "It is my duty and my privilege. I must come, I would never be able to forgive myself if I ignored him, and you, and just turned my back. And you," he urged, "need not forgive me. The injury is all on your side: I was not fair to you, I know that." There was only silence at the other end of the wire. "Mary Jane?"

There was a faint rustling sound.

"Don't come," she said in the same flat tone, and then he heard the click of a broken connection. She had hung up.

"The poor woman," he told his wife, slipping into his jacket and reaching for his hat. "I must go to her."

Sasha touched his lapel with one damp hand.

"You're so good," she said worshipfully.

He brushed her forehead with his lips and hurried off.

A woman in uniform answered the bell.

"Yes?" she inquired politely.

He told her his errand.

"Your name, sir?"

He told her that too, and then quickly inserted his foot between the jamb and the closing door.

"Impossible," he exclaimed powerfully, pushing her aside and entering. "I am an old, old friend. I must see her."

He knew the way without being led; the maid was simply forgotten. He walked quickly into the room, upset and sorrowing, and held up his hand when Mary Jane's face twisted with annoyance.

"You would not shut me out," he exclaimed.

Her face did not change.

"Get out," she directed.

He produced a softening smile.

"I understand," he conceded. "You have every right to be angry with me." He stepped closer to where she was sitting, where she had been addressing a heap of little white cards. Announcements, printed announcements of Dr. Path's death and funeral: had she been going to send him one, did she want to exclude him from that too? "But you can't desecrate my friendship with your father because I have sinned toward you." He shook his head with firm conviction. "You can't."

Mary Jane's mouth twitched.

"You forced your way in," she said flatly.

He nodded.

"The woman must have been mistaken," he said softly. "You couldn't have meant to shut me out."

She rose, her face flushing, her lips quivering. She stood glowering at him, then stabbed for the telephone.

"I'll call the police," she said fiercely. "They'll make you get out, they'll show you what I meant."

He came over to where she stood and gently covered her hand with his.

"Don't," he said warmly, persuasively. "Don't, Mary Jane. For the love you once had for me, the love you shared with me, and for your father's holy memory. Don't."

She let him finish, unmoving, silent, then pulled back her hand and dropped into the chair from which she'd risen. Her back was bent, her head turned down.

"We would both of us be so sorry, later," he informed her, standing just where he was. "We would never be able to forget how we acted toward his memory." He paused a moment. "Don't you think he would have wanted me here? He was my dearest friend; I loved him as almost no other man, and I know he loved me."

She gasped, for a moment he thought she was choking. Then he recognized the sound of laughter.

"You amused him," she said wildly, not bothering to look around at him. "You were a freak, he'd never seen anything like you before." She laughed again. "He used to say he hoped to do the autopsy on you, when you died of an epileptic fit, still talking, talking, talking." Her voice rose steeply. "Jabbering like a monkey, like an animal that doesn't know how to do anything but open and close its snout." She turned and pointed a thin finger directly at him. "Ape, monkey, idiot!" she declaimed fiercely, her face contorting despite the laugh she savagely produced after each word. "Ape!" she spit, swinging back away from him. "Now get out," she said passionately, her voice ebbing slightly.

"It isn't true," he answered slowly. "It could not be the truth."

She began to cry, her face wrinkling like an old woman's, but this time she did not turn away.

"It is true," she said brokenly. "You'll never know how true it is."

Then she looked up at him. "And didn't you lie to me, didn't you cheat me for years, lying and cheating and torturing me?"

She moaned, her sobs returned, and then Harub turned to where the uncomprehending woman in uniform was waiting, just inside the door, and let her show him out of the house. He did not attend the funeral. Sasha noticed the difference at once, for she hung on his every emotion as a hummingbird vibrates above a blossoming flower. But there was nothing she could do, there was nothing anyone could do. Dr. Path was dead and Mary Jane was quite right, Harub would never know.

FATHERHOOD

I

This isn't a life history: I'll spare the world that much. No one has to know when I was weaned, where I got my first complex, and my second. We can skip my mother. My father. My family all. This story begins when the war began. The last war, the biggest war. My work took me to Europe regularly: I had connections on both sides of the ocean, and though the money all travelled west to east, and the goods east to west, my job was to shuttle back and forth from buyer to seller, offering, accepting, the ever-ready conduit. Wherever I went I had something that was wanted. None of it was mine, I risked nothing. In Europe I was money, smart money that smelled the war coming and wanted to pluck the good things that were surely to be had. In America I was the good things willing and anxious to be taken. I knew the people who wanted to turn cash into jewels, and antiques, and paintings. I knew the people who wanted to sell anything that would bring cash. The buyers were looking forward to war and inflation. The sellers thought only of escape, of the German armies and the Russian armies. And because I knew some, the rest sought me out. It was perfect.

But it had never been bad. The depression hadn't touched me. My friends who'd gone into steel and railroads and Wall Street were waiting it out, week by week. The salesmen had nothing to sell, even the lawyers could only shuffle one bankrupt corporation into another, covering the bottomless pit with a spider's web of legal foolscap. They didn't starve, the world hadn't completely stopped on its axis. But they lost their healthy tans and their budding potbellies, they kept last year's Cadillac a year longer, they let their golf clubs grow rusty in the upstairs closet. Wheat and corn were going under, little pigs got no fatter, but how could the market in Old Masters ever break? When could Ming porcelain move as slowly as Woolworth china? It is not the poor we have always with us, but the rich. A few miserable bankers throw themselves out of their office windows, some brokers hang themselves by their garters, a railroad president or two blows his brains out, but very little wealth that is solid melts away.

Which is neither here nor there. All you need to know is that the depression passed over me like a summer shower, only a few stray drops pattering meaninglessly down. I continued to make my annual trip to Europe, my New York studio was discreet, lofty, and rarely empty, and the beginnings of my personal fortune quickly accumulated in one of the banks that nothing short of revolution will ever touch. I kept my dress sombre. I was quite content. And then, before I was thirty, the war approached and, without any special effort, I found myself becoming almost embarrassingly opulent. I had no pangs about my commissions: they were well merited, I earned my pay. But I had no desire for glory: it was with genuine relief that I saw the war fever crawl across the Atlantic and start up the factories and the mines and the railroads, send the ripe wheat and the fattened hogs onto a booming market instead of back into the earth. Money began to flow again, and I was relieved to be no longer conspicuous. I've never grudged my friends their well-being; I still do not, though by now most of them could buy and sell me a dozen times over. What difference does it make, as long as one has enough? I don't think I really know what greed means.

But this too is not my story. Were I spinning a fabricated tale, creating a fiction, it might be appropriate, here, to promise that self-consciousness would be confined in the future, that my plot would firm and not wobble again, that opinionated digressions would cease to intrude. The writer of fiction can afford to offer such assurances, both writer and reader knowing them false. I have no made-up store of incident to rely upon, and surely there is no plot to so much of my life as I shall set down in these pages. I can promise nothing; perhaps where I fail for lack of art I may succeed by virtue of simply telling only and all of what actually occurred. And yet, what a strange word virtue is, used either by or about me.

We can begin in the autumn before the fighting became general. I regularly made my European trips in the fall, after the school teachers and the business men on holidays had gone back to their work, and Continental hotels and cafés were again inhabited by Continentals. And quiet. Also, before the vicious cold of the northern winters had set in, before the lovely self-effacing women were so bundled in great-clothes that they might as well have been men, before the charming greenery that filled even the cities had crumbled away and even the sun had vanished.

My first trip was east of the Danube. Budapest. Rudolf Levi-Zorn was the client's name, a barrister, sometime banker, a dabbler in new products and machines. I was told he'd been largely responsible for two or three of the biggest industries in his country; he was supposed to have built at least one pilot plant with his own money. His collection was reputedly just as up-to-date. I was assured of a good run of Picasso line drawings, several small Matisse canvases, a large Chagall, and quite a bit more. There was statuary, too, though I had some doubt, at that stage, as to my ability to transport safely anything much bulkier than a painting. It was already fairly plain that this was going to be my last European visit for some time. What with the rapidly decaying political situation and the excellence of Levi-Zorn's collection, I was looking forward to my stay at his summer home (where most of the collection was housed) long before I actually arrived at the Budapest station and stepped into the waiting limousine.

Frau Levi-Zorn herself met me at the door.

"Please come in, Mr. Thompson," she said in clear though accented English. She was a short, plain, rather chubby woman, but her smile could not have been more gracious. I felt quite at home from the start.

"My husband is not yet back," she explained.

I was careful to look at nothing but my hostess, though the walls were crowded with bright-colored canvases.

"It's I who am to blame," I assured her. "My train was on time."

She returned my smile, then had a servant show me to my room.

"Dinner will be at nine," she said. It was only a bit past six; I would have an opportunity to change and, if I liked, take a walk about the grounds. I declined the offer, with no falseness of motive: I have never walked, then or now, when it was possible to avoid it.

My room, which I could study at my leisure, was a promise of things to come. The furniture was not exceptional: clean, direct versions of what was then a rather new development, Swedish modern, all angles and planes and rubbed, unvarnished wood. There was next to no decoration. The walls were an off-yellow, and one, the long, unobstructed wall across from the bed, was hung with a really stunning Matisse. If you have been to the Museums which house such things you may have seen it. When I had bathed and shaved I sat in the window seat, with my back to the twilight and to the grounds (extensive and obviously well cared for), and stared at the canvas for a satisfying half an hour. It sent me down to dinner with real anticipation; I even looked forward to awaking in the morning and seeing it there in the half light. I was quite sure it would be every bit as lovely.

Levi-Zorn had returned, when I came down; he greeted me with a curiously delicate handshake. I had expected a fairly large, energetic man, more than likely bearded or at the least moustached. He was as small as his wife, slenderer, his lean, rather yellow face clean-shaven, his eyes deep and ringed, his hands small and conspicuous without seeming to move a great deal. He moved, in fact, with a langour that struck me as convalescent, though I never knew whether it was actual or premonitory. Yet his voice was firm and his manner cheerful.

"You are very welcome," he assured me. His English was still better than his wife's, virtually free of accent.

I joined them in the spacious, dimly lit room. The table had been set and was waiting. And in one corner, perched on the edge of a straight wooden chair, sat a dark-haired little girl, her hands folded in her lap, very still, but looking up at the stranger with evident interest.

"My daughter, Elizabeta," Levi-Zorn informed me. I bowed slightly and the small, dark head inclined forward in return. I was mildly surprised: ordinarily, European children did not dine with their parents until probably twice this child's age. But it was not my affair, and I concentrated my attention where it belonged, on my host and his sweet-faced wife.

"You may have wondered," Levi-Zorn began, with the directness of a commercial empire-builder, "why I expressed interest in dealing with your American clients."

We were seated around a low, rounded table, bearing only a free form bowl with a few green plants sprouting out of it. Levi-Zorn was across from me, his wife to his left. The high windows were open; outside, it was completely dark. After the steady noise of the train (one did not travel by air, in those days, unless the hurry was extraordinary) the evening seemed oddly quiet.

"Surely," I answered, "not out of disinterest in the lovely things you propose to send to my country."

He nodded, his small hands motionless on one knee.

"Thank you," he acknowledged easily. "I'm afraid I forgot that, unlike most of your countrymen, you are not unaware of what is likely to happen here. Soon," he added, nodding again. "Quite soon."

His wife put a hand on his arm. He covered it lightly with his own, then shrugged.

"Well," he resumed, "we have no need to spoil the evening with talk of buying and selling."

I concealed my alarm under gently raised eyebrows.

He waved his free hand briefly, indicating that nothing was excluded.

"You may look about, in the morning," he told me calmly. "Anything you like, at whatever prices you think fair. I quite trust your judgment. Only one thing," he added, as though only then thinking of it.

"Of course," I agreed.

"I should like," he went on, "payment in dollars. Not here: in the United States. And under another name."

I quickly indicated my assent; it would make no difference whatever to me.

Levi-Zorn rose. While we talked the first course had been served.

"Over dinner," he proposed, "shall we discuss pleasanter things?"

We started to the table, he at my arm and a half step behind me.

"Elizabeta," the child's mother said quietly, and mother and daughter came to join us.

And we did discuss pleasanter things. I could not have been in a better mood. And I imagine Levi-Zorn was relieved, if not happy to be prospectively rid of what it had taken years to acquire. We had each done business as we'd wanted and hoped to conduct it; to him, of course, it was more than business. It might even become salvation, if everything came to pass as we were then shaping it, and as we both saw it being shaped about us. For I quite understood that his American assets would be blocked, just as soon as war began; they would still be his, but he would not be able to make any use of them until much too late. His local funds would be even less available once real fighting broke out. It would be dollars, in America, which would lead his family to safety, if anything were to accomplish it. He already saw clearly that nothing less would be of any use. He was right: I can pay him at least that much tribute.

I have some trouble recalling exactly what we did talk about, that evening, as we consumed a leisurely and thoroughly excellent supper. It did not concern art or artists; I can remember that plainly. We would none of us have dared to venture out on ice that might so easily prove too thin. Snatches of the conversation are still clear to me, unconnected but vivid bits such as Frau Levi-Zorn's question about education in America and her thoughtful, unsmiling attention as I attempted to describe our public schools —or Levi-Zorn's gentle mocking of the bitterness and violence of our industrial anti-unionism.

"We solve the problem, over here," he said with a wry smile, "by letting the workingman have a political party of his own. Then he minds his business and we are able to mind ours."

And I remember, too, that one way or another the talk kept coming back to the United States. It was not really strange, articulate Americans being even rarer in Europe than they are in their own country; I am accustomed to being used as a sounding board and traveling encyclopedia of *homo americanus*. And yet, it was more than the usual curiosity. There was an eagerness, a well disguised passion to their interest, which gave the evening a peculiar intensity. We spoke in German, after a time, that being the language of the household. But even German could not conceal the underlying depth of their concern for things American. I remember very distinctly Levi-Zorn telling me that his eight year old daughter was being allowed to stay past her bedtime, and join the adults, solely because the visitor was an American. He added that he had himself been schooling her in English, she not having reached the level where the school system undertook that task. I looked over at the little girl, as he mentioned this: she was looking down into the tablecloth and made no sign she knew we were discussing her. In America, of course, it would have been appropriate to address a comment directly to her, but I was guilty of no such indiscretion.

The table had been cleared, and we were about to proceed to

the verandah (and the little girl, in all probability, to her bed), when there was the sound of voices, a number of voices, from the direction of the outer door. We stayed where we were a moment longer, I at the foot and Levi-Zorn at the head of the table, his wife at his right, his daughter on his left. None of us turned to look, at first, but the sounds persisted and the voices grew clearer and finally we had no choice but to swivel about and see what was occurring. Levi-Zorn did not seem anxious; he showed neither surprise nor concern. His wife did not conceal her distress nearly so well. She reached out for her discarded table napkin and twisted it tightly in suddenly nervous hands.

The voices belonged to two men, dressed in clothes that struck me as something like parodies of a certain kind of military uniform. They were both of medium height, light-complexioned, their faces dark and stubble. One of them carried a sheaf of documents quite prominently in his right hand. The other, in a leather jacket open at the neck, stood beside him, hands empty and hanging awkwardly at his side. Flat, heavy-fingered hands, with short, blunt nails. They might have been workingmen, leaders of a delegation, except for their obvious sense of high purpose. It was too determined, too sure, to be even a wage claim, an ultimatum over protested working conditions.

They stood watching us a moment. No one spoke or moved, there was only the twisting of Frau Levi-Zorn's white table napkin.

"Levi-Zorn?" the document carrier asked, his voice high with excitement.

My host stared at him for a quarter of a minute before answering. One calm, rather fragile hand moved slowly to his breast pocket and then to his damp forehead, the one sign of weakness I saw him give.

"Yes," he said at last.

The document carrier made a mark on one of his papers.

"You will stand," he directed sharply, looking up with a frown.

Levi-Zorn slowly shook his head.

"There will be time enough for that sort of thing," he replied, placing both hands flat on the table in front of him. It was a gesture, I was sure, born in the conference room; I knew it at once.

There was a brief, whispered consultation; ultimately, uncertainty prevailed.

"Your wife?" the document carrier went on, his pencil poised over the same paper, speaking with deliberately rude abruptness.

Levi-Zorn nodded, and though the napkin-twisting did not stop there were no tears. I had expected them; I suspected that our visitors had too.

Attention swung suddenly to me.

"I am a citizen of the United States." I forestalled their inquiry, holding out the passport which, earlier, I had automatically transferred to my dinner clothes. I had made this my habit, several European journeys back, after having been offered a handsome price for conveniently losing so sought-after a commodity. I had refused the offer, and still continued to make quite sure the transaction would not be effected on terms even more favorable to the offering parties.

The document carrier read the unfamiliar names aloud, stumbling badly only on the middle one of the three.

"Mister John Gould Thompson."

I nodded.

He handed the passport back, after a perfunctory leafing through its pages.

"It seems in order," he said, in English not too much worse than Frau Levi-Zorn's. His pride in the feat was unmistakable, but I refused to acknowledge that anything worth noting had occurred.

He turned back to Levi-Zorn.

"The child," he began, but again I cut him off. There was no premeditation; it was, literally, as though some other intelligence had momentarily taken over my voice.

"Is mine," I informed him.

The document carrier was incredulous.

"Do you regularly travel about with women so small?" he wondered, beginning to smile.

In different circumstances I might have struck him.

"My personal habits are not at issue," I answered as levelly as I could. "I happen to be the child's father."

"Quite so," Levi-Zorn echoed briskly. His hands had disappeared from the table, and there was a faint tremor in his voice. I was afraid to look at his wife, for fear she would break down. And all through the few minutes the scene took, I had absolutely no understanding of what had moved me to involve myself in the preservation of an eight year old child I had never seen before that night, and between whom and myself not a single word had ever passed. I am positive I had no real comprehension of what I was doing, nor any effective motivation. At most, perhaps I had some vague notion of making the adults' escape easier by relieving them of the child for a day or two. But I cannot explain even that.

The document carrier turned impatiently to the child herself.

"Are they speaking the truth?" he asked her in English, pointing with his little bundle of papers.

She looked up. Her eyes were very large and very dark, and as I watched she blinked just once.

"Of course," she said distinctly, with her father's fine accent and a great deal of his calm directness. I did not believe that she understood, but her father's wish was plain. There can be no question—the very idea is incomprehensible—of there having been prior instructions to her. I have never asked; there could not be less need for questions on such a score.

My passport was re-examined; I explained that my wife had stopped in Vienna, and that the child was listed on her passport rather than on mine. They wondered why my wife had stopped in Vienna, and why the passport did not indicate that I was married rather than single. I simply shrugged. Their own papers were obviously inconclusive and they finally allowed me to prevail; the important objective, after all, was Levi-Zorn. What did the child matter, one way or the other?

The document carrier motioned for the Levi-Zorns to follow him.

"There is a car," he announced.

Levi-Zorn did not rise from his chair.

"And your authority?" he wondered, his manner once again easy but the tremor still in his voice. It may well have been his last chance to speak normally to another human being.

The second man, till then silent and motionless, suddenly reached for the long white tablecloth and yanked it to the floor. A vase with tall-stemmed flowers smashed into bits; water dribbled over the thick rug and settled into a shining little pool. Silently, the second man wiped the soles of his shoes on the white linen.

"Our authority, Jew!" the document carrier proclaimed.

I took the little girl's hand.

"May I gather up our things?"

When we came down again the room was empty. The whole house seemed empty; what had become of the servants I do not know. There was a taxi, vacant, directly in front of the house. Nothing was said, but I have always thought the document carrier meant, at the last, to go me one better.

And the stunning Matisse that had hung in my room? Its history is typical. It was "collected" by Air Marshal Goering, repossessed after the Nazi defeat, and then, for lack of an owner or any known living heir of the owner, sold (through another dealer, I should add) directly to the Museum where it now hangs. I claim no credit for its post-war journey to these shores. I never got the chance to see it, first thing on awaking, fresh and bold in the morning light. Nor did Levi-Zorn ever collect any of the dollars, payable in the United States, which I was to have owed him for this canvas and a good many more. Of his family only Elizabeta would ever have been able to receive payment in the intended place, though even she only after a long delay. And she did not need it, by then, for she had access to everything I could give her. Money was the least of it, but that like everything else was hers in abundance.

II

In the train, just before we reached the border, Elizabeta turned away from the reddish green countryside at which she'd been staring, and asked me where we were meeting her mother and father. We spoke in English, at which she was already fairly accomplished; her proficiency was increasing almost hourly, as it will with bright children. We used it as a secret language, everyone around us speaking the tongues she had grown up with.

I smiled.

"In Vienna," I said hopefully.

"Soon?"

Her round, dark eyes were still clear, though she had spent the night travelling, first in the taxi to the Budapest station, then in an early morning slow train, and now in an inter-country express. She had slept, both in the station waiting room and in the first train, her heavy brown pig-tails pressed up against my shoulder. I did not sleep, as much from bewilderment as from excitement. I was not accustomed to pleasure and perplexity in so intimate an admixture.

"I don't know," I confessed.

She accepted the answer as I had given it, and went back to staring at the houses and trees sliding past in the soft glow of mid-afternoon. I touched her smooth ropes of hair with what I hoped was a comforting gesture. She did not look around; perhaps she did not know I had offered so tentative a caress. I doubt that she could have felt as uncertain and confused, receiving it, as I felt in proffering and then quickly retracting my hand.

I supposed we would in fact meet her mother and father. If not in Vienna, though that was the closest and the most obvious place, then somewhere else. I had no idea how, or when; there was no way of knowing how long the Levi-Zorns would be detained. Perhaps indefinitely. I knew from the moment I claimed the child that this was a possibility: it was precisely this indistinct but certain knowledge that made it impossible for me to understand what I had done. For there was no wife in Vienna, of course, any more than in any other city. There was no home to take Elizabeta to, even temporarily—and provided we got over the nonexistence of a passport covering the child. And got over the border without one; the problem would shortly become an immediate one.

"Were you surprised?"

She had startled me. I looked down and saw a broad smile. She smoothed the orchard pink dress over her bare legs with rapid, excited motions. It was as though she were suddenly emerging from a hypnotic coma: until just the moment before she had been quiet, reserved, carefully obedient but hardly child-like.

"At what?" I wondered.

She laughed, a high squealing giggle.

"At me."

I smiled back.

"I mean," she explained, "at getting a Levi-Zorn instead of a Picasso?"

I put out a finger, intending to push it against her stubby little nose, but she threw her head to the side.

"I didn't buy you," I finally answered. "I stole you. That's the difference, you see."

"And will you sell me again?" She laughed with delight. "To some rich American?"

I shook my head with mock sadness.

"Little pitchers," I observed briefly.

She did not understand, and was put on the offensive even more.

"Would I look nice," she pursued, "hanging on a wall?"

She spread out her arms and made an agonized face. The burlesque of the crucifixion, which she probably knew mostly from canvases and illustrated books, was extremely funny. That pert, dark little face, its eyes all screwed up and its teeth half bared, lips contorted and pinched, was about as Christ-like as a monkey's. I told her so.

"You're a wrinkled old monkey," I proclaimed. "You'd look fine on a wall, if your tail were cut off first."

She smiled wisely.

"You don't mean that." She shook her head with great deliberation. "You stole me because, when I grow up, you want to marry me. Am I very pretty?" she asked seriously.

It was a difficult game to play. She *was* pretty, even at the age of eight, even with a straight little child's body and round sticks for arms and legs. It was, even then, not decorative good looks. She had from the very first—she probably had when she was born—a quixotic blend of dark loveliness and impish perception.

"I'll marry you right away," I replied. "You can't expect me to wait more than another day or two."

She was bored with the game as suddenly as she had launched it. Perhaps she suddenly realized, once again, that I was very nearly a complete stranger, that her mother and father were far away and in some great trouble. The transformation from imp to small Griselda was instantaneous.

She went back to looking quietly out of the window. I patted her shoulder several times, without hesitation this time, and without any further feeling of impropriety. She was a little girl in a very strange situation, and I was her only link with what, till just the evening before, had been her whole world. I wasn't much of a link, surely, but I was beginning to feel that I knew her. How much, after all, could there be to know, in eight years of existence?

I had lunch sent in to our compartment. The dining car would have been risky: how did one march through a crowded aisle alongside a short-legged, short-skirted, pig-tailed child? Besides, there might be someone who would recognize her. Levi-Zorn had not been an inconspicuous man, in this country. And I did not want her stolen back from me, especially when the adventure was just beginning. Now that I had gotten myself into it I was anxious to see it through. I still had no idea why, but the sense of bewilderment on that score was wearing off, bit by bit, as I grew used to the situation. What difference did it make? Here she was; it was an unexpected delight.

I had great fun feeding her. She insisted that she was not an infant, and could feed herself, but I was not to be deprived of the opportunity.

"In Vienna," I assured her, "we'll find someone to cook your meals and braid your hair and iron your dresses. Until your mother and father come," I added. "Then you'll be their problem." It was easy to smile; pleasing her was extremely important. "Right now you're mine."

And I held out a spoonful of mashed vegetables.

She swallowed it with a face, then made as though to bite my hand. Her tongue licked at my finger, instead; she drew back, laughing. I did not wipe the moisture away. It was a kind of badge of office.

"More," I pursued.

She was laughing too hard to take any, by then. I waited patiently, then held out the spoon.

"And after this," I warned her, "all the meat."

There was a knock at the door. I turned away from the giggling child, suddenly afraid that, having come this far, I would be able to take her no further. It was a conductor, come to collect passports for the border inspection.

I handed him mine; he bowed and was about to leave.

"The little girl is not on my passport," I declared. It had to be faced, now or later. Better as quickly as possible, once it had finally come.

He did not look disturbed.

"She is your daughter?"

"My niece."

It was something of a compromise. A niece might be easier to account for, with respect to missing papers, and the absence of luggage, and all the paraphernalia which closer kin would normally require.

I shrugged.

"I took her with me from Vienna, just for the trip."

He nodded, waiting, I thought I knew why.

"There was no difficulty then," I went on, handing him a moderately large bill. He pocketed it without a sign, made a brief entry in his shabby black leather book, and left us.

When I turned back to Elizabeta she had stopped laughing and was sitting on the edge of her seat, her mouth stretched wide open like a hungry chick's.

"We'll have to give you another name," I explained earnestly. She kept her mouth ajar, expectant. I put down the spoon and, taking her chin in one hand, shook it gently.

"Seriously," I insisted. "I have to be your uncle."

She nodded, very quiet and attentive; there were the beginnings of tears in her eyes and I went on quickly.

"You can be Elizabeth," I suggested. "Elizabeth Thompson. You're my brother's daughter." I smiled fleetingly: "I haven't got a brother, really."

She was looking straight ahead, perceptibly crying but sitting erect and not letting herself sob, not letting the tears spill out as they plainly wanted to.

I reached over and dried the corners of her eyes with my handkerchief.

"Later," I told her. "You mustn't cry now. You can't let them see you crying." I pressed the handkerchief into her hands, which neither accepted nor rejected it. The train began to slow; the brakes shrieked faintly and our carriage bumped. Outside the window the trees moved slower and slower. I felt anger at the child's quiet weeping; she might be giving up her only chance. And depriving me of mine.

"We're almost at the border," I told her, trying distraction where persuasion had failed. "If you look down there you can see it."

She rubbed the handkerchief into her eyes, her hands awkward and trembling. I could see her swallowing hard. Then she pushed the handkerchief back at me.

"Here," she announced. "I won't cry any more."

I tried to laugh.

"It'll be alright, later," I assured her. "You'll be able to cry as much as you like. Buckets full."

She shook her head, then slid the tray closer and picked up a fork. And a knife. And carefully cut herself a piece of meat.

"When I see mommy and daddy," she said at last.

Then she began, slowly and thoughtfully, to chew at her food. It must have had the tastelessness of wax to her, right then, but she persisted. I spread out the handkerchief and draped it over her lap.

"Now you can use it for a napkin," I told her, relieved and a little proud. Of us both, that is.

"I have one," she indicated, looking up at me curiously. Then her lips opened in a very small smile.

"A present?" she wondered.

I considered it. The train had slowed to a rumbling crawl; a few low buildings appeared and drifted lazily past.

"A reward," I answered.

She looked down into the tray, then went on with her slow, steady eating.

"In Vienna," I continued, "I'll buy you some real presents. We'll go to some beautiful shops, and you can pick what you like."

It was her turn to meditate.

"Toys?" she asked.

The train came to a halt. I laughed and nodded.

"Or the real thing."

I don't think she understood. But she smiled back. I wanted to kiss her and did not quite dare.

The border inspectors were casual and brief. They lifted the lids of my suitcases and closed them without even bothering to peer inside. One of them smiled at the little girl with a handkerchief in her lap instead of a napkin; they both smiled pleasantly when I extended a minor gratuity. We were wished a good journey, the compartment door was closed, and in another quarter of an hour the train jerked into motion and we slid safely across the border into Austria. It had all been incredibly easy.

III

The infection had come to Vienna, too. The Nazis had long since been in open command; their time had been well spent. But the war-to-be was still only a distant noise, a sputtering unreal commotion that might never reach this far. The city had already known something like the beginnings of war; in places the scars were prominent. Perhaps it was the effort to ignore the signs of internal combat that kept it still Vienna, no matter how many Brown Shirts tromped its streets, no matter how many Stars of David hung on sleeves and blouses and store fronts. There were still pastry vendors; somehow, though most of the tourists had gone, had they all suddenly reappeared most of the places they had always thronged to would have remained much as they had always been. The shops, especially. Butter was scarce, cheap shoes and clothing had become expensive, but the fashionable places were by some miracle of perversity almost as modish and well stocked as ever. Or it might have been that the new aristocracy preferred it that way.

I was delighted. Strolling easily from one *salon* to the next, buying a bit here and a bit there, I soon had Elizabeth (we kept the new name, to be safe) once again a well accoutred little girl. It was a queer experience, sitting in the comfortable anterooms and having her appear in one stylish frock after another. It was pure frolic for her, all the more because I smiled with such obvious satisfaction at each new transformation. It was nothing at all like outfitting a woman—wife or mistress. Yet there would not have been the same enjoyment in making the rounds with a small boy of the same age, and not simply because little boys imitate the flat, monochomatic dress of their fathers and uncles. A girl's potential is always more tangible, closer to the surface; seeing the ribbons and bows, the careful hints and echoes, one can see a woman even in an eight year old. If the child shows any signs of grace and good looks, the promise of what half a dozen years will do can sometimes be overwhelmingly clear.

And I had another reason for not yielding to temptation, not staying in one dressmaker's chambers from breakfast to dinner, piling up without any arbitrary intermissions the trunkfuls of lovely things I wanted her to have. It was the better reason, I have no doubt, for it was hard to know what was being spied upon, in Nazi-controlled Vienna. Probably everything. By spreading our flurry of buying over a small host of shops, and half the city, we avoided unnecessary, unwelcome attention. It was not remarkable for a prosperous American globe-trotter to buy his small relative a dress or two. But to entirely and immediately clothe the child, from pinafores to underpants, might well have brought the police, with questions that had as yet no answers, with requests for papers that did not as yet exist. They would be forthcoming; I had made the necessary contacts, to be sure. But my requirements were exacting, if not unusual, and my supplier a forger both cautious and painstaking. He would be the better part of a week at creating a passport that only full-fledged investigation could discredit. In the meantime we could not leave Vienna even had we wanted to. Borders were not all to be crossed with such effortless ease; the era of the casual bribe had momentarily gone into eclipse. I could not count on being so ridiculously lucky twice in a row.

Which was also why I first considered and then decided against a temporary nursemaid for the child. Decided against the very idea of one, that is: I never got to the point of interviewing candidates. A nurse would turn my whole adventure upside down just as easily as a suspicious shop clerk. Her opportunities for spotting strange flaws in our story, peculiar sides to our relationship, would be very nearly perfect. We would be away most of the day, most days, on our shopping tours, but that would not save the situation. At least until Elizabeth's papers came, and probably until we were out of Vienna, we would have to get along like touring Americans rather than after the fashion of well-bred natives. Until then, the hotel would iron and starch her frocks, the hotel would prepare her breakfasts and her dinners, and the only nursemaid in sight would be myself.

The very first evening, when we checked into the hotel, it was of course an inevitable role. She had fallen asleep on the train, and though she was quite conscious while we rode up in the elevator and were shown to our room, she was also quite helpless. Her accommodations for the night were a small trundle bed, hastily prepared for her and wheeled into one corner of the room. There were no nightclothes, and probably no longer any hot water for a bath even had I ventured to administer one. She sat up, patient and uncomplaining, while I pulled off her shoes and stockings; she stayed still while I fumbled with bows and buttons and got her dress and underskirt off. Then she flopped down in her underclothes and was fast asleep at once. It seemed an excellent resolution. I covered her with a light blanket and got myself to bed too. And slept: I hadn't realized how completely fatigue had set in.

In the morning, of course, she pretty much managed for herself. I tied the bow on the rumpled, badly stained dress, and did one button she couldn't reach. It was strange, bathing and shaving with her in the adjoining room, but I shrugged it off. But that night there *were* nightclothes, and she was palpably grimy. And she wanted a bath, though I had suspected no child ever asked for the application of soap and water; I had counted on it. We came up, after dinner, both of us weary from the day's round of the shops; I turned down the lights, threw back the covers of her bed, and draped a clean new nightgown over the foot of it.

"There," I proposed. "A little nicer than last night."

She seemed startled.

"Shouldn't I have a bath?" she wondered.

She was right, of course, and I had very little choice. I put a bathrobe over my dinner clothes, while she wandered into the bathroom. I followed, a little gingerly.

I startled her, which for the moment made it still worse. Her dress lay over a chair; she was bent over the antique tub, in her new underclothes, trying to induce the bath water to flow. I knew she would never succeed, even were the queer apparatus more familiar to her than it was. I've sometimes thought such resistant knobs created for, and carefully preserved by, the male employees of European hotels, precisely for the enterprising visitor who strips for the plunge and then finds the wherewithal denied her. I had indeed heard stories, and they were strangely in my mind as I came forward and volunteered my services.

It took a few moments, and the temperature required adjusting. Elizabeth stood to the side for a bit, watching aimlessly, then automatically removed the rest of her clothing and deposited it too on the chair. I stayed bent over the slowly filling tub till the bath was ready, then backed awkwardly toward the door. But not out.

"All ready," I announced uncertainly.

Without looking around, she stepped carefully over the high rim, holding the edge with both hands, then quickly lowered herself out of sight into the tepid water. Only the upper part of her face was still visible. One small hand reached out for the soap; even from where I stood I could spell out the bold letters of the hotel name, stamped into the yellow cake.

She washed herself in silence. I was afraid to interrupt. She knew what she was about; I had no concern on that score. Yet her motions, what I could see of them as her head bobbed and her arms went up and down, were as often the stiff clumsiness of the child as they were the deliberate gestures of knowledge and purpose. Frothing suds, on her arms and hands, gave her all the disguise she needed to seem far older than her years, and I had to remind myself that she was only eight, that in America she would be in the third grade. Jumping rope. Playing with dolls.

Inadvertently, suddenly reminded that I had meant to buy her the biggest doll in Vienna and had quite forgotten to buy any toys at all, too completely caught up with my own pleasures to even think of hers, I uttered a loud, clear exclamation of self-disgust.

Her round, dark eyes peered at me over the edge of the tub. I smiled and shrugged.

"I was going to buy you a doll," I explained. "I forgot. But tomorrow," I promised. I nodded, to reassure her. "Tomorrow."

She stared at me a moment, perhaps smiling, perhaps frowning—I had no way of telling, except from her eyes, and they did not alter their expression. Then she looked away, and one soapy hand reached clumsily down her back. I could not help her; I remember wanting to. I stayed silently where I was.

She got through with it, quickly enough, splashed herself off, opened the catch without any assistance and sat while the water drained noisily away. And after it had all been gulped down the narrow pipes she still sat in the security of the deep tub, not making any motion to come out. Was she waiting for me to go? I noticed a big bath towel hanging from a hook, and without saying anything pulled it down and brought it to the tub, averting my eyes slightly. I quite knew that there was nothing to look away from. She was simply a little girl, dripping wet, newly clean, and incidentally, unimportantly disrobed. Yet it seemed important to look away.

She took the towel, made a few passes at drying herself, then suddenly stood up and quickly wrapped the huge, soft cloth around her body, tucking it in in the front like a sarong. It went around her three full times, giving her a padded, false obesity that, in other circumstances, might have seemed exceedingly droll. Neither of us laughed. I watched solemnly as she began to climb out, then slipped back. The rim was too high. It had not been too high, earlier, but she had not then been swathed in layers of fabric. And the rim had been dry, before. She tried to get her leg over, failed once again, then stood silently, her hands gripping the edge, looking down at the floor and the stray drops spattered across it.

I hesitated, but only for an instant. It took no effort to lean down and lift her out; it took no strength to carry her, a still half-wet little thing who weighed next to nothing, into and across the bedroom, where I carefully lowered her onto her bed. She sat where I put her, the towel crumpled around her middle, its tuck loosened and the material sliding away, then suddenly reached up and clamped her hands onto my shoulders. The towel slipped free as she pulled herself erect, standing on her bed, her face almost level with mine, and, smiling, gave me a grateful kiss. It was quite unimportant, now, that she was undressed. I patted her damp hair, turned and handed her the nightgown. She held up her arms and I helped her put it on. And as I pulled the blanket over her, and said goodnight, I felt as moved as if I had unexpectedly won the affections of some infinitely desirable woman.

We managed quite well, after that. Her passport appeared: a more than satisfactory job, well worth the handsome fee involved. There was only one thing wrong, it was a vital, pressing thing, and it stayed wrong. There were difficulties in our unlikely situation that could be resolved by patience, and effort, and money. I could furnish her with a wardrobe, food, shelter; I could entertain her, lavishing on my new niece the days that might otherwise have gone into elaborate and profitable business arrangements; I could even bathe her, and help her with her nightgowns. I could buy her a huge, delicately dressed doll, the choicest pastries, most anything Vienna offered. But I was a successful art dealer, not a magician, and I could not make her parents re-appear. I could not even get news of them, news either good or bad. It grew harder and harder to believe that they would ever appear, as it grew ever more difficult to pretend, for Elizabeth's benefit, that the happy tidings were always just about to be delivered, the long-awaited materialization of Levi-Zorn and his quiet, sweet-faced wife just about to occur. Not that we spent our time discussing her parents and the coming reunion. It would have been impossible to discuss such things, even with a child as bright and quick as Elizabeth. It was a matter of almost no words, of occasional gestures, smiles, and a deep underlying belief. Hers, not mine.

Exactly how much she knew, or suspected, I cannot say. If she had any clear inkling, it must certainly have been one of those ideas which come to a child's mind like dreams, and are as easily dissipated, as readily put to the side, snuffed into shadow by certain, unshakeable belief. She did not act forlorn. As she had promised, just the other side of the border, there had been no more tears. None at all. She dashed about Vienna with me as though this strange new life was exactly what she had been looking forward to, just what she had wanted, delivered on schedule and in wonderful abundance. She slept long and well, played hard, ate like a Shetland pony. I hoped that she was too occupied with the steady stream of new trivia to stop and wonder what was actually happening, where she had gotten to and how, and when she would go back to her own. I certainly made it my urgent business not to give her time in which she could mope, or any cause for any distress whatever.

Then I heard from Budapest. Not from Herr Levi-Zorn, nor through a messenger sent by him. His power to move men, his power to even put a letter into the post, had been completely destroyed. He and his wife and almost all the prominent and wealthy Jews of the city had been taken together, consigned like so many units of shabby merchandise to await shipment god only knew where. The chances of them returning, whatever the destination might be, were almost nil; if the impending war became as universal as I expected, the Levi-Zorns and those taken with them were as good as dead. Younger people might have had a small chance, either to survive or escape, but not those for whom Elizabeth and I were waiting. There was nothing to wait for.

Still, we lingered on. The news was not definite and I could give the child no reason for moving, for leaving a Vienna which was hardly a sanctuary but was certainly her last link with her parents. This was the rendezvous I had helped her to expect. It had not been deception, then. Nor was it difficult to linger. Service, especially, was beyond compare, in those last days before the crisis split open and *maitres d'hôtel* threw up their hands and went down with the rest. Elegantly formal waiters stood quietly about, the long black tails of their coats hanging like pennons on a dull day. Only the hint of some needed service was necessary; with a war just on the horizon, they all knew that those who might cease to wait would still be expected to serve. Elizabeth and I continued our far-flung shopping, our tours of the nooks and crannies of the city. But the world spun in an ever-narrowing circle. I began to dream of taking the child to Mexico; on crowded streets I found myself planning into which little doorway we would run, if the moment came. The point of excitement had long since passed. It was apprehension I felt now, a growing sick conviction that we would be caught, helplessly enmeshed by our own uncertainties. The child would be taken away from me. Almost worst of all, I could show her nothing of my steadily mounting fear: the more craven and trembling I actually felt the more desperately I had to conceal myself, playing at calm and good humor.

I stood it as long as I could, then proposed a brief trip to Switzerland. I did not give her any reason, though I had thought of telling her that neutral Berne or Geneva were rendezvous spots as logical as Vienna. What was the use of explanations, of more rationalizations piled high on top of a flimsy structure I could no longer sustain? One trenchant question and it—and I—were likely to break down, blown back to earth like a windswept straw briefly hung in the tree tops. After all, it was not a flight: we left most of our things in the hotel, and I gave a forwarding address. It was clear that we would be coming back, or at least I meant Elizabeth to see it that way. And perhaps, though of course I did not dare say it, breaking our vigil would in fact resolve it. I did not know just how, but whether we in fact returned to Vienna or not I felt that, the second time, it would not be the same. I had reached the point where any change was clearly for the better.

We did not go back. We had scarcely gotten out in time. The

explosion began a fortnight after we rolled over the mountains into Switzerland, perching ourselves temporarily in the midst of that universal haven. It became not at all temporary. I had dreamed of Mexico, but her passport would have made that a dead end. The cleverest forgery was not good enough. If we stayed where we were, and the war was not won by Germany, I might well be able to get the child into the United States. There would be universal confusion; no one's papers would be in order. And commitment to Switzerland was scarcely a sentence of hardship and suffering. Nothing on the other side of the Atlantic needed my attention. My staff was capable and relatively honest. And if they were not? Truthfully, I did not much care. I would have a year or even longer alone with Elizabeth; she was entirely mine, now. I could do with her as I wanted. And I did not care as the year lengthened into two, and then three, and still the war went on. It was in fact more than five years before we finally set out for New York, two among many passengers crowded into an overloaded and not very clean ship, but not minding in the least. Elizabeth was thirteen and life could not have seemed better. American officials had been as understanding as possible; her papers gave us trouble but no fears. And in all the five years we had not once spoken of her parents. They had become as dead in name as, surely, they were in fact. She was thirteen and I was exultant with hope and certainty. It was happening, it would happen, at last.

IV

It was a queer voyage. I had suspected as much long before the ship docked at Le Havre and was declared available for human cargo. Elizabeth and I had not had to push and plead our way into consulate offices, but I had seen those who did. The passenger list would include other reluctant expatriates, and perhaps a few soldiers who had asked for discharges in France or Italy and then repented, but by and large, I could see, we would be perfect grist for the melting pot. There would be Jews whom the concentration camps and gas ovens had not been able to eliminate; there would be slave laborers whom typhus and pellagra and Nazi bullets had overlooked; there would be gaunt civilians, neither Jewish nor suspect, but withered by years of German occupation and only interested in seeking a life where the past that had just come to a close could be quickly forgotten.

So it came as no surprise to find that the *Polar Icecap* was old, rusting, and, in spite of the hard-pressed authorities' best efforts, something of a madhouse. At least half a dozen languages were in constant use, as spoken by people of all ages and from every class. The dining hall (we had to eat in hurried shifts) was bedlam incarnate, with half the diners either observing or attempting to observe civilized decorum, the other half scraping with their spoons and clanging their plates like what they were, the long-starved survivors of civilization's lowest depth. Walking about the decks one could see representatives of every ancient European virtue. But one could also come upon men and women squeezed into some tiny deck space, American cigarettes bobbing slowly between their lips and no thought, no consciousness of anything but pure sensation in their eyes. They would sit virtually motionless until their supply ran out and then they would scramble after the crew, to scrounge for more. Worse, some of them would carefully set out to sleep, at night, with a freshly lighted cigarette in their mouths; some fellow passenger would have to pluck it, smouldering, from between sleeping lips. Talking did no good; they had to be watched. And there were a few cases of delirium tremens, the first days out. One man smashed a quarter of the already skimpy supply of wooden deck chairs, trampling them down like a triumphant armored tank in a field of helpless infantrymen. Another climbed to the crow's nest and threatened suicide until we were almost willing to turn our backs and let him jump. He fell unconscious and was rescued before his oratory ran out. But such cases were easier to control than were the tobacco addicts. It was simple to persuade the American sailors to keep their whiskey under lock and key, exceedingly difficult to keep them from liberally dispensing cigarettes that had cost them only pennies. There were a number of virtual lunatics, too, for the most part genial and inoffensive babblers whose intermittent flashes of lucidity were a pleasant or a horrifying surprise, depending on who you were and what you were treated to.

We were all of us to some degree abnormal; the line between sanity and insanity had become as informal and meaningless, for the moment, as had most other categories and divisions. Aristocrats, laborers, lunatics, artisans, professionals and poets, none of us found it particularly strange or distressing to be crammed into close, common quarters with anyone and everyone else. It was not the magic of Cinderella at the ball: we were smeared with an indiscriminate crippling of our cognitive faculties, rather than raised to uniformly dazzling heights. It was differences and distinctions as such that were in abeyance.

Tramping up the swaying, uneven gangplank proved that. Elizabeth and I bumped along behind a short, grey-haired man who carried his belongings in a patched laundry sack too large and apparently too heavy for convenient handling. He stumbled repeatedly, falling back into Elizabeth over and over again, each time giving her a wide, cheerful grin and never once stopping the flow of melody from under his breath. I heard snatches of familiar symphonies, and a can-can I knew well; by the time we were propelled onto the grimy deck Elizabeth and I were singing along with him. He was conducting with his shoulders, dipping them to indicate the beat, and regularly giving us smiles of encouragement.

We could talk, once the deck was attained and we took our places in a slow, sidewards flow toward a harassed group of official looking men; the dockside rumble and clatter gradually faded. Our new friend was indeed a musician, before the war a professional violinist. He was from eastern Europe, so we spoke in French.

"Your grandmother is very well preserved," he observed with a grin.

I protested.

"We have been married over twenty-five years," I explained.

Elizabeth giggled.

"Not actually married, of course," she put in.

We all laughed.

"Are you Americans?" he wondered. I nodded and he somehow managed to extend his hand to me. "Ah," he exclaimed in triumph. "I have now shaken hands with an American who neither gives nor receives but only desires to talk. You have no chocolate bars?" he pursued. "You do not want my birth certificate in seven official copies? Of course," he added gallantly, "you are not interested in sleeping with my daughters or my aunts or anyone else I am able to produce."

"You talk," Elizabeth declared, "quite as beautifully as you sing."

It was even more effective, in French; he bowed his head in acknowledgment. Then he had reached the thin line of officialdom and our talk was broken off. But when he had passed the last official obstacle and been sent into the free inner recesses of the ship, he turned, a white slip of paper clutched in his teeth, and grimaced resignedly at us. We laughed and waved back.

We met him, not very much later, hanging over the rail and watching the last few passengers straggle on board. Or perhaps he was counting the multitude of would-be passengers whom the police were charged with keeping on the other side of the gangplank. There were a great many of them; I was more comfortable watching the watcher instead. He might not have been as old as he at first seemed: half a dozen years of Nazi control turned even children into wizened relics. His eyes were grey and deep-set, his face wrinkled and lean. But he spoke with the eager quickness of a man my own age, and his spontaneous good humor seemed to smooth the lines out of his face.

After a moment he also averted his eyes and broke, as was his invariable custom, into a musical parable, a bright little anecdote out of his past—or perhaps out of whole cloth. It made no difference.

"I went to South America, once," he told us, "on an Austrian ship. There are such things," he assured us. "Or at least there were. I was violinist in a terrible trio. Terrible. We played *Ländler* and waltzes and Lehar until my ears waltzed when I lay down to sleep at night. In Montevideo—there are lots of Germans there, you know—I took two days of shore leave and hunted up some real musicians, men who could play Schubert with one hand and drink beer with the other. 'Help me,' I begged them. 'I have to cross the whole Atlantic with Josef Strauss under my pillow.' So we spent two days playing Beethoven and Mozart and Schubert; every waking moment was a pure delight. The cellist, who had no ideals, recommended ear-plugs, but I knew it was unnecessary. I went back to the ship and played operetta melodies like Paganini himself. My head was clear, I could sleep with the Trout quintet and the Rasoumovskies."

He laughed.

"You know, I played so well on that return voyage that I was flooded with tips, and the steward fairly begged me to stay on. 'You have sold more wine,' he told me desperately, 'than any fiddler we have ever had.' I was offered a head-waiter's salary, and the head-waiter, you know, is second only to the captain. But I wanted to keep my ideals, so I took a job in the pit of an Italian opera house." He sighed. "What a mistake!"

We laughed with him, and Elizabeth came close to tears. We never introduced ourselves, however; if we exchanged names, at any point, I can no longer recall what his was.

There were a few small wooden chairs about, and we scrounged together three.

"Shall I summon the waiter?" he asked with a flourish. "The lady will drink American whiskey, of course."

"If you can produce a waiter," I assured him, "she will."

He pretended to search in his sleeves; I don't know why, but we laughed uproariously.

"You should have been in the movies," Elizabeth managed to gasp out.

He nodded thoughtfully.

"It is not far, is it, from New York to Hollywood?"

He leaned back in his chair, still nodding slowly, then suddenly he turned his head away and his shoulders quivered. There was nothing to be done. Elizabeth and I sat and tried not to watch him; when several minutes went by and he had not turned back I touched her shoulder and we got up and walked quietly away. We were to be on the *Polar Icecap* for almost two weeks: there would be other opportunities.

Still, I took a long siesta that afternoon, leaving Elizabeth to entertain herself. The ship had cast off, just after an improvised and badly served lunch, and I foresaw no difficulties. I was both right and wrong. As she told me the little story, it went something like this. She was strolling about on the deck, having seen her fill of the French coast receding into the distance, and half just rambling, half looking for something to do. Without knowing it, she walked past the crew's quarters, and a sailor lounging out on the deck struck up a conversation.

She told me, later, that it was queerly exciting, talking to an American, in his own language, and all on her own. She had met others, of course, during our stay in Switzerland, but never without me. It was something of a test, an opportunity to match herself against the role I had created for her. For she knew about sailors, and she knew that it was no longer possible to identify her as a child. She was poised and pretty, and her body had been developing for almost a year, curving and rounding into an indeterminate girlhood. But the challenge seemed infinitely more real than the danger.

When he offered her a cigarette she shook her head.

"I'll share a chocolate bar with you," she proposed, "if you have one."

He was in and out of his quarters in half a minute. This was a language, I'm afraid, which he understood much too well.

"Where you from?" he wondered.

She became a little confused, then managed to say that she had never been in the States. He was impressed.

"You're a regular foreigner," he said, and they both laughed. Then he stood up, snatching at her hand. "Come on in here," he proposed, tugging her toward his quarters. "I've got some records of the real thing, Glenn Miller, T.D. Bet you've never heard them." She hadn't but was suddenly ashamed to confess it.

She allowed herself to be led in. There were a number of beds, several occupied by dozing men.

"Don't mind them," he assured her. "Nothing won't wake them up."

He conducted her to his part of the dim, rectangular room, then waved her to a seat on the bed. She sat down, and he began to rummage through a foot locker.

"Want a drink?" he suggested, looking up at her. "I've got some good stuff."

She shook her head and he resumed his search. She sat, as she told me, in a kind of daze, not really conscious of where she had come with him and feeling terribly unsure of herself, a fraud, ripe for exposure. Then, with a quick and quite unexpected motion he pulled her down on her back, his arm around her shoulder, and leaned over her, his lips against hers. She was too startled to protest, though she did not reciprocate.

"I like you," he said softly.

She tried to sit up but his arm held her securely.

"What'd you say your name was?" he went on, and one hand stroked her waist lightly.

"Please let me go," she asked, not frightened but no longer bewildered.

"It's early," he assured her. "What's your hurry?" Then his hand came up and curled around her breast. He had begun to bend his face down to hers again when she lifted her knee and struck out, hard. I think she must have hit him in the groin, luckily, for he groaned and rolled slowly over on his back, clutching at himself. His hand, entangled in the soft stuff of her blouse, made a tear of a few inches as it pulled automatically away, but that was unimportant. She got up and walked quickly out of the room and back to me. It was a good lesson, not too expensively learned. I was not sorry, after the fact.

"Dance music isn't that important, or that difficult," I told her calmly. "You'll know it all, soon enough."

She was not very much shaken; I don't think she had been frightened at any point. And perhaps she'd in fact been in no real danger.

"Who's Glenn Miller?" she wanted to know.

She put on a fresh blouse and I told her.

"Was it good chocolate?" I teased.

She made a face.

"Snob," I exclaimed. "Not everyone spent the war in Switzerland."

She tried to pull me out of bed.

"Afraid to go back out by yourself?" I demanded, resisting.

She gave me a quick kiss.

"No one's better company than you," she cajoled, and I gave in. As I always did.

But I stayed with her, after that. She was bright and capable, and whatever danger there might be was slight, now, but she was thirteen and I wanted to take no chances. My plans for her were quite different. Actually, though, I should not underestimate. In the course of breaking down the differences and distinctions which regularly control social behavior, more than just caste lines was thrown into abeyance. I have read of freed prisoners, men and women, being transported from Siberia in common boxcars, and of how every male capable of crawling would come and go in a virtually continuous series of copulations. It was not so extreme, on the *Polar Icecap*, but much of the same spirit was prevalent. Nor were there any reported cases of rape.

We did not really meet Tanya until the third day out. She called herself Tanya, but there was not much doubt that she was something other than Russian. Her malady, whatever it was, took the form of passionate prevarication. Her only other passion, so far as anyone knew, was for compulsive sharing; she would offer anything she had, it made no difference what it was. Among passengers who were few of them notable for conventional staidness, she quickly achieved the distinction of notoriety. She strode athletically about the ship, wearing clothing suitable for the Arctic winter, and seeking those with whom she could share her great Russian soul, as well as whatever else she happened to own at the moment. She was blonde and plump, close to middle aged, and I suppose she had listened to too much wartime propaganda, picturing the Russians as our heroic allies and their great leader, Stalin, as an indomitable but warm-hearted genius whose crotchets and peculiarities were better not discussed in public. Or perhaps she was an escapee from Siberia. No one ever bothered to find out.

And as Elizabeth and I did everything together, we met her together. It was a quiet autumn afternoon and the Atlantic was behaving. We had long since lost sight of land: there was only the sun, the labored heaving of the *Polar Icecap's* ancient engines, and the high, irregular swell of the waves. We had climbed into the bow and were leaning over the greasy railing, silently watching the green water splitting off, white and hissing, on either side. There was no need for talk. I put my hand on her shoulder, now and then, or bent and brushed back the hair which the wind whipped into her face. She had reached what I expected would be practically her full height: I was very conscious of how nearly adult she was. It would be no effort to wait, now; I was not impatient, it was enough to be beside her and know to whom her future belonged. I did not ask her what she was thinking: could it have made much difference?

"A luffly breeze!" a rich voice suddenly bellowed into our ears. "Luffly!"

She was perhaps an inch taller than Elizabeth, not exactly portly but decidedly fulsome. She wore a heavy tweed skirt and a sweater so woolly as almost to hide the deep curve of her breast. A fur cap was perched on her yellow hair. And she smiled, a wide, appreciative smile that spread over and beyond us and stretched to the quiet rolling ocean and the bright, empty sky.

"I did not think such old boat could make such luffly breeze," she went on, moving to the railing beside us and visibly stretching her lungs. Her hair began to flap but she gave it no mind. "Vat fine this voyage, eh?"

"Fine," I grinned back at her, trapped but not very much concerned.

"You enjoying yourself?" she demanded of Elizabeth, who nodded gaily. We all laughed. "Vy not, eh?" Tanya exclaimed. "Is good."

She turned back to the ocean, her wide eyes staring far ahead of us.

"Maybe eight years," she proclaimed solemnly, "since I was in America."

There was a long pause.

"What were you doing there?" Elizabeth wondered politely.

Tanya wrinkled her lips into a flat pose and nodded heavily.

"I was spy. For G.P.U." She pronounced it "gay-pay-oo," after the European fashion. "They send me."

I suppressed my laughter.

"*Da*." She prodded the railing with one heavy, rounded finger. "I was best spy in all Russia. Tanya, they say, get machine gun plans for us. We need." She shrugged. "I get."

I had to turn away and pretend to cough. But Elizabeth, who surely knew better, seemed to be paying serious attention to Tanya's fairy stories.

"G.P.U.," she wondered. "That's the Russian secret police, isn't it?"

A five minute lecture followed, incoherent but packed with horrific details and punctuated by frequent expletives of disgust and much breast-slapping. I could see, now, that Elizabeth was not swallowing the whole thing, but she still kept her face straight and her attention focussed. I shrugged, but inwardly, and likewise kept up appearances.

"So," Tanya suddenly announced, her face once again breaking into a broad grin, "I haf some good cheese. You like?"

Elizabeth had accepted for us before I could intervene, and we followed Tanya across the cluttered, rusting deck to her quarters. She cut generous chunks and we all sat on her bed—for there was nowhere else to sit—and munched at it. It was indeed good cheese, and I told her so. It was the least I could do.

"I big heart," she informed us, gesturing suitably. "Vat mine, must share." She pointed at Elizabeth, who was sitting in the middle. "Daughter?"

"My niece."

The word seemed to puzzle her.

"My brother's daughter," I explained.

Comprehension lit up her full, heavy cheeks.

"Ah. You not married?"

I could not help smiling.

"No."

Tanya's smile was deeper.

"I marry six times," she told us.

Elizabeth leaned far back.

"Not six," she protested mildly.

"Vy not?" Tanya insisted. "One man go," and she shrugged, "must get other man."

We all laughed.

"Two soldier," Tanya enumerated thoughtfully, counting off on her plump fingers. "One—how you call?—one crook. One vat wrote for newspaper—nice one, oh very nice one," and she seemed for a moment lost in reverie. Then she lifted her head with a big grin. "Haf more cheese," she boomed richly.

We protested, but it was no use. She had already cut the slices and was pressing them into our hands. And it made better eating than the slop served to us at meal time.

"Vat you do?" she asked, turning to me.

"I sell pictures."

Her grin widened, as though we were blood brothers long lost and newly joined.

"Once I very good painter," she informed us. "You know not

my name: police come, steal all paintings, beat me, make me paint not more." She rubbed her imaginary bruises soulfully. "O.K.," she conceded spiritedly. "I do different big things. Vy not, eh?"

She was becoming a bore. But it was easier to let ourselves become entrapped than it was to get away again. Finally, the sun had set and our excuses were entirely legitimate. Reluctantly, she permitted us to take our leaves.

"You come more cheese tomorrow, eh?"

In the last stages of twilight the deck looked quite unreal.

"Why did you let us in for that?" I exclaimed softly, as soon as we were by ourselves. "Good god!"

"I like her," she protested.

I took her arm and steered us around a loosely piled hawser.

"I'm sorry for her, too," I answered.

"She's sort of fun, if you let her."

We reached the stairway to our own places.

"Stop acting your age," I told her with a smile, "and let's get ready for supper."

I put on a tie and she slipped out of her blouse and skirt and into a dress. It was not at all elaborate, but I did not want her to completely lose touch with the non-refugee world.

"She *has* got a big heart, you know," Elizabeth persisted, while I did up the buttons in the back of her dress. "And god only knows what's been done to her."

"You can't be sorry for every stray dog and cat you see."

I took her arm again.

"You don't mean that," she said softly, and I blushed, fully and uncontrollably. I could not turn my face away, and there can be no doubt that she saw.

"She understands what good cheese is," I bumbled.

"Which makes her a connoisseur," she took me up quickly. I squeezed her arm and we went to supper.

Later, that evening, Elizabeth entered us in an impromptu chess tournament. I had taught her to play, in a season of boredom. She quickly outstripped me, for my interest was extremely casual, and though she was not the least bit serious about the game, she could worry a fairly accomplished player into ridiculous defeat. I lost the very first game I played, of course, the ship being packed with devotees and near experts, but she hung on for a surprisingly long time. It was ten second chess, which did not allow for much thought and gave her every advantage possible. Several males much her senior in age and experience fell before she herself succumbed. By then it was impossible to leave, so we stayed on to the bitter end, a hard fought match between a wizened greybeard and a workman who handled the pieces with rough, clumsy hands. The greybeard won, ultimately, but not before most of the defeated entrants—like us, lingering compulsively to the very last—were very nearly asleep on their feet. It passed more than just the evening; we were not in bed till well after midnight. Accordingly, without more than a squint at my wristwatch I let myself sleep through breakfast, which at best was not worth getting up for. When I did yawn myself awake, Elizabeth was dressed and gone.

I was not alarmed: I did not expect to find her in the arms of the lindying sailor. And if I did? I had not been posting guard on her, the last several days, but simply continuing what was, for us, a very natural tradition. How many years had it been, now, that she had had all of my time? I shaved and dressed and then went up on deck to hunt her out. Perhaps we could weasel our way into a shuffleboard competition. But the lines were long and wearisome and she was not there. She did not seem to be anywhere on deck, nor had she returned to our places. It was getting to be lunchtime, and I did not want to descend into the inferno without her, quite as much for my sake as for hers. On a passing whim, and with an oppressed sigh, I headed for Tanya's bunk. The two of them were there, lying across the bed and chatting. They neither heard nor saw me.

"You might be right," Elizabeth was saying.

"O.K.," Tanya answered. "I wrong. So vat?" She laughed. Her

voice was not deep but it had remarkable resonance, and it carried. I was surprised that she hadn't told us of her stellar career in grand opera, but that would follow, in due time.

"Only pretty is important. You pretty."

There was a brief silence. I tried to catch Elizabeth's eye, without making my presence known, but it did not work. I waited.

"Thank you," Elizabeth replied. There was no embarrassment in her voice, though a stranger might have mistaken the softness of her tone for shy reluctance.

The rich laugh sang out again.

"Vy thank me?" Tanya stretched languorously and held both hands up in front of her.

"Now I tell," she began, "how I kill my last husband."

I coughed and came closer.

"Good morning," I called. "At long last."

They both sat up, Elizabeth nearer the foot of the bed and to me.

"You let us miss breakfast," she said accusingly.

I smiled, casually ignoring her companion.

"Why didn't you stay in bed and dream a better one? Besides," I looked down at my watch, "it's just about time for lunch." I touched her shoulder. "We have about ten minutes. Walking shoes, today? Or talking shoes?"

She hooked her hand into my belt and hauled herself up, nearly knocking me over with the suddenness and violence of the motion.

"Running shoes," she laughed, as I teetered and tried to keep my balance. She was up the stairs and gone before I could so much as move after her.

"Little girl," Tanya beamed.

I nodded and started after Elizabeth.

"Stay," Tanya directed, still sitting and looking across at me.

My hand was on the stair railing.

"Talk," Tanya proposed, patting the bed beside her.

I shook my head as graciously as I could. It was broad daylight and I was still less afraid than Elizabeth had been, cornered by her passionate sailor. But I flattered myself that I was also more aware of how vexing such things can be.

"Later?" she wondered, standing, now, beside the bed. "I wait."

I said nothing and went up on deck, firmly resolved to thereafter avoid Tanya, no matter what the occasion. And if I could not avoid her I would have to be rude, in spite of Elizabeth. It had gotten out of hand.

I said nothing to my ward, whom I found combing her hair and preparing for lunch. Her smile may have been vaguely furtive, but I was not anxious to press the point. It was strange, suspecting her of feminine intrigue—but then, less strange than unsettling. I reminded myself that growing up meant more than simply acquiring new skills and a new body. The reminder improved my appetite, or perhaps it was the fact that I had not eaten since the previous night. At any rate, we had a thoroughly pleasant lunch, and I went up on deck again in a fine, sunny mood.

The glow seemed infectious. The shuffleboard lines dissolved as we approached, or so it seemed, and we were soon partners at a winner-take-all venture in which the skillful and the lucky remained to face another team of challengers, and the vanquished departed, at the least to the rear of the lines. They seemed to have grown long again, now that we were immune from them. We were very nearly completely immune: our triumphs lasted until close to sunset. Elizabeth provided the finesse our side needed, and I supplied the brawn; she slipped the wooden disks into odd corners, and I smashed up enemy formations with great glee. We were a great success. And Tanya was nowhere to be seen.

Supper took the edge off the glow, but the night was dry and calm and we were promised a movie. Everyone crammed into some spot from which a part of the improvised screen could be seen, and hung there while a tired projector wheezily gave us a relic of Hollywood's thinner years. We enjoyed it, in spite of ourselves, and clapped and whistled until we got an encore, which turned out to be another showing of the same film. Which was also all right. When the last shadowy reel had finally unwound, we gave up our cherished vantage points and started for bed, groggily content. Elizabeth tried in vain to stifle a yawn.

"Time for good little girls to be in bed," I observed, and then we met Tanya, wearing the same woolly sweater and fur cap, and a new, reproachful smile.

"Did you see the picture?" Elizabeth wondered, rubbing her eyes a little too elaborately.

Tanya shook her head.

"I vait for him," she declared, pointing accusingly at me.

I tried to smile. Elizabeth hesitated only a moment, then, giggling, broke away and bolted downstairs. Tanya took my arm, lightly and a little plaintively.

"Vas promise," she exclaimed, smiling once more.

What was the use of arguing? I walked about the deck with her. It was not far from midnight, but a good many passengers were still up and about. It was growing cool and the stars were incredibly bright.

Tanya had exhausted her small stock of reproaches; it was not her style to express dissatisfaction with anything for very long.

"Vat luffly stars!"

"You're not cold?" I asked hopefully, but without much real hope.

She laughed.

"A Russian?"

We circled the ship until it was almost our own. A few of the deck lights had gone out; as well as I could see, the other passengers had slipped away to their beds. I was tired but I could not just walk away and leave her. It may sound strange, but it was impossible to so directly affront her. Even her.

"We go front?" she suddenly asked.

We went.

It had gotten chilly; at the bow it was windy and quite cold. We leaned over and tried to see the foam. It was not phosphorescent, and the bow was too dark. We straightened, and I found myself shivering.

"Oh," she exclaimed. "I make you cold."

It should have been easy to smile, but I couldn't manage it. Perhaps it was the cold.

She came closer to me and put her arm around my shoulder.

"I make you warm," she declared.

How could I have protested? And, with her body also leaning up against me, it was warmer. I stopped shivering.

"Good so, eh?" she said, lightly stroking my shoulder.

I took a last look at the bright stars smeared across the sky.

"It's late," I began, but stopped when, without warning, her arm slid down to my waist and her head came burrowing against me. I was shaking my head foolishly, but of course she could not see. And then I realized that she was crying.

I took her hands, to pull her erect, and she bent her face back, smiling even as the tears rushed down her broad cheeks.

"Do you like me?" she asked in clear, fluent German. "Do you really like me?"

She freed her hands and pulled my head down to hers. Her lips clutched at mine. She moaned and slid quietly to the deck, taking me with her.

When I got back to my bed Elizabeth was still awake. She made no pretense about sleeping, but half sat up and looked at me inquiringly, her eyes bright.

"Did you?" she whispered.

I pushed her back down, pulled the covers up over her, and got myself ready for sleep.

"Tell me," she whispered fiercely. "You did, didn't you?"

I settled myself into bed.

"Go to sleep. It's late. And I'm tired."

She giggled, high and a little nervously.

"I don't blame you."

I reached over to her bed and pretended to shake her. I could not really be angry, especially with her. I'm afraid she knew that only too well.

"Remind me," I warned her, "to wash your mouth out with soap, first thing in the morning."

She snatched at my hand.

"Did you?" she insisted again. "Tell me. Please." I did not answer. "I wanted you to," she finally conceded.

I pulled my hand away, smiling to myself. It was not a thing I could reproach her with. Perhaps she had felt how deeply the older woman needed just such reassurance; perhaps she was a conscious accomplice. It made little difference.

"Yes," I whispered over to her. "Now go to sleep."

We were late arriving in New York. The wind was against us, the seas were heavy, and the engines developed a tic that made half speed optimum. Still, we crawled forward through the grey weather, and our arrival was sure, albeit chronologically uncertain. We sighted land early one afternoon, after a dozen false alarms, hopeful mirages that turned out to be clouds or high-breaking waves, shapes and forms that kept disappearing into the horizon instead of growing large and green and coming toward us, mile by slow mile. Elizabeth had spent a quiet morning listening to the violin virtuoso tell anecdotes of musical history, perhaps comforted both by his cheerful talk and his abrupt, moody silences. We did without lunch, so as not to miss the first sight of New York harbor. Someone else saw it first, and then Elizabeth made it out and pointed for my benefit, calling, loudly and excitedly, "There it is, there it is!" She was jumping up and down as she shouted. Nor was she, on the *Polar Icecap*, the only one lost in jubilance.

V

Even in peacetime Switzerland's urban centers are something of a hothouse phenomenon. But as we had known them, surrounded by German and Italian armies and ringed in by vast bombing fleets from all over the globe, the Swiss cities became more like extensive sanatoria than places of business. The Swiss tended their little nation like fond, nervous horticulturists; every threat, and especially the forced use of domestic railroad lines for Nazi shipments, wrapped the protective coatings that much closer. German troops on leave and in disguise were difficult, and inconvenient, to tell from ordinary civilians. There were so many refugees, prosperous enough on the whole to be tolerated by a stringent government, that subversion of one kind or another was an ever-present danger. Air raid alerts were frequent and regular; the Swiss army was kept rigorously prepared. And, in the five years we spent in that milieu of mixed fear, suspicion and luxury, Elizabeth had absorbed a large share of my own particular brand of indifference, plus a good deal of the refugee's dogged hedonism. A Victorian governess might very well have labelled her a charming but spoiled brat and recommended strong measures.

But New York was not the place, and I was not the one, to administer anything of the kind. I enrolled her in a good school, for one thing. What were schools for, if not to inculcate the less attractive virtues? And while Elizabeth was learning how to be an accomplished young lady, I was occupied with the task of re-establishing myself in my business. It had not greatly suffered: the swell of war-time profits had created an entirely new group of buyers, in addition to inflating the pocketbooks of the regular clientele. And as the dollar itself inflated, money became much less desirable than, for example, such things as were offered for sale in my salon. The natural result was that my staff had no temptations to resist: they did quite well enough in the normal course of affairs, and without excessive effort. There were still contacts to be re-opened, however, and the uncertainties of the future to be anticipated. I was not crushed beneath an excessive burden of detail, but I did have to sacrifice most of my daytime hours. Especially at the beginning, as much for the general psychological effect as anything else.

Yet not all the daytime hours were, from my point of view,

formalities and make-weights. Elizabeth and I continued to breakfast together. And it was enough to sustain me, knowing that, first thing in the morning, I would be with her across a little breakfast table. I could not be discontented, even though it would be hours before I was to see her again; it was enough to laugh with her, to see her solemnly sipping a cup of steaming cocoa, to watch her hand curled around a spoon or lying pensive beside her plate. She grew prettier and more desirable every day. I tried not to tell her, but I'm sure she knew. There wasn't a great deal I could keep secret from her.

It wasn't long, too, before I could manage, several days a week, to break the office ritual and escape for lunch with her, quiet and necessarily brief meals which we took in a series of small mid-town restaurants not too far from her school. She had no difficulty adjusting to New York; after a few weeks the faint edge of strangeness had worn off, just as it did in her relations with teachers and fellow students. She learned her way about the city quickly and casually, learned how to blend herself into the landscape with virtually no pain or inconvenience.

"And how was school this morning?" I asked her, the first time. She was stirring a small cup of soup.

"I like it," she declared, looking up at me and smiling.

I laughed with what must have seemed an extravagant pleasure, delighted to be with her again without having to wait for nightfall and supper.

"Then it must like you," I assured her.

She nodded.

"Do you mind going to a girl's school?" I wondered. It had occurred to me that perhaps she might feel cheated; it was not so very different, this way, from what she had known in Switzerland, or before.

"Oh no," she answered quickly. "Girls have a lot more to teach me."

I did not push the inquiry any further.

Later that same mid-day rendezvous, I ordered a bottle of mild wine and proposed that she share it with me. She made no objection, nor did her school administration; it became a habit which I continued and even expanded, introducing wines and then liqueurs to our own evening meal. I do not think I was unduly precipitate, although certainly I was as anxious as possible for her to be in all ways adult.

There was a small crisis (internal) when her school arranged a dance. We went to buy her a new dress for the occasion; while it was being fitted I wondered, casually, if I ought to dress up too. She was startled.

"Did you want to come?" she asked, looking around at me. I was lolling on a sofa, watching the shopwoman clamber about, her mouth full of pins, as always relishing the exhibition of Elizabeth in professional deshabilée. I was much more surprised than she was.

"Shouldn't I?"

She hesitated, then smiled.

"The oldest girl will be fifteen," she told me matter-of-factly. "The boys are coming from St. Martin's, and two teachers are going to be chaperones."

I tried to return her smile.

"Of course, then," I agreed. "I hadn't known."

The fitter twitched her about and I lost sight of her face. I hoped I hadn't revealed too much. Somehow, it had never occurred to me that Elizabeth's schoolfellows were, in most people's eyes, little more than children. Elizabeth was probably viewed the same way, though I at least knew better. Nor had I any idea that the girls would require escorts. I knew that it was to be a dance, of course, and I was sufficiently aware of the fact that dancers are automatically paired, male and female. I suppose it was simply an automatic assumption that where Elizabeth went I would go too; if she danced I would be her partner. I don't think the plight of her schoolfellows even crossed my mind.

I saw her off, when the night came, with the blandest demeanor I could muster. The dress was lovely, and someone at St. Martin's had seen to it that every girl was sent flowers. They were impersonal, but looked none the worse for that.

"Don't step on Hugh's feet," I said in farewell.

"As long as he doesn't climb all over mine," she replied quickly. She stepped into the taxi and, when I closed the door behind her, was quickly carried off. I was vaguely restless, riding back up to our apartment, but it was comforting to know that her partner was little more than a cipher, a name and a number assigned to her and very much an unknown quantity. I had tried, earlier, to picture her dancing with a fifteen year old boy. It was inconceivable.

I read for an hour or two, then put on some records and settled myself to await her homecoming. It was not to be quite a bacchanal: the curfew would sound at eleven, and from what I knew of the respective schools involved it would be strictly enforced. Not that I was worried.

She came back, at last, pink cheeked and pleased. And alone.

"Where's Hugh?" I wondered, kissing her and then helping her off with her coat.

"I didn't ask him up. I think he would have been afraid to come. Besides, his dad drove us."

She did a few long whirls around the room; it was an effort, but I kept myself from joining her.

"He didn't take back his flowers, at least," I noted.

She laughed and held out her arms to me. We danced wildly but, I like to think, well.

"He's a nice boy," she confided, and I laughed with her. We went to bed much too late, for both of us were excited and we needed to talk, but I slept the sleep of the blessed. It had not been very serious, after all.

Time passed. That first school dance had served a double function. It allowed me to at least realize how others saw Elizabeth, and it prepared me, after a fashion, for the ubiquitous American custom of adolescent dating. She was immersed in it, of course, within a year from our arrival. I did not like it, neither abstractly nor in its effects upon me and mine; nor did I ever quite accept it. But I did not protest. I treated the succession of red-faced, embarrassed young boys as calmly and humanely as I could. It grew especially difficult when they began to reappear, when it was not too difficult to imagine affectionate ties between Elizabeth and such regular partners. But I felt basically secure.

Yet I did not rely entirely on past achievement and domestic security. Elizabeth was popular and well fêted, but I remained impressario in charge; of all the steady partners I was the most stable and the most constant. Nor did I feel any incongruity in sharing the opera with her, or invading Broadway with only my young ward under my arm. Several times I introduced her, without introduction, into one or another circle of friends and acquaintances, carefully refraining from anything but vague hints as to her origin and ancestry. One prosperous importer, gross but keen, immediately took her for my mistress, and informed me that he was stationed next in line. But it was at a literary soirée, a cocktail party in disguise, that she really shone.

The Parisian guest of honor, by that point well under the influence, began it by demanding to know what she was thinking about, behind that lovely smile. She continued to smile and made him no answer.

"Peut-être aux tendres confidences d'un coeur naïf comme le tien?" he recited. "A ta robe? Aux airs que tu danses? Peut-être à Georges-là—peut-être à rien."

Her smile grew faintly wicked.

"Ce poème," she replied easily, "est toute ta jeunesse. Pas la mienne."

I confess to being surprised myself, though I should not have been. Who could have appealed to her more, at her age, than de Musset? But the Parisian immediately began to circle the room, spreading word of the miraculous phenomenon he had uncovered, a lovely girl—and an American—who responded to one quotation from Musset with another, equally apt, from the same poet. He led over embarrassed strangers who knew neither French nor Musset and some who knew both and found the feat less impressive than did the literary but half embalmed Frenchman. With both sorts Elizabeth behaved beautifully; I could not have asked for a better performance.

I told her so, on the way back; I wanted her to know with perfect clarity how well she was appreciated at home.

She hugged my arm.

"Wasn't it silly!" she exclaimed.

I was doubly pleased.

"It was," I repeated. "But you weren't."

"I read the poem in class," she smiled. "And just last week."

I laughed with her.

"Thank god you didn't say so."

She shook her head.

"I would have embarrassed you," she assured me. "You might not have taken me again."

I protested.

"You're still my favorite dancing partner," she went on, leaning her head against my shoulder.

I sighed elaborately.

"It isn't difficult, being good to you. You flatter so deftly."

She laughed and stayed where she was.

"It's true," she reaffirmed. "I mean it."

I smiled and said nothing. It was enough, then, to feel the light pressure of her cheek on my shoulder, and the touch of her hand under my arm. I regretted our arrival home, and the necessity of dispossessing her. But I could not have felt much closer to a pleasure which transcends description. Which helps explain how I could watch the parade of strange young men with reasonably bland confidence in the outcome.

We were at supper, one evening, when the boy of the moment called and cancelled a scheduled expedition.

"He has a bad cold," she explained, rejoining me.

"I'm sorry."

She nodded.

"So am I. We were going to see a play."

I looked up, but she had gone back to her food.

"Shall I take you?" I suggested.

Her smile was uncomfortably rueful.

"Let's just stay home."

I administered an extra glass of her favorite liqueur, to help ease her disappointment a bit. I think it made her communicative. Or perhaps there were things she simply wanted to say. At any rate, she began talking about the defaulting boy in warmer tones than I had ever heard from her. I was alarmed. She was almost sixteen, by then, and very much her own mistress. I took the plunge.

"Are you considering marrying him?" I wondered, with a big facetious grin.

She wrinkled her brow.

"He's nice," she declared.

We were sitting on a broad, soft couch. The phonograph was spinning, softly. I touched her shoulder apprehensively and she suddenly smiled.

"Are you worried?" she laughed.

I nodded.

"Yes."

She took my hand in hers.

"Don't be. It isn't serious. Besides," she assured me earnestly, "I couldn't. He isn't Jewish."

I had to bite my tongue to keep from exclaiming that I was not, either. I nodded and desperately looked at something else, but it was no good. She saw.

"You knew that, didn't you?" she continued.

I couldn't speak. Her eyes were unnaturally bright.

"Did you want me to forget?" she asked, leaning forward so that her glance would meet mine.

I made an effort to answer, but my jaws would not work. I sat like a mummy, incapable of helping myself by word or motion.

"Did you think I could?" she went on, then answered herself, shaking her head. "You didn't. I know you didn't."

I managed to wrinkle my hands around hers, but it was all I could do. I felt ill. I think I frightened her.

"Are you all right?" she asked, freeing her hands and shaking me lightly.

I nodded jerkily.

"Yes," I gulped out.

She put her head on my shoulder and I knew she was crying. How could I comfort her?

"We don't have to talk about it," I said at last, as the shock wore away and I became more or less myself again. It was not hopeless; I would have done more to have her. Knowing that she remembered had been explosive enough; the fact that she had clung to her memories through all the intervening years, considered herself still sister to Elizabeta Levi-Zorn and all her tribe, had been absolutely crushing. But there was no need for it to be. I would swear public fealty to Judaism and Jews alike, I would donate to synagogues and temples; had she insisted I would have grown a beard and worn a prayer shawl. I sighed with relief and, at last, put my arm around her and tried to ease the flow of her tears. They had been eight years in coming.

She straightened, soon, and put herself to rights. I reached out and took a stray tear on my finger.

"Such pearls," I told her, "to cast before swine."

She sealed my lips with a quick gesture.

"Don't. You've been more like an angel. You're all I've had."

She caught at her lip and the tears did not come. I put my arm around her again.

"I always will be."

She rubbed her hand furiously over my knee.

"I know." She twisted, suddenly, and looked up at me, her

face less than a foot from mine. Her eyes were still damp and her smile had never been more tender. "I've wanted to tell you," she said slowly. "I've always wanted you to know." Her neck was arched like the gentle curve of the heavens, and, through the loose opening of her blouse, I saw the beginning swell of her breasts. My mouth was suddenly dry. I touched her throat gently with the tip of a single finger and stroked it across and down to the soft hollow at the base of her neck.

"I've known," I nearly whispered.

Her hand rubbed against my cheek.

"You could almost have been my real father," she said softly.

I slapped her. And, lest I should hit out at her again, I shoved her roughly away and ran out of the room, leaving her sprawled on the couch and bewildered.

Which was how it happened. We made it up, of course; anything can be patched, in this world of cracked clay. But nothing is ever as good as new. And in my case it never was. Never.

The Drifter

SHORT STORIES

by

MATTHEW CARNEY

The Drifter Stories by Matthew Carney

"The Drifter" was first published in *Points, No. 6* under the title "Unquiet Drifting"

THE IVORY CIRCLE

The Bishop, stout, sturdy, ruddy, in loose purple gown, had his finger on elephants, and always concealed the ivory and his money from Prince Orchard. Now he was masking craftiness behind indignant eyes. "One hour of esoteric meditation," he declaimed to Al, head of the Organic Society Armed Band, "does more good for your confounded society than ten years of machine shops. You want money again, you want my ivory. Well, I have no money to turn over to you. Tell your Prince and your committees just that."

Al nodded, gazing at him wryly. "I'll turn the boys loose on the premises."

"Confound your boys," said the Bishop, looking angrily out the window. "There's no money in this monastery." He turned glaring, and moistened his lips. "You've plundered me again and again this last year, day and night. Each time I replace my golden ritual articles you steal them again. You've stripped the monastery of its sacred ivory decorations. Taxation, pfaw! It's out and out brigandage! In the darkest years of banditry we weren't hounded more than we are now. Because we're not 'organic' with your vulgar society. Thank God at least the enterprises are honest. If they didn't pay us for our ivory work, we'd be starving to death to support your Prince."

Al looked away coldly. "Isn't lying forbidden in monasteries, Bishop?" He walked out of the vestry, into a speckled marble corridor, following it far up to an open-air causeway which encircled the monastery's fourth inner labyrinth. He stepped into the sunlight there and summoned up his group leaders.

"Where are the monks?" he asked.

"By the labyrinth entrance," one man said, "stretched on the ground in ranks of three."

"Any missing, any new faces?"

"All accounted for. We caught five of them trying to duck out of sight. Two in the center, the others in the fifth. The boys are checking for panels now."

Al's face creased with a dour expression. "All right, I'll go up into the center myself. Bring up the electronic equipment, we'll try to swing open a wall with that. Run the squads through all quarters and shops in all seven labyrinths. Complete shakedown. Pick up anything of value, look for the ivory stores." He took a plan of the monastery from his pocket and sighed, tracing his finger over the concentric circles of labyrinths. "Any change in the routes since last time?"

"No, same-same," one of the group leaders said.

"OK, let's move out. We've got a day's work."

Prince Orchard was like a big reflective lion as he frowned, examining the gold chalices and the sun-burst on his desk. "Junk, Al. No one values gold in the whole society any more. What about the ivory?"

Al shrugged, keeping his thin face expressionless. "No ivory, Prince, and no currency. We found a secret panel in one labyrinth, but it was empty."

The Prince grunted and smoothed his heavy yellow mustache. He was studying Al's face. "The Bishop's got a raft of money, Al. He's always got ivory. Now doesn't that impress you as menacing?"

"Maybe." Al tensed his jaw and shifted. "But how much can one lousy monastery drain out of the organic economy? I'd rather ignore the joint than turn around in that maze every month."

The Prince nodded and tapped the side of his strong nose with a finger. "Fifty years of war and politics, Al. I smell a rat hole. I haven't got the figures, can't get them since I gave up my prerogatives with the enterprises, but look here: they're all rich." He arose and paced back to a mahogany wall where he rapped his fingers on a large chart. "Every syndicate and enterprise in the society is rich, but the monastery's getting all the excess wealth, for their damn carved ivory, and I can't get a bean for the Big Center." He returned and eased into his seat, smiling as he fixed his gaze on Al. "Imagine how I feel. I beat the bandits, Al. I founded the organic society, wrote the laws, and then set people free from myself. Take your own syndic. They turn out all the electricity we can use, they're fat, opulent and peaceful, so what do they care if they don't train boys or put up money for a Big Center astro-physics? They want to line their premises with that ivory, OK. But they want *me* to bring in money from outside, or else, no extra work. You see how it is?"

Al relaxed in a chair and lit a cigarette, his face noncommittal. "Prince, no one's really convinced we need a Big Center. May be a little too close to the old State idea."

The Prince lowered his brows. "Now, Al," he said gravely. "My history's no secret. Fifty years of hell to build an organic society won't peter out in a State!" He slapped his hand on the desk. "But organic means dynamic! We need that Big Center, if society is going to produce sovereign, evolving individuals, the kind who give some kind of meaning to life. We don't want to go back and be a bunch of ruin dwellers."

Al flicked the ashes from his cigarette and gave the Prince a casual, sidelong glance. "OK, Prince," he said and took a breath. "But how about elephants? Do you suppose the Bishop has dug up an elephant graveyard or something?"

"That's the thing," said the Prince quietly, leaning forward. "Talk about your empire, listen a minute. As far as I know, or anyone else knows, elephants are extinct. But month after month, year after year that monastery comes up with ivory. It means organization, Al. It goes beyond the valley, or our whole continent here." He stood up to pace back and forth, but stopped and looked questioningly at Al. "You're a young, modern-day buck,

Al. You were educated in a peaceful society, but we don't know what the remnants of people in the rest of the world are doing. The population's so thin maybe you can't imagine good, old fashioned police work having a positive benefit." He glanced around with his eyes and lowered his voice. "But I can tell you this. During the past year I've reconstituted the Eye force. Nothing to reveal so far, but we're poking around for a live elephant empire. An idea I've got. If one exists, we'll grab it for society. It's the only way out."

Al casually blew a smoke ring up to the ceiling and blinked. "As captain of the Armed Band, I realize you've got to use force now and then, Prince. But I'm against the Eye."

"I know, I know," said the Prince. "It's anti-freedom, but I've kept it non-organic. No politics, no spying on the enterprises. You can trust my word. As soon as we get that monastery's wealth working for the organic society, I'll abolish it. That'll wind up everything I need to do for my aim."

Al stood up to go and tossed his cigarette into an ashtray. "You're the Prince," he said. "But nobody wants a monastery organic with society, either. We're through with secret politics and authority." He tucked in the back of his shirt and pulled at his collar. "I've got to get over to the lab. All the tax collecting with the boys lately, I'm behind in my work."

"Right, go ahead, Al, but listen . . ." The Prince followed him to the door. "We want to give you even more work the next few months. Organize unexpected raids on the Bishop. Surprise him, get in there and get hold of some real wealth, ivory or currency. We'll tap that monastery for everything they owe society."

Al frowned as the Prince sent him away with a pat on the back. "All right, the organic society forever."

One evening after the Armed Band had left the monastery with some ivory baubles they'd found planted in a "secret" closet, the Bishop hurried down to the third level of the cool, secure underground. His nine-month initiates were assembled in the spacious chapel, where they sat cross-legged in a semi-circle on the polished stone floor.

"Young men!" he addressed them genially, moving into their midst. "Two minutes and forty seconds! Every last man was concealed, all portage removed, twenty full seconds before they stuck their noses in the front door!" He stood still, hands on hips, smiling broadly. "I am very, very proud of this group. You've shown more alacrity, more promise, more development, under the worst of conditions, than I have ever encountered in my time. Really, you have been splendid. And now, tonight, for that reason, I'm going to reveal a little plan to you. Something I've been considering for some time." He raised his chin, studying the group from one end to the other. He extended a hand as though to pluck something from the air. "Jasper!"

A berobed young man leaped to his feet in one lithe spring. "Yes sir!"

"Come out here, boy. Come out here beside me." He ran his eyes back and forth over the group as Jasper, relaxed and aware, moved to his side. "I'm going to take Jasper, here," the Bishop announced, clapping a hand on the young man's shoulder, "on a little trip with me. You all recognize by now, without jealousy of any sort, how his own rapid advance in the work has really aided the whole group's development. All of you are ready for more important things, for teachings closer to the esoteric circle. Jasper here will be your courier." He leaned toward the group, his eyebrows raised. "I'm taking him to the continental elephant preserve!"

A ripple of joy and surprise went through the disciplined ranks. "You deserve it, you deserve it!" the Bishop called out, beaming down and rubbing his hands. "But!" He assumed a serious attitude of warning. "Jasper will have to bring back a great deal from the Negro monastery down there. It means more is demanded of you. The Negroes are ahead of us in many aspects of development. Their Bishop is a great, venerable saint, and one hundred and fifty years of the most absolute secrecy won't leave anything for the uninitiated eye to comprehend. Symbols, symbols, symbols, that's what he'll bring back. And you'll have to start incorporating them into your carving and your construction. Remember that, and prepare yourselves."

He turned reflectively and strode toward the cavernous corridor. "Ten minutes, Jasper," he said over his shoulder. "West side garage, panel truck."

Silence consumed the misted, fragrant air under the towering roof of interlacing vines and branches. Around the Negro Bishop's inspection party, scattered in quiet attitudes for evening meditation, a wide park faded in somber distance.

The center of the monastery was concealed under hundred-foot spreading branches of gigantic, sparsely planted trees. The Bishop hadn't told Jasper that the Negro monastery was, literally, the living forest, impenetrably girdled and roofed by vegetation. Throughout the week's trek on the inspection tour, traversing all six labyrinths, Jasper had not seen the sun. He had scarcely even heard a noise, but had seen architectural marvels, leafy palaces, titanic corridors, chapels, lanes, parks, bridges, all fashioned from growing plant life. Sometimes he had seen tan-skinned Negro monks and their wives lacing vines in the trees, stooping over gardens, tending smouldering little pots of perfumed pest bane. From time to time the party passed herds of the gentle, white-bodied, silent elephants.

Now, seated apart on the mossy grass, Jasper was relaxing, reaching deep inside for the still filament of perfect attention on his self-remembering. Speech was forbidden above ground, and the soundless communication practiced by the Negroes was lost to him, but still he'd amassed knowledge. It was in his brain, registered, recorded. He had to review the impressions, deepen them, not let them fade or distort, but his attention was pinked with anxiety.

A faint knot in his solar-plexus sent recurring, indistinct warnings to his brain each time he sought to link impressions to his aim. An emotion, a new emotion to him, provoked some wisp of fear and dimmed his fixed aim.

Reverence, it must be reverence. The Bishop said they would all discover it "some day." The living organism of the fabulous monastery, and that ancient little brown man. Reverence was making him taste the incipient traces of that most dreadful suffering, pride's immolation. He sat absorbed in meditation, and a presence took shape in front of him. He glanced up, and his heart froze. The old saint, clothed only in his short yellow skirt and sandals, stood regarding him, a benign smile on his face. He leaned, and his lips moved, whispering.

"You're having trouble."

Jasper's attention fled. He felt control slip away and his limbs began to tremble. He was on his knees, bowing, and the slender, ancient presence loomed above him. He was found out! His heart swelled, his throat constricted, and he knew he was helpless, but a gentle, dry hand, half imperceptibly, was gripping his shoulder, straightening him up. The dark, leathery old face stared down, commiserating, his deep eyes kind and peaceful. "Recite all you've learned."

Jasper's eyes filled with tears and the inside of his nose smarted. "Forgive me, sir. Forgive me," he whispered.

The old man put a slight pressure on Jasper's shoulder and he shivered with a move toward calm. In the turmoil of his attention the week's impressions fell slowly into compartments, and he was able to read them off his mind. It went quickly, in a hesitating whisper. "The outer circle is penetrated . . . where you've built the deep-water port . . . by the promontory. The gate . . . is reached by land along the beach . . . at low tide. Next full moon a marine monastery is coming . . . with elephants from Africa. Inside here the true way . . . through the labyrinths . . . is determined from the relation of . . . the compass to the enneagram. Point 9 at the outside entrance . . . is south . . ."

The saint applied another slight pressure to the shoulder and Jasper, silent, was peacefully aware of kneeling in the misty green spaciousness. He looked up into the old man's face as the lips formed again, half smiling, to whisper: "You have everything for your immediate aim?"

"Yes sir."

Once more the slight pressure on his shoulder and Jasper looked into the infinity of the shaded brown eyes and heard the whisper. "Fulfill the aim with your Prince." He wasn't sure he could possibly have heard that, and the old saint smiled at him. "Fulfill the aim with your Prince, it's time to reconstruct. Listen carefully. I want you to do something for us when you are back in society. It is between you and me only. You will be the messenger."

Jasper bowed his forehead to the ground as he realized his insufficiency, and the new sensation rushed through him violently. He reverenced the saint deeply, and the knowledge he had. He listened to the whisper coming straight at him, and knew he was in contact with the force of the inner circle that ruled the world.

Prince Orchard paced thoughtfully in the headlights of the huge vans, but stopped when Al led up a company of the Armed Band. "Where are the Negroes?"

Al looked at the ground and spat. "Locked them in the ship's hold with the crew, about three hundred. Goes against the grain, Prince."

"Yeah, yeah, I know," said the Prince. "Wait a minute, I've got a word for the boys. Try to get it in your head that this is only a maneuver."

Several men in overalls came up to speak briefly with the Prince, after which he turned to face the armed company. "All right now, boys," he called out. "We're ready to go. The animal men are set, and the carnival up north is waiting for a big surprise. I've got to duck, but remember this one thing: you are picked men. So are the farm boys. Your job is: support the organic society. We'll have to see this maneuver through to the end. Those of you going up with the vans: clam up till we get a formal decision from the committeemen. The rest of you'll be down here for about a week keeping an eye on the monastery. Don't try to go in any further than the first labyrinth till we come down with a crew and some heavy equipment. Another thing. All this stuff belongs to these monks, ivory included. They worked hard for it, they're going to get paid for it. With a bonus. All we want to do is give the elephants a little publicity in organic society."

Motors began warming up down the line of vans, so the Prince broke off his talk. The air was charged for the departure and some elephants began trumpeting in the roar of the motors. Al followed the Prince to his car. "You work out some of the damnedest projects," he said with a grin. "Never thought I'd see an elephant."

The Prince nodded and grinned back. "Good work on your part, Al. Let's just hope those committeemen don't feel too organically moral about it." He got in the car and rolled down the window. "The trucks can follow me right out. See you."

He started the car, waved, and drove out on the webbed steel tracks laid along the beach. Al looked at the freshening blue sky in the east and went over to the lead van. "Go on, take off!" he hollered to the driver.

The news was a sensation up and down the valley, and farther. Farm families not intending to visit the fair packed up anyway and came motoring in from a thousand mile radius. Even the organic communities far flung on the continent were flying people in for a look at the incredible find. The valley lodging enterprise was obliged to erect tent camps in all the outlying sections of the capital. Committeemen from the farm enterprises had erected a huge reinforced enclosure for the herd, and had printed and distributed booklets on the history and eventual disappearance of the species. Elephants had electrified the air and, proportionate to their size, portended big, new events.

In the Valley Co-ordination Building, over a hubbub of shouts, calls, laughter and angry demands, Prince Orchard was spreading his hands for silence among the assembled committee chiefs. He smiled benignly from a refuge behind his desk on the platform and put on a pair of horn-rimmed glasses, gravely lifting several sheets of paper. "Gentlemen!" he addressed them. "Now gentlemen, I wouldn't want it said that we've been asleep on the job." The hubbub died slowly and the Prince looked about before resuming. "We haven't been asleep on the job. No one has to tell you how important elephants are." He cleared his throat and rattled the papers, looking over the group. "You see that a little police work is still necessary for the organic nature of our society."

The chiefs were surveying him attentively so the Prince spoke on, looking at his papers. "The elephants came in by ship from Africa, for breeding purposes. We found out they were arriving at a Negro monastery hidden in the swamps down south, so we sent the farm boys down with an escort to pick them up. The monastery is part of a world-wide religious organization, tied up with the monastery here in the valley. The monasteries have been growing elephants in secret for a couple of hundred years! The Negroes down south, and somewhere in Africa, too, and we don't know just where else. It has to do with the monasteries' esoteric aim."

"Just a minute now, by God," interrupted one of the chiefs. "They've got an esoteric what?"

"Quiet! A monastery," said another. "The monastery raises elephants."

"Let him get on with it. Quiet!"

"Gentlemen," said Prince Orchard, smiling gently, looking over the chiefs. "Gentlemen," he said, collecting all their attention. "It's a big continent. The population is small. Many things go on that we can't possibly know about. There are still hidden regions, still groups of people not organic with society, still ruin dwellers. As long as they represent no danger, you know we never force them to become organic. We even exclude some, namely, as you know, religions, because of their inherently authoritarian and esoteric nature. Here today we have before us a matter of some depth. It requires a decision from you, perhaps a vote of the syndics, on what is esoteric and what is not, on what is socially organic and what is not. I'm confident the farms chief will bear me out in this: living animals are organic with the recognized direction of society. The teeth of these animals are not less organic. Will the farms chief support me there?"

The farms chief rose to his feet impressively. "Orchard, do those animals belong to this Negro monastery?"

"Yes, they do, chief. To all the monasteries."

The farms chief looked about at his colleagues. "Men, those people have got to play ball with society!"

"Now, Bishop, a little self control," said the Prince.

"I am controlling myself, Orchard. Confound you, I say."

The Prince chuckled and leaned back in his chair. "Tell the truth, Bishop, you didn't need all that money, did you?"

The Bishop, grave in demeanor, leaned over his desk toward the Prince. "What do you think we do in these monasteries, man? Of course we need the money. With this nonsense of organic and non-organic, how do you expect we're going to feed ourselves, dress ourselves, move about, study? A religion needs funds, man, for the love of God. And it's not a question merely of money!"

The Prince shook his head with a smile and folded his hands on his lap. "Now don't tell me you really depend on elephants to live, Bishop. Eh?"

The Bishop frowned. "Don't try to snoop into our business, Orchard. We need money to carry on our work, and our work is secret. You blasted one hundred and eighty-nine years of continuous, conscientious and creative toil when you uncovered the Negro monastery's preservation work. In that vulgar shambles you call organic society there's not the slightest inkling of inner work, the divine creation of the self. *That's* really behind our preservation of elephants and ivory. Through one hundred and fifty years of the worst chaos in history we managed to work unimpeded, in a real society. But you blasted it, in some way I'll never know. My young people are even leaving now, disillusioned."

The Prince, nodding pleasantly, took a little figurine of ivory out of his pocket for examination. He showed it to the Bishop and tossed it onto the desk. "You're talking about Jasper, I presume."

The Bishop grew red in the face, but settled back in his seat. "So that's it," he said disgustedly.

"You people, you're in monasteries," said the Prince, "with private, secret aims, ostensibly to surpass our non-eternal public aim. But let me tell you this: *we* conquered the bandits. I moulded a peaceful society, literally out of human clay, and the creation now of our Big Center project is as conscious, as delicate a work as . . . as finely done as your little figurine, and it not only symbolizes objective nature, but it controls it."

The Bishop scoffed. "Don't weary me with your nonsense, Orchard. Savages can run machines. Your society hasn't the vaguest germ of real, inner cultiv . . ."

"One little factor," the Prince interrupted. He picked up the ivory work again and studied the symbol on it. "I organized men and set them free. I gave them possibly centuries of peaceful construction for the earth, because I believe the Big Center will breed a superior kind of man who can run it." He held the figurine aside from his eyes to look at the Bishop. "But I personally lack desire to participate in the society I made."

The Bishop's eyes widened. "You, Prince?"

"Yes, and then I've had some talks with Jasper . . ."

The Bishop was nodding, soberly.

The acres of the Science enterprise were astir as trainees from schools all over the continent were coming in for placement. At the same time a new Lab School was opening for Big Center training. Happy young men and women were wandering loosely over the premises. Al had gone to the recreation house to relax as soon as he had word of his acceptance into the Big Center school. As he eased into a chair with a magazine, one of his boys came up. "Well, Al, going into the big time?"

Al shook his head and winked. "Yes sir, getting organic as hell." He looked beyond the fellow and his mouth turned down. He started to leaf the magazine, but a crease appeared between his brows and he looked back up. The man with him looked also. "What're you doing around Science, Jasper?" Al asked. "Someone told me you left the farm to go join the monastery."

Jasper glanced up pleasantly. "Oh, hello, Al. Yes, didn't you see me? I saw you there, all last year."

Al stared hostilely. "Learn a lot?" he asked.

Jasper kept smiling, but said nothing and Al grunted and turned to his friend. "Guess the Prince is going to take his place over there. That right Jasper?"

Jasper no longer vouchsafed his smile. "Orchard surpassed his aim so often it got too rarefied for feeding on society," he said.

"What's that, some of your monastery talk?" asked Al. "I suppose the Prince is taking your place over there, and you're going to try to take his place here. You want to be a Prince, Jasper?"

Jasper laughed and stood up. "Don't be bitter, Al. You don't know how much the monastery appreciates organic society."

"Well, let me tell you this: don't come around here and try to convert us. We've got a long tradition of being rough on authoritarians."

"I wouldn't think of it, Al," Jasper said and started away cheerfully. "I want you all just as you are. You'll see what I mean."

Al and his friend watched Jasper leave the room, and Al reached in his pocket for a cigarette. He found his hand trembling with fury, because he knew he couldn't rest until he found out what Jasper knew. "We'll see," he said disgustedly to his friend. "Where does he get off?"

ONE MAN

A SWARM of naked devils, skinny, glossy grey and blue with little round faces, spilled out of their corner rat hole in the twilight dimness. "They can't hurt you, they can't hurt you," Evers repeated nervously to the group of us on the balcony. The demons loped over the stone courtyard to begin a dance around the center fire, and a high-pitched howling chant rose in the air.

"What are they doing, Evers?" a young lady asked, frightened.

"Evers, can't we get out of here?" a pompous voice demanded.

The firelight caused Evers' sweating face to glisten as he adjusted his glasses. "These are our own devils," he instructed. "We have to learn what they're going to do. But they can't hurt us." He moistened his lips, watching the devils.

They were hopping about the fire in little groups of three, and suddenly a trio broke from the circle with arms outstretched above them, running loosely to the balcony on which we stood. "Eeee hee hee hee!" they laughed, flapping their hands as they came to a halt, gazing up intently.

"See here, Evers, what is all this?" the pompous voice spoke out again.

"Shh, shh," said Evers, waving for silence.

The devils flapped their hands frettedly, waiting, and then with a cascading chorus of squeals rushed back to rejoin the dance at the fire.

"Now, I've had enough of this pussy-footing around," the pompous voice stated again. "You got us into this, Evers. It's up to you to explain what's going on."

Evers straightened primly then, and for the first time took personal notice of one of us. "Now please!" he said with rooster dignity. "Would you come forward in the light, please, you, mister, who's been speaking so much."

"Arr," growled a round, balding man dressed in a business suit. He stepped boldly through the crowd toward the leader.

"Let's have this clear once and for all!" said Evers in shrill severity. "I didn't bring you here, and I'm not in the least responsible for you. I have my job to guide you best I can, but that is absolutely all."

The round, pompous one stared red-faced at Evers with bulging eyes. "Well, what are we doing here?" he blurted. "Why'd you guide us here, if that's your job?"

"We came here," Evers stated coldly, "all of us together, because we have no place else to go."

"Arr," said the round man, looking out at the devils. "Ought to tell us something about the place, though."

Evers sighed and raised his eyes patiently to the sky. "My heavens," he said, "I can only repeat what I've already told you. It's a ten thousand year old palace. It used to be the dwelling place of kings with their armies."

"Yeah," said the round man, leaning with his hands on the balustrade, taking charge. "Where's all the soldiers now? Use 'em to clean out those devils there."

"What are you yakking about?" spoke up a tall young man at the rear. "Did you hear what Evers said?" He swaggered forward and we all turned to stare at him. "He told us these are our devils. The thing to do is go get them."

"Now just a moment, just a moment, there," fluttered Evers. The young fellow was climbing over the balustrade.

"Here, what's he doing?" bluffed the round man.

The young fellow hung by his hands above the courtyard, then dropped to the ground. At the fire the devils were staring in his direction, and suddenly broke and swarmed over to him in a mad rush, shrieking, "Yee yee yee yee!"

"Oh, my heavens, my heavens," said Evers, wringing his hands.

"They'll tear him apart!" cried the round man.

A mass of blue and grey had inundated the young man below us, and the ladies hid their eyes, except one French one who was wearing a light raincoat. She leaned on the balustrade surveying the struggle. "Tiens," she said. Down below the young man was emerging into view, strong on his feet and unharmed, devils dripping off of him. He turned to us with a jaunty smile, waved, and set out for the fire. Some devils ran ahead with the howling chant, others still leaped about him shrieking. We were all silent as the young man, on gaining the fire, began to clap his hands, rather sportingly. To our amazement the devils resumed the dance!

"Now he's making a terrible mistake," said Evers uncertainly. "He can't have any idea what he's doing. If he'd have been sensible and waited . . ."

The French girl stood at the balustrade and watched the dance out by the fire, admiringly. "Voila, bravo," she said.

"Well, I've seen enough," said the round man taking a seat on a stone bench against the wall, folding his arms. Several men and women went to sit with him.

"There's no telling what's going to happen next," Evers said, a wistful note in his voice. Lassitude had overtaken the whole group of us. No one had much to say, and our interest was waning in the devils, save for that of the French girl. She had climbed over the balustrade and now dropped sprawling to the courtyard, where she quickly recovered and ran to the fire. The young man bowed and smiled to greet her, and she stood close to him as he continued to clap in rhythm for the dancing devils.

"They say the French are so well dressed," one young lady remarked. "She doesn't look so smart."

By the fire the young man had called a trio of devils to him, was asking something with gestures. The three demons paced and fretted under a command, but they obeyed and raced toward the corner rat hole. In a moment their king showed himself and proceeded toward the fire in some dignity. He was heavier than the others, horns protruding ostentatiously from his round little head.

The young man conferred with him, and the horned one bowed, indicating large doors leading into the palace from the far end of the courtyard. The young man strode over, escorting the girl, while the devils all broke from the dance and streamed out to open the doors and crowd along the way. The king followed, and when all were inside, the doors closed, leaving silence over the courtyard.

"You see, they'll come back," Evers said, wetting his lips.

As the fire died down we all settled back to wait, some of the younger men paying attention to the girls, who smiled, but for all that seemed bored. Others took a cue from the round man and stretched out on benches. Presently the creak and groan of opening doors roused some of us, and there from one side emerged onto the courtyard a motley pack of men, heavily armed but in raggle-taggle uniforms. A man's voice spoke up complainingly, "What's this now, Evers?"

The leader cleared his throat and regarded the new sight educatedly. "These are soldiers of the castle. We must wait and see what they're going to do."

"Huh?" popped the round man, sitting up. "Soldiers? What are there, soldiers?"

The raggle-taggle group was enlarging greatly, beginning to form in ranks, setting up artillery and rocket installations which pointed across from them to our left. An endless mob of them kept pouring out of the castle, sloppy, unshaven, dirty, and we began to wonder how such a large number could fit into the narrow space they occupied along the edge of the courtyard.

"Oh dear," a young lady said.

"Doesn't look like much of a castle guard to me," said the round man.

"Please, just watch," instructed Evers. "We must find out what we have to do."

At this point a well oiled door on the side facing the raggle-taggle army opened with a bang, and smart, well uniformed young men double-timed into the courtyard and went busily to work erecting installations on their side. At a shrill whistle, more handsome young men bounded out, in step, rolling machines and well tired gun carriages. With precision, efficiency and accuracy, group after group marched out, formed without hesitation in rank on rank, till their side was almost as replete as the raggle-taggle side. Lovely young ladies were going among the men serving coffee and ice cream, some of them singing, and clergymen went among them also, speaking firmly, laughing in manly fashion.

"Evers, I thought we were through with wars and armies," one man spoke up angrily. "I came up here to get away from all that."

"Now watch, please," said Evers. "Remember, you're on the balcony, not in the courtyard."

"Sure," said another one, "but when those bullets start flying, brother, you're better off down there with some company."

The talk was interrupted by a round of shots from the raggle-taggle army, and a number of the well-dressed boys fell neatly dead and wounded.

"Oh!" went the suppressed cry among us on the balcony, and down below there was shouting, men running with stretchers, clergymen kneeling, and higher echelon officers pacing gravely up and down. At the far end of the ranks several large pieces were being unlimbered.

The raggle-taggle army was guffawing, waving arms and chattering in general disorder when the clean army's field pieces fired, a quick barrage, and machine guns followed sweeping up and down the glutted ranks. Dead bodies tumbled all over the line, wounded were crying out, but the living ones were silent, crouching low to the ground, pushing the dead out in front as shields.

At the end of the firing, the raggle-taggle army, seemingly undepleted, was deadly silent, while on the other side, soldiers marched up and down, saluting, receiving decorations, receiving ministrations from the clergy and the ladies.

"Ha ha!" chortled the round man. "That'll show those bums, eh?"

"Now, now," put in Evers, "remember where we are. Don't take sides in this."

"Yeah, but it isn't fair," an intense young man spoke up. "The ragged ones are poor. They don't have half the equipment of the other ones."

"But remember," another man added in a modulated voice. "It was the poor side which fired the first shots."

"Well, why shouldn't they?" snapped the intense fellow. "The rich ones have got everything."

"Ooh hoo hoo hoo!" chortled the round man gleefully. "Let 'em start it, let 'em start it. Our boys can take care of . . ."

A tremendous volley burst from the raggle-taggle ranks to interrupt him, and the whole army was massed in firing position. They fired and fired for a long time, and smoke filled the courtyard, dimming the light of the fire, until gradually the noise filtered down to a few sporadic shots. As the smoke cleared, the good army was still intact, but was visibly depleted, and they were going through the same efficient rigmarole of pinning decorations, saluting, bearing stretchers, and receiving ministrations of clergymen and girls. Also, new squads of fine boys were being marched out to refill the ranks.

"By God," said the round man heroically leaning at the balustrade, "it's every man's duty to get in there and do his bit."

"I'm with you, mister," another man said stoutly.

"Gentlemen, please," faltered Evers. "Try to remember . . ."

"Sure, you people want to jump in on the rich side," sneered the intense man.

"All those in favor of doing their bit, line up over here!" the round man was commanding. Several younger men were already with him, smoking cigarettes rightfully.

"Remember our job is to find out what to do!" Evers was pleading.

"Just a minute, Mr. Evers," spoke up the modulated voice. "I believe it's fairly clear what we have to do. Those are people we were raised with down there."

"No, no," said Evers, confused. "It's totally another . . ."

At this time a handsome metal staircase had been raised to our balcony from the ranks of the good army, and another young man spoke up. "What the hell, Evers, we'll all get knocked off anyway. This is the biggest thing in history."

Fully a third of our people had moved to the stairway and were descending while Evers stood by wringing his hands. "I don't know what to tell you."

"Can girls go, too?" a couple of young ladies asked the round man.

"You bet your boots you can," he said smiling tenderly. "God bless you, honey."

At the other end of the balcony the intense fellow had stood up on the balustrade waving his fist. He shouted something unintelligible and leaped off into the raggle-taggle ranks, becoming indistinguishable from the mass of them.

Shots began to ring out once more from both sides, and then cannons pounded across the court, and there were shouts with bugles, and smoke rising up, till nothing at all was visible to us. Evers took a seat on the stone bench, shaking his head wearily, and once more our group seemed to lose interest in the events. Evers had leaned his head back and people were talking in low voices to each other, while the noise generally didn't impress us. Gradually the air was clearing, and dawn's grey seemed to silhouette the towers and roofs above us.

When the smoke was dispersed, the armies were gone and the fire burned up brightly. Some young men and women sitting up on the balustrade laughed in a chorus, and a sleepy voice spoke out, "What now, Evers?"

Evers snapped awake and, recovering himself, laughed nervously. "Dear me, almost sleeping," he said. "Mustn't sleep, you know."

"What are there besides devils and armies?" the sleepy voice wanted to know.

Evers straightened up and rubbed his eyes under his glasses with a frown. "We have to wait," he said.

"Wait!" said a stocky young man disgustedly. "That's all we been hearing out of you, Evers." He opened the balcony doors into the palace and poked his blond head into the darkness. "What's inside here, anyway?"

"Now, don't go in there," said Evers yawning. "That's where everything happens after we find out what to do."

"Hell, I know what to do," said the young fellow taking a step inside.

"No, no," said Evers disinterestedly. "We have to wait." He was staring off dreamily over the courtyard.

The stocky lad had taken a few steps inside, and I slipped over to watch him. He was disappearing into the darkness, so I followed warily and perceived we were in a large, bare salon. As my eyes grew accustomed to the dark, I could see the stocky fellow mounting a staircase which led up to some corridors.

Upstairs, on hearing a dull muttering down one of the corridors, we proceeded toward the sound. Eventually, far off, a light was visible coming from under a door, and as we paced the hallway, the stocky fellow came to an uncertain halt. He felt his pockets thoughtfully and turned to me.

"Say, have you got a cigarette, mister?"

I gave him one, and in the light of the match his chin was trembling.

"Good old smokes," he said.

At the door from under which light came, we stood listening but could only hear muttering and cackling laughter. The stocky fellow, smoking intensely, stood with ear pressed against the door. It popped open, flooding us with light, and inside, at a table in the center of a vast room, his back to us, sat the plucky young fellow who had taken on the devils first. Off to his right, in a corner, was a bed in which the French girl, dressed in chaste nightgown, sat up demurely, watching the young man as he ran his fingers agitatedly through his hair.

"You are my man, I am your woman," droned the girl in halting English.

The young man, small in the center of the great room, stood up suddenly, knocking over the chair, and he paced grimly up and down. "The longer we delay the worse it gets!" he cried waving an arm, his voice lost in the high chamber.

The girl, far off in the bed, lowered her eyes and soberly fingered the bodice of her nightgown.

"I can't! I can't!" the young man shouted. He kicked at the tumbled chair, then seized it up and rushed to the left hand corner of the room where he braced the chair under the knob of a door. He turned toward the girl and started forward resolutely, but halfway to her, the braced closet door burst open, sending the chair skittering across the floor.

"Aaaaaak hak hak hak! There he goes!" shrieked a wave of harpy cackling. "There he goes, yoo hoo!" In the darkness beyond the open door their painted chicken heads and scrawny necks were lighted up.

"You see!" cried the young man dramatically, hands to his head.

"Aaaaaak hak hak hak hak!" swept the gale over the room. "Oh hun-nee, don't you want a good time? Yaaaaak hak hak hak!"

He shook his head with teeth clenched, and turned appealing with his glance to the French girl. She reached out her hand to him.

"Hey, stud! Tweeee-tweeew!" whistled a harpie, and the young man gestured distractedly. Then the muttering ceased for a moment, and he walked quickly over to the bed, standing there breathing heavily. Angel-like, the girl gazed up at him, and as he bent to her the muttering broke out again. A harpie head poked into the room on a scrawny neck. "Oh bravo, coo coo!"

The young man straightened and shook his head. He said something to the girl, whereupon she got up and put on her shoes and the raincoat. She stood close to him, and he held her arm.

"Yoo hoo, baby! Coo coo!"

The two of them linked arms and started slowly toward us at the door.

"Yaaaaaaah!" came a nasty shout from the closet. "What's the matter, sugar, you proud?" A wave of triumphant cackling followed and swelled over the whole chamber, but the couple came toward us, and in the middle of the cacophony, the light suddenly went out and silence fell.

The four of us stood facing each other in the hallway, cloaked in dimness and mystery. The stocky fellow cleared his throat uneasily but didn't speak.

"Et alors?" said the French girl at last.

The young fellow drew her to him and fondly kissed her forehead. "Sorry, kid. I guess it takes more than I've got yet." She took his hand and lay it against her cheek, and he smiled. "We'll go on to some more. Try this one again later, OK?"

We went with them slowly up the dark hall and the stocky fellow cleared his throat again. "Where's them devils, anyway?" he asked. "Them other ones you had?"

The young man paused. "What do you mean? Didn't you fellows come in from the fire?"

"No," said the stocky one, "we come in through the door from the balcony. There was a war going on in the courtyard."

The young man shook his head. "Well, you boys stick with me, I'll get you headed back to the balcony. You've got to start this tour with your own devils. They'll show you where to begin."

The stocky fellow and I looked at each other, and we all proceeded along the corridor till the dimness was diminished, and soon we were in the grey light of a large, bare gallery. High windows at one end let in the day, and along the facing wall were seven heavy wooden doors. The young man didn't hesitate but marched right up and surveyed the center one. He smiled back at the girl. "OK?" he said. She nodded bravely, so he seized the door handle in both hands and threw it open.

In a vast stone barn, around a fire, squatted a bunch of devils, about twenty of them, but these were different from the courtyard pack. They were thick set, silent brutes, dog-toothed and menacing as they looked sidelong and secretive at our advance. The young man approached them boldly, but the brutes remained squatting in muscled heaps near the fire. "Yah! Hyah!" the young man suddenly shouted, as though herding cattle. "Git up, there! Hyah!"

The brutes jerked to their paw feet and started in a slow circle about the fire, malevolent in their unwillingness. "Git on! Get a move on there, you morphodite pigs!" The devils started at the command, shuffling around in a half trot, while the young man circled them. "Move! Move! Move! Move!" He skipped in among them and dealt a furious kick to the haunch of one brute. "Dance, you scummy hulk!"

They snarled, but sporadically began stamping the floor, clapping hands over their heads and letting their arms drop in rhythm. The young fellow turned to the stocky lad and me, speaking in a low voice. "Keep that dance going. Holler at them, keep up the rhythm, but don't get too close. The kid and I are going to see what work they can do. We've got the upper hand so far."

While he took the girl into the darkness on the other side of the barn, the stocky one and I mustered our command presence to keep things in order. The shambling, stinking things began a grunting chant, and the stocky fellow showed his spunk by keeping close to them, herding them expertly.

Eventually the young man came back with a stick in his hand, his wife still next to him. "There's lumber under the straw over here," he said. "We'll get the devils to build us a ladder or tower. There's an exit door way up by the ceiling. I'd try to work something fancy with them, but right now we just want to get you fellows started back." With stick in hand he regarded the circle of devils, then suddenly leaped in among them to club one out of the line. The thing snarled ferociously, swiping out a vicious hand. "Hyah! Git on!" the young man cried, clubbing the brute again. "Lead 'em out of here! Over to that lumber.

The creatures shuffled grumbling out of the circle into a line across the room, and the young man whacked his stick on the stone floor to keep a rhythm going. "All right, a tower! Ho! Ho!" he hollered in rhythm. "Build it! Ho! Hyah!"

He moved among them, whacking, cursing, keeping a rhythm, never letting up, and the devils knew what to do. They carried and fitted the lumber, chanting the while, snarling, working, and bit by bit a tower rose, clear up to a shadowy passage just under the ceiling. They were swarming over their work, moving faster, sometimes breaking the rhythm, and at last the young man hollered up at them. "Ho, get down! Back in line! Back to the fire!" For emphasis he knocked the ones nearest him off the construction. "Chant! Chant!" he shouted. "Let's hear some noise!" and the chant swelled up as the devil brutes climbed back down and shuffled in their hand-clapping dance to the fire.

"Let's get that last one down here!" called out the young man. "One more! Get down here, you!" Up above, a devil clung to the rafters and snarled down at us, refusing to move. The young man raised a din with his stick on the tower. "Get down, you blasted eunuch ape! I'll club you out of existence!"

He turned to the stocky fellow. "Take a stick and go up there. Knock him down to the ground. We've got to get them all back into the circle."

While the stocky fellow armed himself and began a wary ascent, the young man kept the other devils chanting and shuffling around the fire, and presently we heard the stocky fellow shouting and the devil snarling. Wood knocked on wood, and then with a great thump the devil struck the stone floor. He got groggily to his feet, limping hurriedly back to the fire to join his fellows.

"You two go on up," the young man ordered the girl and me, and then shouting the while, whacking his stick for emphasis, he followed us up the tower. On the ledge in front of our door at last, he said, "Give me a hand here."

Using the clubs for poles, we got the tower teetering, and with one great shove toppled it over so that it broke apart on the stone below. The devils swarmed roaring from the fire, pawing at the lumber and throwing it about.

The stocky fellow had opened the door, so we went right out, finding ourselves in a pleasant, sun-lit corridor. The stocky fellow, hands in pockets, walked thoughtfully a little ahead of us. He stopped when he reached another gallery. "Say, fella," he said, turning to the young man. "Is that all you do in here? Wander around hollering at devils?"

The young man stood just at the entrance of the massive, bay-windowed gallery, looking bemused. "You boys probably don't understand this like I do," he said. "They're my own private devils, anyway. The idea is to get to know the different kinds, according to their nature. Make them work for you, make them obey. You be the boss, and eventually you'll get some idea how to run the castle." He smiled and looked at the girl. "I don't see anything else worthwhile doing in life."

The stocky fellow shook his head and, hands still in pockets, wandered with short steps over to the bay window where he stood gazing pensively at the distance. The young man had taken me by the arm and was indicating a small hallway in the corner of the gallery. "You follow that straight," he said. "Tell your buddy. It brings you right out onto the balcony again."

I nodded and the stocky fellow called us over to the window. He had opened a small glass door among the panes and was breathing the air in great breaths, his eyes closed. "Boy, what a countryside," he was saying.

We all crowded out on the balcony to look. The air was fresh and the sunlight sparkling. "I wouldn't look at that too long," the young man said, putting a hand on each of our shoulders. He started away, then turned back once more. "Good luck to you boys. You know the way back, eh? Hope we all meet again here."

I waved to him as he and the girl went into one of the doors along the wall, and then the stocky fellow and I were alone with the view on the breezy balcony. "Boy, I know where I want to be," he said, staring off wistfully. Then he looked closer below us. "Sure as hell a man can get down that cliff."

He started over the balustrade, and I said, "Wait, the chap told us to go back to the . . ."

On the grass below the balcony, the stocky fellow got to his feet and waved up to me. "So long," he called. "I'm off to the farm country." He waved once more and trotted out to the cliff. There he found some sort of path and began a descent, waving a last time just before he climbed down out of sight.

I watched and watched for him to appear in the part of a field visible below the cliff, hoping he hadn't fallen, but as the sun began to wane I gave up hope and shook my head. At that very moment I saw him, a tiny ant of a figure, moving rapidly over the yellow field to a clump of dark trees. He turned once, it seemed, toward the castle to wave, but he was so small I couldn't be sure, and at the moment he seemed to wave, I ceased focusing on him. There were simply trees with their branches waving.

I sighed and left the little balcony, closing the window, and went across the gallery to the hallway which I followed for quite a long time without incident. At last I reached our balcony, and as I stepped onto it, I had a moment of shock to think no one was there. Then Evers stood up suddenly, coming awake, but I could have sworn he wasn't there on first glance.

"Oh dear, here's someone," he said flustered, adjusting his glasses. "My word, I really thought you'd all gone. I really thought I was alone. Do you know, when you came just now I believe I was falling asleep."

"Well, well," I said to him. "So you and I are all that's left?"

He sat down again and shook his head sadly. "Yes, they've all gone, one by one." He sighed. "I told them all, time after time, to wait." He stood up again and went to the balustrade. "Some were carried off by the dawn devils, like the fellow at twilight, you remember? Others, poor souls, went out by the fire but dropped right down dead. I suppose they were devoured in that hole."

The sun was set, and twilight was over the courtyard while the fire seemed to grow brighter all by itself. Almost time for the devils of evening to be coming, and my heart beat a little faster.

"Most terrible of all," Evers went on, "was to watch our people here in day time. They went all to pieces. A king had a garden party at noon, and we lost half our people to that."

I was nodding, keeping my eye on the corner rat hole for the devils' entrance, and Evers stopped talking. "What happened to the rest?" I asked.

He slapped his hands against his legs and shrugged. "Went to sleep," he said.

"Ah," I said, and then after a pause, "They were gone when you awoke?"

"Eh? No!" he said. "I wasn't asleep, you can't sleep here. The *others* went to sleep, that's why they're gone. Where they are I'll never know, but as soon as they dropped to sleep in the afternoon sun . . . pop! Disappeared into thin air."

At that moment, out leaped the first devils from the corner rat hole and loped to the fire where they tried the first few notes of their howling chant. Evers leaned his elbows on the balustrade to watch them, and inside of me my stomach began to crawl. The devils were all out now, in their trios, leaping about the fire, devil dance and devil chant. On the balcony, Evers and I, waiting, two of a kind . .

I took a breath at that and clenched my fists, and then a trio broke from the fire as on the night before, running to us arms outstretched, crying, "Eeee hee hee hee!" They stood below, gazing up, flapping their hands idiotically.

I put a foot suddenly on the balustrade as though to climb up and jump, but Evers said, "Wait, wait!" and my foot came down again. The devils had started when I made as though to climb over, but now they ran slowly back to the fire, seeming dispirited.

My heart burned in shame and I couldn't bear to look at Evers. I recognized him now, with his dry, peripheral curiosity. The last ones, of a same cloth. I turned suddenly to look him directly in the eye, and saw myself. "Evers, perhaps I owe you a debt of gratitude. I don't think I'd have wanted to catch up to my manhood if I hadn't seen I was the same as you. We're really the same, you and I."

"How's that?" he asked.

I merely took his hand and shook it, then climbed quickly over the balustrade. As I hung there an instant, I heard his frantic voice, "Wait! Wait!" and I smiled at the instinct which made me want to wait. I shook my head as he reached for me, and wilfully let go my hands, sailing through the air.

The shock when I struck the ground caused me to bite my tongue and made my nose burn, and I couldn't get immediate control of my legs.

"Yee yee yee yee yee!" came the impish squeals, and they were on me, pushing me down. I couldn't get my breath, my tongue hurt, and my feet struggled to touch a bottom somewhere. Desperately, desperately, I had to get hold of myself and stand up.

THE DRIFTER

I TOOK down her picture from the wall and fittingly bowed my head. Devotion and love and ideals are nonsense. None of that had fitted into our lives, but I wanted to savor a momentary halt in the rush of us living people. My brother sat across the room watching me hold the picture and I felt his impatience as he flicked the ashes from his cigarette time and time again. He spilled them recklessly on the stringy carpet, but it was all right.

"I don't want to impinge on your proper melancholy," he said at last. "God spare me from social indecencies at any rate, but what have you decided to do?"

I tossed the picture into my open suitcase and sat down smiling. I didn't wish to appear devil-may-care or bohemian, but I couldn't bring myself to avoid it. "Henry, there's no use troubling yourself about the boy. I'll just creep along my private little dingy track."

He tapped out his cigarette and blew a clot of ashes off the corner of the table, then leaned forward in the easy chair and frowned. "It has been your fancy," he said, "that we've all abandoned you in the family, but it simply isn't that way. Your father's life is deeply saddened by your refusal to come home. He's hoped and prayed you'd clear out of your rut, and he still wants to see you in his house again. You with your child."

"Ah, the child of course," I said smiling. "The sole hope of the generation."

My brother knitted his brow self-consciously. "Not necessarily *the* hope," he said. "Martha and I are quite young enough, you know. In fact we've been talking over the possibility of a son just recently."

"With all due respects, Henry," I said, "little Jill's birth put an end to Martha's spawning days. The poor woman's health is broken, you know it as well as myself."

He inhaled and portrayed a man getting a grip on himself. "Your child," he said, seeking to recall the subject. "Your child and Herminia's, the family would like to see him get a break in life. If you're so rotten and lost we can't do much about that. It's your own business. But that boy deserves good education and decency and a home, and your father and I want to know your plans for him."

It makes me laugh whenever the spotlight of attention is turned on me. Automatically I become self-conscious, but it's so ridiculous to be bothered that I have to laugh. "Well, you'll have to see Neeley about the child," I said, holding down my grin. "He's taking care of him and he wants the kid, too."

"Neeley!" my brother fairly shouted. "Neeley's taking care of him! Jesus, man, have you gone out of your . . . do you realize . . . why, that half-wit might do anything! Why, what do you mean we have to see Neeley? Why do we have to see Neeley?"

I was laughing and waved him back into his chair. "Lord save you, man," I said and he gestured impatiently at me but quieted down. I held up two fingers for a cigarette and he threw me one, and then threw over a pack of matches. "Now in the first place," I said, puffing on the cigarette, "Neeley was in love with Herminia."

Henry tossed his head as though he were about to interrupt, but he relaxed again and tightened his mouth. "In the second place, Neeley's not an idiot," I said. "Or, if you persist in that word let me refer you to Dostoyevsky's idiot. The man closest to Christ and all that. It behooves all of us to seek to emulate Christ, doesn't it?"

"No, the point is," said my brother reasonably, ". . . you see, you've missed the point. Dostoyevsky and Neeley's love or all the rest notwithstanding, we have a child to deal with. A child innocent of all this human error. Think of the child first, and his needs, and then we'll mold ourselves and our entanglements to suit the case. Do you see what I mean?"

"Henry, we're all innocent in that respect," I said, smiling again. "Each one of us, and the boy, must take whatever the Lord sends. The paps of destiny nourish us all indiscriminately. I don't understand any special innocence in children, but perhaps you have a point anyway. As I said before, though, we'll have to see Neeley." I arose, picked up Henry's hat and went to the door.

"In other words, what you're trying to say is," said Henry, obstinately retaining his seat, "Neeley is more important than your own child to you. You want to carry your inanities to criminal ends. The whole soul of your son is being formed."

"There!" I interrupted him, stepping out the door with his hat. "You've missed the point. I don't discriminate in the application of my inanities, like the paps of destiny. What a great phrase, eh?"

As I descended the stairs I could hear his muffled, argumentative tones and I laughed to myself waiting for him outside on the sidewalk. He came down very shortly, looking casual and composed. I gave him his hat.

"Your manners are rotten," he said. "Stinking."

"He lives a couple of blocks over," I said smiling. "Good old Neeley. Never far from where I am, you know."

Henry fitted on his hat as we walked. "God, what an unholy alliance," he said. "How long have you been together with that brute, ten years?"

"Since the war," I said. "I don't have to fight when he's around."

"I'll never forget when you brought him to the house," said Henry, shaking his head. "Mother had to go to bed early, and she's never been well since."

We reached the frame house where Neeley boarded and the landlady opened to us, peering in a disapproving way, which was characteristic of her. "Aw yus, Nilley," she said in her strangely accented, adenoidal voice. "He's gone t' th' pahk with th' little angel. I don't know, gwin, gwin his rum and wait frim in case." She waved us on with her hand and hurried to the kitchen.

Neeley was in the room, bouncing my child about on the bed, both of them with huge grins on their faces, but silent. Henry tightened his lips. "Here, here," I said going over to pat Neeley's shoulder. "How's the old monster? Here's my brother Henry to talk about the child. Mrs. Bradish said you were at the park."

"Aw hullo there." Neeley glanced up at both of us in slight confusion. He arose and pulled out a small chair for Henry. "Yes, I had Cedric out riding him on the merry-go-round. He sure loves that. Shall I see about some coffee for you?"

"No, forget it, old chap," I said. "Henry's here on serious business. We're going to talk over the disposition of Cedric."

Henry was smiling at the boy and he put out his arms to him. "Well, well, come here young fella," he said warmly. "Come on over and see your old Uncle Hank." Like the obedient child he is, Cedric waddled over to him.

Neeley was standing up, looking emotional with his hand out to steady himself. "It's much smarter . . . you'll be smart," he said loudly, but in a way, muffled sounding, "not trying to take thit . . . thus baby. I'm taking care of him the best can be done, and I'm telling you I'm gonna keep him! Now don't forget it."

Henry and I looked at each other and Henry exhibited traces of alarm and anger, but I broke into a grin. "Relax, Neeley," I said. "I'm here to show Henry what a capable handler you are. Show him how you change the diapers or something."

Neeley sat down with his brow furrowed and squeezed his hands nervously. "A boy a year and a half that needs changing ain't been trained," he said. "Cedric don't need that nursing. He's smart, and he's good and trained."

"There, you see," I said to Henry.

"Oh, come on, now," Henry said. "Let's don't evade the real issue. We're interested, after all, in the total boy, a dweller in society . . ."

"That ain't my credit," Neeley interrupted. "Herminia's the one that trained him. She always done everything . . ." He gestured to mask his inarticulation.

"What you might observe, Henry," I said, "is that the two of them are mutually charmed. They can sit stupefied for hours gazing into each other's eyes."

"Lookin' at Cedric he's Herminia all over again," Neeley grumbled, piously brooding. "It's your blue eyes, but he's got her face and black hair; the mouth the way them dimples comes in when he's about to laugh."

Henry was pacing slowly up and down the room, and he stopped to regard the beetle-browed Neeley. "Your devotion to poor Herminia is certainly, we might say, salutary, Neeley," he said. "But don't you think, after all, that the solace from the child, I mean, the child himself, ought more rightfully to go to her husband?"

Neeley looked upward at me till the whites of his eyes showed clean and bright under black brows. "Him, he's a drifter. I'm stayin' in one place with Cedric till Herminia comes for him. Then she'll listen to me, too, if I got the boy with me."

Henry put a hand to his brow. "Oh Lord," he said. "It's worse than I thought." He turned to me with his hands on his hips, frowning with an air of triumph. "It's quite obvious that this fellow is beyond being pixyish. He's unbalanced, and you can't leave that boy with him any more. He'll fill Cedric with some unwholesome nonsense about his mother coming back in spirit or something, and then where'll you be?"

I just smiled and shrugged, to keep from laughing out loud. The older Henry got the easier he became indignant. "That's the truth, Herminia's coming back!" Neeley shouted. "She ain't dead, I don't care. I know she ain't dead and she's coming back after he's gone." He indicated me with his head. "I know a lot more than I tell about, by God, and I'm keeping this kid till she comes back for him." He went over and picked up Cedric who had been looking blankly from one to the other of us, and he hugged the child to his breast as he sat down again.

"Pacify him, will you," Henry said to me. "Before he gets wild or something.'

"Why don't you relax, the whole pack of you," I said. "Neeley, old chap, Herminia was drowned and we identified her and buried her. What's this sad fancy of yours, now?"

"The fish ate that girl so bad when they found her you couldn't tell who it was," Neeley grumbled. "That there was nothing you can identify, just because of the hair . . ."

"Oh, now, we don't have to drag over this, for the love of God, do we?" Henry put in. "Lord, the man was her husband, Neeley, he ought to know . . ."

"That husband stuff my eye!" Neeley said angrily. "She was in bed with me down in Chile before he met her. What do you think, she was any angel when he brought her up here? I can identify Herminia like anyone else, by God, maybe better. She ain't dead I say, and she's coming back for this kid." He folded his arms and relaxed with a clouded brow. His vehemence had momentarily silenced Henry and me, but I caught my aplomb and laughed again.

"Let's say we all rescued her from the Chilean flesh pots, then, eh Neeley? But if she's dead, she's dead, and your uneasy projections can't alter that."

"You know, I think I've heard enough," Henry said with fatuous dignity. "If my brother can't see reasonability about his own child perhaps a court of law will hold out some hope for us." He picked up his hat and walked to the door straightening his clothing. "This fellow is patently incompetent. In fact the fellow is dangerous and, really, out of his mind. So we'd better take some legal action."

He was out the door and into the hall. Lord, I let him go. I might have let the whole thing go it was such a dismal hassle. I turned to Neeley who had remained unimpressed by Henry's threat of legal action. "Well, you go blubbering with your big, fat mouth, and you get into difficulty right away. What I'm going to do is let them take the kid, and to hell with you, anyway. Lord knows I've tried to keep you happy these bloody years. I let you come moping around Herminia, you big ape, till the whole house was insane with the big, sad face on you." I sat down and felt very capable until the monstrous paw gripped my shoulder.

"I ain't kiddin' when I said it. That kid's staying with me!"

I looked into the ugly face clouded into his comic version of ferocity, and I broke out laughing. It was a mistake, because I next remember the landlady Mrs. Bradish holding me in a sitting position and putting a cold towel or something on the back of my neck. "Indeed, indeed, indeed," she was saying. "The poor fella was bond t' turn on yuh. See now, y'd do best t' let 'im take the boy till she comes frim. Now, look't the lump on your jaw, what a shame."

It was a foggy moment, full of uncertainties. Her face was concerned but not exactly kindly, and her heavy brows were stern as she tended me and rubbed my neck. I was thinking of Herminia being alive, and thinking of Neeley and Cedric all at the same time. The phrase floated hazily through my head, ". . . till she comes frim."

"Frim, frim," I said to myself. "Froom, Mrs.," I said aloud to her. "Froom'll she come? She's coming for Neeley?"

"Och, gawd," she said. "Yuh talk very educated, but y've not any sense of th' real life. Who wouldn't know but you she's comin' back f'r th' child!"

It was dream-like hearing her talk as her arms worked busily past my eyes as she sponged my forehead. "Ah, tsk tsk," she said. "Y'r unsettled and a drifter, and 'twill be so till yuh die. I ain't mean t' say this, y've always been pleasant enough with me, but y'd best drift off again right away so's the others c'n do f'r th'mselves. Here, lie down a bit onta th' pilla."

This reminded me of the times as a child when I would change schools. I would go into a new class and everyone had a little smile on his face. Everyone knew what all the smiling references of the teacher were, except me, and I used to feel that everything they said was a secret joke against me. I coughed out a laugh and looked up at Mrs. Bradish. "Would you believe it, my dear woman," I said. "I think you're all playing a big joke."

She snorted and picked up towels and water basin with quick motions. "Aw, a joke, yus," she muttered. "But the joke's y'r own sense, not seein' she's run off with some fella, th' way yuh treated her so casual. A joke, yus."

I knew perfectly well that Herminia was alive all right. A momentary vision of the bluish body I identified faded neatly from my mind and that was all. I laughed as Mrs. Bradish went out the door, and my heart beat a little faster as I thought of exactly where to find the girl. Once she had mentioned with restrained delight, in her South American smugness, that she had been to a garden cafe with music in the southeast part of town. I had absolutely no doubt she'd be around there, and I had at the same time an uncrystallized consciousness of guilt or fear or something I don't know anything about. I got up and went out of the house in an amused numbness. I couldn't see big problems arising and my attention was engaged by a pair of little dogs playing on the sidewalk. I felt the heat of the afternoon sun on my neck and was, you might say, half at ease.

On the bus I asked the driver if he'd heard of a garden cafe with music out on his line, and he sucked his teeth and took a breath. "The *Vienna*," he said. "Broadway and Gordon Place, just off Broadway. Fifteen cents fare."

I was pleased, and I alighted in good time to find the *Vienna* with no difficulty. It was just what Herminia would care for, prosperous looking and modern but with a trace of the dance-hall air which would revivify her sentiment over the old life in Chile. I went through the large, dim bar and out into the garden where I took a small table by some potted palms. Rich, American taste, palms in a cafe trying to be Viennese. But it was pleasant enough, with a fountain in the center struggling happily to appear fresh. I settled down with a large beer and felt some excitement, as though Herminia might come in at any moment. A few afternoon customers were coming and going, most of them apparently friends of the proprietary staff. Little lives striving for happiness in their dry recognitions of each other.

Over a period of hours I drank eight or ten of the big beers, and pored hazily over some ineffectual reminiscences, quite forgetting what I'd come there for. At one point I realized I was light-headed and ate two hard-boiled eggs and a garlic sausage. Also, the place had undergone a transformation. From a loudspeaker floated Viennese waltzes heavily interspersed with popular dance tunes. Darkness had settled outside the walls and the people were much more numerous. My brother Henry and Herminia walked in together looking quite normal, quite in place.

The shock of realizing they were together tumbled the blood from my head all the way down through my body, and of course I broke into a wide smile and flushed as I waited for them to see me. But they sat at a table with their backs to me, and Henry held her hand awkwardly. It occurred to me that I didn't know what I might say. I could only think that Henry was with her, that Henry was not the stable, respectable, monogamous character so directly counter to me. I paced quietly up to them and laid a gentle hand on each of their shoulders.

"Good evening, lovers," I said.

They both turned sharply around and Henry gave a sort of agonized gurgle and was white in the face, while Herminia merely said accusingly, "Oh, you . . ."

I eased around the table smiling and dropped into a chair. Leaning forward on my elbows and leering, I said, "Surprised to see me? Have to get up pretty early in the morning to put it over on an old vet. No flies on the old vet, you know."

Herminia was smiling wryly and the dimples around her mouth were pretty and appealing, but her eyes were full of the old, deep, confident knowledge I never could approach. Henry, still pale, and with lips tightened, looked into an ashtray where he was stirring around his cigarette. "Don't be pained, lovers," I said. "You know me, I'm just a little guy trying to get along. I won't tell anybody. I'm only seeking the heartfelt verity of life's core, and then I'm on my way. My bag's all packed, you know. You saw it yourself, brother. How are you, Herminia, poor little child?"

"I'm not a poor little child," she said, grinning like a cat.

"Oh Lord," I said, "but we're all children under the sky, full of hopes and melancholia. You know the truth of that, eh Henry? I mean as a matter of fact."

"The fact of the matter is, you've discovered things at a rotten time," Henry said, looking up full of strength and purpose. "I don't want you to think we're miserable in some sordid affair. By God, I know the value and importance of taking a hold of things we need in this world. This is something you probably wouldn't understand, but if you want an explanation . . ."

"Oh," I said. "Henry, brother! Herminia, my love! I want to understand. I understand already in my heart. Don't be grim, just tell me a few significant details for my curiosity. Tell me about Herminia."

I smiled at the girl and she smiled to herself, the secret, masterful turning within herself, and she cocked her head at me. "You always told me I was free, didn't you? I went away in secrecy because Henry is better than you and we don't want his wife to know I'm with him."

Henry moved into the conversation, speaking casually. "That drowned girl was an accidental circumstance in the picture. I had read about her being found, conveniently at the time Herminia had left you. Actually I hesitated before I guided you to the morgue, you know, but then I knew you'd leave more quickly if you thought Herminia was dead." He leaned back at his ease now. "We were going to have her come forward after you'd given me the child and had left. Now, of course, something else will have to be done since you stumbled onto us. You can make it pretty nasty for us, you know."

They were both looking at me with the tiniest trace of anxiety on their faces, and I reached out to chuck Herminia under the chin but she pulled away. "Nonsense," I said. "Go ahead with the game. It all looks good to me. I'm shoving off anyway, you see. It doesn't make any difference."

I stood up to go, it seemed rather suddenly to me, and I shook hands with both of them. None of us said a word so I turned and walked out. A Viennese waltz was playing and a light behind the fountain created a gaily jumping shadow inside the bar. It was dramatic to me.

At Mrs. Bradish's I found Neeley getting ready for bed. He looked at me in remorseful fashion and cast down his eyes. "I'm sorry I hit you," he said. "I been thinkin' a lot since then, and I guess . . ."

I slapped him on the shoulder and smiled. "Thinking again, eh?"

"Well," he said, and pointing to the child sleeping in a crib, "this here kid. You know I love this here kid like nothing else in the world, and you can believe me when I say it, but . . ." He sat down and wrung his hands, looking sadly out in front of him. "I guess I know I got no business around here. I guess I know it's about time I shove off." We looked at each other in the dim light from the lamp, and I smiled and took out a cigarette. I nodded and winked and lit the cigarette, but said nothing. Neeley grinned knowingly and pointed his finger at me. "You knew it'd be like this, you old son of a gun. I got an idea you're figurin' on goin' somewhere. Am I right?"

I walked over to pat his head. "Man, you're not dumb, are you?"

He jumped up and grabbed me by the shoulders in glee. "Aw-w baby, that's great," he said. "What kind of an idea you got in mind?"

I took him by the arm and sat him down again. "Right now I'm too tired to talk. But maybe we'll find out if it's really true about Chinese babes, eh?"

"Yeah," he said happily, punching his palm with his fist. "I'll come wake you up tomorrow. We'll cut out of this thing."

I went over to glance into the crib, then waved and walked out, gathering into my spirit the drifter's melancholy. I paced slowly over to my apartment and didn't think much as I put on my best suit and finished packing some things in the small suitcase. When I started to leave I paused with my hand on the lightswitch, looking to see if I'd forgotten something. Nothing. None of that made any more difference.

As I walked toward the boulevard leading to the highway, leading in fact to the big mid-west where I had visions of buxom farmers' daughters, untapped, I reflected that I was old for hitchhiking. It's easier for the youth to get rides. Youth, full of pessimism and gaiety.

"Damn it, I'm tired of youth," I murmured to the city at night. "This'll be the last time, damn it, I leave the others at home." I turned up the boulevard and listened to my footfalls lovely in the vacant night city. A car was coming, and I raised my thumb, but it went past.

"Bourgeois lout. Why can't he give a poor wandering soul a ride?"

WHOLE HOG DRIFTER

The foreman, a pinched little red-head with glasses, was grinning. "Drug that whole reel of copper cable out there in the woods and hid it last night. Cut off thirty-forty foot of it, I reckon, and made off with that."

Cavin tightened his mouth. "We couldn't put a guard here from six to eight. I *figured* that's when they were getting in, God damn it. The reel still out there?"

"It's so heavy we left it out there. Cut off what we needed for the job today. You can see the path where they drug the thing, clear as day in the sand." He pointed. "Right across the road there in the woods."

Cavin made the decision right then. His eyes were grave. "To-night," he said. "We'll put an end to stealing tonight."

"Doin' all right up to last night," the foreman said. "Hadn't been nothing missing since they put you in charge there."

Cavin put the jeep into low and turned it out onto the road. The day shift was ready to quit, and as he drove along the air strip he could see the Arabs on the job sites girdled for action. Ready for the assault on the brass shacks. Beasts. Savages. There was the trouble. If the Arab manuals didn't rush to check out like they were on a raid he could make an orderly and permanent distribution of his guards. Anyway, it was whipped now. He and Perales together had figured out the subtle juggling of guards and posts. Except for a few unavoidable holes like last night.

He drove up to the brass shack at the batch-plant, just as the Arabs came whooping and charging across the fields. He was going to handle this one alone. The guards were over by the line of big bird-cage trucks, ready for the nightly shakedown. Cavin hated this. He hated handling Arabs. It was like running your hands through hundreds of greasy, stinking rag bags, and the wild, yelling assault was on. Brown human tatters with shrieking mouths and frantic eyes banged up to the shack and clawed at each other to get their brass chits into the window. Cavin leaped among them, hauling, cursing, shoving. The clamorous animal mass squeezed down quickly into a semblance of line, and he stepped back and held them, with his eye and presence. The ones he'd been tossing around and cursing were the most jolly as they clutched tenaciously in line.

"*Hey, Kipitan! La bess!*" The big gap-tooth smiles they had. One little rat was trying to sneak in front of his buddy. Cavin went over and tapped him and pointed to the end of the line. The Arab laughed, and the others all laughed. "*Ahhh, Sikitty! Sikitty shoof bien! Wa-hah!*" The little one went back waving happily. The damnedest thing, these guys liked him. They couldn't say Security, and they couldn't say Captain. *Sikitty* and *Kipitan.* Cavin shook his head.

As the line dwindled he pointed his finger at the Arabs. "*Wa-hada-wahada,*" he warned, and they all laughed happily. He went over to the bird-cages. Turmoil behind every truck. The French guards were cold and calm, and the Arabs didn't joke with them, but didn't stay in line very well, either. Cavin looked over the pile of loot the guards lifted off the workers. Saws, pliers, hammers, wood, pipe, the usual; anything they could get their hands on. Miscellaneous junk, too. Cavin didn't want to let them have the idea *anything* could go off the base. He straightened out the lines behind the trucks, and the loading proceeded. A sea of humanity, eighty men, crowded standing into the caged back of each truck. Skull caps and turbans. Like political prisoners, for a lousy ride home.

He took off then for the office. Perales would be getting the Security night shift organized. Have to scrape out four or five men for the trap. Traffic was thick toward camp, trucks, jeeps and pickups, full of French, Arabs and Americans, all sweaty and grimy. The maintenance of order and the protection of property. Cavin grinned with clenched teeth and leaned into the steering wheel.

He found Perales with the night shift ready to go ten minutes early. Exploitation. Perales kept a tight hand on his boys. He alone was worth all the Americans Cavin had working for him. He wished to God he could pay Perales an American salary. The guards, French and Arab, were peeping out of the back of the truck where Perales had stuffed them. He'd put four in his jeep, against safety regulations.

"I need five men, right now," Cavin said.

Perales was a little alarmed. "Ah capitaine, ne ees possible. We can't leave any-sing inoccupy, specially ri' now."

"I know that. But they got away with a spool of cable at the tanks last night. Must have been right between six and eight o'clock. I want the men for a trap. The spool's still out in the woods nearby."

"Ah la la!" Perales looked worriedly over at the truck. "Lenoir ees on tanks. You take heem." He kept looking reluctantly at the others in the truck.

"Give me the man on the batch-plant, and where's the boxer, the Spanish-Jew?"

"Mendoza. He ees on lumber."

"OK, give me Lenoir, Mendoza and the one for the batch-plant. And I'll get Kinsey. Where's Kinsey?"

"He ees gone to eat."

God damn Kinsey. He was all right. He was sincere. But he was so stupid. Eating supper during the shift change. "OK, Perales. I'll let you know how the trap works out. Send those men into the office."

In the office he broke out the battery spot-light and had Ballouard explain carefully to the guards what they were going to do. He opened the iron cabinet and brought out two of the Mab 7.65 automatics and checked them. He checked the rounds in the clips and then looked up at the guards who were staring casually at him.

"OK?" he asked, and they all broke into smiles and nodded bashfully.

"You're Lemaire, aren't you?" he asked the third guard. The man was young, growing a fuzzy little mustache. He looked up, polite and willing. *"Oui, mon capitaine."*

"All right, let's get in the jeep. Be sure you've got your clubs with you, and those tie-ties." He belted on one of the automatics and carried the other, along with the spot-light.

Darkness was falling rapidly as they drove down to the mess hall. Cavin went in and hauled Kinsey away from a plate full of fried chicken. Kinsey, about forty, was surprised, with his big nose and yellow hair. "Bring a piece of that with you if you want," Cavin said. He wished Johnson wasn't on his night off.

"Yessirree, Cavin," Kinsey said, hurrying right along. They went out to the jeep and started directly toward the strip. Cavin explained the deal to Kinsey on the way. He gave him a club and the other automatic. "Now don't shoot it, except in self-defense. That's the law. These are just supposed to scare them."

A few hundred yards from the asphalt plant he cut off the road into a sandy depression. He chunked into four wheel drive and rode up the gully till they reached the wooded area. The trees were thin young mimosas and eucalyptus, but they gave some cover. He cut the lights and drove up out of the gully into a sandy basin in the ground. There he stopped.

They found the spool about fifty yards into the woods. He got Lenoir, Mendoza and Lemaire spread out and concealed in bushes beyond the spool, and he shouldered the heavy battery for the spot-light himself. He staked Kinsey on the near side of the spool. "Now, when I flash the light," he told them, "come out swinging. Hit hard, for the old kayo. *Compris?* We'll get a little prize for ourselves."

He got down behind a small clump growing at the foot of a mimosa, and relaxed himself for the vigil. He figured they'd be in before eight to get the spool. He smiled to himself. A Security man. A success. He never thought he'd be anything like a cop.

That's playing the game. You can be a bum and a drifter, but only on the condition that when you *do* work, you go whole hog. Well, he was whole hog, and lucky he had a job. He heard Lenoir shifting out there.

"Ssh," he warned. Lenoir was a good head. A big easy-going kid with a dark crew cut. He was the one who had spotted old Kraft with the new tires and batteries in the back of the pick-up two months ago. Poor old Kraft, in jail. A hell of a note. Funny, Cavin had never had the slightest remorse getting the evidence in secret on Kraft. A damn nice boss, too, old Kraft. He'd made Cavin acting shift captain, along with the ex-cops Johnson and Morris. A nice old reprobate. Cavin knew he was putting a knife into him. He could have warned the old thief, and let him resign and get out before he put the finger on him. But the wily old bloke might have turned the tables, and besides, that wouldn't have been playing the game. That wouldn't have been whole hog, according to the contract he'd signed.

"Hey!" Kinsey whispered.

"Ssh."

"I hear them!"

"Ssh." Cavin heard them, too. Way out there. They were murmuring their gutteral Arab talk, and making noise in the brush. He knew what he was going to do. Little rat-like thieves. They were tough, and good, but he was beating them. When the office had put him in charge after Kraft was arrested, he'd gone right after the stealing. His first day in he'd re-organized the shifts to fill the gap between six and eight. It took just a little brain work and pushing, and it paid off. He was getting the foremen and superintendents on his side, too. A construction stiff detests Security, but Cavin was going out of his way to do them favors. And he was getting them to lock up their gear and to report thefts right away. He was a good Security boss, he knew. And the office knew it, too. And so did the Arabs. They weren't getting away with too much now, but they were still slipping onto the base. Tonight would take care of that. He eased the automatic out of the holster and drew the slide to put a round in the chamber. He pushed off the safety. With his other hand he gripped the handle of the spot-light.

The Arabs were closer, muttering in low voices, coming right on with a rustling in the branches and brush. They didn't suspect anything. Only one was going back out, a lot faster than he'd come in. One thief to get away and spread the tale of terror to the others outside.

Cavin fixed his eyes on the shadow of spool on the grey sand. As soon as they were all there, busy with it . . . a shadow slid past Mendoza's spot and came to the spool. He called in a hoarse whisper. Cavin recognized a word. "*Ajee!*" It meant "come here." The whole group floated in and clustered around the spool, jabbering in muted voices. They were gleeful. They hauled at the spool, trying to get it into a position to roll. "*Wahat! Hnn!*"

Cavin flashed the spot. Five Arabs, raggedy and muffled to the ears, stared for one panicked instant right into the light. Lenoir and Mendoza were on them before they broke and scattered. The white clubs gleamed and two were down. Everything was silent. Lemaire was late and leaped on one as he went by. The other two were high-tailing it back into the woods and Cavin was on his feet after them, keeping the spot right on them. He paused and leveled down. A hopping figure in skull cap, black vest and baggy purple pants. The little Mab hardly jumped at all. He smelled powder and kept pulling the trigger. It wasn't loud. First time he'd ever fired a Mab. Behind him Kinsey was shouting, "Halt! Halt or I'll shoot!" The idiot. Baggy pants was down and Cavin emptied the clip after the other one. He heard a yowl but didn't know if it was fear or pain. Either way was all right.

Kinsey was hysterical. "You got him! You got him!" He was running out into the beam of light. "Did you see him? You got him!"

"Shut up, you jerk!" Cavin snapped. "Come here!"

Kinsey was dancing up and down waving his arms. "You got him, Cavin! You got him!"

"Shut up! Get back there with the others!" He jerked Kinsey by the collar and sent him backwards. He jogged out along the beam of light till he reached the Arab lying rumpled in the sand and brush, half on his side. He was just a kid. No more than eighteen. He was dead. His baggy purple pants had blood all down the front. Cavin put away the gun and grabbed the boy by the scruff of his neck. The eyes were open, white, and his mouth hung loose. Cavin dragged him back through the trees to the spool and let him flop on the ground. The other three Arabs were lying face down with their hands tied behind their backs. Mendoza squatted and examined the dead boy. His eyes were big. "*Mort*," he said.

"Yeah, *mort*. Kinsey, come here. Take the jeep and go back in and get the pick-up. Drive it around to the road there opposite the tanks. You understand? We'll be waiting by the road, so hurry."

Kinsey was staring at the dead Arab, a little awed by it all. "And listen," Cavin said, "don't tell anyone what happened. Wait till I get in there, because we've got to report this thing as self-defense. You get me?"

"Yeah, sure, sure," said Kinsey and took off, glad to get out of there. Cavin lit the way to the jeep for him, and the motor roared right up.

"All right, get those guys out to the road and wait there," Cavin told the guards, and they prodded the prisoners up onto their feet. Cavin kept the spot off the dead one. When they were gone, he went through the dead boy's pockets till he found a knife, a big one. There was bound to be a knife. He opened the blade and clasped the handle into the dead hand. It wouldn't stay there, so he put the knife in his pocket and dragged the boy out toward the road.

The office was in an uproar. The three prisoners had started moaning and wailing in the pick-up when they saw the dead boy, and were still at it crouching inside the office in a corner. Cavin had Ballouard explain the story precisely to the guards: the Arab had attacked them with a knife and so had been shot. They nodded soberly and loyally and went out to the jeep. Kinsey was driving them to their posts. A small crowd was gathered around the pick-up looking at the feet sticking out from under a tarp. Cavin cleaned the Mab himself, then checked off the used rounds on a special card, and then Bob Richards came in. He was an old time office manager on construction jobs, and he took it real easy.

"So you killed one," he said, breezily, with half a smile.

"Yeah, self defense, Bob," Cavin said. "Here's his knife. He was attacking the guards with it and I shot him. I'll get my report out in half an hour."

Richards bounced up and down on his toes, still half smiling, with his hands behind his back. "Got your bags packed?"

Cavin looked up sharply. "What?"

"You're moving out tonight. Before the local cops get here, boy."

"What's the big idea, Bob?"

"Company policy. Probably have a spot for you down at Bel Kivir. If you want it. Less noise that way, you know. Don't worry about the report. We'll write it up."

Cavin had a little sinking feeling. "Listen, Bob. I just got the place organized here. When the news of that punk gets out, that'll be the end of the stealing."

"Oh yes. Yes, we know that. It's a mighty fine thing. Mighty fine." Richards kept his half-smile. "Better go on down and pack your gear now."

Cavin didn't say anything more, but went right down to his hut. When he was ready, a grey Plymouth station wagon was waiting outside, and he loaded in his two suitcases. Just two suitcases. Richards himself was going to drive him down to headquarters, and he waited calmly behind the wheel. Perales was there, on the other side of the station wagon. Cavin flipped his hand at him. "Goodbye, Perales," he said. Perales didn't say anything, but stood with an odd grin on his face. Cavin got in and slammed the door and Richards gunned right out.

They were speeding along through the black night. There was nothing Cavin could do. His energy was running out and he couldn't shake the image of baggy purple pants flopping along as he dragged that boy. Whole hog, whole hog. He was slightly sick and didn't want to close his eyes. Richards was humming a little tune as he steered along. So, back on the vag with a lousy grand in his kip. And old Kraft behind bars. *Sikitty. Kipitan.* He placed his head in his hands, and noticed then how badly he was trembling.

DRIFTER'S PROGRESS

HER lovely turned-up nose quivered with the flair of adventure, and the blue eyes danced in distrust as I made my move. "Don't," she said, pushing, but then was kissing back as hard as she could. Arab music on the radio strained and strained its chords and she clutched me frettedly around the neck, and at first I didn't know where the voice came from. "Well, Lena," it said.

There stood Deluard, in a dark grey flannel suit, closing the door from the vestibule. I'd have known him anywhere. Young, slender, tall, deep-set eyes. Everything about him was familiar. In fact, I could have sworn I'd already lived that very instant. Music was whining, Lena looked stunned, staring at the Arab rug, her short dark hair tousled. The atmosphere of Tangier, especially, fitted in the scene, the feeling of the bay and ships' lights and tumbled town mystery outside the big window. Deluard was sober, restraining anger, very, very continental, and I jumped up happy and ready and turned off the radio.

"Well, Deluard," I said cheerily. "Glad you're here. You do speak English?"

He was glancing from me to Lena, trying to catch her eye, trying to get a line to take. "Ho ho!" I said. "Don't imagine the worst. Lena and I are just having a little interlude. I really came to see *you*. Coincidence, what?"

The handsome, abused face went dead pan, the green eyes staring into me. The smile on my face seemed awfully foolish, so I dropped it. I felt a wild urge to lug out the .38 and shoot him as he stood there, to get it over. But I hadn't figured what to do with the Swede girl. Then the noise, and the neighbors. He was permitting a sardonic twist to his mouth. "So you are still at large," he said. "Cavin, isn't it?"

Now, that was a shock. He shouldn't have known anything about me or my business. I hoped the dismay didn't show. "Yes, Cavin. As large as I can be."

His face tried to recapture the dead pan, but he couldn't make it. "Overgrown children," he said in disgust. "How did you think to play at such games?"

I looked back at Lena but she was still sitting there dazed. "Games?" I asked, turning to Deluard. "Who, us?"

"A naive American. Just forget the pretenses. We know you're working for Romilliac, but I'd like to know what connection she has with you." He nodded toward Lena.

Ah, he wasn't sure of the Swede. I felt a sense of victory there. And he was spooked on Romilliac, whoever that was. "What pretenses, Deluard?" I said. "Lena and I just met today and were overcome by passion. As for me, you know us Yanks. Just big, overgrown kids, like you say."

He really felt superior. His face could hardly contain all the smugness, and then I hated him. The head of a traitor. Up till then he'd been an abstraction, but now I read the vanity of a dogmatic intellectual. He was the kind of jerk the Party rubbed out once he served their purposes. His lip was curling. "Children depend on guardian angels. You always play on your innocence. But now you must pay the price an adult pays for meddling where you don't have any business."

I felt anger invade my organism in a hot wave. "Don't talk about children," I said. "The Aubrys kids outside Oran in Algeria were deserted by the guardian angel." I stepped toward him and he stiffened for action, so I thought better of it. Look out for French feet. "Deluard, you led a pack of Fellagha to the Aubrys farm. You watched them slaughter your own countrymen. Innocent French babies with their throats cut, Deluard. And the lovely daughter, Marie, the blonde one. You must have seen them open her throat, too. Well, she was mine. I was going to marry her. So you know what that makes you."

He was pale as skim milk with fury. I watched his supreme inner effort to get back the dead pan and breathe normally. I heard the Swede come to life, too, and tossed her a quick glance. She was looking at me bug-eyed. As I turned, Deluard was already moving toward a cabinet by the door. I outed the .38.

"Hold it, Deluard."

He stopped and peered at the .38, then at me. Damned if my hand wasn't quivering a little. He wasn't a bit afraid, and started edging on slowly, daring me. I thumbed back the hammer. "Dead still," I said. "Not a muscle. I don't mind killing you right here." He stopped, then, his pants legs jimmying. I got him to turn and face the wall, then pulled out my sap and went over and swung. He swayed, and floated to his knees, looking back at me. I swung again. His eyes rolled up white as he flopped, and Lena gasped behind me. I got out his wallet, some loose francs and pesetas, a comb and a key case. Car keys. I put them in my pocket. I checked Lena Christina. She was sitting there staring like she didn't know what to think. I indicated Deluard.

"Don't fight it. The guy's a filth. A traitor. I'm going on the assumption you didn't know it. I'm sorry I had to get to your boy friend through you, but if you don't want to be mixed in this, better quick pack your gear and shove off."

She was a picture of bruised loveliness and shook her head indecisively as she stood up. I hauled Deluard to the center of the room, got his coat off, loosened his belt and put his hands in his back pockets, under the belt. I cinched it tight, put the coat back over his shoulders and buttoned it. I turned. "Lena, are you one of them? Are you a Red? Better tell me now."

She hesitated, shook her head dumbly.

"Then get me his top coat and pack your gear." She obediently went into the bedroom and came back out with a top coat. "That's adventure for you, kid," I said. "Go pack up now."

I put the coat around Deluard's shoulders and buttoned the top button. Not bad. Bulgy and humped, but he might pass for an arty stroller, coat on cape-like. He was coming to and I sat him up against the table. I waited till he blinked and licked his chops. "Listen carefully, Deluard," I said and stuck the .38 six inches from his nose. He awoke and stared right down the barrel. "I would like to kill you, but I'm going to bring you to some people for questioning. If you want to live, don't make one wrong move, one wink, one peep. If I even think you might crack, I'll kill you on the spot. You're going to walk me to your car, and if any of your buddies are around, just smile and say *ça va*. And be convincing."

He blinked at the barrel, flashed his eyes on me, then nodded glumly at the floor. The Swede came out of the bedroom slim and gracious in a black tailored suit and set down a suitcase. Her blue eyes were full of light and trouble. "Will I leave with you?" she asked.

I nodded, so she went back to the bedroom and rustled around awhile. She brought out an overnight bag, a coat and a huge purse. "There are some little things I'm leaving. I guess they're not important." She looked around worried but game. I was glad she was OK, and glad to help her out of the mess.

"Get me his gun," I said. "You must know where he keeps it."

She went over, fumbled open a door to the cabinet and brought out a Mab 7.65 automatic. "Slip it in my pocket," I said. I took the overnight bag. "Now turn out the lights and follow us. If any shooting starts outside, hit the deck and scream, loud as you can."

She was real cute. She'd taken time to fluff up her short brunette hair and had an interested, excited expression. I found myself wanting to appear good, to impress her. I figured I'd drive to the airport, let her out to grab the first plane anywhere. Then I'd park in a far, dark corner of the lot, wait till a plane was revving up, gun the car motor and shoot him in the head with his own pistol. I'd set it up for suicide, get a cab to town, and from there . . .

Lena doused the lights and I opened the vestibule door, pushing Deluard in front of me. I had just eased down the hammer of the .38 so it wouldn't go off too easily. Something patted the left side of my head, the gun was yanked out of my right hand, and I was drifting to the deck with liquid knees. I saw a huge foot heading toward my eyes. At the same time the back of my head split apart and I never saw the shoe hit my eyes.

An intense feeling of disappointment eased. An airplane was revving. Ah, the plan was going through. Then I realized. The airplane was a groan. My groan. I was lying on my right side, arm cramped and numb under me. Something was telling me to wake up, but I didn't want to. I rolled slightly, and pain stabbed into both my sides and my back. I was sick. Throbbing head. I started to frown in pain but it felt like my nose was going into my brain. Lying real still it all came back. Disappointment mingling with the ache. Flubbed, like I expected. Didn't think they'd be in the vestibule. I was going to look into the outside hall from a peep hole they had in the front door. God!

Elie would be waiting, disappointed. Elie the Tangier guttersnipe grown up smooth, tall and bemused. He'd done so much to help me with the job. I was just a punk after all, a hypercharged zero he'd found wandering around the medina looking for Deluard. I'd let him down, and let myself down, and let the Aubrys family down. My sweet people, dead and buried. Unavenged and forgotten. My lithe blonde Marie, and I was afraid to wake up. A worthless punk. And Chuck, my buddy? He'd take my gear back to Paris and tell the lads in the quarter I was dead. The Reds were too tough for me. They knew I was here all along. Some little slob trying to crowd them. My nose burned with sadness.

I'd have been so proud to tell Chuck the story about Deluard. He hadn't liked me hanging around the Reds in Paris, but I couldn't tell him or anyone I was out to avenge the Aubrys, to perform one brave, real, non-cynical, non-drifter act. Josette with the long nose and honest brown eyes in Paris had believed I was a fervent comrade. She'd got hold of the name Deluard of Tangier, the "mystery man" commanding the Fellagha around Oran. Very big secret. It took Elie two good weeks to locate him for me. Ah, happy, busy Elie, his mouth like a little o when he was bemused. He'd made all the contacts and was sure I could make it. Get the brunette Swedish girl on the beach. Deluard's mistress. Sensational Lena Christina, and I'd made good. Charmed her on the beach and got up to Deluard's apartment. It would have been so great to tell Chuck. Chuck and Elie and I in the Black Cat, and the wild gay fillies. I'd have recounted it all with dash and bravado.

Tears were leaking out of my eyelids and my nose burned. Chuck would go on drifting around the world, never knowing what a good effort I'd made. His buddy would be dead. Chucky boy and I, drifters. Big, blond, easy-going Chuck. Followed me innocently down to Tangier to do some high drinking with me. He didn't know. And the hard, tough, organized guys had me. Maybe Elie would tell Chuck the story after they found my body.

My head started throbbing again. They'd known about me! Deluard was surprised I was still at large. They'd been to my room after me. God almighty they must have got Chuck! They killed Chuck figuring they had me!

I was really sick. But it wouldn't be long. I wished I could stop thinking or go to sleep or die. I was already busted up, I could feel that. I wouldn't be afraid to fight them still, if I could fight. I just hated so much to lose. *They* got me, my first time trying to do something big. Like they got the Aubrys over in Algeria, and poor Chuck. Chuck was my fault. Little individuals, wiped out, a small job well done, no trouble, and that's all there was to me and everyone I loved. My head throbbed from the base of my skull right up into my eyeballs, and then I knew the throbbing came from voices. I wanted to see this. I made an effort. Light grew red to my eyes, and only the left one opened. It was blurry.

I was lying partly under the table in Deluard's place. At the divan stood two Arabs, dressed European fashion, one skinny, one husky, and another Frenchman, a *pied noir* North African French by his look, stocky, dark hair, bad complexion. Deluard sat next to Lena on the divan. They were all watching her, and she was scrunched up, scared, her brow furrowed into a V pointing between her eyes. I felt ashamed. Another part of the foul up.

"But I really don't know, Claude," she was saying. "I only met him today. I was frightened. I don't know anything else."

Deluard was restrained but grim and his voice clacked metallically. "Why do you protect these fascists? Why do you persist? We only wish to know what Romilliac plans in sending people down here. If you have undertaken the job for adventure, it is not too late to change over to us." His voice softened and he put a hand on her arm. "We could remain together."

She stared at him with all the confidence a mouse has in a rattlesnake, and her eyes began to puddle up. She just shook her head back and forth. Deluard stood up abruptly. "*Bon, ça va. Elle ne veut pas être raisonable.*" He took a couple of steps away and kept his back turned, his mouth a thin, hurt line.

"*J'irai, chef?*" asked the stocky Frenchman.

Deluard nodded. The stocky guy moved fast and walloped Lena hard on the face. She yowled. He grabbed her hair and flung her to the floor. I must have croaked something. One of the Arabs came right over. Yellow face, purple lips, thick neck and narrow eyes. A hunter. He hauled an ugly pistol out of his pocket and raised it high. I tried to move but just got a riot of pain all over.

Darkness was disintegrating a long way off, and I came rushing out of it terrified. The skinny Arab was poking a knife into my throat!

"*Non, non! Pas de sang!*" came Deluard's voice. The knife stopped.

I tried to scream but only got a muffled sound that sent skyrockets through my head. I was gagged. Jagged shadows on mud walls, reed mats for floor. Four men standing, the Swede huddled in a corner by her suitcases, in the pale white of a kerosene lamp. The men moved and I stirred against the wall, sitting, hands tied behind me. My right arm was numb.

"*La garrotte?*" asked the stocky Frenchman and Deluard nodded. The thin Arab who'd had the knife was twirling a big white cloth into a choker, his black eyes fixed on me. The other Arab squatted down in a far corner.

Good God! Don't take it like a dumb hulk! I felt like crying. I was paralyzed. Jesus, remember the Aubrys. Fight it! The cry-baby stayed in my chest. Yes, me and the Aubrys. They got us. The Arab was moving toward me, the choker neatly rolled. He had a delicate way of moving. I started trembling, my brain wild trying to make me move. Move! Jesus Christ, what's worth anything!

Feet snapped under me and blindly I sprang up into the Arab's face. I felt the squish of his nose on my head and he toppled with an anguished snort, but the stocky Frenchman was on me. He seized my head, which tore off the gag, but I caught him in the crotch with my knee and brought my forehead down on his nose. The other Arab was coming up, colliding with Deluard, which gave me time to kick him in the gut, but they were all hup-hupping around me in French or Arabic. Deluard started plowing lefts and rights into my face. He knew how to hit, and I was against the wall, barely keeping my knees stiff. I bobbed once and he pounded the wall. I got into the opening and sunk my teeth into his cheek. Teeth are sharp, but cheek is tough. He backed off carrying me with him while the others hauled at me. The cheek tore partly but I had to let go when one of them plowed into my back and I was conked. It was an effort, one hell of an effort, but I kept my feet and spun over to the wooden door. I turned to face them and yelled, really yelled, levelling frenziedly on them. They hesitated, staring. Deluard was clutching his cheek. Then the door whammed into my back and

I pitched forward and draped helplessly over onto the Swede who was just sitting up.

I heard the roar of the guns and got my head turned to see Chuck in the doorway. Big, blond Chuck, two pistols in his hands. Two of them! God, he could shoot. Thunder all over the hut, and they toppled like ten-pins. I saw Deluard's brains spatter red and white over the thin Arab's face as they both went down. It only lasted a second, and Chuck was up there like a conquering god. Easy-going Chuck. He closed the door behind him, grinning at us in the corner, his teeth dark from wine drinking.

I couldn't grin back. I could only sprawl there trying to get air into my lungs and trying to soak in the joy of a miracle. Where did he come from? The Swede was under me squirming, but I couldn't move off her and she whimpered. Chuck was still grinning when a shot boomed from the dead men. A big chunk of mud flew off the wall, and Chuck leaped away. Another shot caught him, folding him up, and he slumped down on his seat, dropping the guns and clutching his gut.

I couldn't believe it. The stocky Frenchman was struggling to his feet, face all bloody and desperate. He stood there a moment getting his bearings, my own .38 in his hand. Blood on the hand, too. He went over to Chuck, wobbling a little on his feet. One more move. Once more, I was telling myself. The Swede had half crawled out from under me and I felt my weight shift. My feet grabbed bottom. The Frenchman was pointing the .38 at the top of Chuck's head. I yelled again. I was scurrying, low to the ground. The Frenchman and I went down together as a shot rang out. I was stretched flat, the Frenchman sitting on me. I thought how nice it would be to lie there and sleep, but my body was making little spasms trying to get up. I twisted my head and saw the Swede's big suitcase conk the Frenchman flush in the face. She was wresting the .38 from his fist. She got it and began striking his head with it. Funny, like a woman beating a cockroach with a towel.

I was sinking again, wanting to sleep, but a nicer feeling broke around my wrists. I was liberated, like joy in the hands. "Work your wrists," the Swede said holding a knife in her fist. "Your hands are all swollen."

Anything I moved caused agony, but she got me on my feet. She had the efficient, ready-to-go look, though her right cheek bone was puffed out of shape. I eased down to look at Chuck. He was tightened up in a ball sitting against the wall, his face like grey stone.

"Chuck," I called softly.

He grunted and opened his eyes on the floor. I couldn't move my right arm, and it cost me something torn in my side, but Lena and I got his back on the deck and started to straighten out his legs. He groaned but let go till he had his feet down. I unzippered his jacket and the metal tab came off in my hand toward the bottom. The belt buckle was fouled up, too, and Lena cut the belt with her pig sticker. I pulled open the pants and eased down his skivvies. A little red-puling mouth sat below and a shade to the right of his navel. No guts coming out, not too much blood. The bullet had gone through the zipper, the buckle, and the top button of his pants. "Something clean in that suitcase?" I asked, but Lena had it already there, a pair of panties. Chuck was breathing with a hiss.

"It's nylon," she said.

I laid them on the red mouth, plus a towel, and she was tying it with one of her slips when the door opened slowly. Something exploded in my noggin as I dived for Chuck's pistol. Elie stuck his long head into the hut. The little o mouth.

"OK?" he asked.

I passed out.

Lena set me in a shiny new Dodge taxi parked behind a black Citroen and she left. In yellow light from the open door of a cruddy mud hut two men were carrying bodies to the Citroen. Two Elies. That didn't surprise me, but I was lost. Everybody knew what to do and everything was OK. But I felt like crying.

They all *knew* everything. The car door opened and they crowded in and out, muttering, and Chuck was braced in catty-corner on a little plank, coats tucked around him. "Give me a smoke," he was saying and the car was moving slowly. I was sick and stuck my head out the window to heave. Elie came running toward us as a thin streak of fire raced away behind him to the Citroen. We gunned out as he piled into the front seat. The two Elies were muttering in Arabic when a fire at the Citroen billowed up orange and black with a boom.

"Two Elies," I said. "Where you come from?"

The real one turned around smiling. "My cousin," he said. "How you feel?" He was laughing, in high humor, in top shape. "Had to check on you. We go to Deluard's in the cab, me and my cousin, and wait around." The cousin turned briefly and grinned. He looked like Elie in disguise. "We see them drag you out. She's crying."

The Swede looked back with big serious blue eyes. "I'm sorry," I said, but she laughed and turned away.

"Came got me out of the Black Cat," Chuck wheezed. "Little blonde Spaniard I had there."

"First we follow the Citroen," Elie said. "From the highway you see the hut there. I figure what Chuck did to that Arab so we drive back . . ."

I glanced at Chuck and he was smirking, both from the joggling and from amusement. What was so funny? "Thought they got you, too," I said. "They were waiting for me."

He screwed up his face to keep from laughing. "Little Arab did follow me from your joint. Stuck a gun in my ribs, right in the alley. Took it away from him and booted him in the seeds." He winced and put his hand over his gut. "Begging for mercy on his knees and I kicked him in the head. Jesus, those teeth!"

I was sick again, but only retched and Elie was chattering. ". . . maybe it's too late, but we drove out. Chuck run all the way down from the highway."

I gagged again and Lena was reaching back holding Chuck's

arm tenderly. "Old Chucky boy," she said full of affection, and I dimmed out.

Elie, with a full black mustache, in a doctor's smock, stared detachedly down into my face. "Is fine, is good," he said and disappeared.

"All right, old horse?" asked Chuck. He was lying on a cot next to mine, smoking a cigarette. "Got a real jolt of morphine. High as hell. You got six holes in your head, concussion, cuts, contusions, broken nose, four ribs and right arm busted." He was happy. "Slug of morphine, too."

"Elie's a doctor," I said.

"Cousin," Chuck said. "Cut out my lead, sewed up my gut, sewed up the skin, sewed up the whole goddam thing." He was yammering, gleeful. "Elie told me they had you, I felt guilty. Should have warned you when I first came down. Didn't know you were planning a move yet." He yawned. "Was with a little blonde Spaniard, Elie came in told me the story. What the hell, we got plenty of iron. Went down in there shooting."

"Warned me?"

He was holding his gut laughing and trying to smoke. "In Paris you hung out with those Reds. Josette, right? Well, she told me you were a Party man coming down here to hire on for the cause in Algeria." He laughed silently again, bringing up his knees to slack tension on his gut. "And I convinced her you were a spy. To foul you up. Convinced her."

"Oh."

"Goddam spy. How was I to know Romilliac really had something going with the same lash-up?" He grinned sloppily, dragging on the cigarette. "Did you wrong, buddy. Funny in the hut, you like a tall dog on little Lena. Knock me down with a feather when I saw Lena. Crazy Swede in Tangier." He was slurring now, dropped his cigarette on the floor, eyes half closing. "Work with little Lena two years ago in Yugoslavia, for ol' Romilliac."

I blinked my eyes. "Romilliac? Who's Romilliac?"

Chuck sighed and smacked his lips drowsily but I knew even before he said it. "Ol' Romilliac? Frog Intelligence." Elie was leaning over me, a hand on my shoulder. "It's OK, she got a plane to London." The real Elie.

If I could have squinted the tears would have stopped. "How d'you all know so much?" I said, trying to keep from blubbering. "You all know everything and see everything and do everything, and I can't do one single goddam thing in this whole wide bloody world!" I felt tears running into the bandages and I couldn't squint.

Elie was looking down with the little o mouth and I heard Chuck gurgle a drowsy sound in his throat. I was miserable, and it didn't even help knowing it was the anguish of new birth.

DRIFTER'S MAGIC

IN RECONCILING myself to the magic ring, I had knocked off twelve *piscos,* and felt a bit seagoing on my way up *calle* San Ysidro in the dark. Not a glimmer of light. Black velvet houses crouched behind walls and shrubbery.

I felt the note through my shirt pocket: *buena senorita, calle San Ysidro.* No street number, but it went with the ring, and with the voice I'd heard in the foam at sea. And by God that ring had appeared on my finger! At twilight, down near the docks in Callao, all of a sudden the Indian money-changer was asking for twenty-five *soles,* and I was wearing the ring, a gold sun-god sunk in white silver. I hadn't even dreamed of a ring, but there it was on my finger. It was a sign. I felt its unaccustomed weight now, and I believed in Lima's magic.

I wobbled in the dark, for quite a while it seemed, and then was aware of light peeping through a silhouette of iron grille and shrubbery, just a thin line of it from the shutters on a house. *Buena senorita, calle San Ysidro.* The customs man, with his powder blue uniform on, *had* given me the note when I handed him some free soap that afternoon. Afterward the steward was sarcastic as usual. "Tapping the vanilla extract, eh? No customs been aboard yet, boy. The gangway's not even up. And for your information, Peru doesn't have powder blue uniforms!"

My hand moved to the gate and the latch lifted with a clink. I had the note. I didn't dream the guy up. My feet were feeling through blackness, my eyes on the crack of light. "Can't tell a pimp from a customs man," the Stew had said. I laughed. Some low lying object was insistently blocking my toe. The mass of me was heading through space and I cursed out loud as I thudded flat onto soft dirt and bit my tongue.

A dim light some yards away lit up the door of a big stucco house from which a frightened voice had murmured. I was getting to my feet, brushing off my white pants. "I'm sorry, God damn it!" My voice broke the black stillness and I spat. "I lost my way in the God damn dark, but I'm getting out of here right now!" I poked for the gate in the shrubbery, and felt dirt on my clean blue wool shirt. How did I ever get touted onto this deal? The voice from the door murmured again, and finally I got it. "English? You espeak English?"

"Yes, I'm sorry, but I'm getting out if I can find the blasted gate!"

The house door opened and an arm in delicate red wool was motioning. "Don't go! Come in, quickly!"

My heart began beating fast and I felt flushed as I weaved up the path. I went straight up the steps to the door, and in. Through the door was darkness, warmth and fragrance, and something female. I followed her perfumed long hair down a small corridor and into a softly lighted living room. Beige walls and wine colored furniture. She turned, smiling. She was young, sixteen, maybe seventeen. "I expected you tonight," she said. A big, wide smile. "My family have gone until tomorrow."

Sheer sequestered beauty. Large, slanty hazel eyes with long lashes, full, pale pink lips over crystalline teeth, and her skin was delicate ivory with faint veins at the temples. I could feel the heat rise to my face. Her long brown hair, like silk with oaken grain, caressed her cheek. The young breasts and haunches swelled under her red sweater and olive skirt.

"I am so happy," she said. "Please have a seat." She reached out to touch my arm and I felt it to the marrow. "You will wait one moment?" The bright hazel eyes were full of confidence. "I shall come right back."

My grin felt foolish and my arms swung slightly. "Yes, I'll

wait. Where shall I sit, here?" I eyed a squat, antique-looking armchair.

"Anywhere," she said. "I shall return immediately." She spun gaily, and the skirt and petticoat flounced with her fleeing steps. Tender legs, firm and ripe in nylon.

I sat staring at patterns on the rug. What? I'd stumbled onto the sailor's all-time deal. No. I pressed my temples. The thought forced itself into my head. It was the magic. It must be. I was forewarned. At sea, in the foam of the ship, an intimate voice had been whispering all the trip, in a beetly-beetly rhythm, "Lima, Lima, magic Lima." I'd courted the foam's voice. I was pushing thirty, still looking for the fabulous, all-time deal to haul me off the fatal drifter's track. Some tricky inner sense was going to lead me to the moment where life was grand and true and continuous. So here it was, the customs man's note, then the ring, and now the girl, on a silver platter. I twisted the ring and blinked my eyes at the rug. There was an answer somewhere. There was payment somewhere.

She had a small bronze tray with two shiny slender glasses and a green bottle on it. She wore a satiny red housecoat. "Some wine," she said, setting down the tray. She was aglow, and fragrant. She handed me a glass of tawny liquid and went to the divan. As she half-reclined, one length of leg emerged in soft, rippling contours. My gut burned, and the wine was rich. She was smiling quizzically.

"I suppose you know everything," she said. "A woman in a tea-house informed me last month. You would arrive to bring me special knowledge of which I have need." She cast down her eyes, but her lips turned up in a cat smile. "It is very, very special. And, you see, I speak English."

"Yes," I said. "Very good English." I drank part of the sherry and nodded. "By God, it's magic. It's a miracle in this day and age." I blinked at her. "Do you know a customs man in powder-blue uniform? I heard a voice at sea, in the water alongside the ship."

Her smile was pleasant and confident. She shook her head. "*La magìa.* Of course it is powerless if we don't seek a way through life. You know?"

My eye went to her leg. She had all the information, and so young. I nodded again. She giggled. "I think you are American, not English, yes?"

I sat up straight and fingered the glass. "Yes, from California."

"Ah?" She cocked her head. "California is not bad. I am from Lima. You must call me Maru."

"Maru," I said. I felt flustered and drank the sherry. "I'm Lee Cavin."

She stirred, and a sensuous half-smile played on her face. "Lee Cavin. It's nice, on the ear, you know. What kind of name is this?"

"Irish. My parents are both Irish. Liam Patrick Cavin."

"Ah!" Her eyes lit up. "*Muy bueno!* When you said California . . ." she pouted, thinking it over, ". . . not bad of course. *Pero, Irlandès!*" She closed her eyes and kissed the air at me.

My heart began to pound as I leaned forward in the chair. "Maru," I said, staring at my glass. I felt a self-conscious grin on my face. "What is it supposed to be? You know, between us?"

"You don't know?" She was surprised, and childishly innocent. "What have you wanted, Liam Cavin? What special thing from life? I thought you would know."

That whipped the old nameless haunt into my gut. "Why . . ." I said. What was she asking questions for? Those hours on a silver sea-path, hung up under a tantalizing moon, and my knotted tongue . . . here it was again. The hot question paws the edge of my mind, so I go below and stare at the bulkheads. "I suppose I know, but I can't say what I want, Maru."

She was waiting, with her long-lashed eyes. She lay reclining and stirred the heart-rendingly naked leg. A tenacious point of reality. "It's just . . ." I said. She smiled and started. She wanted me to have some weight, some manly component. My gut relaxed a little, and I saw her there, a full little female unity. The words came cool to my mouth. "I want to see something in life itself,

Maru. I want to find some way of looking at life." I finished the sherry and dawdled with the glass in my fingers. "I need to see life in such a way that, all alone, I'll give myself wholeheartedly to it. Permanently. I don't know if. . . ."

She was patting the divan next to her, her eyes glistening. I set down the glass and floated over. I could feel tension down my spine. I loomed above her and she watched me, a pink flush of fright and daring on her cheeks. "To be alone in the universe, Liam Cavin. . . ." Warmth and perfume emanated from her as I sat down. I took that sublime delicateness into my hands and drew her close. The firm lips melted.

It was a sudden plunge to new vision and there were swirling planes in the glow of her, her cries filtering through me, a burden, colored turquoise. I myself was shimmering red dedication. Nothing would ever change, but I was moving. I piled through golden concentric lines, through Maru and the world. That was how it looked.

She was cradling my head on her tender, silken breast. "Oh, Liam Cavin," she murmured. "Oh, Liam Cavin." I bore her fragrant weight in me. Her face, the nakedness, made velvet, waxen colors. We spilled to further levels. I understood. I wanted her. I yearned to give everything to Maru. She was the world. I loved her passionately and exactly. It was strange music. Lofty possibilities lay in my gut and my hands, and time drifted out of sight.

She was shaking me, her muzzle soft at my neck. "You must go." She wore the housecoat, sitting on the edge of the divan where I lay, her face shadowed and relaxed. My heart took a dive. The dreary ship was anchored in Callao. Schedules. A gap lay between Maru and the world.

"Get dressed," she said, and she hovered behind me till I was up and back at the front door again.

"Liam, this cannot happen to everybody. Remember what you loved."

I turned. "I remember everything."

"It is sacred," she said. "To love what we saw is sacred. It is not you or I."

"It's sacred. I understand that."

"Never speak of it, never mention it, even once. Be very careful, Liam. To be not reverent would make us forget, and worse."

"I'll always love you," I said. I solemnly pulled off the magic ring and gave it to her. "I'll always love life."

"No, you must have it," she said, but I folded her fingers around it. We kissed. Her mouth was silken and bruised. I was out on the porch, feeling my way to the gate. Cold air struck my head and I was dizzy. The gate clanged behind me. Still drunk. The iron tanker sat implacable in my mind. I could hardly believe I'd just left Maru, and I didn't dare turn my head. Bridge the gap. I staggered as I walked. A sailor was one thing, a drifter another. I knew.

The taxi sped back to Callao and I tried to review, to believe the magic, but weariness slugged me. I was awakened at the dock gates. Music floated over from a string of gin mills lining the street, and pink and green neon lights. I punched my drowsy mind as the cab drove off. Maru. Rushing concentric circles winged out of my static burden of existence. I loved Maru. I had to think the answer into my life. Plans, set values, stood just outside the picture.

"BR! Hey, BR!"

It was the steward, in starched khakis, hilarious, at the dive nearby. "Told the sons of bitches!" he yodeled. "Twelve straight! Come here show the sons of bitches how to drink *pisco!*"

I laughed and ambled over. One last drink, the sign of parting from the old rich life. I shook my head. The steward was beckoning to someone inside and pointing. "Here he comes! The sunbather!" His white baseball cap was tight on his head, his lined face happy. I laughed again.

He crowded me into the joint, whacking my back and hollering. It was full of smoke and noise. The sailors were drunk and caterwauling. At the bar a wild-eyed gypsy B-girl got hold of my arm. "You buy me drink, I give you for love!"

"Ten of 'em! Ten *piscos!*" the steward was shouting.

This was my night. I stared into the depths of the clear *pisco* in a shot glass. There lay the gold of Maru's beauty, and the lovely blue of her burden. The clamor swirled around me. "Stew, I'm a child of destiny."

"Line 'em up!" the steward shouted. "Twelve before. You bastards going to see him drink ten now!"

The ardent, blank *pisco* went down. It was familiar and warm. The steward was still shouting in the hubbub, and smoke from a cigarette clouded his mouth. Another *pisco.* The boys were crowding around me. Noise beat on my ears. Farewell. I drank. The empty shot glasses glittered on the bar and sharp, nutty *pisco* taste was strong in my mouth. I was confident, and detached. Blue smoke whirled in the music and the wild-eyed B-girl was dancing me around. Smoke billowed and I was whirling. The steward's handsome, beat-up face was creased in laughter and from a great distance I was coming up deep, deep out of the depths.

The four-to-eight Ordinary, who was my good buddy Bridgman, held a cup of odorous coffee under my nose and a damp cloth on my forehead. His voice was droning. ". . . skipper doesn't like you anyway. You'll get fired. Still need dough for Europe."

I thought I couldn't move, and peered through a glaze at the gaping port hole. Bridgman tugged my bare legs off the sack, was pulling me to the deck. ". . . get your clothes on, some chow into you and get to work."

I stumbled trying to get into my trousers. I knew there was something important. I let Bridgman haul me up the black iron ladder to the crew mess and slumped into a swivel chair and closed my eyes. Sandy eyes. When I opened them a stack of buttered toast, a cup of coffee and a dish of prunes stared up at me. I got a prune into my mouth and the thick sweet taste put color in the world. My throat ached from the hot coffee. I wanted to remember the night before.

". . . shock of red, curly hair. An Octoroon." Bridgman's bland young face was smiling. "First time I ever saw three breasts on a woman. Said she could turn people into dogs, like a witch. She liked me and didn't want any dough, but what the hell, it was almost all night. I gave her twently *soles*."

I bit into the salty buttered toast, and coffee washed my tongue clean. Bridgman was smiling, proud. "Most fabulous piece you or I ever had, boy. You get it? A witch. She said she could turn people into dogs."

I blinked, stirring the coffee. Where had I been? Lima. Her white, naked leg in the housecoat and the flush of daring on her cheeks. Some promise lay beyond her, but the mechanism had me gripped. My voice was talking by itself, and something was wrong. The words went on and on before I finally caught them. ". . . then it popped like a fresh, full, sweet grape. She was crying, and I saw visions you could never imagine. . . ."

Bridgman was smiling sardonically. I caught it. Every sailor with the same classic story, and no one believes him. I shut up. I knew something was wrong as hell. The remorsies, on top of everything.

I was dead, toiling through officers' cabins, sloshing a swab here and there. My arms had no strength and I cursed the second engineer for messing up his sack again. I thought of magic by the end of the morning, but was too beat to worry it. The steward found me at noon, dozing miserably on a fantail bit. I'd been dreaming of a raft on the desert.

"You look terrible, BR. Go on ashore and get a drink. You got an hour or so."

I forced a smile and patted my pockets. "Never mind, Stew. I'm dead."

The steward clinked a bunch of brassy coins in his hand and held them out. "I won't be going again. Twenty or thirty there. Go ahead, kid."

On the tank deck the sun was warm. Out of nowhere I was considering Maru's tender youth. I'd got a virgin. There was something else to remember. The gangway was steep and trembly leading down to the dock. I waved over a cruising cab and started to get in when someone called. The big deck hand Paul Gay was teetering down the gangway, hurrying in his drunk fat man's shuffle.

"God, I made it, BR," Gay said sweating. "God if you knew how I'm suffering."

I was suffering, too. We rode in silence. I was brooding at the futility of all those extensive docks. At the gate the two of us paced out to the closest bar. It was the one from the night before. In the bright sunlight it looked chill and empty. The owner sat sulking behind his cash register, but his eyes lit up when he saw us. "Ahhhh!" He extended his arms. "*Mucho pisco! Sí, sí, sí, sí!*"

He had five shot glasses glittering on the bar, delighted, and I weakly tried to restrain him. "*Sí, sí, sí! Mucho pisco* las' night! You pay nothing."

"Some beer. Get me some beer," Gay was pleading.

I carefully held up a brimming shot glass in salute. He was a straight little guy to buy me a drink. *Pisco* started my heart beating and improved my vision. "*Sí, sí!* Drink! You pay nothing!"

At a table in the back of the room sat a yellow-skinned woman in a green satin blouse, about thirty five. Negroid features, hair like crinkled copper threads.

"Oh, you don't know what this means to me, BR," said Gay, sprawled in a chair, amorous of his beer.

A third *pisco,* and I looked into the depths of the fourth. I remembered, as though it were a step to clarity, the voice which had whispered to me at sea. I smelled something precipitous in my destiny and glanced at the red-headed Octoroon. It could only be her. Bridgman said she could work magic. And she had three breasts. She was watching me, and I went over.

"You know my friend Bridgman?"

She smiled, and from the eye teeth back, on both sides, it was all gold. "*Sí!* Las' night. I see you, too. You loco."

I looked her over, and could see Maru in my mind's eye. Two creatures, Psyche bright and the cured hide. They were tied up together in the cosmos. That was depressing, but amusing. What the hell, it's a losing fight. I didn't have much time. I tossed down the fourth *pisco*, feeling smart. "Twenty *soles* OK, you and me?"

She was gay. "Ahhh! *Sí, coco.* You bad boy, ah?" She reached out to chuck me under the chin. "I ask *el dueno,* ah?"

She got up and was over whispering to the owner. Paul Gay was watching soberly and he winked. "Might as well get it while you're young, BR."

She was beckoning from a door in an alcove off the back room, and I strolled in with her to a dim, warm, shade-drawn enclosure. "Naked," I said when she sat on the bed, and she laughed. "Ah, you bad boy. You funny boy, ah?"

When she took off her blouse, there it sat, below the saggy right one, a full-fledged nipple, but no swelling. She saw me looking. "This a mole," she said. I laughed and she tousled my hair. "You bad boy. Oh yi, yi, yi, you bad boy!"

At the bar again I was staring into the fifth *pisco,* into crystalline blue, and concentric whorls surged up at me, engulfing me. My mind teetered on remembering Maru's weight. Give myself eternally to the world! I thrilled in my gut. An effort inside me and I could love Maru, I could see to love Maru! But someone was tugging my sleeve, insistently. I floated out of the reverie. An Indian with a tray of silver rings strapped to his chest was indignant. "Twenny fi' *soles,*" he said. I had another sun-god ring on my finger, like the day before. I was stunned, and drunk again, God damn it. I hauled out my coins and counted them. "Twenty two. Get out of here." It felt good to be salty with the Indian.

"Little souvenir, BR," said Gay. "You're smart. A nice little souvenir."

I descended into the *pisco* again, righteously, but the Octoroon was at my elbow. Gold flashed from the corners of her mouth. "You give me twenny *soles* now, baby. I go eat."

That was it. I felt my pockets. I looked around for the Indian, but I knew he was gone. At my frown the woman's face went blank. "No got. Next time," I said.

Her face was stiff and pale. "What you mean next time? Twenny *soles,* now!"

I was more bothered than concerned and I turned to Gay. "Paul, have you got twenty God damn *soles?*"

Gay was amiable. "Just enough to pay for my beer and a cab, BR."

I faced her grim, darkening presence. "Look," I told her. "Give me your address, I'll send it. But don't get excited, for Christ sake."

She had backed off two paces, staring with sunken eyes, the bright, crinkled copper hair standing on end. Her yellow face twisted. "You son of a bitch!" she hissed. Her arms extended toward me, fingers lean and bony. I watched her as some realization started to come alive in me. I tossed down the last *pisco,* and suddenly was trying to claw the burning ring off my finger.

The ship's whistle hooted mournfully, impatiently, and I reached the green cab as big Paul Gay emerged on the run, leaving the door open. His quivering fat shuffled up the gangway, and the young blond second mate on deck hollered at him. "Get that God damn dog away from here, Gay!"

Gay turned around on the gangway to look, and gave a cry of horror. I was running up behind him. "Second!" he shrieked, hauling his bulk feverishly to the deck. "Get the skipper! It's the BR!"

"You rum-head, Gay!" shouted the second mate. "We been

holding up this ship for you! Catch that dog! Lower the God damn gangway, you people!"

The steward was there, his face white, his mouth thin and eyes anxious. "Where's the BR, Paul?"

The crew were crowding around Gay. "It's a pup, an Irish setter." The skipper elbowed his way through. He was cursing Gay, pointing his finger at him. Gay stood there with his arms out, sweating, horrified, dirty-faced. "I swear to God almighty right before my very eyes, like the lights went on brighter, and I swear to God, right where the BR stood. . . ."

"Get his buddy, get Bridgman!" the steward was hollering, but Bridgman was down beside me. I couldn't keep from quivering and panting. Everyone grew silent and looked at Bridgman. A sense of awe settled over them. My rhythmed panting was all that could be heard. Bridgman arose, pale, his eyes bright but serious.

"I think so," he said. "I think it's Cavin."

They all stood watching, no one saying a word, and then the skipper roared and the crew dispersed to get the ship out onto the sea.

The Perfectionist

SHORT STORIES

by

JOSEPH SLOTKIN

THE PERFECTIONIST

At the intersection of Central and Glenoaks the red light stopped his car, and Harvey glared over the shining hood at the pedestrians in the crosswalk. He nudged his wife, Jennie.

"Notice the dirty looks," he said. "They hate me, because I have a new car. You'd think they'd see it, and admire it, and maybe smile because it's a pleasure to look at. But no!"

His lips curled, and his rather regular, squared-off features seemed to jut forward like the metal indestructible grille of his modern streamlined vehicle.

"It isn't theirs," he mumbled, "and I can just *feel* them wanting to kick it, or scratch it, or do something to hurt it."

He turned a little, his neck stiff. ". . . *Can't* you?"

". . . It's green now, honey," Jennie said.

Out of the corner of his eye he sensed the Mercury in the right-hand lane edging, and heard its motor snarling. Deliberately, he shifted into low, let out the clutch slowly. The Mercury growled ahead, leaping, and he spoke out of the corner of his mouth, disdainfully.

"The hell with'm. They see a new car, right away they wanta challenge, all the time challenge.

"I coulda beat him."

Jennie smiled. "I'm glad you didn't race with him," she said.

They were winding through the sinuous stop-signed area past the tracks. Lightly, she laid her hand on his arm, adding, "I wish you would always do that when they want to race with you."

Not roughly, he shook her off, grunting, "Honey, don't do that, you know I gotta keep my arms free for driving."

Crossing Glendale Boulevard his car bobbed and dipped, like a giant chrome-nosed robot, over the raised center section of the street that made two troughs for the California spring rains: up, then down, curtsying with fluid knees of oil and a warm metallic drone of gears happy in their viscous baths.

As the shocks took up the vibration with liquid grace, Harvey glanced at Jennie. "Doesn't squeak now, that door, does it?" he said with satisfaction.

She shook her head, and he muttered, "Had to take it back to those guys three times, though."

Now they were on Colorado Boulevard, purring along. He looked over at her, smiling broadly. "Really rides, huh?"

He became conscious of something vibrating at him in his rear-view mirror. He felt the pushing, dodging grayness of a shape behind, and his foot slammed down on the accelerator. Then he looked squarely in the mirror, smiling inwardly.

At the next light, without turning his head, he knew the older car was coming up on him, holding back, ready to shoot past as the signal changed. He gunned the motor, and as the amber light flashed, shot ahead in low, shifted rapidly, then permitted himself a quick look back.

His swiveling glance caught Jennie, her fingers laced in her lap, not saying anything.

The older car came up fast, behind, and he grinned as he heard its horn. So it wanted to pass. Harvey stuck out his left hand and made large, elaborate gestures indicating "Go ahead."

Then his foot on the gas went relentlessly floorward. And again, in the rear mirror, the other car receded. Harvey slowed for the next light, saw that he would make it, and accelerated again. Behind him the pursuer was gaining.

"Aw, t'hell with'm," Harvey muttered, and disdained to push ahead. Gray-shaped in his mirror, the car caught up, bearing down on his rear. "Let him go," he growled, and began to pull over to the right. But as he shot over, he pulled away again, too. Behind, he heard the honk, and then, outraged, felt a bump in the rear as the pursuer contacted, and fled away to the front.

"He hit me!" Harvey raged. He shot in pursuit, horn blaring. "My new car!" he shouted. He overtook the offender, motioning to him wildly, glaring.

Just before Figueroa, both cars pulled over, Harvey parking ahead. In the mirror he saw a chunky figure emerge, remove his coat, and stalk toward him.

He felt a chill creep up his back, and the short hairs on his neck rise. He leaned across Jennie, slammed open the glove compartment, and snatched out a three-cell, chrome-plated flashlight.

"That car murderer!" he cried. "I'll teach him!"

They met halfway, and Harvey flourished the flashlight, some calm part of him examining his foe. He saw that his adversary was a man quite his own age, light-complexioned, becoming bald and, from the way he was blinking, he too must have just pulled off his glasses.

With a sense of surprise Harvey realized he wasn't, couldn't be angry with this man who looked so much like himself. But the stocky man was waving his arms threateningly, and Harvey brought the flashlight down with a thunk on the bald head, just over the brow. The man stopped, staggered, shook himself and cried, "You hit me!"

"You hit my car!" Harvey answered, and found himself dodging rather skillfully the inept sweeps the other was making with his arms.

They both froze suddenly as the wail of a siren swept toward them. Abandoning attack, the chunky man seized Harvey's arm, and pulled him toward his car.

"It's the cops," he was saying. He got into his car. "Listen, when he comes up, we'll say it was just a family argument. Okay?"

"Okay," Harvey said.

As the policeman dismounted from his motorcycle, the stocky man put on his glasses, and Harvey leaned as casually as he could against the door. In the second of waiting, he surveyed the man's car, estimating it. A 1941 Chevvy, he told himself.

"What's going on here?" the policeman said. Harvey's opponent leaned out and said, smiling, "Just a little argument with my cousin here, officer, no harm done."

"Yeah, it's all settled," Harvey heard himself adding.

The policeman stood for an instant, looking from one to the other, then reluctantly returned to his motorcycle. "Do your fighting on private property, not on the street," he said.

Harvey found his head bobbing in a helpless nod, and he was saying, "Sure, sure. . . ."

The policeman kicked his motorcycle into sputtering life, and roared away. For a moment Harvey leaned against the old car, in the sudden quiet, and he was wondering, what would this man's cousin really look like?

"Look, fella," the man in the Chevrolet said, "I was only trying to pass you."

"I signaled you to go ahead," Harvey said.

"But then you started to speed up, and—"

"Just a minute," Harvey said. He had suddenly remembered with a shock the feeling of the impact in his rear. "You hit my car. That's why I made you pull over—"

"It was only your bumper," the other said. "It was only your bumper."

Harvey was striding rapidly to his car. He bent down, urgently, and examined the shining chrome of his rear bumper. The metal gleamed smoothly, untouched, like satin. He squinted at the spot where chrome joined paint.

"Look fella, I didn't hit it." The stocky man had come up behind Harvey. "It's okay."

"Yeah," Harvey said slowly, straightening and feeling a bit dizzy as he did so. "Yeah." He looked at the man, at the faint red mark on his forehead, and said, "I guess we better not get upset."

"I'm not upset," the man said.

Harvey felt a flood of remorse sweep over him. He saw the

man's heavy breathing. His hand dug into his pocket and came out with a box of aspirin. "You sure you feel all right?" he said.

"Sure," the man said.

"Look, I guess we both got upset. Here, take an aspirin. Take a couple. It'll calm you down."

"I don't need it," the man said.

"Take it, go ahead," Harvey urged. He thrust two tablets into the man's palm, and felt a shock at the sweating clamminess of it. "Promise me you'll take it when you stop to drink some water.

"You should take a whole glassful of water with it. Promise me—"

"Okay, okay," the man said grudgingly. Harvey was walking him back to the Chevrolet. "Look fella, you got the hottest car on the road, but you gotta be careful," the man said.

So that's it, Harvey thought.

"I am careful," Harvey said.

"You gotta be, with a hot car like that. Everybody knows it's the fastest thing on the road."

"Now will you wait a minute," Harvey said. "This isn't the Hornet, you know. This is the Pacemaker. Only a hundred and twelve horsepower, see?"

"Oh?" The stocky man seemed confused. "Well, it's a good car, but you gotta watch that cutting in and out."

Harvey couldn't stop himself now. "It's not the big Hudson, fella. It's the cheapest of the line, see? I got what I could afford. You got a good car yourself. I had a Chevvy just like that before I went in the Army."

The stocky man started the motor. He didn't say anything.

"No hard feelings," Harvey said.

"Okay, okay," the other said.

Harvey watched him drive off. He stood there a moment, before starting back to his car. He could see Jennie sitting as he had left her, looking straight ahead. Even in profile, he thought, helplessly, she can look more like a cool, efficient nurse—it's as though she put on her professional manner at will.

But she hasn't got her uniform on, he told himself. He got in the car, slamming the door hard and watching Jennie's face. She didn't flinch, he didn't think she would, when she was like that she could assist at surgery, or give medication, needles, tubes—perfectly.

He eased away from the curb, feeling her rigid beside him. They glided along past Figueroa, toward the Arroyo bridge, silently.

Harvey began to loosen up. He looked at Jennie. "You know what was eating that guy?" he said.

Jennie didn't answer.

"He couldn't stand it because I had a new car. That's all. He was just asking for that argument. Think how people are eaten up by envy. Why, he was so guilty, he probably felt satisfied when I conked him one with the flashlight. Probably what he was asking for."

He was silent a moment. Then: "That was the first time I ever hit anybody. Like that, I mean."

"How did it feel?" Jennie said carefully.

"I didn't like it," Harvey said. "I felt sick. He looked so much like me, it was like—like hitting myself. I felt—sorry."

"Then why did you do it?" Jennie said.

"He hit my car," Harvey said.

"What would you have done if that policeman had put you in jail?"

"He didn't," Harvey said. "I have a right to protect my property. Now let's forget it."

His right hand stole out to the seat, where he had put the flashlight. When they stopped for the signal at Orange Grove, he looked at the chrome case. It was dented.

"I had that flashlight for eight years," Harvey said. "Got it as a gift. And now look at it."

"Think how that fellow's head must feel," Jennie said.

"Ha, I didn't hurt him," Harvey muttered. He put the flashlight in the glove compartment. "Maybe I can straighten it out. Must be soft material, to bend like that." He glanced at Jennie. "It dented easy," he said, urgently. "Because it dented doesn't mean he got hurt.

". . . *does* it?" he asked, after a moment, and still Jennie said nothing.

"You still want to go to Bullock's?" he asked.

"Of course," Jennie said. "Isn't that why we came to Pasadena?"

They were going through the city now. Harvey shifted behind the wheel. He looked at Jennie. "Some guys, all they think of is envy," he started again. "They see a big, new car, and right away they hate the guy who owns it. Ha!" He snorted. "I won't even own it until next month."

His lip curled. "They don't realize the struggle it was, getting a trade-in, going easy on food to make the payments, all the things we did without—all they see is a new car, and right away they start hating.

"Well, I'm telling you right now, nobody's gonna get away with it. Understand?" His chin jutted, and he stared over the hood, not looking at Jennie. "If people want to hurt my car, let 'em try. Just let 'em!"

He pulled up suddenly because Jennie was saying, "We're at Bullock's." He let her off at the Lake Street entrance.

"I'll meet you by the fountain at noon," he called after her.

"Be careful," Jennie said, as the door was closing.

"Don't worry," he mouthed through the window, and waved as he drove off. At the California Street intersection he hesitated and then surprised himself by turning left. He had meant to go right to the garage to see about the seat covers.

But he had plenty of time, he told himself, and without quite knowing why, he pulled into the driveway at Caltech. After he had parked as far from the other cars as he could, so that anyone entering the lot wouldn't chance grazing him, he sat there, with the windows rolled up.

And then, he thought he knew why he had come here, where it was quiet.

He was shaking.

He sat there, and all the dim possibilities of the recent angerless encounter flooded over him. What if the cop *had* come up a moment earlier?

Or what, he asked himself, if one of the passing cars had stopped, and someone had wanted to be a witness, testifying he had used a weapon?

He saw himself in jail, being sued for assault; he saw the stocky, flush-faced man with the hurt, shocked face, and felt again the sickly thunk of the impact as the flashlight hit.

And he felt the nudging contact of the pushing car against his rear bumper, and experienced again the sick sense of dread that the shining newness of his car had been ravaged.

He sat there, shaking, and took out two aspirins, gathered a little saliva in his mouth and swallowed them that way.

He thought: Maybe it would have been better to keep the old car. That way no envy, no worry about scratches. Just a second-hand LaSalle. . . .

He remembered how he had taken Jennie for an evening's ride along the Arroyo Freeway after he'd bought it. And she had moved closer to him, because it was their first excursion in their first car together, and he had carefully explained to her that he couldn't put his arm around her because it wasn't safe to drive that way. . . .

At the garage where he'd bought his new car, they got used to him returning for adjustments. "It's in the door," he had told the mechanics once. "The door goes 'cre-e-k,' and then the dash goes 'cra-a-ck,' and there's a sort of groaning sound in the rear. God! When they all go together, it's enough to—"

The mechanics had looked at each other. "A regular Silly Symphony, eh, Mr. Russell?" the tuneup man had commented, but when Harvey looked at him he didn't laugh, and they all took him seriously after that. At least to his face.

The tuneup man was a huge, stout fellow they called "Tiny," and he had once told Harvey that roses were his hobby. "I got them damn roses growin' all over the yard, all kinds," Tiny had said.

Harvey had taken him a sample of his own Heart's Desire red climber. He felt that if he got on a friendly basis with the men in the garage, they would treat his car with special consideration.

Like the time Ed, the lube man, helped him figure out just where to put the side-view mirror. He always brought Ed a cigar. And he remembered how he had been talking to the service manager as Ed brought up the drill to make the hole in the door for the mirror.

As the buzzing tip bit in, Harvey had felt his talk waver and vanish away, sensitively, as though if he were to do a distracting thing he might make the hand of the mechanic, the hand that held the drill, slip; as though in a barber shop the thin, naked, pinging razor were going around his ears. . . .

. . . That was the way he felt about his car, Harvey thought, sitting behind the wheel at Caltech, perspiring in reaction.

He noticed some tennis players on the court, and they looked cool and relaxed in their shorts. For a moment, he wished he were out there, playing, in the dappled shade, instead of here, in this hot thing of oil-smelling metal. Then he smiled to himself, remembering how much more power was here, at this wheel—how puny his arm holding wood and catgut compared to the impatiently leashed horses under the wax-mirrored hood.

One of the players hit wildly, and the white ball soared over the wire fence. Nervously, Harvey saw it bounce close to his car. A thing of soft rubber and fuzz, he told himself. Still, it could smudge if it hit. His finger went to the starter button, and he drove back onto the street.

He made himself relax, and gave himself up to the intricate fretwork of city traffic—gauging lights, computing the speeds of competing cars, braking, shifting, accelerating—and he was at the auto supply store and garage which advertised the seat covers. He parked by the curb—it was safer there—and went into the store.

The seat covers were picked out and paid for quickly. Then he drove into the store's garage to have them installed. He sat in his car, waiting, and watching a young mechanic doing something to the motor of the car next to his.

Harvey was thinking he ought to pull over, the cars were too close, when the young mechanic turned, the wrench in his back pocket narrowly missing Harvey's car. The boy started to open the door of the other car.

Through the open window, Harvey reached out and blocked the door from swinging wide. The mechanic's head swiveled up, and around.

Grinning ingratiatingly, Harvey said, "Want to watch it, pal. Almost nicked me."

"I was just turning off the ignition, mister," the mechanic said.

"Okay, sure, but be careful," Harvey said.

"Sure, okay, don't worry," the young man said, closing the door.

Harvey got out carefully, looked around, and spotted a water cooler in one corner. Over his shoulder, he saw that the young mechanic was all through and slamming down the hood of the other car.

Hurrying, trying to keep the two automobiles in sight, Harvey slipped his metal box out of his pocket, tapped an aspirin into the palm of his hand, and bent over the cooler.

As he was straightening he heard, far off, the click of a door latch, and his glance darted to the car next to his. Some people were getting into it. Trying to appear casual, but walking as fast as he could, he reached the two cars just as a man was climbing into the back seat.

Harvey's hand thrust out, his mouth opened, but he was too late. The back door crunched against the side of Harvey's car with a solid thunk; the man was in, and sitting down.

Urgently Harvey bent over, looking, looking. There, on the side, was a long, deepening scratch, ending in a nick where the tip of the door had gone through to the metal. Harvey saw the man sitting there, waiting.

A woman was sitting behind the wheel. Stiff-legged, Harvey walked over to her and said, "I beg your pardon, but this gentleman has damaged my car with that rear door. I'll have to make a claim to get it fixed. You see, my car's new—"

The woman looked at him. "I'm just driving this for a friend," she said.

"Well, who does this car belong to—?" Harvey started, when the man in the rear shouted, "I didn't touch his car, he's a damn liar!"

Almost gratefully, Harvey turned. "I beg your pardon, but you did, sir," he said elaborately.

He felt a woman coming upon him from behind, around the fender of the other car. "I'm the owner," she said. "What's this all about?"

"This gentleman damaged the paint on my car," Harvey said. "It will have to be fixed."

"He's lying, I tell you," the man called out.

"Doesn't look hurt to me," the woman said.

"I'll have to have that whole rear panel repainted," Harvey said. "So if you'll just tell me the name of your insurance company, and give me your name and address—"

"What for?" the woman said.

"So I can make a claim," Harvey said. He took out a pencil, and jotted down the car's license number.

"What are you trying to pull?" the woman said, becoming angry. "You're imagining things. Your old car looks all right to me."

Harvey bent over and pointed to the spot, the exact spot. It hurt him to look at it, but he had to get this woman to—

"If you'll just examine this place where the door hit," he said, trying to smile courteously at the woman.

"There's nothing the matter with your old car," she said.

"It's a new car," Harvey said carefully. "I'm trying to keep it that way."

He moved toward the man. "If you'll just take a look at my side panel, sir, you'll see what you've done."

"It looks all right to me," the man said, staring straight ahead. "Nothing wrong with it."

"If you'll look—" Harvey began, when the woman grabbed his arm.

"All right!" she said. "If you want to know about that poor man you're pestering, he's blind! He's blind, that's what he is!"

Harvey looked at the man, seeing that he was old, and that the pupils of his eyes were milky and opaque. He felt as though he were caught in some sort of invisible, sticky net, but still he persisted, stubbornly.

"Then someone should have helped him in, and not let him nick my car."

"Oh, your old car," the woman said. "I had one like that, once. They're nothing but tin cans anyway."

Harvey kept himself from becoming angry. He looked up. Several of the other customers were watching the scene. He went toward a man and woman who were about his age.

"You saw that," he said. "How about being a witness? You heard her call my car nothing but a tin can. . . ."

"Sure," the man said. "These people with Cadillacs get too rambunctious anyhow."

Harvey jotted down the man's name, then his wife's name, and their address. He heard the Cadillac start up, and whirled.

"You haven't given me your identification!" he called, as the woman's face floated past him, framed in shining chrome.

"You've got my license number, get it yourself," she said.

Helplessly, Harvey watched the Cadillac roll out of the garage. He bent down and looked at the scratched place again.

"I will," he muttered, feeling the garage whirl as he straightened, still seeing the scratch, staring straight ahead. "I will."

When Harvey met her by the fountain, Jennie smiled. He trudged with her to the car, and her smile widened as he opened the door for her.

"Oh, the seat covers look fine," she said.

"Did you notice anything when you got in?" he asked her.

"You mean the seat covers? I already said—"

"That's right, it wasn't on your side, you couldn't see," he said.

She looked at him inquiringly. "Did you buy something else, too?"

"Never mind," Harvey said. "Never mind."

He drove home quietly, thoughtfully. The man was blind, he told himself. Or almost blind. They should have watched him, he argued with himself. He was still quiet when he put the car away, and went into his den. He sat at his desk, staring at the piece of paper with the license number jotted on it.

He took out his fountain pen and wrote a short, detailed description of the incident, including the license number, folded it into an envelope, enclosed a dime, addressed it to the Motor Vehicle Bureau and got up slowly.

"Where are you going?" Jennie called from the kitchen. "Supper's almost ready."

"Just to the corner," Harvey said.

He walked slowly down the front steps. The letter was in his pocket. He walked into the garage, started up the motor, and backed out carefully.

With the motor still running, he got out, bent down, and looked at the scratch again.

He stood back and looked at it. Then he drove the car back into the garage, walked to the corner and put the letter in the mailbox.

"I got the most lovely pair of sterling napkin rings for Rita," Jennie told him at the table. "They'll make a nice wedding present."

"What?" Harvey said.

Jennie picked up the plates. "Something else happened, didn't it?" she said. "To the car?"

"When we drove away this afternoon, I had a new car," Harvey said. "Now I haven't."

"Do you want strawberries on your ice cream?" Jennie asked.

"You let a couple of those things go," Harvey said, "and before you know it, you've got an old car."

"What happened?" Jennie said.

Harvey told her. "Blind," he said. "That makes me the villain, I suppose. But I've got witnesses," he concluded. "*They* understood."

"What are you going to do?" Jennie said.

"I don't know," Harvey said. "I just don't know."

He took another aspirin before he went to bed. Still, sleep was slow in coming. And when it did, he woke several times to find himself tossing and clawing at the pillow. Jennie murmured and moved beside him, and he lay rigid, closing his eyes.

It wasn't dreaming, exactly. It was just a great sense of taking away, of drawing, of something having been complete, and then part missing.

When he awoke, he knew what it was, because waking was something like driving out of fog that held on with stretching tendrils that broke reluctantly.

He went out, in his bathrobe, before coffee, to see if it were really as bad as it had seemed in the night.

In the yellow light from the huge bare bulb in the garage the car gleamed quietly, authoritatively, and for a moment he didn't see it and was glad. His eye followed the eager lines around to the curve of the shining bumper, and it was all right.

Then he leaned down and looked, and the glowing perfection was broken, and he thought: If I were blind I wouldn't see it, but I do.

Jennie had his coffee heating when he came in. She smiled, not saying anything, and started to lift the coffee pot. Harvey said, "Be sure it's hot enough now," and she set it down again.

"Maybe a few more minutes, then," Jennie said.

She poured some hot water into her cup, and he said, "You're having tea. Why aren't you having cocoa? You usually have cocoa."

"I felt like tea this morning, dear," Jennie said. She put in sugar and milk, and began to stir. He listened to the spoon clinking, and said, "Do you have to keep stirring?"

Jennie got up and poured his coffee. She looked at him.

"Honey, these things are bound to happen," she said.

"People should be more careful," he said. He took a quick mouthful of coffee and she looked inquiringly at him. He said, grudgingly, "Yeah, yeah, it's hot enough," and she smiled.

Jennie picked up her spoon and began stirring thoughtfully, then quickly put it down. She looked at him, and said carefully, "Does it look as bad to you today, as—"

"Yeah, yeah," he said. "It looks like hell."

"You've taken it too much to heart," she said. "You've got to expect your car to get a few scratches."

"Why?" he said. "Why does it have to get—pushed around? A lot of careless people . . . that's what makes a car look old."

"Even people," Jennie said softly, "get old."

He looked at her. He sipped his coffee. Then he said, "Go ahead, stir your tea. Go ahead."

"It's all stirred," Jennie said.

His fingers traced the rim of the cup. "Why do I get all—worked up about a thing like that?"

"Why do you think?" she said.

"I don't know," Harvey said. "I guess a guy has a right to have *something* of his nice, and new, and shining. We expect things to go along in life, you know. And they don't, and each time we get a setback it takes some of the shine off. I don't know.

"And pretty soon we're sad sort of slobs, I guess. You know, things we want, that don't happen—we get used to it, kind of. I don't know," he said, "I don't know."

"And so you put everything you have into a—machine?" Jennie said. "You think it won't ever disappoint you?"

"At least," Harvey said, glaring at her, "I can control what happens to it. That guy that bumped me—I showed *him,* didn't I? Just because *his* car was old—"

"It was new," Jennie started, and then her voice dwindled so he had to lean forward to hear, ". . . once. And I've got news for you," she said, smiling. "How old do you think the things they made your car from are?"

"What?" he said.

"The iron," she said. "It looks new in your car—only because it's been changed from where it was in the hills. For centuries," she said.

Harvey's lips pressed together. Not looking at her, he said: "All I know is—it's something of mine that's new, and I can take care of it."

"Maybe," Jennie whispered, and yet in a way that brought Harvey's head up, "you might find it better to take care of something—human."

"That's the nurse in you talking," Harvey jeered.

"You'll be late if you don't get started," Jennie said.

On his way to work, his eyes were blinded for a moment by a flash of sunlight off the windshield of an oncoming car. Instinctively he turned his head, and when the haze cleared he saw a sign:

PAINT & BODY SHOP

ESTIMATES CHEERFULLY GIVEN

He swung onto the driveway. A man in a gray workshirt, bending over an electric motor vised onto a bench, straightened, wiped his hands on a bit of brown waste, came forward and said, "Somethin' I kin do fer ya, mister?"

Harvey got out, squinted in the morning sun, and reluctantly pointed to the side of his car. "I'm—I might make a claim against somebody for damaging my car, and I wondered. What would it cost to fix this?"

The man looked at him, then squatted on his haunches, his glance following Harvey's pointed finger.

"Well, I dunno," he said.

"You can match the paint?" Harvey asked.

"Sure, sure," the man said. His greasy hand went over the panel, and Harvey made a mental note to wipe the panel as soon as he was out of sight. "Went through to the metal. Have to do the whole side over."

"Yeah, yeah," Harvey said. "How much?"

"Wouldn't do to spot it," the man said. "Would show even worse.

"That's what I thought," Harvey said eagerly. "It's a new car—almost new, you know. I want it to look that way."

The man straightened, and, following his streaked face as it went up, up, and the yellowed teeth showed, Harvey thought, The School Bully. The man put his hands on his hips and surveyed Harvey's car.

"A bastard make," the man said

Carefully, Harvey said, "I've heard of a bastard file, but they usually don't refer to cars that way. You mean—it's made by an independent company?"

"Yeah, a bastard make," the man repeated with rough good humor. "American public, they get their minds made up on a car, can't change 'em." He showed his dirty, broken teeth. "Oh, it's a good car, but you know the public."

"Sure," Harvey agreed warmly. "They even give me dirty looks because my car's different."

The man turned toward his grubby office. Harvey followed. There was the big calendar with the nude, smiling blonde over the grease-spattered desk, and for a moment Harvey's eyes helplessly followed the perfection of contour and unbroken pink skin, and his lips dried a little.

"You just write out the estimate," Harvey said. "Then I'll let you know."

The man coughed, spat out into the yard, laboriously figured with the stump of a pencil, and handed Harvey the greasy, finger-marked paper. He eyed the car again.

"That's a lot of automobile," he said. "Big car."

"I like it," Harvey said.

He drove out of the yard, and in the rear view mirror he saw the man shaking his head before turning back to his bench.

"Dirty slob," Harvey thought.

When he parked at his usual place near the office where he

worked, Harvey went to the side of his car, took out a piece of Kleenex, and carefully wiped off the fingermarks. He looked at the scratch.

He came back and looked at it during his lunch hour. There was a card stuck behind the windshield wiper. He clawed it out and looked at it.

It was a blue-inked duplicate of handwriting, on a postcard. "I can give you more for your car on a trade-in," it said. "See me first. . . ."

Harvey started to walk away. He looked over his shoulder at his car, thought, It gets dusty, just standing, tore up the card and threw the pieces on the street.

He told Jennie about the estimate at the supper table. "I'd hate to get started with that guy," he said. "He'd never match the paint."

He laughed, and Jennie turned to look at him. "Can you imagine saying that about a car?" he said.

"Remember when we had the LaSalle?" Harvey said, and Jennie smiled. "Once I drove it into a garage, and the fella said, 'That's a lot of car for you to handle, sonny.' What are they? *Afraid* to be human? Jealous of a guy with a big car . . . ?"

He broke a piece of bread thoughtfully. "Still, there are advantages to a smaller car. Before the Army, when I had that Chevvy—"

"How do you like the gravy?" Jennie said. "I used less flour."

"It's good," he said. Absently, he pushed the bread back and forth on his plate.

"Fellow at the office has a brother-in-law who has a Chevrolet agency," he said off-handedly.

"I like the Hudson," Jennie said. "It rides so comfortably. I feel good in it."

"But it's such a big car," Harvey said. His eyes gleamed. "It's too big for a little woman like you to handle. You could drive a smaller car easier—park it easier—"

"You never let me drive our car anyhow," Jennie said.

"Not when it's so big," Harvey said.

"You mean if we had a smaller car, you'd let me drive it?"

"Sure," Harvey said.

"Eat your supper," Jennie said.

Before he went to bed, Harvey backed out the car . . . took a soft cloth and wiped the paint again where the greasy man's fingers had defiled it. He worked a little rubbing compound into a damp pad and dabbed into the scratch, over the scratch, around it, gently, wiped it off, then stood back and looked at it.

When he came to bed, Jennie was curled over on her side, her eyes determinedly closed. He sat on the edge of the bed, scraping some of the compound from under his fingernails. He felt the dull ache behind his eyes, got up, washed his hands again, and took two aspirins.

When he came back, Jennie was really asleep.

She was still sleeping when he left in the morning.

As he drove past the paint and body shop where estimates were cheerfully given, he glanced into the yard and saw, as though in slow motion, the greasy man padding toward his bench like a big-buttocked bear.

When he pulled into the driveway late that afternoon, he wondered what Jennie would think, hearing the sound of the strange horn. He leaned on the horn again, savoring the sound, and saw her flitting behind the screen door. She was wriggling a T-shirt over her head.

He leaned out as she opened the screen door, and gave her a big smile . . . just like in the magazine ads, he thought, helplessly. She stood on the porch, her forehead wrinkled.

"Where's our car?" she said. "Did you—it—?" And he laughed at what she must have been thinking.

"It's okay," he said. "Nothing happened."

"Whose car is that?"

He grinned. "It could be ours."

Her hand went out to the porch pillar, where the vine grew, and it wasn't as though she were leaning against it, but growing into it, rooting there.

Harvey got out, leaving the door open invitingly. "You know that fella in the office I was telling you about? Whose brother-in-law has that Chevvy agency? We got to talking, and on the way from work today, I—"

He stopped, watching the way she was twisting the vine.

"Oh, I didn't buy it yet, monkey-face," he laughed. "I'm just taking it for a spin."

Her hand disengaged from the vine, tentatively. "You left our car there?" she said.

"I couldn't drive both of them, could I?" he said, gawping at her comically, and she smiled. "I'm going back to pick it up now. Want to come along?"

"I was ironing."

"Let you drive it back if you want to," he said.

"Just a minute," Jennie said. He watched the screen door slam, then began to walk around the new car, in a slow ellipse. Once, he bent down to examine the paint, and straightened, smiling.

It was smooth, all smooth. Unbroken, like a fresh egg.

Jennie came out, wearing a skirt and sweater, her hair combed up and her lipstick bright against the whiteness of her face. He motioned her behind the wheel but she shook her head.

"No," she said, "I'm not used to it."

"Maybe I better take it first for awhile," he conceded, casually, and rolled carefully down the drive. "It's got that automatic shift, see?"

"It's a pretty color," Jennie said.

"Sure," he said eagerly. "Even better than the Chevvy I had before I went in the Army. That was maroon too, only not as deep as this."

Jennie looked at him, he felt her sideways glance. "You hated to give up that other car, didn't you?" she said.

He leaned back against the new-smelling upholstery. "Yeah. It was like—well, when the guy I sold it to drove it away, it was like the last link to my civilian life being broken.

"I often wondered where that car was, when I came out," he said.

"Getting it back would be like—taking up the pattern again, wouldn't it?" said Jennie.

He looked at her, his jaw dropping a little. He watched the road, squinting, thinking. Then he shook his head.

"Somebody else had it," he said. "It would be all kicked around, the guy had three kids, it wouldn't be the way I kept it.

"No," he said. "It wouldn't be the same.

"You can't go back like that," he said.

"You've got a newer car anyhow," Jennie said.

He was silent, sensing the movement of this other car. Then his head shot up. "My God!" he said. "I left the keys in it."

"They'll be watching it," Jennie said.

"I never did that before," Harvey said. "If it was—if it was stolen. . . ."

He braked up to a light, and looked at her. "Good thing it's insured."

"My bobby pins are in it," she said.

He grinned. "Outside of that, it would be one way of switching to this car without losing anything. We could use the insurance money to—"

"Oh, we wouldn't have to do that!" Jennie said, and then bit her lip.

Inside himself, he grinned triumphantly. "Rides nice, doesn't it?" he said. From his eye-corner he watched her fighting a nod.

"Handles like a baby. I tell you these small cars have got it all over those big ones. Of course, this is plenty big—a full-size car," he added proprietarily.

"Fella told me this is the wise time to trade," he said.

Jennie was scrunched into herself on the seat next to him. Her voice sounded small and quiet above the croon of the humming tires.

"We've owed things for so long. . . .

"I hate to owe things," she said.

He didn't say anything, and then Jennie said, "They've been calling me from the hospital. I guess I could—"

Harvey turned, eagerly, then caught his eagerness half-way around.

"It's up to you," he said casually.

"I don't want you to go back to work just for this," he added.

Jennie shook her head. "I get feeling cooped up, in the house, anyhow. They want me on Third South, seven to three. I always liked working on the medical floor," she said, and added, ". . . anyhow."

She fingered the knob on the handle that rolled the window up and down.

"That way we could catch up faster," she said.

They were coming to the dealer's now, and Harvey saw his car, the one he'd traded the LaSalle for, gleaming and yet not gleaming as he passed it to pull into the garage, and his look flicked over it, and he could see, at least *he* could see, the long uneven scratch on the side.

"If you didn't like nursing, I'd say no," he said.

"I want to do whatever will make you happy," Jennie said.

For a moment Harvey's mood coincided with the movement of the car he was driving going from daylight into the dark of the garage, and he felt as though he were taking his mate out of the sun and into a waiting, unknown cave somewhere.

He looked at her, sitting there, and smelled the newness of the car he was driving, and said, "I'm not good enough for you, not near good enough for you."

Jennie smiled and said, "Oh, I think you are." She looked around, in the big garage, just before the smiling salesman, swooping, reached them, and said, "It's just that you're like a little boy about some things.'

And she didn't say much except "Yes" or "I'm employed as a nurse—that is, I will be, and I have been—" while they were treading through the necessary papers, until they walked toward the deep maroon car that was theirs now, and then she said, "You said I could drive it."

"That's right," Harvey said. He opened the door for her, grandiloquently, and helped her adjust the seat. "You can even drive me to work and take it to the hospital if you want to," he said.

Jennie, busy with the mechanics of becoming part of the traffic's flow, tensed forward behind the wheel. Harvey's hand stole to the glove compartment, to which he had transferred the accumulation from the other car. He opened it, the light went on courteously, and in the soft glow he could see the areas of darkness on the chrome of the flashlight, the dented flashlight, and he thought, I'll have to try to straighten that, now.

Then everything will be fixed up, nice and shining, he thought.

He felt Jennie's elbows, rigid beside him, and blurted out, "Keep to the right," and felt her go even stiffer.

"You get so nervous when I drive," she said.

Watching her neck craning forward, Harvey said, "Why don't *you* relax?"

"Maybe because you never let me relax when you taught me," she said. "Now it's part of my pattern of driving."

He drove the car—silently, dually, tensely, right along with her for the next mile, fighting to keep his hands still, his feet beating a frantic, sympathetic tattoo on the floor mat whenever she slowed down. Until finally she pulled over and sat there, by the curb.

The car crept forward a little, and he said, "Use the hand brake, or shift into neutral."

"*You* drive," she said.

"Had enough, huh?" He got out, and by the time he had come around, Jennie had moved over and was sitting with her hands in her lap.

He grinned, slid behind the wheel and pulled away smoothly. "That's how it's done," he said.

As he pulled into his driveway, with Jennie sitting silently beside him, for a moment out of time the garage seemed to float away and the gray ribbon of drive uncoil endlessly toward it.

And the house inched a little away and shrank into itself, so that

Harvey wanted to take his hands off the wheel and clutch at it, to steady it. But he found himself clutching at his head.

Jennie was on the porch, looking at him, he saw between his fingers. "Come on in," she said. "Have some coffee."

"In a minute," he said. "I want to see if I've enough wax for the bumpers."

He heard the screen door close, and stood by the new car. He looked at the garage and it wavered again, and he put out a hand to steady everything. He felt the cool, satisfying surface of the car beneath his palm. He examined the place his hand had been, and thought, I'll have to wax the whole car.

When he went into the house, Jennie was trying on a nurse's uniform—a flame of white against the dark living room wall.

"It still fits," she said.

He heard the clatter of the mailbox lid outside, and went out to the post by the gate. He stood there, looking about, at the house, at the garage, at the new car in the driveway. He saw that he was holding a long envelope in his hand. He knew what it was.

It was a receipt from the finance company for the last payment on the other car.

There was another envelope, from the Motor Bureau, giving the Cadillac owner's address, but he tore it up, thinking: At least I won't have to call up about a blind man, now. I ought to be able to sleep the sleep of the merciful, letting that woman get away with. . . .

It took him a week to wax the car the way he wanted it—working on it evenings and wishing Jennie would watch instead of going to bed right after supper. But, he considered, maybe she was tired, too.

He hated getting up mornings in the dark. He hated to hear Jennie's voice telling him, "We'll have to start earlier today. I have a staff meeting." He rolled down the drive in the dark, wondering how soon it would be light.

A new pack of drivers were out at this hour, he noticed—

pushing, voracious, scrabbling, frantic to dart under the closing fingers of dawn before they became the hot, hammering fist of day.

He adapted himself to the arhythmic scuffle, telling Jennie, as he did every morning, "This automatic shift makes it easier, doesn't it?" He added, "Wait until the sun really starts coming up. You'll see how that new wax brings out the maroon."

Jennie's fingers laced and unlaced in her lap. Noticing, he said, "I can't go any faster. Seems to be a jam up ahead."

He found an opening and went through it, and a contorted face framed in rusted metal floated past him, barking, "Watch that cutting in and out, what do you think you—?"

This was something he could push against. Harvey leaned out, seeing the oldness of the yammerer's car, correlating it with his hard-won knowledge of the nature of envy, and lashed fiercely, "Aahh, go to—"

He felt a jolt, and read the unholy gleam of anticipated satisfaction in the red face glaring evilly at him.

Afraid, but needing to, he turned his head to see the front of his car cuddling intimately, overlappingly, with the rear of a flat-bed truck.

He heard the clanking dissonance of a metal fan striking the radiator honeycomb, and was out of his car, running.

Savagely, he raced, afoot, trying to overtake the gloating face that, feral and fiendish, fled away laughing. He turned, heard the broken sounds of the metal, clacking, abused, and shouted to Jennie hoarsely, "Turn it off, turn the motor off!"

The truck began to move ahead, a few feet, and Harvey, standing there, wanted, for a wild moment, to leap onto the back of the platform and let it carry him away—away from his ravaged car, and the end of its perfection, away from what he would have to think, and feel, and do, now.

But the truck stopped, and everything was more silent than Harvey could have believed possible with all that traffic, as the first of the cars behind his turned out of line and moved away quietly, almost reverently as one tiptoes past a house with a black wreath, except that he caught the curious, almost consoling glances of the people floating by framed in unbent, shining, not-hurt metal.

He stood there, by the driver's side of his car, and didn't want to go around to the front because, from where he stood, it looked all right, everything looked all right, and there was no knowing what it looked like up ahead.

And he saw Jennie, sitting quietly in her car, her hands folded in her lap, there in her nurse's uniform, and he thought: If I hadn't had to hurry for her this wouldn't—and, if I hadn't met her, if I hadn't married her—and now, up ahead, it's all ruined. And then his thoughts were a jumbled dissonance echoing the death-song of his ruined metal-car, and he saw the truck driver coming toward him.

He felt Jennie getting out and hurrying around to be next to him, and he thought: She's afraid I'll fight.

But all he wanted to do was have everything the way it was, or have somebody tell him it was all right.

The man coming toward him was not so tall, but wide, and his shoulders inside his blue-gray workman's shirt were hunched forward. Then Harvey realized that the big, wind-burned face wore concern and regret, and the glance, as it passed the car's front, mirrored what it meant to a machine to be wrecked.

And Harvey reached out and put his hand on the big shoulder, and said, "I try to do the right thing, and then this happens, it wasn't your fault. I wasn't looking.

"I didn't hurt your truck, did I?" Harvey said. "It's all right, isn't it?"

Somehow this man's shoulder radiated a brotherliness, and Harvey thought with a helpless feeling: He knows all about me.

Softly, the truck driver was saying, "You should never drive so close to the back of a truck, fella."

Then another part of Harvey answered: He can be calm, I didn't hurt his truck, that's the way you can be when you're too big to be hurt, the big Brother.

And Jennie and the truck driver were talking in low tones,

arranging things, so he felt like a patient beside whose bed the doctor and nurse are in conference.

He forced himself to walk over to where they were standing, and then he turned and looked. And maybe because he had expected anything, it was only as bad as the end of the world, and not worse:

His hood, the shining hood, was crumpled and pushed back, and both headlights were dented and broken. Some inside part of him was trying, with thoughts only, to put it back together, to make it perfect, the way it was.

He heard the truck driver say again, in that amazingly sensitive, low voice, "You'd better pull it off the road, bud," and he got in and sat behind the wheel, but felt powerless.

And when he started the motor, he felt it wasn't to go anywhere, but it would drag itself, crippled, away from where life was going on and on, and he found a gas station driveway there by the side, so he pulled into it.

The station attendant, a short, fat little man waddled over and spoke to Harvey through the window. "You'd better park by the side, so you're out of the way," and Harvey thought: If I were buying gas he would say "Sir."

But Harvey moved dully, in his car, to where he would be out of the way.

He thought he would sit and wait for Jennie to come back, she was still talking to the truck driver. But he wanted to get out and look again, too, because maybe it wasn't so bad. But it was, because he heard a new sound as he got out, the sound of water splashing, and there was a puddle under the front of the car, a rusty puddle, so he knew his car had been hurt internally.

And the water sound acted on him, standing tight there, so that suddenly, helplessly, he found he was shaking, and his cheeks were wet.

He was still trying to stop crying when Jennie came up. He took out his change purse and thrust a dime at her. "Here," he said. "Call the auto club. They'll take it away."

Jennie looked at him. She took the dime, went to her side of the car, fumbled in her purse and took out a small white tablet. "Here, honey, take this," she said. "Go ahead, take it."

Meekly, he took the barbiturate, swallowed it dry, and it burned bitter on his tongue. He looked about and saw a water fountain beside the station. He went over and bent down. The liquid spurted into his hot mouth.

He straightened, hearing shuffling feet coming toward him. It was the fat attendant.

"It ain't gonna be there long, is it?" the attendant said.

"They'll take it away," Harvey said. He had to talk. "Look at it," he told the attendant.

"Yeah," the fat man said. "Wrecked, all right."

"They'll fix it," Harvey argued.

"Oh, they know how to fix things, all right," the fat man said, adding, "only it ain't never just the same."

"It'll look all right," Harvey said, hating the fat man, wondering why he was talking to him. He saw Jennie, a flash of white in the phone booth. He went to the booth and opened the door, pushing at it, saying, "Tell them to hurry. Hurry, hurry!"

He went around the corner of a shed next to the station, sat on a packing box and looked over the unkempt, weedy fields bordering the airport. There, with no one to see him, his shoulders began to shake, and he moaned.

Just as he felt he would begin to howl, raging, in that open space, Jennie came to him and said, "Don't you want to sit in the car?"

"I want to go home," Harvey said.

"We will," she told him. "Just as soon as the—as the man comes. We'll both take the day off."

"What about your meeting?"

"I called them up and told them."

They heard a horn, and it was the tow truck. Harvey watched the giant hook, and the chain, gripping his helpless car, attaching it in odious familiarity to this whining crane, and he didn't want to look any more.

Jennie was talking to the driver of the tow truck, and then she came over and took Harvey's arm. She had his arm, and some iron hand had his temples pinched between pressing fingers. The barbiturate burned in his stomach. He trudged dully with her toward the bus stop, hearing the tow truck turn and maneuver out of the driveway.

A gray shape they were passing stirred, and it was the greasy man, astride his driveway, wiping his hands on his buttocks. His eyebrows went up as he saw Harvey, and his head jerked toward the tow truck going by, with its helpless freight still shining newly.

"You in that?" the greasy man asked. Harvey nodded. He saw recognition crawl into the greasy man's smile, and heard the words from a long way off.

"What happened to the Hudson?"

Harvey felt Jennie's fingers on his arm, and he looked at the man, the greasy man, and said, "The ash trays were full."

The bus bore down on them with a loud, cold swooping of dirty wind. He fumbled in his pocket, stumbling up the steps, and the driver muttered something about how much the fare was. Harvey had a quarter and a dime, and he dropped them both into the grinding, ruminative box, and told the driver, "I got some change coming," but Jennie said, "Never mind," and pulled at his arm, so they walked back, past the iron-jawed driver, and he slumped into the soiled seat.

By the time he was sitting at the kitchen table, sipping his hot coffee, the pill he had taken made a gentle haze behind his eyes, and relaxed the hand at his temples. He looked at Jennie.

"They'll fix it," she said.

"It'll never be the same," Harvey said. "You'd think I could keep something the same, without having it banged up. But, no."

"It's only a material thing," Jennie said.

"It means something," Harvey said. "It means—"

"What?" Jennie said.

He looked out the window, at the clouds, and at the trees

against the sky. The pill was making him sleepy, and he felt a little sick.

"When I was a kid, and I got sick, my mother used to get sore at me about it, like I was letting her down," he told Jennie.

She didn't say anything, but got up and poured hot water for her tea and sat down again. She spooned sugar into the cup and started to stir, then she put the spoon down, quickly.

"You didn't know my mother," he said. "You didn't know my father either, really, just when he was an old, old man.

"I used to wait for him to come home from work, when I was little," Harvey said, "and I'd run to meet him. And one day he brought me home this kite, in the Spring. It was a big kite, all the other kids had little kites with plain brownish paper, or else some market would give them a kite with the market's name all over it.

"But this was a beautiful big store-bought kite, with pink tissue paper.

"He never gave me stuff, usually, my father, or paid much attention to me, it seemed, but this kite—"

Jennie spooned sugar into her tea, started to stir it, then realized she had already put sugar in. She watched Harvey listening to something, to the wind, or the trees waving, or to a little boy that was, carrying a big pink kite that rustled and skittered in a whisper, a delicious whisper of tissue.

"That same afternoon," Harvey said, "right after my father gave it to me, I took the kite, and with a little string tied to it sort of trotted along, pulling it. And it flipped over, sideways, and hit the ground.

"I ran over to it and when I picked it up maybe my thumb went through it, but there was this hole in it. Just a little hole you could hardly see the sky through, in one corner.

"There was this big, beautiful kite, that my father gave me, but now it wasn't perfect any more. It was hurt, and not whole any longer, I don't know.

"I could see that it needed a patch," Harvey said, "and I saw how the patch would look on it, not smooth and pink any more, and that got me sore, so I started to pull it, and tear at it, and it hurt *me* to do it, but I couldn't stop.

"And then I just ripped it apart, crying, because my father had given it to me, and it meant he loved me, and now here I'd taken this beautiful perfect thing and ruined it."

Harvey put his hand up to his hot face, and felt that he was smiling. He looked at Jennie, wishing she would smile, and grateful to her for being there, and sorry because she looked as if she couldn't smile and it was his fault.

"My father came out, and instead of getting sore, he saw me crying and promised to get me another kite, just like it.

"But I knew it wouldn't be the same. It would be the *second* kite. And I wanted *that* kite, *that* kite. . . . but I had ruined it, the first kite.

"Then this kid in the neighborhood came up, and he'd been watching, and he asked me what I was going to do with what was left of my kite, the sticks and what was left of the tissue. I told him to take it, he could have it. He said he'd patch it up. He said I should have put a tail on it, and it wouldn't have flipped over."

He laughed, coughingly. "The little scavenger!"

Harvey put his hand up to his hot face, feeling the muscles working, felt them tighten against his palm in a kind of humorless grin.

"What am I?" he said, not knowing quite what he meant, wanting to keep talking, and maybe the pill . . .

Jennie picked up her spoon, then put it down again.

"A perfectionist," she said, so quietly he had to lean forward.

"That's what I am, a perfectionist," he said. "Is that good?"

"Look what it's doing to you," Jennie said.

"I can't help it," he said. He looked at her. "How about you? You can't stand to get your hands dirty. Always washing them, and you a nurse."

"Everybody's funny," he said. "About some things, anyhow."

Jennie looked at her hands, with their long, slim white fingers.

"You're a perfectionist," she repeated, half to herself. "And you think because I'm a nurse I don't mind seeing things broken. Because people come into the hospital that way . . ." her voice trailed off.

"You think I don't know about wanting things beautiful?" she said, and Harvey, half drowsing, felt he needn't answer. He heard her through a thick blanket of warmth and haze, and her voice had a strangely ethereal quality he had never heard before.

"I've thought about . . . being beautiful," she went on. "I know I'm not. You think I don't know anything about what some poets say. But I do. I know someone said beauty was truth. I don't care.

"I think nothing is beautiful unless you use it," she said. "I think that . . . beauty is *use*. And that use is beauty.

"People grow old," Jennie said, "and things, houses, cars, get used, and the scratches are all right, and the—the wrinkles mean you've lived."

Harvey's head felt heavier than he could support, and the hand had left his temples and was pushing him down, down in his chair. He thought he heard Jennie going on, and on, but wasn't sure, and thought he saw her pick up her spoon and begin to stir, and the milky-brown liquid swirl in her cup.

He felt caught in a whirlpool, and knew he would stay that way, half drowning, until he saw his car again—until he saw it, nice, and new, and shining—

And Jennie's voice was a thin thread of sound still, like one high note in his brain:

"I almost wrote a poem about what we talked about once," she was saying. ". . . about how your car was *never* new, but made from old things changed. . . .

"I thought, People are made of materials old but changed, too. People are born, and what are they? Made of things that were changed—from a bit of flower, their skin, a piece of lettuce, for each finger, or eyelash, once, maybe, a sprig of heather grew on a mountain. . . .

"For each hair, something of a Brown-eyed Susan, for each toenail—" She laughed. "I almost wrote a poem, once. Once, I almost —I almost. . . ."

And in the land where Harvey listened, part drawn to darkness, he may have heard a woman crying, but when he woke, later, in their bed, he was never very sure what Jennie had said. Or that she had said anything at all.

He had paid the fifty-dollar deductible to the man called "Ernie" in the little office of the garage the auto club had sent his car to; and then Ernie had said his car was waiting, "just as good as new," parked by the school playground, across the street from the garage.

It was the children's lunch hour, and Harvey saw them hitting a ball around near the row of parked cars. He made himself watch them, steadily, until he was closer, then he forced himself to look.

And there it was. His car. He saw the front, all fixed up, just as Ernie had said. And it was the same, yet not the same, because he knew about it.

Did the curve of the hood seem a bit sharper? Yet it was smooth. Smooth and gleaming. Ernie came up, and yes, Harvey told Ernie, it was a good job.

And for a moment Harvey felt free and good, knowing that things can be fixed up, like new. Just like new.

But with Ernie talking to him there, he knew he wouldn't be able to *really* examine his car until he got alone with it. And maybe then he would find a thousand little imperfections he wasn't noticing now, with Ernie there, telling him, "If it isn't exactly right, you just bring it back."

And it *wasn't* just exactly right, because when he was in the privacy of his own driveway he saw that there was a lighter spot on the hood, and one on the fender, and another, when the sun hit it, at a certain angle. So now he would have to go back to Ernie who, whether he liked it or not, would have to make it right.

Harvey chose a time to go back when he figured the sun would hit it at an angle sure to show up the defective spots. He didn't want to have to argue with Ernie. Ernie somehow reminded him of the truck he had crashed against—immovable if his mind were made up. And Harvey didn't want to get into a rage and have to go crashing against anything.

But Ernie was all right. Surprisingly, he saw the light spots—"holidays," he called them, and sure, he'd take care of it. But his wife's father was ill, and so it would have to be a while from now.

It would be fixed, though, Harvey told himself. It would be as good as new. But when he went to work and parked by the usual curb, he got out and left his keys in the car and had to go back for them. Then he stood on the sidewalk, watching the way the light made pools of difference on the formerly pristine gleam of his car.

He drove to the hospital to pick up Jennie, hating, as he did every day, to call for her because she looked so tired coming toward him through the black arch of the high, wrought iron gates.

Waiting for her, he saw the student nurses swing across the street on their way to classes, their bright, high young voices lilting, and their strong, tireless legs flashing in the white stockings. He scrunched lower behind the wheel, following them in the rear-view mirror, thinking how Jennie must have looked at that age.

Not that she wasn't still young—younger than himself, he amended. He recalled suddenly, for no reason, how oddly she had acted when they had sat in the kitchen after the accident. Had she said something about beauty—and how it was good to grow old and be useful?

Or had he, under the powerful pill's influence, been imagining that his good, practical, useful nurse-wife had been talking poetry, and about people being born from old things? . . .

He shifted uncomfortably because she'd never been this late. Then there she was, and he couldn't be angry because she was smiling.

She was still smiling, dreamily, as he pulled into their driveway. Opening the door for her, he pointed to the imperfect blending of paint and said, "Look, see how the sun shows it up?"

"Let's go inside," Jennie said, and her voice was soft.

"You didn't look at the car," he said.

"Never mind the car," Jennie said, and he followed her into the house, looking at the car from the porch, to see if it was noticeable from there.

"Well, what is it?" he said, because Jennie was standing there, in the living room, looking at him expectantly.

"Sit down," she said.

She stood there, smiling at him, and then she said, "I had to go down to first-aid today. I got dizzy and started to faint."

"You're working too hard," he said. "You take nursing too seriously, maybe you—"

"I'm going to have a baby," she said.

He looked at her. She was standing there, smiling at him, and he was trying to recognize her words. He wanted to say, Where are you going to get it? But he thought of something, and he said, "How could that be possible?"

"Something must have slipped," Jennie said.

Harvey felt that he should lift her up and whirl her around, and then be comical and pretend she was made of filigree glass, just like in the movies. He wanted, too, to argue with her, to tell her to wait because he didn't feel ready yet.

But because he had to do something, he got up and put his arm around her shoulders and said, "You'd better take it easy now."

"Oh, I'm all right," Jennie said. "I can even keep working."

"You don't really have to," he said.

"It would help," Jennie said. She glanced at him, then away quickly. "How do you feel?" she asked.

She was looking at him again, and he knew she expected something, so he pulled her to her feet, and lifted her, grinning helplessly, holding her tightly, and then whirling her around, in her white uniform, whirling her around and around, until she was laughing, and in the circle of his arms, as he turned, watching the walls spin, the colors flashing like a child's Fourth-of-July firewheel, in a dizzy tourbillion around, around.

Ernie's father-in-law felt worse for a week, so Harvey had to wait, and then the week after that, the old man died, and Harvey fretted through the mourning period, his glance sliding over his car, pondering how all these things, these people he never knew, kept perfection from him.

But in time, Harvey knew, people adjust to death, he had only to wait. And he wondered, the day he finally *did* drive his car to Ernie's to be repainted, why he felt that somehow that old man's death had made him wait until it seemed it was too long . . . too long with an imperfect car.

Then, the next day, when he came toward his car again, seeing the children in the playground, he looked at them and tried to smile at them, feeling fatherly, while he was wondering what the car would look like this time. They were hitting the ball close to the parked row of automobiles, and he kept smiling at them until they saw him, and his smile, when they moved away to where their ball couldn't hit the cars.

Ernie, who was walking with him, was saying, "I repainted the front fenders and hood—the whole thing. There's plenty of paint on it now."

"It looks fine," Harvey said, knowing he couldn't look at it until he was by himself.

"Remember," Ernie told him, "bring it back, if you're not satisfied."

He repainted the whole thing, Harvey kept telling himself as he drove to pick up Jennie. I don't even *have* to look at it. It *must* be all right. It's like new. . . .

. . . And there was Jennie, still slim, but not smiling as she came toward him from the hospital.

He didn't want to ask her, because he knew, but he said, "How was it today?" And she said, tonelessly, "All right, just a little nauseated."

"Does riding in the car bother you?" he asked her. "Is it a little rough?"

She was looking at her hands—the long, slim fingers waxen and white in her lap. From his eye corner he saw them, too quiet, as she was.

"Doesn't quite ride the way a bigger car would, does it?" he said. "Of course, it's safe enough," he added. "It's plenty safe."

Jennie went into the house quickly, and he lingered in the drive, fighting to keep from looking back. When he went to put the car away, he took a quick look.

And the "holidays" were all out; it seemed all right.

"It seems all right," he said in a low voice to himself, parked at his usual place before work in the morning. And when he stood back, looking at it, the sun shone on the maroon, and where the fender ended and the door began, it was darker. The whole front was lighter, on the right side.

"The whole front's lighter," he told Ernie, and the big man stood back, squinting, hands on hips, chafed red elbows out like the danger lights on a truck.

"It'll darken down," Ernie assured him. "You just give it a trial and see. Wait—oh, say, three months, and then if you're not satisfied, bring it back."

That's reasonable, Harvey told himself. That's as much as anyone could ask. And when he got to where he parked for the day, he walked away from his car. Then he turned, came back, opened the glove compartment, and took out the dented flashlight.

It jingled against the keys hanging from the ignition as he turned to leave.

He put the flashlight in his desk at the office. And all through the day he heard the keys jingling until, in the late afternoon, when he came to where he'd left his car, the jingling stopped because the car was gone.

Jennie came toward him where he was sitting on the bench outside the hospital gate, and he said, "We'll have to take the bus home. The car's been stolen."

He helped her up the high metal steps, with the cold gaseous wind of the bus exhaust beating about them. And Jennie didn't say anything except, "I wish it wouldn't jiggle so much," until they got home, when she said, "I'm going to lie down."

Harvey came in and stood at the bedroom door, looking down at her. She was smiling at him, in the semi-darkness. "It's nothing," Jennie said. "I just had a little emesis at work today."

"It was the bus," Harvey said. "Riding on that bus—we'll get another car, and it'll be easier on you."

He sat on the edge of the bed and took her hand. "The insurance money will take care of the down-payment. We won't lose anything.

"How did it happen?" Jennie said.

He shrugged. In the dimness, she might not have seen the whole meaning of the shrug, so he shrugged again and said, "It was a good-looking car. You know how car thieves operate."

She looked at him. "Did you—"

"What?"

"Nothing." She clutched his hand tighter. "Maybe a little soup—" He had to lean close to catch the words.

From the kitchen, he called in to her, "This time I'll make sure we've got plenty of weight in the old bus. That's how you can depend on safety.

"We might as well get the best. Then you know you've got something," he said, bringing the pan with the canned soup in it along, so he could stand by the bedroom door, looking at her, and stirring it.

And as he stirred it, around and around, everything was whirling again, the earth turning, and circles inside circles, wheels within wheels. . . .

When Jennie said, "I can't get up," the next morning, he called the doctor.

"She's having some difficulty, Mr. Russell," the doctor said, but Harvey had heard Jennie saying, in a small voice, to the doctor in the bedroom, "It's *hyperemesis gravidarum*, isn't it?"

"That's the way it is sometimes during the first three months," he told Harvey. "She'll need intravenous fluids, and care—I think she'd be better off at the hospital."

"I don't want to go to the hospital," Jennie said, and the doctor smiled.

"Never saw a nurse that did," the doctor said, and as he shrugged into his coat, he added, casually, "I'll arrange a room."

Harvey followed him out, and stood watching, as the doctor got into his car.

He stood in the driveway, watching the doctor's car float away, thinking: that's the kind of car to have. Big. Strong. Shining.

He went back into the house, and Jennie's face was white against the whiteness of the pillow. "I've got to go to work," he said.

"I'll be all right," Jennie said.

He poured a spoonful of her medicine into a glass, added some water and stirred, watching the greenish liquid swirl and turn, and he looked at it, one part of him thinking: How can she drink that stuff, it smells, I hope it cures her. . . .

. . . And he was thinking, too: Green is a good color for a car.

He left work early, to visit the dealer he'd phoned from the office, and it felt good standing on the shining floor near these big, new machines.

The salesman had said, "Try it, Mr. Russell, go ahead, show it to your wife."

He drove it home carefully, in no time finding himself floating, in the slanting sunlight, up the driveway in this car that gleamed as though it had been dipped in honey, from its exhaust the sound of a thousand happy, swarming bees.

He got out, slammed the door, listening to the solidity of it, and stood back, devouring the eager lines, thinking: There's nothing like a Cadillac, wait until I tell Jennie.

She was lying the same way, against the pillow, as he came into the darkened room, and he thought: She won't be able to get up to look at it, she may not want me to buy it, it's more than the insurance on the other car.

"I never thought having a baby would be this tough," she was saying.

"You'll be all right," he started to say, and the phone was ringing in the hall.

"If that's the hospital, I don't want to go to the hospital," Jennie said when he came back into the room. "It's hard enough to wor—" and she stopped, her eyes big in her white face, looking at him.

"It wasn't the hospital," she said.

He sat on the edge of the bed, looking at her. Her hand was moist against his.

"It was the police," Harvey said. "They recovered the car. They called to say they're sending it over."

He turned away, because Jennie was smiling, so she couldn't see the draining away that was going on in him. He went down the front steps, and down the drive, past the quiet, gleaming machine in its glowing perfection, to where the *other* car was being parked by the curb.

There it was: the *other* car, no longer radiating possession to him, being vacated now by a big policeman who walked up to him, explaining.

"Some kids got hold of it. Took it on a joyride. A real bender. They didn't do too much to it. You're lucky to get it back so soon."

He saw the dent in the fender, the right fender where the maroon darkness had changed in the sunlight, and the cop was saying, "It can be hammered out, all right. Guess your insurance will take care of it. Sign this, please."

And as he stood there, in the dark, signing the white sheet, he could smell the stale beer odors, and sense the pocking cigarette burns and blotting stains, the finger smudges and scuffed, kicked places—all the savage brands that had ravaged a perfection that was no more.

He didn't get into it, but stood by it, the car that had returned, listening to the creaking of the motor as it cooled.

Then he walked up the drive and opened the door of the Cadillac. He sank behind the shining wheel, enwombed in silent, seamless strength, cradled, drenched in the aroma of shining newness.

He stared over the lengthening hood. It was quiet, and there was only the wind, with the leaves scudding on the sleeping street, skittering and skipping and going to mold somewhere, so the earth could remold them—

He released the handbrake gently, so that it slid back soundlessly into its oiled slot. A leaf crunched, crackling under the wondrously-treaded tires as he let the big car roll back down the drive and into the street.

But a leaf that moved with the wind might never turn to mold, he told himself. There ought to be something in the world that could be kept safe and inviolate. . .

. . . And maybe if he and this machine kept moving, nothing could harm them—they could move like planets in their orbits, like meteors—

In the west, the clouds were purpling among panels of golden light. He saw the trembling needle of the gauge on the dash rising to the full mark as the key turned.

. . . Even dust could not settle on them, if they moved fast enough, away, and if anyone or even anything got in the way, they would go faster. . . .

. . . Faster, and if this machine, that was a part of him now, got hungry, it could feed from his own blood, he felt it—

The big motor awoke to young, eager, unprotesting life against his fingers on the new-minted key. As he passed the house, he saw that it was silent and dark, and he tried to tell himself he wondered who lived there.

He had a lot of driving to do before it would become light. His foot lifted from the accelerator, as he thought: Fast enough, and even light can't hurt us, we can stay in the dark, safe there, forever.

Then his foot pressed down on the accelerator, tentatively at first, then welded to it in a mounting kiss as the perfect car glided westward.

Faster, faster and faster. Away from hurt and imperfection, and the sounds of leaves breaking and women's voices Harvey drove, and the gray road unfolded endlessly into the night, away from the sun forever.

No dust, or moist or molded leaves, or mud to mar their journey now. The quivering needle telling speed pressed hard around the dial, the swift soft wind was dry and cool on Harvey's forehead.

Smiling triumphantly, he closed his eyes.

YOU GET SO HUNGRY

SOMEONE, shrieking miles of pulsing wire and tortured air away, had managed this broadcast braying now—this bobbling of larynx and brass-captured wind, just as someone had managed to put him here, on his back.

But he could still fight (Ted told his fighting self). He reached out to smash the glowing glass-and-copper-wire guts that were warm, human warm.

Being a machine, *it* might have to accept this—this "song." Not he!

And then he remembered where he was.

Oriented, consequence-knowing, he only leaned forward to turn the radio lower, so that he could hear the doctor's answer. What had he asked the good doctor? "Who is managing this farce, this program I never wanted to create?"

No.

It was something else: a question about the second drive.

"The insulin," answered the doctor, "draws the sugar from your blood. And that's why you get so hungry."

Ted said, "I see."

He was lying in the downstairs front room of the private nursing home in Sacramento. Through the window's heavy screen he heard the papery, protesting rustle of the fiery liquid amber leaves: scarlet palms bled of their green summer's blood, pointing accusing fingers in anger at the slanted sun.

He saw them, skimming and skittering, reflected from the bureau's mirror. The waver of the quicksilver made them like the mortar flames he had seen as he lay face down against the ice of a rutted Korean road. The flames had burned against the ice in brief ballet.

But the smell now was not the acrid sulphur of exploded powder; it was the dust of musty curtains, unwaxed hallways dark and airless, bathtub rings unscoured, stale unstarched sheets and nurses' sweat.

Now that the radio's bleat was muted, visiting voices on the porch mingled with the clatter of kitchen crockery, and the doctor's voice had said again, quite patiently: "That's why you get so hungry."

Yes, the insulin, of course. It wasn't appetite, then; not his stomach nerves sending signals up through axons and dendrites, telling synapses of emptiness and a longing for fulfillment, but something squeezed from a dead hog. Or was it a steer?

The doctor watched him picking at the dry chicken the nurse had brought.

"Of course, you're not getting any of the deep shocks. We have them bring you the sweetened orange juice in plenty of time."

What would happen, Ted heard a voice from the center of the earth say; but from the doctor's face he knew no voice had spoken. The doctor was watching him, sucking on his stout, curved pipe, his stout, curved lips moist under the bulbous nose, and between them the shaggy mustache.

He wanted to ask the doctor another, very important question. Was it about his dream: of the way someone was managing his life's program, the long table in the nightmare office and the empty, dissected body on the table, its too-familiar face not authoritative now, and Ted was stuffing the moist cadaver with pages neatly lined with dialogue for radio?

No. "What would happen," Ted said, "if they didn't bring the orange juice in time?"

The doctor slapped together the sides of his shiny little black bag. "Oh, you'd go into a coma. But that isn't necessary. You're coming along fine."

"That's good," Ted said. He liked this doctor. Much better than the other one. The other one had never given him a chance to talk much, during their brief conferences; he had always taken his incoming calls, which were from richer patients (possibly managers of better programs), while Ted sat there, and the slaughtered tatters of foetal phrases went wailing away somewhere so that when the doctor turned back to Ted and folded his hands over his paunch and said, "Now, where were we?" Ted didn't know where they were.

This one had a paunch too, but his broad fat face smiled, and the head nodded, like a benevolent Buddha, nodding and nodding when Ted put the hard coins of his neurosis into the slotted belly.

"Now be sure and get up after your meal, Ted. Get some air. Your father's waiting for you in the back yard."

He watched the doctor's broad back move into the hallway, and the room became a little smaller, and he suddenly felt the cold spoon in his hand, the tray heavy on his knees. Spooning and spooning, he chased the syrupy bread pudding that was dessert. It slid around the dish. He slipped off the bed.

Voices in the hallway reached him faintly; he turned the radio even lower.

"I want to see you before you go, doctor." It was the big blonde Angeline—restless occupant of the room across the hall. Her voice was high and light, and if Ted hadn't been so aware of her appearance, he would have imagined a birdlike woman with tiny, darting eyes.

But Angeline was tall, a Callipygian goddess to grace the prow of any surging man-of-war. Her eyes were large and pale blue—usually open a little wider than seemed necessary.

Ted liked to watch her move away from him in her tight blue skirt. He had watched her phantom sisters move away from him across the rutted rice paddies and frozen marshes near Combat Hill, and known they weren't there, then, only the earthswelling hills and people to kill.

Angeline: A Valkyrie hovering far from Valhalla, frenzied by who knows what mad whims of Loki, lost and looking for Odin, here in this nursing home in California—and jolted daily through paste-smeared temples by bolts of Thor from uncaring cathodes.

"You can go home next Friday, Angeline," the doctor's voice drifted through the open door.

"There was this fellow before I met Fred," Angeline was telling the doctor.

"Yes, Angeline. We talked about that in my office."

"And I wanted to marry him, but his mother wouldn't let us. Then I met Fred."

Ted turned off the radio.

"Every once in a while I keep thinking of him. This fellow before I met Fred."

"That's only natural," the doctor's voice said.

A *natural hunger*, some voice from earthcenter was saying.

"Maybe I should have waited for him, doctor. Until his mother died."

Or killed his mother, the voice from the center of the earth said. Ted turned the radio on, and the radio said, *Thou shalt not covet thy fellow nursing-home inmate*, before it warmed up. But Ted was too smart, he knew it was just someone managing the program again, daring him now to reach in and claw out the trembling wires that hummed and sang. He turned the volume up, and the sound washed over him, helping him to the earth, now . . .

. . . now voices from the back of the house sifted through the hallway.

"I'll drive you back, doctor," Fred's voice said. The voice was tenor, the man, small; Ted remembered his blondness, his good, strong masculine features, molded to smile beneath a crisp-visored cap on any billboard, the eye-corners crinkling and Fred saying, "Fill 'er up, sir? Check your oil? Well now, it all depends on what we find when we take it apart."

Ted had seen Angeline sitting on the lap of this sturdy, small garage-mechanic of a Fred in the back yard one afternoon. His thighs had throbbed as he watched her, squirming and turning to talk over her shoulder to her husband.

Listening now, he heard Fred; he heard the doctor, not meaning to overhear, but listening because they were *real* voices (or were they part of some giant program, being managed by a not-caring director who—the name, it almost came through, now).

The name of the one to blame.

Fred: "No, doc, I ain't worried about her, not the way I used to."

The sound of water upstairs for a moment, a patient taken from a rubber sheet, and sweat washed off onto ringed porcelain, bubbling gurgles, then Fred's voice again:

"I guess the only time I was worried—really worried, you know, was when she was going to have the first baby. You know, how they say about it being inherited.

"And then I kept thinking, the closer she got to having it, how she was so—well, when it was born, that would be it. I mean, I'd have this kid, and with her being my wife, and all . . ."

Yes, expressive, coherent Fred, that would be it all right, Fred. *And all the other hungers going hungry?*

Ted heard the voices moving off through the front door and away. He wanted to call out to Fred, to tell him: You inherit it from people who manage their lives, it isn't the blood, not the blood! Then he remembered that his father was waiting for him.

He let his bare feet slide into slippers, and padded through the dark hallway, down the echoing wooden steps into the back yard.

His father was sitting in the swing, which had two seats and a slatted floor, letting it sway gently back and forth, bending and bowing in the structure, the wood going *creak, creak* as if it were the old bones, amplified by a prankster engineer, the old bones scraping across dry tendons.

In the middle of a bow his father stopped, seeing Ted.

"Did you see the doctor?" the old man said.

Ted slumped onto the other seat of the swing and nodded.

And, nodding and bowing, they moved in the wooden womb of the device, the old man's gray hair wisping and fluttering, the thick veins on the spotted knuckles pulsing, the sun glancing off the thick disks of his horn-rimmed glasses.

He saw the papery skin stretched thin over the shining forehead, pinkly bare, his father's shadowed temples, and the wasted, wrinkled wattle under his sagging chin. Ted breathed deeply of the November air, took a walnut from his pocket, placed it between his palms, put them in a praying position and tried to crack it.

The shell hurt his hands, and he felt his fury mounting. If he became angry enough, he thought, the strength would come to his hands.

His father waited, then smiled. "Here, let me try it." He took the walnut, cracked it, then handed the pieces to his son.

"You get weak, all right," Ted said.

"Does it hurt?" his father asked.

Ted shook his head. "You just go to sleep. Sort of a warm, buzzing sleep. Then you wake up, after awhile. And you're hungry."

"Very hungry?" The old man was frowning.

Ted looked at him, and the voice said: *The deer in the forest and the papa deer, and the papa bird to the nest, bringing food, and why should you work all your life and care for your young and worry, and pay money just to get hungry?*

Loudly, to drown it out, Ted said, "The first morning I didn't know why I was so hungry. The male nurse who gave me the first shot told me it was Vitamin B. But I had a sort of an idea that this was 'it.' "

It was only his own voice now, so he said more quietly, "I woke up sweating a little. Later I was just bathing in sweat—that's part of it, the sweat. But—"

The center of the earth interrupted: *cast out of paradise, now, by the sweat of your brow, in the sweat of thy face shalt thou eat bread . . .*

"But," he said doggedly, "it was the hunger that woke me up.

I started to dream about food. Not just dream, you know, but I *wanted* to eat. More than anything I ever wanted before in my whole life."

Angeline, the voice from the center of the earth said.

"It gives you a good appetite?" his father asked.

"That isn't the idea," Ted said, thinking of the dry, hairy chicken he had just forced himself to eat. "It's a desperate kind of hunger. I started to think about food. Any kind. Then sort of concentrated on hamburgers. I wanted a million hamburgers. All with the works on them.

"Then I wanted marshmallows—the candy-coated kind with the fudge centers. I felt as though I'd do anything to satisfy that hunger."

He looked at the old man, not seeing him.

"Anything," he said again, and the old man's pasted-on smile slipped a little more.

"You mustn't eat until they bring you the orange juice," his father warned. "The doctor told me that."

"I know," Ted said.

He felt tired. Talking was hard, he thought. Maybe because his father was so hard of hearing. He'd been raising his voice, and that took too much energy now.

He saw that his father had been leaning forward on the edge of the swing, and thought vaguely that perhaps the old man would have felt better if he had told him, "I hurt here, in my head," or, "My back hurts."

He sat back in the swing, and let his father's restlessness move them back and forth in an arc.

Two doors down, across the green yards, Ted saw a man and a woman emerge from an apartment house. He saw they were carrying beach chairs, and saw them set up a little table.

He watched them idly for a moment. Then he stiffened, and the swing lurched abruptly.

"What is it?" His father looked up, his hearing-aid cord slapping the side of his neck.

But Ted had slumped back. He didn't care. Maybe it was that damned insulin. Maybe it was everything he'd been through that had given him this new state of mind.

Mind, he thought, and his lips curved.

His father started the swing going gently, tentatively: (*from hand on the cradle to knife in the rib; run soon as you're able, the killer from crib*) Ted knew the rhyme had been soundless, though it had reverberated inside his skull, and was clanging still, like gongs struck in an endless cave, shivering and vibrating from each other, *woom, wooom!*

"Know who's over there?" Ted asked quietly. Too quietly.

His father craned his neck in the familiar arc of the deafened.

"Reese," Ted said. "Norbert Reese." (And the gongs in the cave sang *Reeeese,* like a furious wind through iron trees.)

"Oh," his father said. Then he sat up suddenly, and the swing lurched.

"Oh," his father said again.

"Yes," Ted said. He added, after a moment, "He doesn't see us. That's Mrs. Reese with him."

The yard was quiet. Bees murmured in the dusk, and a few crickets prodded ajar the gates of evening with tentative, atonal creaks of their hinges. An ant ran up a blade of grass and then ran down again on the other side, and Ted remembered an ant that had done just that an inch from his nose as he crouched in a Pyongyang foxhole at dawn.

Reese, Ted thought. Three years of radio. Big deal. Program manager Norbert Reese, giving him a break as a network writer.

Ted had been just a kid, too poor and too tired to finish his last year of college, and radio had seemed like the spires and minarets of the promised city—distant, golden, hunger-fulfilling. So he had begun:

A few playlets sold to a local station, and then:

"How'd you like to write a soap-opera?" Reese's reedy voice on the phone, the lure of ready cash, the promise of some recognition, some yes I am working, I am writing for radio, for the Associated

Broadcasting Company of America Incorporated and their big buildings and their smiling secretaries, and I belong, yes!

Coast-to-coast, over the jagged blue mountains, with lightning tourbillion, across the crackling black wire-nerves on killed-tree poles, with millions of mosquitoes dipping humming needles, I belong!

"I'll help you along with it, at first," Reese had said.

That's how the collaborating byline got in the script: "By Norbert Reese and Ted Cotting." But it hadn't been too long before Ted had been writing the story, knocking out all the scripts . . .

SOUND: OF JENNIE IN THE KITCHEN, AND THE HUNGRY SCRAPE OF DISHES BEING CLEANED . . . OF JENNIE IN THE PARLOR, AND THE HUNGRY LICKING OF THE CHOPS OF THE SLICKER FROM THE CITY.

MUSIC: RISING CHORDS, SUGGESTING THE SOUL'S HUNGER, YEARNING FOR LIFE, LOVE, AND THE PURSUIT OF JENNIE, THE BEAUTIFUL YOUNG HEROINE . . . MORE CHORDS, MOUNTING, STING, STING . . . STING AND SUCK, STING AND SUCK . . . THE SOUND OF BLOOD ON THE LONG OFFICE TABLE . . . DRIPPING . . . DRIPPING . . .

More scripts came later. Variety shows, straight dramas, commercials. Reese would call him into the office, give him that dreamlike stare (compounded of a Koala bear-like amiability, fish-like indifference and main-floor-walkerish superiority), and tell him about the next script:

"As I see it, we could have the story of cotton, straight down from the fields until it's all packaged and made into shirts—great selling idea."

That was all Reese would say, and he wouldn't even admit that this "great selling idea" was really given him as an assignment by a local department store's advertising man.

Then Ted would knock out the script. He would lie across his bed, and wake in the early morning, hungry, the script not yet finished, the winged words not written yet, and go to the nearby tavern and order a big steak and look at it and tell himself, I haven't earned it yet.

Then he'd go back and write the winged words about cotton and singing shirts and everybody so happy.

And all the big shows carried that double byline. Yet, Ted thought, Reese had given him a break. Was it his fault that everything had to be so snide, so neat, so—uninspired and yet smoothly, tritely inspired at the same time?

Is it the rifle's fault that it is aimed? Any North Korean would do it, any enemy in Indo-China . . . any enemy . . .

. . . It probably would have been the same with any program manager. With anyone, Ted knew, he would have come to hate the slick insincerity, the preening announcers, the shrill-voiced frustrated-actress receptionists, the whole damned rotten phoney show.

"It's nice and cool," his father was saying.

"I wonder what he'd think if he knew I were here," Ted muttered.

His father shifted anxiously. The swing slowed down.

"I think I'll go over," Ted said.

"Want me to come with you?"

He turned so suddenly his father winced, cringing away from him. And Ted remembered with a rush of shame and remorse that he had turned just like that once (how long ago?) when his father had said idly, as if speculating, that there were kinds of writing more "dedicated" than that of commercial radio.

His hand had come up, not a part of himself, that once long ago, and his father had crumbled, he could feel it, the love-hate falling apart inside, and though the fist had stopped short of the indrawn belly that had lain against his mother's and created him, Ted knew now, the pattern was there, and in a red rage now, he cursed Reese silently, though he knew, helplessly, who was to blame.

"No," he told his father now. "I'll be just a minute. You rest here, Pop."

As he walked, stiff-legged, across the intervening driveways, Ted thought of the last time he had seen Reese. It had been in Reese's office, a few weeks after Ted had been discharged from the Army hospital.

He had known, after the little interweaving tentacles of personality had meshed into their old familiar patterns, what it would be: the double byline; the same old gaff.

"I think I'll try New York," he had heard himself telling Reese, and remembered now, the satisfaction of seeing Reese's eyebrows go up.

Yes, he'd tried New York, he'd tried. And in the reception room of two broadcasting companies he'd learned without going any further that it was not the size of the station he hated.

It was the fact that he had been geared up to fight a war, and now he just couldn't go back to living in the slick, smooth, artificial world of dreamed-up commercials, of lying to himself that everything was all right again, there were no corpses in Korea, there would be no sudden word that an Army buddy was dead now in Indo-China, just get the deluxe model with the three-year guarantee—

He couldn't go on manufacturing the false promises of excitement, of smiling voices, of insulin for empty desires (he told himself now) to make hungers that were impossible of attainment, he couldn't now, he couldn't.

The evening after the second reception room, they'd picked him up wandering the streets, babbling to himself, trying to find a foxhole in the uncaring pavement of the neatly-curbed ways. He guessed he'd been lucky, though: only a couple of days in the observation ward of the city hospital, and then home, and his own private doctor.

And the doctor had leaned back in his chair, one visit, looked at Ted, and said, "I believe we'll give you a few insulin treatments. Just to calm you down a bit," he reassured quickly as Ted frowned.

So now, here he was. And he had never known that it would be possible for Reese to live so close by the nursing home the doctor had chosen.

"Hi, Bert," he heard himself say, and heard his companion voice mock: *Hi, lo, shift into slow, upper, upper class, class . . .*

Reese turned suddenly, his knuckles whitening around the sweating-cold beer bottle, and a long moment passed in which the only sound was the metallic clattering of the steel capclaw hitting the table.

"Why, it's—why, Evelyn, look who's here!"

Mrs. Reese picked up the bottle opener, shifted it to her left hand, and held out her right (in the time it took, she became, for Ted, not real, as though she were pasted on the cover of a box of expensive candy in a perfumed store, and he guessed, snapping back, that that was how she saw herself).

"We thought you were still out of town, Ted," she said. "Glad to see you back." Her glance was cool, inquiring.

Ted took the clasp of the limp, slim hand. "No, I'm back."

"You'll have to look us up," Reese said. "We can't have you a stranger, now that you're in town again."

Do people shun you? Do you want to be the life of the party? Friends, here's what to do. Yes, try our product for one week, just one week—

"I haven't been back long," Ted said, while another part of his mind was saying: What would commercial radio do without the word, the magic word, "Yes"? The ingratiating, affirmative, clinching word, yes, yesssss!

"Can't see why you didn't come right back to work when you got out—"

You learn things in the Army, Ted thought. That's why I didn't come back.

"Here, sit down." Reese was surveying him, now. Had he heard? His cool, sizing stare caught something. "Are you—visiting around here?"

"No," Ted jerked his head toward where his father was watching across the driveways, craning his neck and smiling sociably, nodding and bowing in the swing.

"Over—" Reese set the bottle on the table and carefully wiped the frosted sides with a napkin. "Well, say. What's up? You're not—? Just resting up, are you?"

"No," Ted said. "I had a nervous breakdown and I'm getting insulin treatment." He was annoyed because Reese was still wiping the bottle, so he added deliberately, "Shock treatment."

He concentrated on shifting his chair around so he could watch his father, and felt them exchanging glances.

"Well, say. I suppose the Army hitch—" Reese left it hanging.

"Oh, I don't know. I guess maybe some of it."

Ted thought of Reese—the shows he'd written for him on assigned basis. Ideas from Reese. Bare, hungry skeletons, with joints and sinews missing. He'd added the marrow and the flesh, the warm blood, sometimes lifting himself away from the typewriter at four a.m., sometimes later, earlier, the days and nights a whirling blur.

"Well, say. I'm sorry. But you seem . . . I mean—"

"Oh, I'm all right, now. Just a little tense, yet."

"Of course, of course. You know," Reese got chummy, "living so close, the way we do, we can't help seeing, and occasionally even hearing a few things."

Now I'm being accepted, Ted thought. Taken into his confidence.

"Some of those nurses are certainly Amazons, aren't they?" Reese leaned forward, grinning.

"Say, when one of those patients gets violent, how do they handle them? I'll bet none of them are as big as those nurses, eh?"

The reddening sun slanted against his moist high forehead, and Ted thought he might have been bleeding sweat and that his teeth were too pointed and his nose too narrow but blunt at the end, nostrils working, like a muzzle, and he wondered what Reese turned into when the moon was dark.

Ted wanted to say, "They shoot them. Or else stick them in strait jackets and hide them under the bed or in a closet. Don't you know what happens to loonies like me?"

He heard what sounded like a shout, and realized, surprised, it was the thunder of his blood roaring on adrenalized command against his temples.

For a moment he almost savored the fury rising, felt it clench his hands and bathe him in a warm sense of power, so that, looking at Reese through the new pinpoints of his irises, he could almost see his fist wreaking a change in the blunt, working nostrils (and would the pointed teeth bite back?).

But he said, "I'd better be getting back. Early hours, you know."

"Of course. And say—when this is all over . . . I mean, you know—well, come around and see us."

"Yes, do," Mrs. Reese said.

"I will," Ted said. They were still looking at him and smiling, so he nodded his head and said again, "I will."

He had to keep himself from saying it once more, or it would have been like an echo chamber inside his head, resounding like the commercial at the end of a jingle, resounding: *I will, I willll . . . l . . . l . . .*

"Well, it was nice seeing you," Ted said.

"Sure you won't have a drink?" Reese reached for another bottle of beer. "I mean, is it allowed?"

"No, thanks."

"Special diet, and all that?"

"Not exactly," Ted said. "Just that I've got to be careful."

"There's no pain, or anything of that—sort, is there?"

"No. You don't even feel the needle. It's just that you get very hungry after the insulin."

"The—oh, yes. Yes, of course," Reese said.

Ted saw his father smiling sociably toward them, turned his back on Reese and his wife, stiffened, and centered like a radar missile on the old man in the swing, then walked away, trying to make his knees bend in a natural manner.

He didn't look back, but he wanted to flop down, seeking cover, and wriggle back on his belly, so the small sharp pellets of the people who had already eaten part of him without even being hungry would be fired over him.

But he could feel the pellets, feel them go through him.

I did it, he thought, not quite sure of what he had done. He felt oddly relieved.

Relieved, because you didn't do it? his earthcenter voice said.

Why? Because he had promised himself something one night in Korea, thinking of Reese, because, there in the rutted, frozen earth one night as he lay listening to the hungry steel wind pluck at him with fingers of fire, thinking of managers of programs, the sky had turned white with the small sun bursting over his head, and as the shell fragments ate hungrily around him, mashing flesh and making bloodflowers, he'd seen the beasts lurking there, and knew the answer then?

His father rose from the swing as he approached. "Did you have a nice talk?" the old man said.

He glared at his father. "What did you expect?" he muttered. "Think he would offer me a contract or something? I'm through; he's used me.

"They picked my brains, I wrote their damned soap-opera, they've got their fouled-up plaques for public service on their soundproofed wall, they don't need me, what do you think, I—"

He stopped, and looked at the old man, seeing him now. He wished he could straighten up the cringing shoulders, the worried crouch, quiet the blinking, confused eyes so aqueous behind the thick glass.

But there was nothing to say, now.

He thought of the walnut the old man had cracked between his knuckles, and the secret voice said, *You didn't go to war. Maybe if you'd gone to war, you wouldn't be able to crack walnuts either.*

But he was glad the old man couldn't hear the voice. There was a tone about it now that frightened him, even though he was a part of it.

His father walked him through the dark hallway into the house.

He watched the old man clump down the front steps. He stood between the narrow walls, feeling alone.

A nurse, pushing the kitchen swinging door with one hand, wiping her mouth with the other, flamed white in the dark corridor.

He took the pill the nurse gave him, looking at her. The Amazons were lithe, proud and free, he thought. They weren't pear-shaped, with corns on white-shod feet, legs like bologna in bleached casings. They wore crested helmets gleaming gold from filtered sunlight, not ridiculous bits of starched froth, and they didn't have their shining hair coiled and caged under a hairnet in a bun at the back.

He closed the door of his bedroom, turned the radio on low, and settled under the covers.

On the other side of the windowshade, he knew, was the still, soft dusk, kept carefully out. And he thought of the little poem he had read as a child, about having to go to bed before dark.

He heard the crickets calling, making small noises like a lover kissing his lady in the hollow of her throat. Somewhere, a mocking bird trilled and warbled mournfully among the flaming leaves. He closed his eyes, listening to earthsounds diminishing, letting them lull him. Thin music trickled over him.

Through the half-open window by the front porch he heard stealthy footsteps, and then the unaccustomed clamor of the door bell.

Drowning the crickets came the rapid pad of calloused feet from the back of the house, the garglings and blowings of the nurse with sinusitis, and the front door opened to the tune of a phlegmy, annoyed, "Yes?"

The other voice brought ice to Ted's spine: "You—have a Mr. Cotting here? A Mr. Theodore—"

"I'm sorry, visiting hour's over."

"Well, say, I didn't mean to disturb him. I just thought—"

It *was* Reese! Was the moon darkening? Was his muzzle wet?

"You kin come back tomorrow."

"No need of that. I—that is, Mrs. Reese and I, we thought it would be nice for him to have this."

"Don't know if he's allowed to have candy."

"Oh, I'm sorry, I didn't know." Reese's voice lowered and Ted leaned forward, his breath held, listening. "He—*is* quite ill, then?"

"He's coming along." The nurse's voice, firm, unrevealing.

"Well, say, that's fine. I—that is, Mrs. Reese—well, we thought perhaps it might be necessary for him to have—well, *you* know those more *drastic* therapies—"

Without insulin, Ted felt his hunger rising, and the sweat spurt unbidden to his clenched palms.

Solicitiously, Reese's voice: "I'm certainly glad he won't need anything like a prefrontal lobotomy. You know, I've heard—"

"I'll take this box, Mr.—?"

"Uh—Reese, Norbert—that is, the card's right in there."

"I'll take this, Mr. Rice, and tomorrow when the doctor comes I'll ask him if Mr. Cotting—"

"Oh, I wouldn't want him to have it if he's not supposed to."

The nurse, rheumy guardian on bunioned boots, assuring the invader, and the invader's voice fading, fading, the door completing its wooden curtaining of the outside, and Ted sitting bolt upright in the damp bed, pinpoint pupils raying through the dark, ready to repel the pointed teeth.

But what if they had hollow, numbing pockets, those fangs, and Reese bit him, emptying the poison into his tissues?

Then he would be anesthetized, unaware of the leucotome under his eyelid, severing the connection between the thalamus and frontal lobe, the thin blade twisting, like a wire, twisting . . .

. . . darting inside the skull, the dark skull, like a metal viper, the tongue flicking the blood-bathed flesh forever apart, andnomore! No more the music of Haydn stirring, or the frozen blue fire of a Sibelius crescendo sheering upward soaring to the mountain top alone in the clear free Finlandian sky like an eagle soaring, but falling now like a sparrow to the dead earth.

The radio, through some freak of the heavyside layer, suddenly blared forth. He reached out to turn the volume down. Tomorrow, another hypodermic of insulin, he thought.

Pouring over him, the bitter syrup of a jingly commercial scorched like new lava; the announcer's voice was serious, with the seriousness of someone who is sure he sounds serious:

"With these crystals, you won't *need* that extra slice of toast tomorrow morning, friends. They *control* your hunger. Yessss, try them for that hungry feeling," the announcer announced.

And Ted thought of all the kinds of hunger and all the kinds of control and what caused the hungers and knew, suddenly, how to make a million dollars; he heard his secret voice give the formula:

Create things to make people hungry, then make things to take the hunger away. But don't satisfy it, don't ever satisfy it.

Ted turned the dial again, and Frank J. Savolney was singing the song of civilization, telling Jack Benny:

"I get so nuhrr-vuss—yah, ahhh, hahd, aiyeeee!" And everybody laughed.

You get so hungry, Ted thought. He snapped off the radio. Then, just before he slipped into the blue, sightless depths of the sleeping pill, he murmured, "But what—if they didn't bring the orange juice when I get so hungry? What then . . .

"How would it feel, getting hungrier and hungrier?"

He thought of Reese, and the box of candy they probably wouldn't let him have. And from somewhere near the center of the earth, the strange, prodding voice he had been living with lately reminded:

Hunger is your enemy. Who has made you hungry? You have learned to eliminate the enemy. Anyone who gets in your way is the enemy . . .

But I get in my own way, Ted told himself uneasily.

It would be so easy, the voice urged, *to slip across the driveways and stop him before he stops you. He might come back, and they might listen to him and cut your nerves across with a knife—*

And then the voice was silent, but in the blackness sudden warmth came from the turned-off radio, and the tubes flared and blared, and the radio came to life, and the speaker was an endless glass funnel smoking and clearing.

From the funnel started to come Angeline, but she belonged to someone else, and Ted reached out to turn the radio off, but it wouldn't stay off, but kept playing music that sounded like bombs and bones breaking, and Ted saw that it was his father, red-hot leucotomes snaking from his nostrils, playing tympanic tunes on his shining pink forehead with cracked walnut shells.

Then everyone had leucotomes, and Mrs. Reese, her head porcupined with them, Medusa-like, offered him their slicing peace, but he twisted away, running under a sky black, then shot with starshells bursting fire that froze and burned.

He felt the bed slipping away from him, and fumbled for it, clawing away shapes that were hungrier than he, running over a sucking, pulling marsh of soft, dead, upturned faces with grinning, open, unhungry mouths.

And when he opened his eyes, his bare feet were wet and dew-fresh grass caressed the sides of his toes, the little green spears tickling the flushed skin, peeping like pointed emeralds prodding his flesh.

There was a scarlet smear on his arm, and redness dripping from the jagged edges of the broken beer bottle in his hand.

And far off, a woman was screaming.

TRAUMEREI

He walked into the store his mother and father kept for the sale of "Ladies' Cloaks and Suits." His knee was skinned, and the mud was caked over the khaki. He hoped his parents would be busy with customers. If they were both busy, he could walk right through the store, into the back, through the partition that separated the store and the rooms where they lived. But there were no customers.

"Here comes the soldier!" his father said, looking up from the copy of Engels' *The Origin of the Family* he had open on his knee.

"Bolshevik!" Jerome's mother glared at his father. "There's nothing wrong with being a Boy Scout."

"Militarism," his father said. "They march. They line up and march."

"What are you doing home so early?" his mother said.

"I don't feel so good," Jerome said.

"Your new uniform, and already you got it dirty," his mother said, inspecting the knee with a seamstress's care.

"I'll be all right." He turned away. "I just didn't want to go back to school."

Miss Fitzgerald, the salesgirl, undulated from the back of the store. Jerome felt that hot, dizzy feeling again, and he tried to keep his eyes away from what his blood was telling him to watch.

Miss Fitzgerald had once told him he was "cute." He knew why she had said that.

His parents were her boss. It would be just too bad if she knew the power she could have over him. But she would never know.

No one ever called him cute. Not at school, or anywhere else.

"You had your lunch?" His mother was still inspecting the knee.

"I ate at school," he said.

A customer came in. His mother's eye wavered from the knee to the customer. The customer was wavering between the fur coats and the bargain dress rack. His father was deep in *The Origin of the Family.*

"Then go back and lie down," his mother said. "Mrs. McMann is cleaning, so don't get in her way." She bore down on the customer, her smile coming up and focusing like the radar-operated gun of an intercepting destroyer.

Miss Fitzgerald inspected the uniform, her long-lashed eyes surveying him. She put her hand on his shoulder, and he tried to keep from trembling. "My, but you look nice. All grown up," she said.

He didn't want to say it, but he said, "So what?" He wanted to look at her and say, "Take me, I'm yours." But the slight smile of possession on her full lips, the little smirk of pride, and she became one person, and he was another, and his self was at stake. And besides, he didn't know how.

His father looked up again. "Soon you'll be carrying a gun," he said, and lowered his eyes to his book and he wasn't there anymore.

Jerome walked rapidly toward the rooms behind the store.

He could hear Mrs. McMann moving about upstairs. He didn't feel like going to his room. The parlor was dim and cool. The old phonograph was open. Trying to ignore the feeling about his new uniform and the stinging of his knee, he cranked up the machine.

From the belly of the phonograph, which was slotted to hold the recordings, he picked out the one he liked best, and put it on the turn-table.

As the violins and clarinets came nasally through the old

diaphragm, shaped to the tune of Schumann's "Traumerei," he settled on the couch and closed his eyes.

The clarinet moaned, the violins sang, the familiar vision swam dimly across his closed eyelids . . . A lacy cool green forest, where all the trees and shrubbery were soft to the sight and to the touch.

The forest surrounded a little clearing where a silvery little lake reflected the drooping branches. Into the clearing floated a creature gowned in gossamer white . . . a beautiful woman. *His.*

The one he would find, some day.

She was beautiful. She was good. She was better than Una of the Red Cross Knight. Better than the Good Fairy of Tinkle Bell. Better than Wendy of Peter Pan. Moving through the soft green haze, she was more lovely, even, than Miss Fitzgerald.

She was—and this was most important—she was *his.*

There was no trouble about it. He didn't have to talk to her. She *knew.* And he *knew,* and they would be together for always after, just he and the beautiful creature in white and the needle of the nasal phonograph slid clackingly onto the grooves at the end of the record.

He got up and started the record again. He could have brought the vision back once more, if he had wanted to, but something else was forcing the blood into his head again. He felt that dizzy, powerless surging.

His head felt light. His limbs felt endless, and ending.

Although he knew what would happen as he got up, he wanted to think that he could stop any time he wanted to. This doesn't have to be this way, he thought. Yet, his own will was nothing.

He started to pray as he headed toward the hallway between the store and the back rooms. "Please. Not with me wearing my uniform." The uniform should make everything different. His skinned knee burned and the mud was heavy on his leg, and he thought of the Boy Scout Handbook.

Onmy honor Iwill do my bestto do my duty toGodandto-Country . . .

He couldn't remember the rest of it. Why couldn't he remember the rest of it?

He had reached the alcove. Then the hallway.

His legs were taking him there.

Lined up neatly along the baseboard in the hallway, they were just where he had expected them to be. If they had not been there, he would have been dismally glad.

But now that they were there, they summoned. Just as Miss Fitzgerald summoned.

He thought of her in her work shoes—the low-heeled shoes, and how lovely her legs looked even in the low-heeled shoes. But when she came to work in the morning before changing into low-heeled shoes she wore these—the ones that were now against the baseboard in the hallway.

They were black and shiny and patent leather. They gleamed and beckoned when she wore them. As she teetered on them, her smooth, shiny calves curving upward, she looked wonderful in them. Wonderful—and terrible.

He had once asked his father, "Why are men so—indulgent with women? Why do they—well . . . *take* as much as they do from them? Why do they, for instance, smile when a woman does something, but when a man does the same thing, they might get sore, or not smile?"

His father had got uncomfortable, cleared his throat, and he knew that because his father had taken time to think, his father would tell him what he had just been thinking rather than what he was first about to say.

"Women have been the playthings of men throughout the ages, Jerome—" And it hadn't meant anything to Jerome to have his father say that.

. . . But there they were. He stood watching them, at first. As though there were a life of their own about them. In a way there was. They were bright, with a light seeming not altogether from the unshaded hall bulb. The heels were slender and delicate—like *her.*

He speculated for a moment, thinking about turning around and going back to the parlor and the phonograph. But just the thought of turning his eyes away sent the blood coursing through his head and along his arms.

Now he sat down, with his back to the baseboard, the shoes beside him. The wonderful shoes—

He leaned toward them. He picked up the nearest one. It was real in his hand. She had been wearing it a little while before and it felt warm and alive in his hand. Her foot had been in it. The lining was still moist, and scented with her presence.

Then he picked up the other shoe.

When he went upstairs, Mrs. McMann was just coming out of his room. She smiled when she saw him. "Well, you're home early," she said. There was a challenging glint to his eye. He always felt as though Mrs. McMann knew something he could never know, even about himself.

"I know you," her glance seemed to say, "and I know where you belong, no matter how uppity you try to act. You can't fool me. Oh, you're coming along, little man, aren't you?"

As he lay on his bed, he heard her in the spare room, getting ready to leave. He knew she was changing back into her street clothes. She would leave her work clothes in the closet.

He thought of Mrs. McMann. She was about his teacher Miss Grover's age, and Miss Grover wasn't so very old. But she was different from the prim Miss Grover. Mrs. McMann seemed to carry something precious and a little unusual with her, gleefully, secretly, glad of it in a glinting way. And Mrs. McMann seemed to dare you to discover it. Miss Grover seemed the guardian of all that had died or was dying and laying it respectfully, acceptably, to rest.

He thought of Mrs. McMann's mouth. There were hard lines about it. It was always heavily rouged. And her voice had a harsh rasp.

And that hidden smile.

When Mrs. McMann left, he went into the spare room in his uniform still, and opened the closet door and stood looking at the clothes Mrs. McMann had left behind when she changed into her street clothes.

There was an old skirt, old silk stockings full of runs, a pair of old rayon bloomers, an old blouse, an old pair of shoes. His eyes were riveted on the shoes as he moved farther into the closet.

The shoes were black and old. They were cracked, and old. And they were full of Mrs. McMann who was, after all, a woman.

The closet was strong with the smell of her, the stale, sweaty reek of perfume and body and the dirt of Mrs. McMann. She was a woman and she had been working hard in the bloomers and the blouse and the skirt and the shoes.

And the bloomers were slithery to the touch and almost warm, and laden with the memory of the woman who had worn them.

And who challenged him, in every move of her, to discover the mystery . . .

Later, from downstairs and beyond and far away, from another place through folds of silk that obscured his hearing, his mother's voice came to him. He hurried out of the closet and lay down on the bed in his room, trying not to think. "There's someone here to see you," his mother called.

He came downstairs in his uniform still, and Mr. Ferris, his Scoutmaster, was at the foot of the stairs, smiling up at him.

Mr. Ferris was a beefy man much too large for his wisp of mustache. Mrs. McMann had once remarked, after one of his visits, that he acted "like Godalmighty." The Scoutmaster said, "Hello, Jerry," and slapped him on the back.

His mother laughed, and wriggled coquettishly. "Come into the parlor," she invited.

"I asked Mr. Ferris to stay for supper," she told Jerome. "But he has to go somewhere quick after this. Anyhow, you'll see him at the Scout meeting tonight."

Jerome's face felt hot. His hands felt clammy. Why was Mr. Ferris here?

"I just thought I'd drop in," Mr. Ferris was saying. Jerome felt sure he was looking at him, but he kept his eyes riveted on the floor.

"Sure, sure," Jerome's mother said.

Jerome felt there was something behind all this, but he knew that Mr. Ferris couldn't lie.

"Well," said Jerome's mother, "I wanted to talk to you about Jerome."

Her voice was reaching the boy vaguely, as though it were coming from the cool, distant forest, filtering through the green ferns, birdlike.

"I didn't mean to stay home from school this afternoon," Jerome said. He looked up, and felt relieved at the puzzled expression on Mr. Ferris's beefy face.

"I hope you're feeling all right, Jerry," the Scoutmaster said.

"Oh, yessir."

"Oh, Jerome's all right," his mother said. "But sometimes he doesn't appreciate what we do for him."

The boy looked at his mother. Why was she saying that?

"Oh, I'm sure he does," Mr. Ferris said, looking uncomfortable.

"Not all the time." Now his mother was smiling at Mr. Ferris the way Jerome had seen her smile once at his father when he had passed by their bedroom door and glanced in.

"I thought," his mother went on, "you could maybe have a talk with him—tell him about the sacrifices his parents make. It isn't so easy to keep up a store and a home, too."

"Why, I'm sure he knows that," Mr. Ferris said, not sounding at all sure.

"I do, really I really do," Jerome said. He noticed Mr. Ferris's tight smile. Why was his mother tearing down his world of Mr. Ferris? How could Mr. Ferris like him if she said these things?

"Sometimes I think he doesn't know the struggle we put up to give him things—things other boys don't have." His mother leaned toward Mr. Ferris. "He wanted a Boy Scout uniform, did we say 'No, we can't afford it'? No, we didn't. He needed a Scout Handbook? All right, he got one. Neckerchief, shoes, belt—a Scout knife, even. We didn't say 'No.' What other boy's parents would do that? And in our circumstances . . ."

Mr. Ferris absently reached into his pocket and started to fumble for a cigarette.

"But do you think he appreciates it?" His mother leaned farther forward, looking intently at Mr. Ferris, smiling. The Scoutmaster scratched a match against the folder in his hand and looked at her through the flame, puffing and squinting.

"Jerry, get Mr. Ferris the ash tray," his mother said.

He fled from the room, his face burning, feeling the air cool on the hot skin of his forehead. When he returned he found his mother and Mr. Ferris both staring at opposite ends of the room, the smoke from their extinguished conversation smouldering between them.

Mr. Ferris smoked his cigarette rapidly. There was a moment's silence. Jerome still felt afraid to look at the Scoutmaster.

"Well," said Mr. Ferris, rising, "I must be running along."

"A little tea first, maybe?" His mother rose, too.

"No, thank you, just the same. Well, Jerry, see you tonight. Won't be long before you'll be a full-fledged Tenderfoot."

"Oh, I hope so," said his mother, smiling at Mr. Ferris.

Jerome stood alone in the parlor while his mother saw Mr. Ferris out through the back way which was really the "visitor's entrance" since the front was through the store. She returned in a moment.

"Such a nice man, that Mr. Ferris. I really enjoyed talking to him. But what was the matter with you?"

"Nothing, Mama. I—wish you hadn't told him that," Jerome said.

"Well, Jerry, if you would learn a little appreciation—" his mother called back over her shoulder as she headed for the kitchen to prepare supper.

He heard the scratch of a match, and over it, her voice. "I never saw you so white before, though. You got white as a sheet."

Jerome crept up the steps, the steep steps, and when he reached his room, he threw himself face down across the bed. He was lying like that when his sister came home from high school. He heard her throw her books on the couch, then the quick, impatient whir of the phonograph crank as she wound it tightly.

The record that was on the machine spun. And, filteredly, from far away downstairs through the deepening dusk, the strains of "Traumerei" reached the white-faced boy in the muddy-kneed Boy Scout uniform, lying tensely face down across the bed.

YOUR BEST INTERESTS AT HEART

PUSHING ahead of his father, he slammed himself against the ponderous hospital door, and it swayed outward into the whipping wind. A cold blast struck him as he stood waiting on the concrete steps, waiting until he heard his father's labored breathing behind him.

They descended the steps, he listening to the meticulous voice in his head counting them: *one, two, three, four, five . . .* They trudged across the soggy earth. The snow-soaked ground under their feet squushed and, as he bent his head under the weight of the barracks bag on his shoulder, he saw the winter-withered tan grass that had been stamped into the reddish clay earth by many feet, so stamped in that it had failed to spring back.

They reached the road, panting, and he let the heavy burden slide shapelessly down. His father watched the faded green canvas bag plop against the earth. "It's too heavy for you to carry, isn't it?" his father asked.

The old man was peering at his son through thick bifocaled horn-rimmed spectacles that made his nose sore, but he wasn't thinking about the weight of the spectacles; he had another weight, now. He had to get his son home, and he was wondering, looking at his boy, if he would have trouble getting him on the train.

The son, Ernest, turned slowly, like a toy not wound tightly enough, and faced the sharply-angled, trim brick building which housed the ward they had just left.

"It isn't too cold for this time of year, is it?" Ernest's father said. He craned his neck toward his son, and the black cord of the hearing device he carried in his vest pocket rubbed against the loose, mottled flesh of the aged throat.

He fumbled a spotted, wrinkled hand through the folds of his heavy, resisting overcoat to reach the volume control on the instrument panel, and turned his chunky, tired-out body toward the younger man. His foot stumbled against the barracks bag, and he coughed dryly. He thought he heard Ernest speak. "Huh?" He spoke too loudly, and peered fluidly at the sullen, expressionless face with its two-day growth of beard.

When Ernest didn't answer, he raised his arm against the weight of his coat and said, "Why look back? I should think you'd be glad to see the last of that place." His old arm groped, and the worn hand descended, patting his son's shoulders as he said, "After six months . . ."

The red-brick, sharp block-shaped structure loomed over them, each ward protruding from the mass of the building and ending in a cross-barred, black-shadowed porch. Iron-barred porches of wards jutted from either side of the massive middle entrance door of the hospital, like great vacant, commentless eyes. Ernest's father felt no movement of the shoulder under his dry, papery palm, and the wrinkled hand tremored. He let his arm drop to his side. "It doesn't look too bad from the outside, does it?" the old man said.

Ernest turned suddenly, and the old man winced into himself a little more. He looked at his father, at the stiff, awkward overcoat, at the black, shaking cord dangling from the snail-like piece of plastic thrust into the mottled ear.

He saw the white tufts of hair over the warm brown eyes swimming in the fluids of age and irritation, filmed over and blinking, but blinking with love, a love he could feel, an ill-controlled, nervous, anxious but undeniable love.

Then the meticulous voice echoed the word *outside,* and he thought: I'm outside of there, but what am I inside of now? It's cold here, here where I'm not a part of anything.

He looked at his father. *Not a part of him, not yet,* the voice reminded him. But I've got to be a part of something, he argued back, voicelessly.

He looked over his father's shoulder, seeing someone wave to him. A young man and woman, walking toward the hospital, had altered their course and were heading for Ernest and his father. "Going to see Dominick?" Ernest called to the plump, swarthy man who had waved to him.

The plump, swarthy woman holding the man's arm nodded, smiling. "Is he in?"

"Yeah. I just said goodbye to him."

The dark man glanced at the barracks bag, his eyebrows lifting. "Going home today?"

Ernest placed a hand on the bag, rubbing the heavy, shapeless canvas experimentally. He nodded, and said dully, "Yeah, I guess I am."

Then he lifted his head, and his eyes almost came alive. "I heard Dominick's getting out soon, too."

"We hope so," the man said.

Ernest stared intently at them. "I hope so, too."

He turned, and noticed his father peering at the man and woman. "This is my father," he said.

The old man lifted his hat, smiled timidly. They nodded and Ernest said, "Can't they do anything about his mouth?"

The swarthy man frowned. "No," he said, "they figured it wasn't any use trying to operate."

The four people stood there silently for a moment, on the wet ground under the looming brick of the muscular building with its bulging, empty porches. "We're waiting for a taxi," Ernest's father contributed.

The three turned and looked at the old man, who was standing there breathing hard. Then the woman shifted the shopping bag she was carrying to the hand that had been resting on her brother's arm and said, "Well, I guess he's waiting." The couple smiled. The woman said, "Well, good luck." And they left the father and son standing by the side of the road.

Ernest watched them walking toward the huge hospital door. As though feeling his gaze, they turned together, looked back, smiled and waved. Then they went ahead, not looking at each other, toward the massive, waiting door. Ernest looked at his father and said, "You saw Dominick. He was the fellow with the open mouth. The one in the supply room."

The old man nodded, grinning sociably, helplessly. "Yes, I remember, the open mouth, yes. Yes, well . . ."

"Taking him to that hospital didn't do any good," Ernest said. The old man turned and looked at the hospital. "Dominick was a baker in the Army."

"He was?" The old man shook his head with great interest, to indicate that he realized how important bakers were in the Army.

"Yes. He was at Pyongyang. A bomb dropped near him, and he got the shock. His mouth fell open . . ."

"Yes, I saw him," his father said.

"He can't close it. We used to work together. We lived in the same dormitory."

"He seemed like a nicelittlefellow," the old man said, running the words together.

Ernest nodded, thoughtfully. "The last four weeks, after treatments, I worked with him on the rolling litter. We carried treatment patients from bed to the shock room. They'd got insulin first, then when they were in a coma—"

A taxi swung around the bend of the road, and the old man waved. "Hey! There! Hey, you, cabbie!" the old man called, hoarsely. The taxi braked before them, and Ernest's father scrabbled at the door latch, until Ernest said, "You push the button." The old man pushed it, saying, "I know, I know."

The driver got out, unlatched the rear compartment and reached for the barracks bag. "Going home?" he commented cheerfully, swinging the bag in and slamming the lid down with competent energy. He slid behind the wheel, whistling breathily.

"That's right," Ernest said. The car shot forward. He settled back in the seat, but suddenly he sat bolt upright and stared hard through the side window, his head turning to keep the hospital building in sight as long as possible.

His father watched him. "Why look back? That's the last of that place," he said hoarsely. He coughed, and leaned forward to speak to the driver. "Say, what time does the next train pull out of the village, mister?"

"There won't be any for quite a while," the driver said, slowing the cab carefully, and speaking out of the corner of his mouth. "There was a wreck just down the line. Freight got sideswiped, holding everything up."

"Well, we can have something to eat then," Ernest's father said. "I didn't have any lunch."

"There's a hotel serves good meals just next to the station," the driver volunteered, picking up speed.

"What did he say?" the old man asked Ernest.

"He said there's a hotel that has a restaurant. It's near the station," Ernest said. "Okay," he told the driver, "we'll go there."

The taxi hummed past the hospital powerhouse, past older brick buildings housing wards Ernest had heard about but never been in, then crept down the main street of the village, a village Ernest had last glimpsed from the hospital-bound bus in which he had been a strait-jacketed passenger. He didn't remember much about the trip, except a goat-faced attendant, who, somehow, had become, in his fantasies, the experimental goat which had been found alive on the ship after the Bikini bomb explosion.

The village, he noted now, was like some of the small towns which had been boomed by nearness to the Army camps he had trained in: extra drug stores, groceries; neon-sign-fronted, chromium-plated taverns, bars . . .

The cab pulled up before the frame building opposite the shabby depot. Whistling tunelessly, the driver swiftly unlocked the trunk and swung out the barracks bag. He deposited it with a plop at Ernest's feet. "Good luck, son," the driver said, grinning.

The old man fished under his overcoat and produced a quarter.

"Thanks, for helping my son," he said, not quite knowing what he meant, and pushed the coin at the driver.

Ernest watched the taxi drive away. He looked at the bag on the ground before him. He saw his name and Army serial number stencilled on the canvas in big black letters. He read it over silently. He knew that within the barracks bag, on the waistbands of his shorts, on his socks, on the neckbands of his shirts, on all his clothing in neat black stencilling was his name and the number of the ward he had just left. In his mind, he read it over, silently.

And he heard the meticulous voice asking: *Why didn't they stencil "insane asylum" on your forehead, too? So that all the neighbors will know?*

They'll probably find out anyhow, Ernest answered the voice, soundlessly. Maybe the Chinese laundryman on the corner where he took his shirts would decode the neckband and lay down his hot iron and pad shufflingly to the back of his shop where his wife was nursing a slant-eyed baby. And there would be a sing-song in the air, and questioning glances, and the Chinese equivalent of the words "crazy boy" would quiver in the hot, steamy air of the incense-laden room.

Or something he might say or do would start them talking, the neighbors. And then maybe Mikie, the neighborhood clown, would tag along after him, yelling out, "Looney, looney."

His mother had always warned him, when they raised their voices in an argument, "The neighbors, watch out for the neighbors. What will the neighbors think?"

Well, some smiling men around a big table in the brick building had reached a decision that he could go home, so he must be all right. But he knew he would be watched.

I have to say what I think they want me to say. Act the way they might want me to act. I'm under suspicion. I even suspect myself. And I'm outnumbered.

Or are you? the voice wanted to know.

Yes I am, he answered. But some day there might be more of us than there are of them. Then it will be all right.

But meanwhile, I'm guilty, he reminded the voice.

He looked at his father, and thought: And even love isn't strong enough to give me a blanket verdict of "not guilty."

In his mind, he read the black stencilling over, and began to shiver. His father nudged him. "Let's go inside. It's cold out here."

"So I'm out," Ernest said.

"That's right, you're out. Let's go inside. We can sit down," the old man said.

"I never thought I'd get out," Ernest said.

"I had a hard time getting you out," his father said.

"You didn't get me out. I had to work to get myself out. Sweeping floors, mopping, cleaning, polishing. Working with the attendant—"

"You ought to see the letters I wrote the director of the hospital, asking him to help my son," the old man said, shaking his head.

"Letters!" Ernest's lip curled. "Why didn't you get me out when they first took me to Bellevue six months ago?"

"How could I? You ran down naked in your hotel lobby. I was home, five hundred miles away. You never should have left home so soon after the Army. It was a mistake."

Ernest tittered mirthlessly. Then he glared at his father. "I'm not so sure I like you. Maybe I ought to go back to the hospital," he said too loudly.

His father smiled twistedly and extended his hand toward his son, patting the air with his other hand. "Now, Ernest, don't be that way."

It's an experiment, the voice said not quite so meticulously. *He's not quite sure how to handle his crazy son.*

"What way?" Ernest demanded. "What way do you mean?"

"You know," the old man said vaguely. He tapped his breast pocket lightly, grinning to show he was making a joke. "I'm your custodian, at least for a year. I had to sign the papers. Otherwise they never would have let you out."

"Maybe I should have stayed," Ernest muttered, his eyes

sliding over the old man's rapidly rising and falling chest. "There were people there who understood me . . ."

He heard the whistle of his father's breathing over the insistence of the meticulous voice that was saying *He doesn't seem to understand. I thought some of them in there understood. But now I'm not a part of them any more.*

I need to identify myself with someone, something, I can't be alone, he was thinking, while the voice was saying *Maybe now you'll always be a part of them.*

He watched his father trying to give a casual shrug in his too-big, weighty overcoat that couldn't hide the tremulous breathing, heard him say, "What's the use of talking out here? Let's go inside and have a nice cup of hot coffee."

Ernest tugged at the shapeless bag, swinging it onto his shoulder, grunting. The old man fumbled awkwardly, trying to help his son hoist the bag, his brittle nails slipping on the rough canvas.

"They understood me," Ernest panted. "We had it tough in there, but they understood me, those fellows . . ."

"Now look, son," the old man said, and Ernest saw him glance about to make sure no one would see this argument, this argument so soon after those papers giving his son his freedom had been handed to him at the hospital.

"Son," the old man said, and at the way he said it, Ernest suddenly felt the canvas bag weighing on him heavily, heavily. "Everybody understands you. I understand you. We're all trying to help you. We all have your best interests at heart. You should know that."

Ernest gazed toward the railway yards, noticing the gray clusters of people outside the station, waiting for the train to take them back to the city. The bag pressed down hard on his shoulder, and he hesitated. He turned toward his father, squinting at the old man so that he couldn't see the aged face under the brown felt hat.

"You say you didn't have any lunch?"

"I didn't have time. I had to hurry to catch the early train."

The old man was still trying to make a joke. "How would it be if you got all ready to leave that place, and then there wasn't anybody to take you home?"

"If you had caught the later one, you would have been in the wreck." Ernest shifted the weight, plopping the bag on his shoulder. "Let's eat."

His father held open the door, and he entered the small bar outside the dining room. They walked through to the tables.

Ernest plumped the bag down against the wall, and they sat at the nearest table. His father reached for the menu, and he picked it up and handed it to the old man.

Across the aisle, Ernest could see two tables, at one a man and a woman; at the other, two men. One of the men wore a gray business suit, the other, in a black overcoat, was hunched forward over his plate, his face a dull red as he maneuvered confusedly with a knife and fork, handling them clumsily, like a child learning how to eat properly at the big table. As Ernest watched, the gray business-suited man picked up a forkful of food and thrust it at the red face of what might have been his brother, brother-in-law, son, nephew or uncle whom he was treating to a Sunday's airing on a temporary hospital pass.

"Now, eat!" the gray business-suited man said, and from the impatient way he said it Ernest guessed that Redface must be a close, loved relative.

The loose lips in the red mouth opened to receive the thrusted food. Ernest watched the red face gobble a moment, then he turned to his father. "You must be hungry," he said.

The old man looked at his son. "I guess I am," he said.

A plump waitress bustled up with two glasses of water, and said, "I'll be with you gentlemen in a minute." Ernest nodded.

The old man said, "Your mother, do you still feel you don't want your mother to be in the house when you get home?"

Ernest's head jerked up. "I don't know. She might start asking me a lot of questions like she does. I don't know."

"She was all upset when I telephoned her and told her you

said you didn't want her to meet you. She has her heart set on meeting you at the door."

The old man was clutching the menu tightly, so that it trembled. Ernest reached over and took it out of his father's hand.

"You sure you won't change your mind?"

"Well," Ernest fumbled with the menu. "Maybe she can be home. But what if she starts asking a lot of questions the way she does?"

"That's her nature, that's your mother's nature, but she means well," the old man said. "She took it hard when you went to the hospital. She'll be so happy to see you. She promised me she would do anything to make you happy, your mother," the old man went on, beginning to run his words together. "She's got your best interests at heart, your mother." The old man smiled. "You still have time to write her a card and tell her you'd like her to meet you at the door."

His father fumbled in his coat pocket and brought forth a postcard. "Here. You can write her now, if you want to. I picked up some cards in the city."

Ernest took the card and turned it over. There was a picture of the United Nations General Assembly building on the other side. "Have you got another one?" he asked. "I promised some of the fellows I'd write . . ."

"But you just got out." His father was frowning.

"It would make them feel good to get a card right away. I've got their addresses. I promised to look them up when I come back to New York. I'll be back to look for a job again some day . . ."

The old man shook his head, and his voice was hoarse. "I should think—" He cleared his throat and started again, "I should think you would never want to see those kind of people again."

Ernest half rose from his chair. "Those kind of people! I'm those kind of people. Don't forget that. Why can't you look at it like it was a broken leg—" His voice rose. "A broken leg that got fixed, or—or something like being deaf!"

His father's eyes shifted uneasily about the room, and again he extended his hand toward his son, patting the air placatingly. "All right, all right. Sit down. I didn't mean anything. I'll give you another card if you want it. But first write your mother. She'll be so happy."

Ernest turned the card over, and took the fountain pen from his father's blue-nailed fingers. For a brief moment, his intense, dark gaze met the puzzled, worried, age-filmed eyes of the man opposite. And his moist hand brushed the dry, loose flesh of the old man's hand. He looked at the fountain pen and remembered that he had given it to his father for a birthday present, that his mother always borrowed it because she was forgetting her own somewhere about the house. And he bent his head, and began to write.

The waitress fluttered back to their table, and said, "You'll have to excuse me, but I'm so nervous. I guess you heard of the wreck. About five of the people who come in here every Sunday were in it. They brought some of the ones who were hurt in here. I'm all upset. They were all bandaged . . ."

"It's all right. My father wants a dinner," Ernest said.

The waitress looked at Ernest and smiled. "And what'll you have?"

Ernest fumbled with his chin. The rough, uneven bristles scratched against the tips of his fingers. "I just ate," he said.

"Have something more. Have a piece of pie," his father suggested.

"Pie," Ernest agreed. "Apple pie."

He watched the waitress's bulging hips as she moved away, and he thought, *So I'm free.*

His father ate slowly, concentrating on the thin slices of beef under the thick gravy. Ernest idled indifferently with the slab of pie.

"Now, eat!" the gray business-suited man was saying again, and the ice cream dribbled around the corners of the loose lips onto the red chin.

Ernest looked away, gazing out the window at the growing crowd around the railway depot.

"Lots of people," his father commented, watching his son.

"There are ten thousand patients at that hospital. This is visiting day," Ernest said.

The old man carefully mushed a piece of bread in the gravy and held it up, dripping. "Your mother can hardly wait to have you home. She told me she'll do anything you say. She wants it peaceful.

"I told her the doctor said you should have it peaceful," he said.

Ernest looked down at the knife by the side of his plate. It was the first time he had had a knife by his plate in six months. "I suppose Selma's anxious to see me, too."

"Your sister has been terribly worried about you," his father nodded. "You know," he added, mouthing the bread slowly, "her divorce is final, now." He wiped his chin and put down his fork. "Your little niece, Diana, all she talks about is her Uncle Ernest."

"It's probably crowded at home."

"There's always room for you," his father said. "Besides, that's where the doctor said you have to go. Home."

"I'll go home. Where else is there to go," Ernest said.

"Some day you'll be a big success. You shouldn't lose courage. Remember, everybody has a struggle. My life hasn't been a bed of roses either," the old man said.

The waitress came over, smiling at Ernest, and said, "Is everything all right, a bus is coming up to take you passengers to the next village where you can get your train fer the city, that's good pie, ain't it?"

She wiped around his water glass and wobbled away. "Hurry up and finish," Ernest told his father. "They're sending up a bus."

"My teeth," his father said. "They're not like the real thing. Food gets in between."

Ernest watched his father mouthing the food. "There was an old lady there. I helped wheel her into the shock room, from insulin therapy. The student nurse told her to take out her teeth, sometimes they clench too hard when you go into convulsions, even with the cotton between them. They slipped out of her hand and broke on the floor. She was too far gone to know. I picked them up and gave them back to her, the pieces."

Ernest was gazing out the window, and his father had to lean forward to catch the words.

Two weather-beaten busses pulled up outside the hotel, and the gray crowd surged around the doors. The old man looked at his son, then put down his fork, and dabbed at his mouth with the napkin.

"You haven't finished yet," Ernest said.

"I'm not hungry, now. I ate enough," his father said. "Let's go."

They hurried outside. People were stamping on the mushiness of the yard, milling about, pushing each other, boiling about the two busses. The old man shook his head, and the black cord of the hearing device swayed. "It's no use. Let's wait. There will be other busses."

The two vehicles roared away, filled with people standing and people sitting, people who had paid their daily visit, or their weekly or their monthly visit, and who seemed to be anxious to escape back to the city, now. A few minutes later, two more busses pulled up.

The bus doors hissed open, the crowd surged toward them, and the old man padded through, calling out hoarsely in a faded voice. "Here, let my son through. He's carrying a heavy bag. He doesn't feel so well."

"It's all right, it's all right," Ernest said. The bag shifted as he carried it, pressing against the cords of his neck. He followed his father into the bus. The doors hissed closed.

Ernest sat, the bag between his legs, his head down, eyes half-closed. He opened them as the bus lurched, once. He looked at the draw ropes of his barracks bag, tied and retied over the top. He saw the black floor of the bus. The floor swayed and rubbed against his feet, creaking.

He heard his father's hoarse mutter, close to his ear. He

looked up, and found that the bus had swung up against the wall of another depot, as crowded as the wreck-isolated one they had just left.

"We're here, in the next village already," his father was saying.

People were lined up along the track. A few railroad cars stood at the end of the line. Ernest plumped his bag onto a bench next to the depot. He waited for his father to catch up to him.

"It shouldn't be long now," the old man said, beaming through his spectacles. He was breathing heavily, and fumbling under his overcoat. He dragged out a handkerchief and blew his nose. "You walk fast," he said.

They stood around the barracks bag and watched the crowd thicken, as more busses pulled up and spewed forth their loads. Ernest looked at the crowd along the tracks. He saw a ruddy-faced mustached young man lugging a big suitcase, holding onto it with both hands. "Hey," Ernest called out. "Are you going home, too?"

The mustache tilted, the suitcase dropped, the young man looked at Ernest. "Yeah, this is the day," he said.

"I didn't know they released them from your ward," Ernest said.

"Hey, where do I know you from?" the young man asked.

"Shock therapy," Ernest explained. "You came up with the other out-patients from some of the other wards. I helped wheel you fellows into the electric room—"

"Oh, yeah," the young man said vaguely.

"I guess you wouldn't remember," Ernest said. "Those treatments—"

Ernest suddenly found a sharp picture thrust into his mind: the man with the mustache lying on a movable litter, a circular gauze bandage pressed between his teeth. Tremor under the shock, the face purpled, then as Ernest bent over to hold him back against the pad, a wet, foul breath blew into his face. The glazed eyes with the red-veined whites staring blindly open upward. Thrashing arms, and the deep-throated growling—

"You going home too?" the young man with the mustache said.

Ernest nodded, and the other said, "I guess quite a few are. I saw a couple more from my ward."

"How you doing?" Ernest asked the young man he had wheeled into the shock room.

"Well," the young man looked around and jerked his head toward a lean, stooped figure approaching them. "I had a argument with my father already. I dunno . . ."

"Well, we gotta take it easy," Ernest cautioned. He smiled, "We got to get used to civilians. The whole thing . . ."

"That's right." The lean, stooped figure had reached them and overheard. "Tell my son that. I already told him."

"Okay, pop, okay," muttered the young man with the mustache, nodding his head hard. He reached down to pick up his suitcase, turning his eyes up to look at Ernest as he did so. The whites were still red-veined, Ernest noted.

"Well, good luck," said the young man with the mustache, tugging at the suitcase. Ernest watched him and his father vanish into the crowd at the back of the depot.

Ernest's father was craning his neck forward, fumbling with the volume control of his hearing device. "What did they say?" he asked sociably. "Did you know them?"

"Yes," said Ernest. "I knew him." And he recalled how the young man with the mustache had lain on the litter, how Dominick, the Army baker from Pyongyang, had taken off his shoes and shoved them under the mattress of the litter. How the brown-stained socks had looked, toes up.

"Was he in the hospital with you?" his father asked.

"Yes," said Ernest. He remembered how he had helped lift the young man with the mustache off the litter onto the ward bed. He remembered the feel of his sweating, oily, thick-haired head under his clenched hands.

"Their feet almost always smelled," Ernest said.

The old man smiled vaguely and said, "It's cold out here. I'll go into the depot and see what's doing. Is it all right if you stay here?"

"Go ahead," Ernest said. He watched his father shuffle through the crowd. A round, rouged face outlined itself from the dimness of the shapeless group. A small, grinning woman trotted up to Ernest. The woman licked her lips, still grinning.

"Why, Ernest, are you here? Don't tell me you're going home today?" she said. Unspoken questions slid across her face like one of these credit-title drums on a television program.

"Yes," Ernest said. He remembered how the woman's brother had begun bothering him in the ward. He looked at the woman's grinning face, and saw her brother staring back.

In the ward, on visiting day, when no one had come to see him, the woman would call Ernest over to where she was feeding her brother lox and bagel sandwiches, and halvah, and she would slip him a banana and say, "Be friends with my brother, Ernest. Be friends with him."

Ernest remembered the short, pudgy little creature with the slyly grinning face, who used to walk around and around the dayroom, chanting to himself, refusing to talk to anyone, running from the barred porch to the dayroom benches, rubbing his dark, hairy hands together. The attendants would laugh, when he began his chant. "And the coach of the Brooklyn Dodgers said, 'That runner is out.' *And do you know what he said?*" Over and over, broken by a snatch of song, or a bit of the Gettysburg Address. Ernest remembered that he had been a lawyer.

His sister would remind everyone, when she made her visits, that her brother had a law degree. She would listen to the long list of abuses he would pour out, things that had been done to him by attendants, by patients, by nurses.

"Yes," Ernest said. "I'm here."

"Well," the woman said, licking her lips again, "you must be anxious to be getting home."

"Yes," Ernest said, "I'm anxious."

"Well," said the grinning woman. "Good luck, if you make

it." And she trotted back to an aged, wrinkled woman whose face was shadowed by the huge shawl over her head and shoulders.

Ernest saw the two of them crouched toe-to-toe, looking at him, turning to talk to each other in short, rapid phrases, then turning to stare at him solemnly, shake their heads, and turn to each other again. He began to wish his father would come back. Then, suddenly, he was glad his father hadn't been there. Because maybe the grinning woman might have reached into his father's pocket and snatched the precious paper that allowed him his freedom. He felt their glances slide away from him, and dared to turn toward them again. They were walking toward the depot, still shaking their heads.

The meticulous voice in his head speculated: *They're jealous, because somebody got ahead of their son, their brother again. Maybe that's why they made him a lawyer, because lawyers are looked up to.*

Why couldn't I like him, back there? Ernest asked himself. We had a lot in common. We were both sick.

Different kinds of sickness, the voice replied, primly.

I don't know, Ernest answered soundlessly. Maybe because I don't like lox.

Suddenly, Ernest turned, and saw that his father was standing by him, watching him. Quickly, the old man smiled and said, "There's no train in sight, and the waiting room is too crowded for comfort. We'll just have to stay here."

Ernest toyed with the rope at the top of his barracks bag. As the old man was about to say something, Ernest nudged him, and pointed to two people getting off a bus.

"See that fellow? The fat one, wearing the Navy jacket? Now he's helping his mother get off the bus," he said.

His father automatically smiled the confused, sociable smile, the uneasy smile that had been flickering like a faulty searchlight ever since they had left the hospital. He looked from his son to the couple Ernest had pointed out, and nodded.

"That's Luca," Ernest said and his voice began to pitch higher.

"That's the fellow who went through everyone's drawer in the dormitory, taking food that didn't belong to him. He slept in a separate room, but during the day he would roam through the dormitory."

The old man watched the bulging mass of fat boymanhood carrying a little satchel, and the little, bent-over fat woman in a gray coat, and coughed. The old man began to reach out toward his son, as though he were about to make another placating, patting gesture in the air, a preventive gesture, to ward off trouble, anxieties, but he coughed again, and the hand flew nervelessly to the sagging mouth.

Luca had caught sight of them, and waddled in their direction, leaving his mother's side. She turned to follow. Luca was moving toward Ernest, and yet seemed not to notice where he was heading.

"One of the men told us it was Luca who stole, and we got him in a corner when the attendants weren't around, and asked him why he took out stuff from our drawers that didn't belong to him. We said we would have given him some candy bars if he'd asked right out.

"We asked him why he stole our stuff, and he would just smile and say he was hungry. But look at how fat he is.

"He was let out today, too, and from my ward, and a lot of good guys still in there," Ernest complained.

Luca pretended not to notice him, settling his little satchel on the ground near them, and shoving his hairy hands into the pockets of his bulging jacket.

Ernest began to raise his voice. "He admitted he took our food, the food our parents sent us from home. We asked him to stop it, but he kept on taking our food."

Luca turned, and the massy fat cheeks bulged, almost closing the black, glaring little eyes. When he spoke, his voice was oily-rich and guttural. "Oh come now, Ernest," Luca said. "Surely you're exaggerating."

Ernest was surprised at the way Luca enunciated each word

calmly, clearly. He had never heard Luca speak much in the ward, only seen him in action. He began to wish Luca had shouted at him, and felt foolishly defensive.

Luca's mother had almost reached them, and Ernest glanced toward him, then toward his mother. "Does your mother know what you did?"

The fat little woman reached them, and her smile was like her son's. Luca extended a pudgy hand, placatingly, toward Ernest. "Well, Ernest . . ." he began.

Ernest stared at the hairy paw reaching out to be shaken. He glared at the fat young manlittleboy. "After all the trouble you caused me, I'm sorry, Luca, but this is once I'm not going to say goodbye. I can't find it in my heart to say goodbye to anyone like you."

Luca dropped his hand and glanced at his mother. His grin was even broader. "You see?" it seemed to say. "He's sicker than I am."

His mother's smile caught the infection as she looked up at her son, adoringly, and she burst into a smiling laugh that gurgled like olive oil being poured from a jug. Luca began to laugh hissingly, like thick hot grease hitting a heated griddle. He turned away. His mother followed him.

Ernest's father looked at his son, watching the play of expression on the stubbled, weary face. He shook his head, and the hearing aid cord waggled, opened his mouth, closed it, then opened it again. "Let them go," the old man said, finally. "They both laugh like fools."

"He'll be back," Ernest said from between clenched teeth. "Wait until he gets hungry enough. He used to say he took our candy whenever he got a burning feeling in his stomach. Wait until he gets that burning feeling. He'll do something, and they'll put him back in the hospital. Just wait.

"I don't know why they let him out," he grated. "The attendants used to treat him like a violent patient. He'd hit the walls with his fist, and then just look at you as though it was you, and smile that way. If a patient is violent, he should be kept locked up," said Ernest loudly.

"Maybe he was just hungry," his father said, trying to be sensible. "Maybe he needed the food."

"Hungry!" Ernest snorted. "You never saw him in the shower, his fat body covered with hanging black hair. The fat just hanging in gobs on him, almost falling off him. He's hungry, sure, but not for food—"

"He was wearing a Navy coat," the old man said as conversationally as he could. "Was he in the Navy?"

"Huh? Yeah. Yeah, I guess so." Ernest was remembering the fat paw held out to be shaken, and the way Luca had told them, when they had backed him into a corner, with a lookout watching for attendants, that he was hungry.

He stared, leaning forward, toward the part of the station platform where Luca and his mother had melted into the crowd.

"Maybe we could take a cab to the city," his father said uncomfortably.

Ernest felt someone tap him on the shoulder. He turned and two tall, skinny, dark young men were smiling at him. One was wearing a light gray broad-brimmed felt hat. The other was hatless, and his dark hair was long, and combed oilily back behind his ears. "We heard you saying you just got out of the hospital," the hatless one said.

"That's right," Ernest said.

"Cripes, if ya'd just tell us how ya did it. Our brother's in there. You ever been in Ward Ten?" the young man with the long hair and the broad-brimmed hat said.

Ernest felt himself tense, even though he was on the outside. "Ward Ten? No."

"You was lucky," the hatless one said. "They got a attendant in there—big guy, almost bald, got a broken nose?"

"I heard of him," Ernest said.

"The Killer," the young man with the broad-brimmed hat said.

"That's what they call him, 'The Killer.' We're gonna catch up with that creep one a these days—"

"We was visiting our brother today," the hatless one said quickly. "We been trying to get him out. Maybe you got some ideas how it could be done. How'd you get out?"

"I got well," Ernest said.

"In *that* place?" the hatless one said. "How'd you get well in *that* place?"

"They gave me treatments," Ernest said.

"That's what we been trying to get the doctor to fix our brother up with. But he says it aint's no use. He says our brother's in bad shape," the young man wearing the hat said.

"Maybe they'll observe him and give him treatments later," Ernest said.

"No use," the hatless one said. "Know what that doctor told us? He said he should try to use some kind of pull. If we knew anybody that was important, he said, maybe we could get him out. But cripes, who do we know?"

"Here's my father. He doesn't know anybody and I'm out," Ernest said.

His father was craning his neck, the side of his head with the flesh colored earpiece turned toward the conversationalists. He smiled and nodded sociably when the two young men turned and looked at him.

"We was almost gonna take a poke at that doctor," the hatless one said.

"That wouldn't help," Ernest said.

Ernest turned to his father, and when the old man leaned forward carefully to hear, he said, "They've got a brother in the hospital."

He turned back, and saw that the two young men had gone off toward the far end of the depot, arguing with each other and making large gestures in the frosty air.

"They're worried about their brother?" the old man asked.

"He's in a bad ward," Ernest said. "They just keep him there. They call it observation, but they don't do anything, just keep him there."

The old man's head tilted and his eyes gleamed as he glanced at Ernest's troubled face. He had found his chance to make a joke. "So let them go. Are you their brother's keeper?" he chuckled, sociably.

Ernest looked at him. "All men are supposed to be brothers," he said in a way that brought the old man's neck craning forward. "But I couldn't look at that guy Luca that way. If you'd ever seen him in the evening, when they gave us milk and jam sandwiches. They'd all be on one plate, the sandwiches, and Luca he'd attack that jam sandwich, tearing off a huge hunk with his teeth and chewing it spittily, not a bit of expression on his fat face, his wet lips just going 'smak, smak, smak' and those beady eyes watching the plate, him getting ready to grab more than his share . . ."

Angrily, the old man said, "You had no right to associate with such people."

"I had no right to be born," Ernest said. "If you think it was easy all those months in New York, living in a dusty, dark little hotel room, eating in greasy hash houses, being shoved around—in the subways, on the streets . . ."

"You could have found a good job," the old man said. "You knew you were nervous from the Army. You didn't have to try to be a big success, not at first. If you'd of struggled along, being patient, starting small—"

"I started small," Ernest said, "and I got smaller and smaller . . ."

The old man shifted uneasily in the frosty dark. He said, "Let's have a cup of coffee. I'm so cold I don't care even if we do miss the train."

The restaurant was decorated with colored neon signs in the window advertising the food. Menus were Scotch-taped against the glass, listing the specials. Ernest slammed the barracks bag against the door, and the door swung open.

Through a wide entrance to the left, Ernest could see a bar. There were a few imitation leather-backed booths and a black glossy counter with high stools in the restaurant part. An automatic coin phonograph stood between the bar and the food counter.

Ernest glanced at the bar and the humped-over protuberances on the stools. He looked at his father. The old man was panting again, and his sociable smile was a bit twisted now, his eyes blinking fluidly behind the spectacles.

He thought, My father could use a drink. And then he saw his father looking at him, and he thought, He's studying me, wondering what I'm going to do. He sees me looking at the bar, and he's got custodian papers in his pockets, and ex-patients aren't supposed to drink.

He didn't really want a drink, but stubbornly, the meticulous voice said: *This is a celebration, really. You got out of there.*

We could sit at the bar, he thought. Then I'd belong to the barfly class, anyhow. I'd belong somewhere. It's a club. And he's looking at me now, knowing I'm thinking it over. I see the little smile. He's thinking it's all right, it's his son, and he deserves a drink on a day like this, the day he comes out.

Ernest sagged his bag down and picked a booth in the restaurant part nearest the phonograph. His father settled back against the imitation leather cushions. Ernest stretched out his hand, palm upward.

"Give me a dime," he said.

"Haven't you got any money?" his father asked.

"Where would I get it?" Ernest asked.

His father unbuttoned the awkward coat and reached into his pocket. He pulled a handful of coins and selected a quarter. He extended it toward Ernest.

"I said a dime," Ernest said.

"Take a quarter," his father said, patting the air. "What difference does it make?"

Ernest took the quarter and slid out from behind the fixed,

glossy-chromium black-topped table, his eyes fixed on the melting, shifting colors running through the plastic of the automatic phonograph. He pushed five of the round knobs and slid the quarter into the slot. He pushed the big round knob in the middle, and the first record slid out of the chromium-edged pile onto the turntable.

He stood for a few moments, leaning against the warm, plastic top of the machine, listening to the brassy orchestra weave its ten-inch brittle blanket of blare; then he turned and plumped into the seat across from his father. He rested his elbows on the black-topped table. "We had a radio in the ward," he said. "Sometimes it was on too loud. Sometimes we would argue over what program to tune in. Sometimes the attendants would make us turn it off. They said it interfered with the game of cards they were playing."

"You played cards with the attendants?" his father asked.

"The radio was way up on a platform. You had to stand on a chair to turn it on. One of the attendants was too short to reach it, even on a chair. He always made us get the programs he wanted."

"A short attendant," his father said, shaking his head to indicate how unusual it seemed, to have a short attendant in an insane asylum.

"He was squat and short. He was fat and short. His body pushed against his arms so they stood out from his sides a little. But he knew how to use those arms. I saw him take care of a patient who got out of line once," Ernest said.

The needle slid off the brassy record with an amplified "whomp," and the machine was thoughtfully quiet while it searched its intestines, reaching into its electronic subconscious for another nickel nightmare.

A waitress came up to their booth and rested her palms on the black top of the table. "We haven't been so busy in a long time," she said, lifting a moist arm so that the hand hung loosely, and brushing back a limp wisp of hair with her wrist.

"Soup," Ernest's father said. "We want hot soup."

Facing the door, Ernest could see more and more people entering the restaurant. He saw the clock on the wall over the counter. He smiled. "At this time in the hospital they're having their milk and jam sandwiches," he said.

"Forget the hospital," his father said hoarsely. "You're out of it, I tell you."

"For how long?" Ernest asked.

"What?" His father's face was drawn and gray in the fluorescent lights.

"I said, 'For how long?' This attendant, this short fat fellow, he predicted I'd be back in six months. He said he's seen them come and seen them go. He says most of them come back."

"Why should he say that?" Ernest's father demanded. "You're young. The Army made you nervous. You had treatments. You're cured, now. You're going home."

"He says I'll be back."

"The doctor didn't say that?"

"The doctor said it was up to me."

"Well," Ernest's father settled back against the imitation leather cushions. "You see? How does that other fellow know? Is he a doctor? How did he get his job? How does he hold it? Just a common ordinary attendant."

"He says he sees us more than the doctors do. He says he knows us better. He says you don't have to be educated to know what's wrong with somebody. He says he can tell by the way we walk and talk, and the way we sit down. He says—"

"He was just trying to scare you," the old man interrupted. "Trying to have some fun at your expense. Don't you care what he says."

The waitress brought the soup and two glasses of water. The place was becoming more and more crowded, and Ernest glanced at the latest knot of travelers spewed through the door. He saw two women enter, and he recognized the woman in the brown beaver coat. He called to her. "Mrs. Costello!"

The woman in the beaver coat hesitated, glanced their way,

said something to her companion, then bustled to their booth.

"Did you see Blase, Mrs. Costello?"

"Hello, there," she said a bit doubtfully. Then her head tilted a bit, and she smiled. Her features were small, her cheeks prettily curved, her nose arched and delicate. "Say, weren't you in the same ward with my son?"

"That's right," Ernest said. "I was there when they took him away."

"I'm so worried about him," Mrs. Costello said. "Was he as bad as they said he was? He couldn't be as bad as they said he was."

"He was a nice fellow, all right," Ernest said.

"Of course he was," said Mrs. Costello. "He was the most gentle, likeable, friendly boy in all the world. You were there when they took him away. What happened?"

"He got into a fight," Ernest explained. He turned to his father, saying, "This is Mrs. Costello."

His father nodded and smiled sociably, glancing at the beaver coat. Mrs. Costello smiled absent-mindedly and said, "How do you do, what kind of a fight?"

"There were two other fellows," Ernest said. "Luca and a big tough guy, Jimmy. It was in the cafeteria. I heard a lot of dishes hitting the floor and the metal trays being knocked down, and when I turned, Jimmy was halfway in the air and Blase was jumping around, and two of the attendants had Luca pinned down."

"I'm sure it wasn't Blase's fault. I know it couldn't be his fault. He was always so friendly," Mrs. Costello said. "Now they've got him in the violent ward."

"Maybe they'll let him out after a while. He might go back on shock treatments," Ernest comforted.

"Oh, no," Mrs. Costello cried, rubbing the collar of her beaver coat, roughing it up then smoothing it back down. "I tried to tell the doctor in your ward to give him more treatments and he got excited and told me to get out of his office. He said the treatments wouldn't help Blase any more."

"Maybe you said something to get him excited," Ernest said.

"All I did was tell him to give Blase more treatments," Mrs. Costello insisted. "Isn't that what we pay our taxes for?" She leaned forward and looked at Ernest intently. "And what kind of a doctor is it who gets excited, anyhow? Doctors aren't supposed to get excited."

Ernest's father leaned forward and said, "Were you visiting someone in the hospital today, lady?" And he fumbled with the volume control of his hearing aid. In his anxiety to hear, he turned the knob too far, and the feedback squealed in his ear. The others could hear it as a dull squeak, somewhat like the noise a child's rubber toy makes when it is squeezed.

The old man squinted in agony, and half-opened his mouth as though to cry out. Then he readjusted the knob and looked about apologetically.

"He uses one of those things, doesn't he?" Mrs. Costello remarked. She inclined herself toward the old man, bending from the waist, mouthing the words with her pretty red lips. "I'm worried about my son," she told Ernest's father loudly.

The old man leaned further forward, smiling sociably as she began to speak, but at the last word his smile wavered and he slouched back, nodding rhythmically, to indicate that he knew what it was to be worried about one's son.

The waitress bustled up, leaned across Ernest and stretched her bare arms to pick up the soup plates. He could see the fuzz on her flesh, and he could smell the sharp sweat, the pungent perfume and the woman scent of body.

"Everybody's in a hurry," the waitress commented, and smiled a sweet, impersonal smile at the beaver coat. She smiled at Ernest. "Will that be all, sir?"

"Give us a couple of ham sandwiches," Ernest said.

Mrs. Costello glanced around. "I came in with a friend. Oh, there she is," she said, pointing to a fat, approaching-menopause woman near the front door.

"If you can't find a seat you can sit with us in our booth," Ernest offered.

"That would be nice," Mrs. Costello said. "I want to hear

more about what they said Blase did." She glanced at Ernest's father and raised her voice. "I'm so worried about my son," she said loudly.

The old man nodded, grinning sociably, helplessly. "Yes, of course, your son, yes. Yes, well . . ."

The delicate features relaxed in a smile, and she turned her back on them, seeking her friend. Ernest watched his father wiping his mouth on the paper napkin and gazing meditatively after Mrs. Costello.

"What are you thinking about?" he asked his father.

The old man peered across the table at his son, his lower jaw sagging in a tired smile. As he started to speak, the waitress brought their sandwiches wrapped in waxed paper, and he began to fumble with the wrapper. "I was remembering when you were a little boy, how you would never eat your mother's soup if she put cooked carrots in it," he said.

The automatic phonograph was devoting three minutes to a baritone who was asking for just one more chance, because he was willing to serve his sentence but wanted to prove he still cared, and Ernest said, "It's hard to believe she's the mother of a fellow about my age."

"Raw carrots you would eat," the old man said. "But cooked carrots, never. You liked raw carrots so much, you'd even promise your mother to take your castor oil if she would give you a nice peeled one." He chuckled, shaking his head, the hearing aid cord waggling and rubbing against his vest.

Ernest looked at him sharply. The baritone said that he was back now to cry his heart out. The old man leaned back and bit experimentally at the firm, resisting crust of the bread, blinking up at his son over the sandwich and still smiling.

Ernest bit into the dry sandwich and chewed thoughtfully. "I remember when she was visiting her son the day I was transferred from the observation ward to the treatment ward," he said. "I was thin and hungry, and she had food spread out on the table. I went over to where she was sitting with Blase, and she said,

'Now let's see, what can we give him to eat?' And she gave me a twisted-bread sandwich."

"Why were you hungry?" his father demanded. "Didn't they give you enough to eat?"

"In the observation ward, most of the time I ate in the ward kitchen. The food was served by a patient they called Jehovah. He was big and black and wiry, and used to sing voodoo songs all night near my bed. He looked so fierce I was afraid to ask for more food. Sometimes when I came into the kitchen one of the attendants would say, 'Kick him, Jehovah!' and he would kick me, hard."

"You wrote me something about that," his father said hoarsely, pulling the crust off his bread.

"I didn't think they'd pass that through the censorship," Ernest said.

The old man leaned forward. "You say this lady who just came over, her son,—were you friends with him?"

"Nobody could be friends with him. He'd roam from one bunch of guys to another, a sort of smile on his face. He was built like a panther, all smooth muscles, and when he walked over you could feel the vibrations like he was fierce in a forest, and I'd get scared. He'd just walk over and look at you and smile," Ernest remembered.

Mrs. Costello was hurrying back to their booth. Behind her was the fat overrouged woman, who seemed to be toeing an invisible mark on some sprinter's track. "This is my friend," Mrs. Costello introduced. "Someone took the table we were going to sit at. But we have to catch the train soon anyhow. I just want to know—did you ever see Blase get violent in there?"

"You remember the time he shoved his fist through the glass in the dayroom door?" Ernest said. "They told you about that?"

"Oh, that," Mrs. Costello said. "That. Yes, well . . ."

"I heard you telling Blase to take it easy, once, when you were visiting him after that."

"He cut his hand," Mrs. Costello explained.

She blew on the sleeve of her coat. "I thought God was good, when Blase came through the war and back to me. He was my only child. And now I've lost him again, and forever," she said.

"Maybe they'll take him out of cold storage," Ernest encouraged.

"No," she said. "They've got him in a ward where he sits and sits. Just sits and looks at the wall. They don't do anything there."

"Did you try to see anybody important on the outside?" Ernest asked, remembering the two tall, dark, skinny young brothers with the long hair.

Mrs. Costello looked at him sharply, her pretty red mouth still pursed to blow the fur of her coat sleeve. "I've been burning up the wires to Washington all day," she said. Her eyes slid away, and she put her slim, soft little hand on Ernest's arm for a fleeting second, pouting; then the hand flew away, fluttering onto the table like a little bird. "You have no idea how lonely it is in my little apartment, now. I come home at the end of the day, tired, restless, unhappy, and my Blase, my wonderful big son, he isn't there."

The fat woman with the heavily rouged lips had slid onto the imitation leather cushions next to Ernest's father. She had looked at the old man quickly, then looked down at the black table top. Mrs. Costello, sitting beside Ernest, plucked a little rhinestone-studded compact from her purse, her elbow brushing his ribs for a moment. She began to apply rouge, in swift, darting dabs.

A large man wearing a heavy black sweater and an old visored cap stopped at their booth and said, "It'll cost you ten dollars apiece to take a taxi into the city from here."

The man looked at the two women. Mrs. Costello's glance slid imperceptibly across that of the fat woman's. Ernest saw Mrs. Costello nod slightly in the direction of the old man. "You can cash your train tickets in," the man suggested.

"Shall we taxi back?" Mrs. Costello said lightly to her companion.

She smiled, looking at the fat woman intently, snapping shut her compact with a little click. The fat woman shrugged, "It doesn't matter to *me*."

"Maybe we will, too," Ernest's father said. "We could all take a taxi together."

Ernest looked at his father, and the meticulous voice said, *He's not that tired,* and Ernest answered it indignantly, He is!

Maybe he knows how I feel about leaving there. Maybe he wants to be good to people who were friends with me, in there, Ernest thought, recalling the tip to the taxi driver who had driven them to the village, and how his father had said, "Thanks for helping my son," when the driver had said, "Good luck, son."

"It wouldn't be so much, all together," Mrs. Costello said prettily.

"You make up your mind, and I'll round up a few more passengers," the cab driver said, moving away.

Mrs. Costello shoved her compact into her purse. "My Blase is lost, I tell you," she told Ernest.

"If he can only stop being so tough," Ernest said. "He was always walking around with that superior smile of his."

"But Blase never feels superior," she protested. "He's got an inferiority complex. He's afraid of everybody. That's what's wrong. People frighten him. He'd never hurt a soul."

"The only one he ever seemed to talk to much was a little fellow you know, that Allan Preston," Ernest said. "Allan used to call him 'My Blasie,' and give him candy, and he'd ask Blase to use some of his cologne, he used to finger Blase's ear and put his arm around him and say that Blase was the handsomest man in the ward."

Mrs. Costello knotted her slim fingers together. Her delicate brows crinkled in a frown. "He was a fairy, that Preston, wasn't he?" she said.

Ernest shrugged. "He walked around like one."

What does she want of you? the meticulous voice said, and Ernest said soundlessly, I don't know.

What do any of them want of me? he said voicelessly. They all asked me questions, wanting to know how I got out. Why, why why?

He looked at Mrs. Costello, and felt her shoulder brush his, and he heard the small squeak her nylons made as she crossed her legs under the table. And he started to speak, and he realized suddenly it was the hidden meticulous voice speaking, only it was making the sounds, and it started to say, "*What do you—*"

The shuffling crowd in the restaurant began to hum and murmur, and Ernest saw several people nearest the door look out the window. He saw them dart to the door, and someone called, "The train's ready!"

Mrs. Costello rose, motioning to the fat woman. They began to thread their way through the crowd, toward the door. At the door, Mrs. Costello turned, for a fleeting moment, smiled, and waved hastily. She turned, and the two women ran out the door.

The meticulous voice was not so meticulous now, but it spoke silently again. It told Ernest, *Do you call that a mother? Maybe she isn't even Blase's mother. The way they held hands in the ward—*

Ernest's father was looking down at the pieces of hard crust he had torn off his ham sandwich. The phonograph was vibrating to the rhythm of a martial beat, as a young girl, harmonizing with herself, sang "Retreat, retreat, retreat . . ."

"We'd better get out there. If the train's ready, we won't have to take a taxi," the old man said. He craned over his shoulder, searching for their waitress.

Ernest reached for his barracks bag. He hoisted it onto his shoulder, and they plodded out of the restaurant, through the muddy streets to the depot. Through the dark windows of the depot, Ernest could see the railway cars backing down the track. The train stopped, and the cars loomed up out of the darkness. The travelers were straggling into the coaches.

Ernest stopped by the doorway of a car and waited for his father. The old man plodded up beside him, puffing hard, his eyes blinking and watering.

In the smoke-smelling, creaky dusty old coaches, Ernest's father found two seats together, and the old man slid gratefully onto the dirty plush cushions, licking his dry, blued lips.

Seated next to the window, Ernest saw the lights of the little village waver and swiftly melt into the night, then disappear. He felt the train lurching, gathering speed, rackety-racketying and pounding along the rails.

He peered through the darkness, and the unseen, blackened landscape poured over his aching eyeballs like thoughts unspoken.

Unspoken thoughts of his wardmates lying in the snug little steel beds with their thin, striped mattresses all in a row. Of Dominick, the Army baker, bomb-shocked at Pyongyang, trying to close his mouth, gasping for breath in the darkened dormitory, and of the Greek, Kaxon, who snored heavily under one of the dim blue lights that made the dormitory seem all the darker—

Of the soft little bobbysoxed Aileen, whose snub-nosed, flushed face was close to his, as he held her carefully under the serious scrutiny of the methodical, big-hipped occupational therapist during the weekly dance-and-lotto sessions on the fourth floor, while the nasal, two-dimensional music of the scratchy donated phonograph played Sometimes I Wonder Why I Spend The Lonely Night . . . and how purple her face had been as he wheeled her from the shock room, gauze packing between her teeth, to deposit her gently on the wrinkle-sheeted bed from which she would rise dizzily in a few minutes so that another could be so deposited—

Aileen, who had offered him her last stick of gum, who had tripped up to him in her bathrobe, her red face tear-streaked on the day she had learned he was leaving, and how he had wanted desperately to clutch the rough stuff of the hospital-issue bathrobe and kiss her beautifully-moulded, red little mouth—

To kiss her goodbye, but he had been afraid to, because it was so close to freedom now, and they might think he was attacking her, you had to be so careful—

Of the grinning lawyer, who had cheered the Brooklyn Dodgers from his seat in the dayroom, of the red-faced schizoid in the sailor coat, whose buttocks rose and fell as he rubbed himself, face down, against the dayroom benches, and the Russian refugee, Carnovsky, who had been a doctor, and who discussed over and over the merits of estrogen and corpus luteum.

Of the two Mahatma Ghandis, three Winston Churchills, five Satans, one King of Saturn, a Martian bug-eyed-monster, and four Joseph Stalins he had encountered in the wards, and how he himself had been Jesus Christ for a while . . .

Of the pretty nurse affiliates from the New York hospitals, fresh from having kneeled before an altar while their Big Sisters placed the rounded, starched white bits of cloth on their heads, reciting the Florence Nightingale oath—getting their required experience in their first mental hospital, standing by in the morning at the zero hour in their crisp blue-and-white striped bibs and watching wide-eyed as he poured sugar water and starchy potato soup down the gullet of a moaning, comatose wardmate who had been murdered and was being reborn by a couple of hundred units of insulin—

The rose-cheeked affiliates, squealing excitedly, "Hey, I gave my first hypo today. Hey, the Doc let me flip the switch on the shock machine. Gee, it cuts off so fast, but what if it didn't—"

His father coughed, adjusted his spectacles, and said, "In a few hours now, we'll be in the city. Then home, and will your mother be glad!"

Unspoken thoughts of the patients, and friends and relatives of patients he had met in the last few hours, and how easy he had thought it would be to talk to them, having so much in common, but how no one seemed to understand, now.

And of the questions his mother would ask, and his sister would ask, and the people he would meet who might wonder how he got out, why he went in, whether he was all right, now.

Of the restaurant they had just left, with its jukebox moaning about one more chance, and Mrs. Costello moaning about her son who had been given his last chance.

And how fierce and muscular her son was, how, secretly, Ernest had always been afraid the tightly-smiling, wire-taut Blase might lash out at him in frenzy released. But one blue-lit night in the dim dormitory it had been the hard-knuckled fist of an ex-Marine patient which had knocked Ernest down.

Knocked down Ernest, the newly-arrived treatment patient who had been sent up from the ward where Jehovah had given him kicks instead of food.

And how the curious treatment patients had clustered around Ernest, as he felt his jaw, crouching on the floor, clutching a package of cigarettes in one hand, a candy bar in the other, crying, "I was only exchanging things! See, cigarettes for candy!"

But neither the cigarettes nor candy had been his, and the husky ex-Marine who had knocked him down knew it, and the others knew it, though they couldn't know how hungrily he had nibbled at the chocolate, right through the wrapper, because Jehovah hadn't let him eat.

Yet one of the others had interceded, "Well, he's sicker than us. And he seems to have some sort of idea of fair play, trading ciggies for candy."

The meticulous voice prodded, *If people together in one sickness can't understand each other, how can you expect strangers to understand?*

Indignantly, Ernest answered the voice, silently trying to silence it.

Mostly, in there though, we got along.

But he thought of Luca's fat paw held out to be shaken at the village depot, as they both stood on the threshold of the frightening unknown, and he shuddered.

He looked at the old man, and wanted to say: I think I know why I didn't have my chance to stay in the city, but why didn't you? And where is the holiday smile now? But he looked back at the window and couldn't see the outside but only his reflection, blurred, and the dim shadow of the father beside him, and suddenly he wanted to look out very much, but could see only mirror-images, faintly lit while the world streamed on blackly beyond the glass.

Ernest mumbled something, and the old man coughed, shifted, and said, "Huh? What did you say?"

He turned away from the window, and said, "In a few hours now, back at the hospital . . ." And then he saw his father, not smiling the holiday smile any more, and looking very small inside his thick coat.

"In a few hours now, back at the hospital," Ernest said, "somebody else will be taking my place, feeding the shock patients potato soup." And he knew, turning back to the black window, that if he went back he would be changed already, and his ward fellows would know it, he had to go on.

Up ahead, the train shrieked for a crossing. The old man smiled sociably, and licked his blueing lips, blinking and nodding, and hoping his son hadn't just asked a question, because his hearing-aid battery was dead.

The train hurtled on, taking them somewhere, but always away. Ernest put his forehead against the cold, vibrating glass of the window and closed his eyes.

The Musicians

SHORT STORIES

by

ROBERT CREELEY

The Boat

The Gold Diggers

The Unsuccessful Husband

3 Fate Tales

Jardou

The Seance

The Musicians

THE BOAT

No one was moving but for William, and they paid him little attention. He came, now, down through the trees, and behind them, very carefully, to a huge rock that overlooked the water. The boat was too far out to see who was in it, but the sails looked beautiful, tight out and driving the boat through the water in a series of chopped lunges. He climbed up on the rock, took a stick he found there, and leaning out, dabbled it in the water. He wrote his own name three times, then his wife's, then those of their three children.

Way off up the field Mrs. Peter had talked of the weather, and she repeated herself, endlessly. The heat came, the sun rising very high and white in the sky, and beyond the field the trees in the orchard looked wilted and dull. She cried. Her face grew very tiny and alone, and with a sense of relief the other man, her friend, bent over quietly with a white handkerchief and dabbed at her eyes. He implored her to have reason, the conversation had been so tiring, and if they were to be together, ultimately, they must have the necessary courage. But she cried, again, until her face was wet, and he held the handkerchief on her cheeks, rubbing them, hopelessly involved to be sure, but some small part of him seemed heroic and manly, and that was the part she looked to.

William, on the rock, knew nothing much more than the heat, and if the sun got any higher, he said, he would lose his mind entirely. The trees rustled slightly, the wind went past them with a murmur, but it was a hot wind, and William crawled down lower on the rock to wet his face in the water. And feeling it cool, he quickly took off his clothes and left them there, and jumped in.

All this the children were aware of, and in the boat they prepared to attack him, not sullenly, but as quickly as he had thought to go into the water like that, they as well saw him and wanted to surprise him by bearing down on him with the boat. They tacked, and the boat shuddered. For a minute the smallest boy's legs were covered with the foam, and he shouted to them all to look. But coming off, the boat righted itself, and again they watched William who swam beyond them.

Hence, in a vague way, it was all, Mrs. Peter said, a question of the heat. William could not hear her, he would not have heard her in any circumstances, but to her friend, recovered, the comment was apt and sensible. Weather as an inexhaustible subject, or he answered her, that this as well they would have to consider, and above all its effects on William's nerves. The right time would be precisely the time when, at an impasse with everything, and with, particularly, the heat, he should no longer give much of a damn about anything, and if he did treasure her, or anything, even so would give it all up quietly enough.

Supposition, she said, was not accurate. The wind blew. But to be in love was to be something, and if heat were elemental, they were likewise of nature's force.

It was a ridiculous time for anything. She couldn't really say that she loved him, and had to think quickly, which one. Her friend looked at her, her eyes were a little red but the face was not for him. He took her hand, because he wanted something, and she let the pressure come, then relax, and squeezed back a little and smiling, wondered again what would become of them.

William was not the question, she knew, or at least she thought it, and then kissed the other man, in almost trite fashion, saying it is very like it always is. And, do I now think what I think because I think other people have thought it. For this there was no reply, the kiss being remote, and very near insult. The speech, anyhow a question, which the friend wanted to answer, but could not. He dressed in a loose shirt, worn outside of his pants, and with a check-like design. The pants were brown, something like khaki.

He had black hair, and a small clipped beard on the end of his chin. To be romantic was to be insular in one's concern for others, and in love he acted as though he were looking in a mirror.

Against all that, viciously, the boat went on and in it the children hung one to the rudder, and one to the jib lines, while the third kept hold of the rope for the boom, and sighted William for the one sitting behind him. They were almost there. William's head showed itself a little off to the right, and with a sudden push, the rudder went over, and they were on top of him.

At that moment he saw them, and why he hadn't before, or heard them, he had no time to think of, but dove, the boat's bottom hitting his head. He went down and down, and in spite of it, thought of them all up there, on the surface. The boat had gone over, the water again grew light, and from his mouth a very thin line of little bubbles. Time passed, the weeds shone blue and green in the depth, the mud felt cool and close on his body. Then he gave a push with his feet and felt them sink in, then lift, and then he swam, up, and broke the water with a kind of gasped cry.

They were on the shore, and called out to him, and he answered by a wave of his hand and swam to them, slowly, feeling his head ache but had no resentment. The three children were there, the boat was now anchored and the sails rolled up, and tied. The rudder had been taken off, and lay across the back of the boat, drying. At the top of the mast a small red flag flapped in the breeze and the boat lifted and dropped in the ground-swell.

It was very lovely, he thought, but even more, this immediate solicitation, and pulling himself out of the water, he let himself fall into their hands, and be carried all the long distance to the house, as the friend took the bulk of the load by holding him under the arm-pits, gently, and lifting him very carefully so as not to joggle his head. He swore at the children, and they came behind him, somewhat afraid. He made no conditions, the sound of his own voice was ugly, or seemed ugly, to him. When he had been lowered to the sofa, he wanted to cry, and let them see it. But their faces were too far away, and he found himself asleep.

He dreamt of three tigers, in a forest. Their bodies were striped as he had expected. Their faces were long, with, on each one, a red tongue lolling out over white teeth. He gave a banana to each one of them. They ate the bananas, and put the skins to one side, whereupon he grew frightened, shifted his position, and began to snore.

Mrs. Peter continued with the business in hand, and she had no doubt that it was, despite the difficulties, an act that could be transacted as elaborately and as completely as the buying of potatoes. In the garden, she drew up a chair, close to the friend whom the matter of the boat had frightened. He felt himself now an outsider, or, more simply, unable to recover his own place with quite the same manipulation. To quiet him, she took off her sun-hat and began to fan herself, then fanned him, so that the moving air lifted the collar of his shirt, which he had left unbuttoned to the middle of his chest, and blew it against his beard.

Now, she said, that there is quiet, now we can settle all of this. He raised himself to listen, and to say what he himself would have to. She said, do you love me. To that, certainly, he replied, yes. They kissed.

But, she said, being married and all, does it matter to you that another man has had my love. And that was not a fair question. The woman who loves is beyond it, she does not see anything more than what she does have, just there and then, in front of her nose. He said, if it does not matter to you, it does not matter to me.

It was enough, and might have been for anyone else, but not for her. She wanted to go away, a long voyage, or anything to get away from him, and from both of them. Well, she said, I love you, but you don't love me. For my own part I think we are not so much in love as I had thought, but, seeing that we have no reason to hurry, take a walk to the beach, and in an hour I will come and join you.

Once he was gone, she went back into the house to look at William. He lay with an arm down over the edge of the sofa, and she could see the place where the boat had hit him. The bruise began at the edge of his hair, back of his ear, then went into the hair itself. It all looked swollen and painful. But she was not sure that she loved him.

If she whistled, or cried out, one of the two might come. Otherwise, she then thought, I have three children. Who would have killed their father this morning, and not even meant to do it.

So it was impossible not to think about life, or the sense of the kind of life she herself might find possible. The room came in, a picture of her own father, or someone, hung at an odd angle over the cold fireplace. There was no fire and yet she screamed. But did not scream. In the emptiness she saw William coming toward her, carrying an oar. He was about to found a city.

As an alternative she left the room, and went out again into the garden. The remains of their lunch were still there, and, over the plates, she saw a swarm of flies. Looking past them, she saw a briefcase, on the seat of a chair, with gold initials just over the lock. She went over and picked it up, and tried to open it, but could not, and threw it back in the chair in anger. It was the life of a dead man, not to have kindness, and openness, in each person met or dealt with. To have secrets was finally to have desires, and if she could not satisfy them, to keep them like that was dishonest. She picked up the briefcase again and threw it into a bed of yellow flowers. What she gave was open, and all air, she thought. But for them it was the careful locking up of each particular, because they thought they were men.

The children used another way of things, and taking in the friend, now they played with him, and soon he was exhausted, panting after them, foolishly, up and down the beach. He had taken off his shirt, but they ran too fast, and if he caught one, another suddenly pelted him with a handful of sand, and, in trying to see which had done it, he lost hold of the one he had had, and found his eyes full of sand and tears.

He wanted her to come very badly, he saw their future life together floating over his head, and, as the wind might take it, blown away from him. He indulged in this metaphor, and was like a man lost in himself completely. If he wanted her, then, he thought, it must be that they leave together right away. To have the children, he said, and a stone hit him, and a small spot of blood appeared on the inner side of his ankle.

Mrs. Peter watched all this, and again was powerless. But, coming down, she told the children to stop, and from their own audacity, which they felt they had perhaps taken too far, they stopped, and ran down the beach and out of sight. Then she said, love me, very simply. And, as she asked it, he brushed off his pants, and came to her, and then led her back to the field, where they lay down. I want you to be for me, she said, but she hated him. As his hands touched her, she felt cold finally, and thanked him for that.

THE GOLD DIGGERS

West of thc mountains, the land rides out on a flat and open plain and continues for more miles than any one man ever knows of. The light is high, it comes from the farthest point of the sun. If you put a man here, already you find him lonely. If you put two, then what happens is not so much what either one man decides on, but what happens to them no matter.

For both of these reasons they built the shed in the shadow of one tree, which was the only one. To the back they put another slight covering for the machine, that is, the machine which dug for the gold. Sometimes it covered an acre a day, and on others, meeting with less, over twice that area. Their car stood back of it all under a thin canvas. In one of the rooms of the shed there was another machine which gave them electricity, and it ran on the same gasoline which they had provided for the other, at the first, making a cache of fifty large drums of it, at the far end of the site. That much was all safe, and because it had been regulated at the beginning, it now went on without significant interruption.

Only this night one of the men sat by himself on a chair leaning against the tree. He had pushed back with his feet, and the chair lifted, and rested against the tree's trunk. The car was gone, and had left two days before, making a dust cloud far out over the dry ground to the east, and at last leaving him there, as now, sitting on the chair and watching. He said he could drink, and did drink, and left a single bottle, empty, on the ground. It was unpleasant. He sang to himself, and his voice rose out into the air, and against the sun he sang one thing that he could remember, which he called a lament. But he knew this loneliness.

Toward seven or eight the car came back, and at first he saw the small cloud of dust, which might have been made by some incredible stray horse, although there were none. It came closer and closer, and as it did he felt himself aching, and beginning to cry a little not much caring. The car came finally into the yard, and slurred past his chair to stop back of the shed. For a few minutes the doors stayed shut, and from behind the dusty windshield he could see the other man watching him. He tried to smile, but the skin of his face felt too cracked, so that he called out, in protest, and let himself wait for the other man to answer.

Getting out of the car, the man spoke, and motioned him to come over. Now he could smile a little, and saw the packages in the back of the car, piled up as high as the window. Reaching in, he took an armful and followed after the other man into the shed. He watched while the other man put his load down, by the table, but not on it. Then he put his own down.

There was nothing to say but he looked at him, knowing the face so exactly he could see the eyes pushed back into the narrow and quiescent head. He tried to say something, of the sitting there, but the other began to talk now, and they sat down together, facing, while the other paused to open one of the boxes, taking out two small bars of chocolate, and ripped the papers off both, first the shiny and smooth label one, and then the silver under it. He listened.

At first there was only a sort of low and discontinuous obscenity, the phrases marking out a street of the city he could not remember. He knew it was late. There was a bar, open, on the corner. The other man went in and sat down there. There were women.

One of them came up to him. He saw her head nodding under a high light, and some of it fell off the hair, glancing down to the glass in his hands. She was smiling at him or trying to also, and her hand had come forward enough to find his own. Speaking to her, his mouth was like the substance of his whole body, and twisted itself to answer. The low phrases continued, marking again and again each act of the meeting.

In her room she went completely into him, against his own will tearing at him, so that he left her, he thought, unconscious. The obscenities were now actual, they surrounded him. He thought of each thing, and could not even say who he was, or whether this had happened to him, or had not. When he made supper, because the other man was too tired and hardly ate it, he went in a daze, and even the food which the other had brought was almost something he could not taste.

The next day the sun cleared early, and getting out the machine, he oiled it. It looked black, and squat, on the ground. It moved like a tractor, and was long and low. The earth broke under it, shovelled into the front opening, and then ground down and down and down into small, and sortable, fragments. In a hopper at the back the gold itself slowly collected, in a half pure state. To some extent a man could become rich, insofar as the nature of the place allowed him that, and let the gold come up without difficulty. Here they found it uncertain, and some days travelled mile after mile without much of anything.

Because of practice he rode it easily, and without concentration. Before him the land spread flat. The mark of the other days was on his right, and there the land looked chewed and broken. In front of him it was utterly smooth, showing only a trace of rock, here and there, as something too far under him to be important perhaps came up to declare itself. But the gold was there. To that extent it was a job he had chosen for himself, although he had not known then what it would be. But that sort of argument he had the same contempt for he would show against any alternative, to the chosen thing, and had not as yet needed it.

Riding high, he set the steering wheel against his knees, and held it loosely with his hands. He kept his eyes low, clear of the glare of light from the horizon. Under him the machine moved along, carrying him straight forward.

So it went on. He didn't forget anything, but lumped it, now, altogether. He thought the light killed the woman, or the idea of her. He didn't know whether his companion was lying. Perhaps he was. There was no way to prove it. The machine grated on rock, then lifted and slid off, to dig in again ahead of it, and continue. He never looked back because he thought he would not be able to bear it, like a cut on his hand when the blood came too fast. Now he rode it, or drove it, regardless.

Then he stopped. He got down from the seat, swinging clear of the treads with a push of one hand, and landed hard on the ground. For a moment he crouched there, leaning against the machine, and then looked around the back of it to the shed. But for the car again, there was nothing different. The tree was there. The shed stood over from it only a short distance, and the door was shut. He couldn't see anyone, and thinking to call, stopped himself, and got back up on the machine.

But it was a persistent thought. Somewhere in the screaming, still under him, the sound alone enough to kill out any other, even so there was something else. He would have driven a tractor the same way, and could see no difference possible. He made as straight a furrow as he could, and at the end, let it rear on the turn, to settle again to the run back. Forcing it only a little, he judged he could make it in an hour, and settled himself back to watching the shed reappear, at first a small and indeterminate blur, then larger, until at last he saw it almost clearly, and the tree again beside it.

When he came in, the other man started to talk to him. He told him more of the trip, with the car, and took each mile as it had come, the rabbits shying in front of the lights at night, then the flat emptiness of the day, until, at last, he saw the first towns coming up to him, and then the city. But it was not really possible to believe it. Together they knew everything, and nothing, because one false thing and none of it was true. He thought, he didn't even like the other man, and was with him because he needed him, but not in a way that he might. He poured out the water, carefully, and got the bottle the other had brought from the cupboard and put it on the table beside the plates. Drink, he said, damn you. You have all the fun.

You want to know a real woman, the other said, some real fine thing. Because that's why I stay here at all. To earn money.

He didn't answer him. He put the rest of the things on the table, and pulled up his own chair to sit down. A real woman, the other man said. One with real hair, and real legs, and real eyes. Real, he said.

But the plates were clean, the food left, unavoidably, dried, and hardened, on the tin. The other man got up and pushing them all together, he picked them up and carried them off to the bucket. He sat down beside it, and poured some water into another tin, and sloshed it over the dishes.

There was nothing to say. He watched the other man's hands, he saw them take the dishes, rubbing them. The water poured over them, back to the tin, then repeated, until the other man got up, and wiped them all with his hand, shaking them, and put them beside the tin on a shelf to dry. It was time to go.

Once again on the machine, the sun came down, clearing his head, he thought. The noise came again. It started as the motor started, then ground deeper into the final sound of the machine moving, and the earth lifting into it. He whistled, and high above the sound could hear the thin, sighing noise. Now he rode the machine, letting it take him, like a horse. Perhaps the gold rattled into the box. The lumps were as big as his fist, he scooped them up, and let them fall through his fingers. Somewhere the whole noise was constant, and became a continuity through which he rode the afternoon.

So he drove carefully. Now and again a ragged patch of mesquite, or some bush, passed him, or else he struck it head on, eating it up. Far ahead sometimes the sun glinted on rock, and as he came up to it, he eased the machine, then hit it. There was the lifting motion, and then they went on. Time after time the plain blurred, and to his eyes it was an ocean, or a place without any disturbance at all. The sun flattened it, it pressed hard in, and down, and forced the nature of the ground itself out.

Then, turning, he saw the woman, not really as even he knew, but there she was even so. He felt embarrassed by the noise, and the nature of the work he was doing. He wished the dust might be not so thick, or the roar so heavy he could not even speak to her. He had no hat that he could rightly raise for her, since the cap he did wear seemed impossible to him to lift. All of it was impossible, he saw her float for a moment, clear of the ground, then she was gone completely. He let the idea stay inside of him. He thought he would never speak of it. He let the roar come back, and drove ahead, sighting the shed, and watched the tree grow larger beside it.

But that night he spoke of it. It was night in the shed now. They ate. The other man got out the bottle and they drank, and he sat there listening to the other man talk again. There were other things to be said. The pictures came, faded, and came back. The woman was all alone. It was an echo coming again and again, back, and in the words of the other, with no intention, continuing until he spoke at last himself, telling all of it, of her being there, and then not there, and finally fell down himself, crying and crying, until the other pulled at him, to make him stop.

You should stop, the other man said. There's no good in that, you wait a minute.

He heard nothing but the sound of the other moving away from him, back to a corner of the room. He waited. His eyes were wet but he made no move to rub them. He lay still forward on the table, keeping his head covered with his hands. Behind him the sounds shifted to a rattling of some paper, something unrolling, and then again he heard the man walking across the room to him. The hand pulled at his shoulder, lifting him, and light hit his face, while the other said, look, pushing it at him, the odor incredible but certain, and again the light fell off the silk and the hair into his eyes.

He went forward, grabbing at the cloth. The other man fell

down still holding it, and then sat, on the floor. He kicked at him, and the other fell over completely and rolled flat on the floor, then quiet. The room was quiet. He bent over and picked up the table, and lifting it as high as he could, he let go.

THE UNSUCCESSFUL HUSBAND

SUCH a day of peace it was, so calm and quiet, with the haze at the window, beginning, and from there going far out over the fields to the river beyond, a morning haze, such as the sun soon burns and has done with. Yet all through that day there was quiet and the haze of calm. It was not the first of many such days. None followed. But it became the reminder of something somewhat better than what one had, the stasis of peace, which, once found, can always remind one and even be found again. Such a day, a peaceful day, so calm and quiet, one is never done with no matter how long . . .

We were married fifteen years ago, at a quiet ceremony attended by a very few people, close friends, and following the ceremony we travelled to a place where I had not been since my childhood but where, as it were, I had always lived or at least wanted to. My wife was then a very pretty woman, a quiet face with a smile of destructive calm, and a figure which, at the very least, provoked one to thoughts not at all in keeping with a usual intention. I cannot say how it was but it was simply that she could not be won, not in the usual manner. Although I do not remember it as deliberate, still I can see now that it was a matter of giving in the old sense such as I had believed no longer to exist. Nothing so much suggested it as when, after we had eaten and had spent what was left of the evening reading, perhaps, with some time of quiet conversation, she would at last turn to me with an air of permission and would then rise and set about the task of going to bed. What I had expected was not necessarily something more, but certainly something different, and when on that first night I was so permitted, I saw that nothing again would ever be as I intended it, or ever what I had hoped for.

I am not a successful man in any sense of the word and if my wife has permitted me in her own way, the rest of the world has allowed me to live in another. I have never been openly molested, not with the intention of the sort I might imagine for myself. I have often thought that an open attack might be fairer for all concerned but I can see now that I was only thinking of myself. Others seemed not to care that much and I suppose that they had every right not to. I have annoyed them but, after all, I have never essentially disturbed their lives. Let live, they say, and they know what they are doing.

The fact of my failure can be seen in many instances but it is not so much this fact as the other of my not having been a success. Because, after all, I haven't failed if it was my own intention not to be successful, although to anyone else it might seem that way. I will allow that I am not successful, but I confess it is more difficult to admit of my failure. I agree to the compromise but must reserve the choice for myself.

When it was that I first gave evidence of my intention to be an unsuccessful man, I do not remember. In any event it was a long time ago, and quite probably not long after our marriage. Before that time I was not quite so sure as I am now of the fact that it is at all costs necessary to oppose oneself to the determinations of one's destroyers. I had not then thought that my wife would be in some sense their general. But it turned out so and soon after I began the task of opposition on whatever level they should choose. Though I have never been successful, even in this, I have the eventual satisfaction of a life so empty that even they will be hard put to it for praise.

At the time of our marriage my wife had a small sum of money with which we intended to make our start. This sum she put at my disposal, to use in whatever way I thought best. She had given me this sum or rather she had given me a check on her bank for the amount and told me that it was now mine to do with as I pleased. So, taking the check, I set out toward the business district of the town and when I had come to the first bank, I went in and deposited the check in her name. And there it has been ever since.

This gesture, which was to be sure very much a gesture, began the understanding between my wife and myself which was never obscured in all our years of living together, which did in fact survive those years more gracefully than we ourselves. It was an altogether simple act, half-understood and at best angry, but it served us better than any of the more deliberate ones that followed. Nothing made it quite so plain to each of us where the other stood, and there never was a better reminder.

I would often say to my wife who was not so well controlled that she could forbear mention of the money at all times, that when I had at last made my fortune, this money we would use to make a wonderful time for ourselves, spending it on a trip to the Bahamas or some such nonsensical place. On such occasions she would smile and laugh a little but the success of my wit had really more to do with the fact of my certainty that even should I have had those tickets in my hand at that very moment, she would have laughed just as delightfully and would not have moved one inch from her chair. The surety with which we grew to deal with one another was actually what delighted us and we always knew exactly what to say. If it had not been for the money to begin with, it would not have been so easy and this first gesture of mine served as model for many more. Still, if my gesture seemed the first, and the money the source of all our understanding, as time passed I began to understand my wife a little more acutely than at first, and also to see that if it was I who had put the money to such good use, it was nevertheless she who had had the good sense to give it to me.

In past years I have often had called to my attention the constant infidelities of husbands and wives which marked them much more than they would have, had they been confined to the flesh only. Because the flesh is at best flesh, and would look as poor as any hanging in a butcher's window. But these whom I have watched were dealing primarily with other values, with lives in a more total sense, and they could only be condemned for their lack of understanding. Their bickering was constant, never-ending, and the wives waited only for the moment when their husbands would return from their various jobs so that it could all begin again. And I suspect that even the husbands hurried a little faster on their way home from work, to get at it and to miss as little as they possibly could. For myself, perhaps a month or two would pass before either my wife or myself were aware of our differences. Perhaps they were not even differences but rather our unholy similiarities, our understandings. We were not thought to be unhappy, to be fighting all of the time, and to tell the truth we weren't. But I suspect that each of us was sure that there was, after all, something better, though we had long since given up trying to think about it. It was the suggestion of this which reminded us, which gave us all our pleasure.

Yet we did live together in a way which few people do nowadays. We dealt with one another constantly and were never put off, never refused, unless it were a condition of our understanding that was in question. We knew one another as well as anyone ever knew another and, if it had not been for our loathing, we should have been happy.

Other people, although I don't for a moment believe that what they say is true, at least claim a continuity in their lives, a going up or a coming down. The rise or fall which they maintain is their way of saying that they have lived and even those who stay in the middle suppose that they narrowly missed worse or very nearly achieved better. For me this doesn't apply, and I find it very hard to believe that it does even for others. If I say that I got to know my wife better during the time we lived together, what I intend to say is that after a time I knew her whereas before that time I did not. Neither of us lived for much more than ourselves, one another, though not in the usual sense. God knows we lived long enough, both of us, though I can't say we grew older or younger or that we grew at all. If one lives at all one lives for the kind of things that my wife and I lived for, understandings, the security of knowledge. One certainly does not live to grow old.

But now for my purposes it is necessary to suppose a continuity although none comes readily to hand. What my wife said a year ago is no more to the point than what she said on our wedding night. There is nothing to suggest that we have lived in between. No, for both of us it was like going past some beautiful spot, stopping to look, and then never leaving, always looking to see more and more and more. We never tired of one another and we spent our lives in such looking though at times we might wish to be gone. But still we stayed where we were.

Taken only as years our life seems very uneventful. After our marriage we settled in the town where we spent the days of our honeymoon, an acquiescence on the part of my wife which I was then still too confused to understand. Now I see that it was for her purposes, not mine, that we settled there for it was intended that I should fail on home-ground, so to speak. It was to be the place of my failure or at least the place of my giving proof. But my failure was never what they intended or, because they so deliberately intended it, it was not really mine. I was an unsuccessful man to be sure, but the failure was all theirs. Had they intended my success, it would have been something else again but, as it was, the failure belonged to them.

I can remember the occasions of the first trials quite well just as I can remember almost all of my relations with my wife. A friend would sponsor me, set me up in business, and then quite quietly I would fail. It was always the same, always followed by the half-expressed reproaches from the friend. They could never say that I did not try because I did, but what they forgot was my own intelligence which made each of my efforts consistently contributive to my ruin. It was a way I had about which they really knew nothing. My wife knew though, perhaps, not as well as I, but it was for her own purposes that she never said anything and always expressed her confidence in me with the same sure tone, just as if nothing had happened. If at first I was tempted to tell her why I so often failed, I soon saw that she knew quite well without my telling, and it was better for all concerned to keep silent.

Such conduct on my part was never very simple and I always envied my wife her own part. She was never obliged to come and go as I was, never forced into tedious misrepresentations, never compelled to show failure if not actually to fail. On some evenings I came home as tired as any honest man, no matter what I had been up to, but never was there anything more than what I had left in the morning. Gently my wife would question me about the day's work and I would answer that it had gone well and that I was sure that soon everything would be all right. It was our particular joke, this question, and it never failed to bring a smile from my wife. But it was never quite so simple for me because there were those evenings when I wished that my own work had gone for something more than jokes whose humor was not always so apparent.

It was wrong of me to worry and I did worry quite often during the middle of our life together. At that time it became more difficult than I had thought possible for me to keep my own attitude free of the suggestion of failure directed at me from every side. My wife's friends came frequently to call during that time, and when I came in from work I found them there with my wife, waiting no less than she to see how my day had gone. Perhaps my wife agreed after awhile to the more private engagement I had intended because after some time had passed, her friends were no longer there when I came in, and once again it was only my wife I had to face. To me this seemed fairer and moreover, it was she whom they had chosen.

It was wrong of me to worry because, as we went on, I began to see that I had very nearly won, at least so far as my wife was concerned. Perhaps it was that her questions concerning the businesses I so carefully guided into failure seemed more genuine, more tired. My own answers were never more cheerful, more full of hope, and I told her each day that perhaps tomorrow would see the final victory and, I would add with a smile, the long-promised trip to the Bahamas. I don't know if it was wrong to take advantage of her growing weakness but I was sure that if it had been I who had been first to give in, she would have been no less kind. There was little chance to do more than I had always done, those things upon which we had so long ago agreed, and I am even inclined to think that my wife would never have respected a response to her own weakness. And I wonder even now if her weakness, so persuasive in its own way, was not, after all, just another trick.

In any event the time after that was a great deal easier for me because I could begin to relax though not too much at first. I had lived with my wife too long not to realize the infinite resources at her disposal and I could suspect with some justice that at any time, a time when I should least suspect it, she would again attack and my long-built defenses would fall in ruins. In consequence I was careful, very careful, at first and then I did relax a little but she gave no sign that she noticed it, my relaxing, until at last I was almost sure that what I did no longer concerned her and my time of trial was at an end.

One evening I came home as usual with much the same news and when I came into the house, I called to her but she did not answer. It did not surprise me very much because she had begun to show signs of deafness and although I was not altogether convinced that it was not her last attempt to defeat me, it did seem that she could not hear as well as she once had. Calling again, I went into the room where she spent most of her time and there she was, sitting in her chair. But I could see immediately from the slack position of her hands, fallen beyond the arms of her chair, that she was not well and then, when I came closer, I saw that she was dead.

The next day I have already spoken of, such a calm and peaceful day, and I spent the greater part of it arranging for her funeral. Needless to say, I had only to express a few brief wishes and the rest of the matter was taken out of my hands. The day of her funeral passed without event and I found myself watching her go into the ground without much feeling of any kind. I knew that her part in it was over, and my own very nearly so. In any event it was something to think about.

3 FATE TALES

I

I PUT it this way. That I am, say, myself, that this, or this feel, you can't have, or from that man or this, me, you can't take it. And what I would do, with any of this, is beyond you, and mine. But for this time, yours too.

I haven't always lived here. I used to live in the city, in the middle of it, straight, tall buildings, some of it, but where I was they were cramped, squat, four stories. There was a trolley-line ran down the middle of the street. Noise. Each day the iceman came, under the windows. I could hear him shout. I even waited for him to shout.

Thinking of that time, as it comes here, here and now, I think of the other, somewhat different. I say time. I say time, to mean place.

Let me put it another way. What have we got but this which is myself, yourself. Or that word, self. You figure there's more, some way to make it more, but what you keep is the means, the ways. Make them the end. And that's the end of it, what might have been more.

But nothing more strange, taken or not, than just that, the self which is single. And I make it such, so call it, because it is so. I only call it what it is.

One day, any day, there could be these people, or make them three people, this man and this woman and this little girl. They live in the next place to mine. I see them go down the steps, out on to the street, there, the three of them. I don't say, look for yourselves, see them, or what you may take as enough to convince you. They are there. That is the fact of it.

The days are long, as it happens, hot. The sun in the city is a hard thing, up, inaccessible, hangs over the hardness of the city, out of it. Hot. I hate it but that is, again, my own business.

The woman sits there by herself, in the place with just the girl. They work out the day the best they can. Make the time pass. I know there are at least a hundred and one things anyone can do, to get through these days. Hold to, the actions, the little things done. I have my own things. I get up, eat breakfast, sit around, read, look out the window. There are these ways.

They wait, the two of them, in the place next to mine. The noises come through. The little girl has a ball. It bounces on the floor. Its noise is exact. The woman calls her for her dinner, she complains, doesn't want to come. There is some sharpness in the voices. I listen. I hear all that I want to hear of it.

Then, as it happens, there is this one day, again, one day out of the number, fifty, twenty-five.

The chair slides across the floor. I hear the girl push it.

There is no other sound. Just what comes up from the street, what I have grown used to, the trolley, and the cars, the people, below me, out the window, down. This is what I am sure of, what is down there, that I can speak of without looking, seeing, any of it. It is the one pattern which cannot be broken because it is the general, the collection. The numbers.

It is still quiet. But then out, it goes by me, and down. Stops. But I can't do anything, sit only for a moment, and then, jump, and look out, see there, down, the girl and the people already around her. Nothing of the woman until her head is just opposite mine, the mouth wide, scream, and someone I see the face of below, looks up and calls to her. It's all right. She isn't hurt. A miracle.

It's all right, or right is what they have said, that it's all right, but myself, I can't find their answers or even what they answer, to say it's all right. To her, or myself, or anyone, or even looking straight down at it, after it happens, what happens?

It isn't known. I make that sense of it, that it isn't known, any of it. This woman or this girl or what has happened, and how I would have it, or my hand there. To feel. To be felt. Which they want, or I want, more than the seeing. Any day of the week this could happen, to any, this girl, to others, me, you. I suppose it is something, even, done with. As it turned out. Past, and even complete. I am left with it, made different, because of it. Or, am I? We are back to that.

II

I take it another way, since in this or in what is around is, perhaps, some of it, that such can come to interest, or finds, so, some place in the attention. Let me begin.

There is an old woman who lives in the country and she is very old indeed. Her husband, somewhat younger than herself, has grown tired of waiting but being an honest man, he cannot bring himself to the act of deciding just how old she should be before she is ready to die. It is to be thought that this old woman's days are inaccessible, even to herself, and though she is certainly alive, for the most part she is dead because she cannot remember anything and when she talks, her words slide into one another and the sentence breaks down before it is even half begun. It is a practice of her husband, a rather cruel one, to have the old woman do the week's shopping, so that each Saturday she arrives in the village and totters from store to store, usually led by some old friend of the family who has happened to be standing on the street corner at the time when she is let down from her husband's car. Often the job is divided so that one begins it and then another goes on with it while a third appears at the end to guide her to the car where her husband sits waiting. And behind them comes the clerk carrying the groceries. It is a common sight each Saturday.

This is, it can be supposed, one of the old woman's horrors, but her joy, which is equally distinct, has to do with something which for others would be even more horrible. In the cemetery where she is, once dead, to be buried, her stone is already set in place and her name with all but the final date has been carefully cut into it. She is often taken to the cemetery to see her stone, perhaps with a certain willingness on the part of her husband who may think that if she sees it often enough, this place where she is to be laid to rest, she will hurry up the process of getting there once and for all. For some years she worried about the possible annoyance her choice of a final resting place might cause another member of the family but when with reluctant decision, she made her choice known to the family, she was overjoyed to find this doubtful one quite approved.

In any event this old woman seems to be doing it all by herself, so that when it does come time to bury her, one would not be too surprised, should the knotted old hands reach up and, pushing the shovels aside, pull the dirt over all by themselves, for at least that's one way to think of it.

III

I think we deal with other wisdoms, all more real than our own, which is to say, I think we have to do with others. Sometimes, sitting in a chair by the window, I see a man go by on foot and I wonder at the precision with which each foot advances, so controlled and so sure. I would hope that if the man and I were to trade places, he might think the same of me going by but I am not at all sure that he would.

I think it is always a question of where we have come from and where we are going. I think they are important in just that order and I think there is little else to think about. Of course, we are ourselves. It would be foolish for us to believe those who tell us different. But to know exactly, to know each time and all the time, about that I am not so sure.

After all, what do we have to do with that is not ourselves?

What can exist that we are not part of or that we do not in some sense *allow* to exist. This is an old story but a true one. The world is my representation. So it is, all of it. And what is more, this world belongs to us.

But the order is important, the grasp of the keys and the lay of the land, so to speak. One must know these. Like the man with the car I see each morning, racing its motor, tearing down the road over bumps and stones, what does he know about his own possession? Certainly not enough to make actual use of it, not the use of understanding. This, then, should be criticised, such misuse, and avoided at all costs.

But it is true that everything becomes our own. It's what things are for. We see them and they are ours. It's as simple as that.

The story I have to tell has to do with familiar objects in familiar relations. Unlike the others, it does not suppose a stretching of the usual context. It has to do with a usual reality.

I am in the habit of feeding our cat each night before I go to bed after I have put coal on the fires. This is my usual procedure and one I rarely vary. Both the cat and I are at home in it. When it comes time, if the cat is indoors, she will be sitting by her dish, waiting for me to put food in it. If she is outside, I have only to open the door and there she is, waiting to be let in and fed.

On the night of which I am speaking, or at least now I am speaking of it, I had let the cat out earlier and so when it came time to feed her, I went to the door and opened it but the cat was not in sight. But do not take this as something altogether unusual. I am not such an automaton that I cannot vary my movements at all. It is often the case that I am a few minutes late with the cat's food. And the cat, too, has her differences.

I opened the door but the cat was not to be seen, so I called to her, once, then twice, but she did not come.

On that night there was a full moon. It was very bright outside, almost like day but still very different. The tall pines at the edge of the field beside our house cast their long shadows over the snow and each object in the field itself that was big enough to have a shadow had its own. But though it seemed very light and the shadows black and distinct, still there were no sharp details such as are to be seen, when a bright sun is shining.

I stood for some minutes, looking out over the fields, and then, because she made a sudden, brief movement, I saw the cat not too far from where I was standing, crouched, her own shadow black and irregular on the snow. I called again to her but she gave no notice, so I walked over to where she was, thinking to pick her up and bring her into the house. When I came to her, however, I saw that she had a mouse and although it's no pleasant sight to watch a cat and a mouse together, one, in fact, which I remember always with unpleasantness, my wife and I have decided that since we have the cat in order to catch the mice which bothered us previously, we have to put up with the unpleasantness, even though it's difficult. So it was that I started to walk away from her in order to let her finish the mouse but as I did so, I was caught by the strange sight of their shadows, the mouse's, though smaller, very distinct and the cat's, like some horrible shadow trying to erase it. I stood there, absorbed, completely caught, until suddenly the mouse's shadow was gone, but no, it appeared again, coming toward me uncertainly, jerkily, until I saw that what it wanted was to hide in my own shadow, which I now saw to be there, just as their own, long and black on the snow. It came toward me, the mouse, and then just as quickly as I had seen it, I lost sight of it again. So again I started back to the house but as I did so, I felt something wriggling on my sleeve and with a sudden brush of my hand, I threw it back on the snow. Only then, because the cat jumped on what I had knocked from my sleeve, did I know it was the mouse.

I don't think that story much more than unpleasant but still it has the point of all I believe. For these things, so powerful in themselves, in their own way, are there to be looked at, I expect, and with more than the eyes. It's a case of making them ours the best way we can. I can remember that as it happened, then, even as it was happening, a good many things occurred to me, each with its relation, and if these things did, as they did, lessen that first impact of horror, they also made it my own.

There are other stories, some with more purpose, and one, perhaps, bears hearing here, tacked on though it is. In any event, it's short. After that snow and before the next, I went out, as usual, to do the chores, and found one afternoon, patches of blood on the snow. And seeing them there, I guessed that the cat had cut her foot and was able to find her and dress the wound before there was chance for it to become infected.

A short time after it did snow and the patches were covered and I forgot about them. It stayed cold for a week and then it turned warm and the snow began to melt. And going out again I saw the patches of blood on the snow and without thinking twice, I went off to find the cat, supposing she had cut another foot. But finding her, I found, as well, that none of her feet were cut and then saw it was the melting of the snow had caused the old patches to come back. I expect that all this might suggest is that a reality, before it becomes our own, is often tricky and can be easily mistaken.

JARDOU

. . . .und leise tönen im Rohr die dunkeln
Flöten des Herbstes . . .

TRAKL

Clearing, the wind left, and the sky was very light, and walking along behind them, he sang, but softly, saying, you want to pick all the olives, but I will pick them all. And sang, again, feeling very good, the sky now altogether clear, and from behind the high house in front of them a single white light climbing down and falling all over them in one heap.

But she was in a hurry, and had the boy's hand in her own, to hold it, pulling, as they went on. We are late, she said, and looking back, found him still there behind them, and waited until he had come up to them, to take his hand too. Opening the gate, he went in and they went in after him.

I love you, he said, and stopped to shout, hello, and heard it echo around the building to be answered from the field, another shout, and they started, calling, the boy running in front of them.

He had expected some diligence, to put it that way, or some aspect of determination. But he now saw them almost finished, the mother by the furthest tree, reaching up and pulling off the olives. There was no hurry, he thought, and saw the trees were very old, the branches filled with the fine leaves, fluted, and still wet from the rain. He waved again, to the husband by himself, in the wet grass, and listening, heard the first sounds of their speech not understood, but it was, she said, *le jardin des olives.*

He listened, then went to the mother saying, hello, again, not caring that she would not know it. I love you, he said, but to the other, coming up now to join them, and she made a face back, laughing, the woman standing still nervous, her skirt held out to catch the olives which he began to toss down. Straining, he raked them clear, then dropped them to her, not looking, and saw the olives above him he could not quite reach.

Those, he said, and pointed at them, and his wife explained, the speech wavering, breathy, and she said, he thought, even things he could not understand. Bringing the chair, they both held it firm, and he got up on it, quite safe. Stretching, he picked more, leaning back to get them, and found himself among the higher branches. He picked what were left to give them to the woman, and shook the branches. Getting down, he looked at her, then felt the chair give and put out his hand and touched her, quickly, then stood on the ground.

Once there, they all sat down, and he lay back against the tree's trunk not caring about the wet. The father still sat past them, over to the side, and watched the children. They did not think to bother him at first, then called, and getting up, he came to sit with them.

They grew quite content, under the tree, the father stretched out by the women, an old hat pulled down to the back of his head, nearly reaching the ears. His hair fell very straight beyond it, curling slightly at the neck.

But he was not, even so, unformidable. There was a very precise weight present. The younger man might not have budged it, he thought, but thought then of the woman, and looking, saw her dress almost worn out, and pulled tight about the shoulders.

I love you, he said, and echoed it in invariable silences saying, each time, I love you, but never feeling very much.

Shall we begin again, his wife said, and translated it, to them, so that they both stood up, waiting, but the father was not very interested.

You are not concerned, he said, but could not think of the right words, and his wife repeated it, to the man, smiling and he shrugged in answer.

I had thought to pick olives, he said then, to his wife, and grew angry. This doesn't seem very close?

And laughed. One didn't care. And got the chair and brought

it to another tree, placing it under the high branches, and then climbed up on it, to stand there. Following, both women took hold, so that he might have been their own, held there, in some attitude of attention.

Still the children ran by them, shouting, and played, very happy, the boy tagging after them to join in. Above them all, he looked down, thinking to pronounce any spell, perhaps, saying that it could be that way, but they waited, and he went back to picking.

He gave it, now, all care, parting the leaves with his fingers, and trying to find all those which might be left. It was difficult because the colors were too similar, and hiding in all shadows, it seemed there might be one more. But, below him, they pointed, and following their hands he saw the olives, and picked them, dropping them down.

All done, he said, but asked, and looking down, saw them pointing, and he reached out, to get it, then tossed it down to them.

Are you done, she said, and he got down off the chair, falling down beside them, then took the bag from the woman, smiling, to look at it.

Back of them, the father, came back, and stood in a tangle of brush, and lifted a camera, holding it steady, to point, the hands very quiet. But the children would not hold still, and all crammed together until the father shouted at them, something, and they stopped and grouped themselves nicely, the grass brushing against their legs. He took the picture, then bent to wind the film, and went off to the house to leave them, there, by the trees.

Let go, the children would have run off but the mother held them, pulling down the youngest to sit on her lap, and he saw the cloth pull tight, watching, and called to his own boy to come.

Sitting him on his knee, he stroked the hair, the boy chafing, but held quiet there and let him do it. He would have spoken, but couldn't, and looking to his wife, wanted to push, then, at her, to explain, but did not know what he wished explained.

The woman watched, even so, intently, and smiling, he thought, or perhaps she smiled. Behind her, the other children stood all looking at him, and he wished to say something, but knew no words to.

She spoke to his wife, and listening, he heard them wander into sounds so very distant he could think of nothing they might mean, and said, stop it, and hearing him, his wife stopped, to smile, and getting up, he pointed again to the trees.

Some left, he said, but the women still sat and looked after him, and would not come. Behind him, their voices grew alien, and broke too far away to make him listen, so that he walked to the field's edge and turned to see no one but the children, still running among the trees. He watched, then brought them to him, calling, then sent them up into the trees for no reason, and they brushed past him, climbing up into the branches.

Waving, he tossed up twigs, and old bark, and looked for more in the trampled grass, then threw what he found up to see it fall, past the children, to the ground. One, now above him, sang, and he looked up to see her there, braced tight against the crotch of the limbs, and white along the ankles, and up the legs, to the skirt, and waved to her, crying out.

But she said, come, and turning, he saw them there now behind him, and nodding, he took the bag they had given her, and put it into his pocket.

THE SEANCE

SOMEWHAT colder, the wind came in at the door, and with a quick turn, shifted and moved down the hall. There, they were sitting, waiting, at the table, backs to the fire, the shadows of them on the wall, against it, big black shapes there which, because they were talking, they didn't see.

A ghost story. An involution back into what was, he said to the other, remember? I give it to you straight, listen.

You see the face, say, that face there. What is it gets on it, I mean, the fact of it coming over & thru, now, as you are looking. Or, how it dies, perhaps, or softens, the thing gone relaxed, like a dying. My hands are cold. I move them a little, flex & wind the fingers together. The coldness. Or rub them, perhaps, one with the other, chafe the skin a little. A charm against what harms them. The coldness. Not so much to laugh at this, or to be laughing, as to see, simply, what it is I am about.

Perhaps, then, in some ways something, something different. Someone is moving. The chair, itself, edges a little, & grates, the legs of it, against the floor. Listen. Unmistakable sound. The slight shifting. The slight noise in the ear. Enough to prove it. Something there. Well, someone. A person, like they say. Man, woman, or child. Who is cold? Not so much cold, as there. That is itself a character.

But even with that, it is still not there, or better, it is away from where we are. Where I am. Or put it simply. I am alone.

To move from this to that. That shift, from here to there where the weather is softer, warmer, & the sun already grows big against the edge of the hills, where the eye hangs, to look at the sun, against it. Strikes out. The trees, green but soft green in the rising fog which the rising wind pushes. He said, never a morning without the slight wind. Clears this fog, cuts thru & lifts it, clears sight.

So good to be stretching. Out, lifts over the edge of the bed, one leg, looks down at the foot, then gets up. Stretches. Through the window, the sun works clear & up, moves higher, & the air is warm.

Lucy sings in the garden, two hours before him, gropes for the weeds, is mad. Tra-las, echoing song. Lifts high as the sun these symptoms of the desperate sound. Weeds, where they grow, catch to her flowers & crowd. She, meticulous, takes each, one by one, carefully, & pulls, lightly, works them loose. The flowers. Color & the morning sun.

Not much more than that, he was saying, I was thinking, again. My head feels thick as a bag of barley. Thick? Well, barley not so much that as slippery. That too, in my head. What was it you wanted to know about—let's get clear on that. At this point it's hard to think straight. I'm in a hurry.

Colder & colder. He rubs his hands more frequently, puts them to his mouth & blows on them, thru. The warm breath. Is uncomfortable & the fire burns out. But flickers. The shadows even more.

The sun, higher & higher. The day burns out. Along. And she is still in the garden, still pulls at the weeds. Which move thru her hands. Counters. Lucy, green, Louise, green. Lionel, green. Lilacs, purple. Purple. Moves her hands with exactness, picks & pulls.

Behind her, thru a chink in the wall, he is watching. Takes after a time, a small pebble & throws it, tosses it, at her. It hits her back & bounces, lightly, down. She shakes & keeps working. He takes another pebble, & throws it, she shakes & keeps working. Another. Throws. She keeps working. Another, larger, throws, harder, another, larger, throws & harder another. She keeps working.

The whistle, far-off, a kind of long screech. All over, they stop.

Put down the tools & move in long lines, past the tools & out. A digression.

But the wind shifts, again, comes down the hall, and finds him. Close to the fire, what's left, he puts his hands out to catch what heat is left. Cold, very cold. No moon but out on the fields the weather. Light light. He rubs his hands.

THE MUSICIANS

He walked out with her behind him. At least she stood there, still, hidden from the doorway but to the side, listening, as he went past her, and out into the hall. She was saying, he's there, although the hall was empty. If there was someone there, then he was not there now. He stopped to say, you see, and continued, no one. There is no one here at all. But she closed the door, hard, and left him standing, facing to the stairs.

So at this moment he saw the other man, like, as he thought, that now of course there he would be, to be alone with him. It was where he hadn't looked, above him, the stairs going up obliquely, to the roof, and now the man came down them and said, good morning. He answered, good morning, John. The sun was bright, what was it, eight or nine. One could go out, on the street, walk two blocks, go into some place, sit down, buy perhaps coffee, black perhaps, and a roll or whatnot, and that would be that and nothing more. But he had something else to do. Look, he said, John, come with me, that is, can't we get out of here? He thought, I knew you in school, one time I slept on top of you, with a mattress between us, which is love of a sort, is it not. His eyes filled, with tears. We're friends still, he said. You don't kill all that that easily? But caught himself, because how easy was it, to do it, anything, anytime, even with anyone.

Behind him the man walked down the stairs very quietly, his face down so that it could not be seen. This was simply protective. They went out, at the bottom of the stairs, the one in front of the other, expecting, at least the one in front did, to be there mowed down, a sudden abrupt barrage of machine-gun fire, cutting them precisely in half. The sun dropped past them, to the flat concrete of the courtyard. And tonight you will do the same thing, he thought, you. Getting up makes no difference whatsoever. To anyone. He walked across the courtyard and opened the door into the other half of the building. The hall was yellow, an ochre. They went along it, past the boxes for mail, and out into the street.

Here it was somewhat simpler. Forced, if there were anything, to happen, then a sidestep, or a push, could bring him past it, hidden against a doorway, or jammed into strangers who might, he thought, help him. This was a story of violence and murder. Three found dead, in a bed. Which, bitterly, the bed itself prevented, being not big enough. What would you like to eat, he said, and added, John, have you eaten? The man came up, then, and walked beside him. You know, he said, it wasn't easy. The man walked, beside him. How could it be easy, he said. Words poured into him, from everywhere. How, he said. Look, you know me.

As they went past the door of a cafe, the man made a sign, to go in, but would not go in himself. So he went in, and bought coffee, to go out, then some rolls, which he also thought indicated, and went out when he had them but he saw nothing of the man, and remembered he was to walk back, and up to the man's room, and they would eat, then.

He used this time to reconnoitre, which phrase he got, or had got, from the account of a British, he remembered, spy in Germany during the first World War. The man wrote, at length, of how he had managed to break over the line, between the two armies, and then by virtue of a straight face, hardly more, and a knowledge of the language, which was also given, he worked his way up and up, till at last he was actually in the very top group of the German Command itself. Work and work, keep at it, you too will be on top. An irony. But nonetheless where he both had been, he thought, and well might land again, helpless as he was to stand against it.

But, opening the door, he saw this plan was useless. The room in front of him scattered, fell into, many patterns. There was a picture of a long low car, an old one, tacked on the wall over a table. There were records, and beyond them, a small black phonograph. Simply enough, this was his friend. Well, he said, do you want proof? Which photograph shall I show you. Or, simply, the first, of a man, standing by himself in a street, somewhere in Mexico City. Or rather he walked along the street and because he did, or John did, his picture was taken, a small card given him, which he, John, must have remembered later, and he got the picture and he, John, sent it home. A fact. He had seen it certainly. He had admired it. How nice to live in Mexico! There was another, as well, a man sitting at a table, in a long low room, a round one, which seemed unusual. On the table there were some plates left over from eating. A girl, a pretty girl, sat past him and had her head bowed. The picture was large, the whole feel of it seemed to mean that someone had both cared to take it, and, having taken it, cared also to print it like this. So that it could be something not just a cheap snapshot, however much that is all right too, but something also better, more durable, simply more careful.

Are you hungry, he said. He put the food and the coffee on the table, and then, unwrapping it, offered it to his friend. Where shall I begin, he said. Perhaps I could tell you a story, too? Let's put it, two men, ourselves, we live in a long black house, like that one. He pointed to the car, on the wall. Every morning at ten o'clock sharp we take it out of the place, wherever we keep it, and we drive it, like hell, up and down, up and down. We love it. We think there is nothing either greater or any damn thing else. By God, we enjoy ourselves. Then one day, because some idiot turns left on a street where there is a huge, huge sign saying, do *not* turn left, that's it, the end of us. The goddam car so smashed, broken, disintegrated, that really we have nothing at all left. So we go out and so on, maybe to a hospital, where a beautiful nurse in a long black uniform, I think, sews us up, good as new, and then we get another car.

Can't we get another car, he said. Can't we do it? The man drank the coffee, lifting the cardboard cup very carefully. Are you listening, John, he said. Can't you hear a goddam thing I am telling you? But then he sat back, and also drank his own coffee, slowly. Look, he said, John. There are other ways than this to tell it? He stopped. Are you listening to me? The man smiled, and got up, and turning on the phonograph, put on a record, and sat down.

At that the room became still, though there was the music, a low quiet thing, perhaps a trumpet, he thought, if I can still remember. You play the piano, don't you, he said. He thought. A face, John's face, hair cut short, clipped. A man's funny odd hands, on a piano, that is, on the keys of a piano. Even, if it mattered, Boston, Mass. The end.

Play it for me, he said, *me*. He stopped. Did you ever hear the one about there must have been three of them, people? He said, there were three people, a man, a man, a woman. God knows where they lived, a house? Ok. Not long and black this time, this one is snow-white, has clapboards like in the movies, roses, the works. Every morning not only the milkman comes, he brings two dozen milks, the greatest, but also, mind you, at least the plumber, the mailman, the electrician, the hairdresser, the modista, the maestro who fixes the walls when they fall down on your head because you will pound on them. Ok, he said. What can I do more than that?

The man sat, watching. Behind them both, and through the window, there was the upper side of the building opposite, breaking off into a line of others, the roofs of them, even more broken. Looking, he caught sight of a small crouched figure, on the roof next to their own, above their heads, and it was her, sitting there, with some kind of pajamas on, with a bathrobe over them, to cover her.

Look, he said. See this. The man got up and went over to the window, then sat down again.

By god, he said. You know, John, I haven't really tried and let me do that at least. He stopped again and coughed, and added, what the hell do you like to drink, at which the man bent over and pulled a bottle of sherry out from underneath the bed, uncorked it, and handed it to him. He swallowed, quickly, and handed it back.

It's never easy, he said, never. What should I say, that I was walking down the street? When suddenly, and from out of nowhere, comes a truck and hits me? That's love, John. Nothing more, nothing less. You had a mother?

The man said, don't talk about my mother, saying it carefully, so that he stopped, again, to listen to him. Because he did not know John's mother, but wanted to, not for maudlin reasons, but there it was, something unknown, and a pleasure. Why don't we go to Mexico, he said. He watched the man carefully. There's a bus, he said, it's not impossible?

Or work, he said. Look, I would like to work, I would like to do something outside. He made a movement of his hands, and there it was, perhaps a big hole in the ground, in which others sweated, but never himself. I would like to get out of this.

John, he said, for the last time, look. Nothing is easy. Because, he said, three things matter. That one eat, that one sleep, that one make it. Three finite actions, which can, I think, be accomplished?

The man got up, coming toward him, saying, to go, as he knew, and behind them, also she moved, on the roof, and seeing that, then it was ugly, unsimplified. Don't cry, he said. That doesn't help.